On Thin Ice

Also by Caperton Tissot

Kicking Leaves;
The Contrarian Life of a Yankee Rebel, 2018

The Beat Within;
Poetry, Another Round, 2017

Adirondack Flashes and Floaters;
A River of Verse, 2014

Saranac Lake's Ice Palace;
a History of Winter Carnival's Crown Jewel, 2012

Tibetta's World;
High Jinks and Hard Times in the North Country, 2012
(Out of print)

Adirondack Ice;
a Cultural and Natural History, 2010

History Between the Lines;
Women's Lives and Saranac Lake Customs, 2007

More Information and contact at www.SnowyOwlPress.com

On Thin Ice

THE LIFE AND TIMES
OF A NORTH WOODS CARETAKER

A Novel

Caperton Tissot

This book was previously published as
Tibetta's World: High Jinks and Hard Times in the North Country

ISBN: 978-0-359-17965-7

PublishNation LLC
www.publishnation.net

Author's Note

On Thin Ice: the Life and Times of a North Woods Caretaker was first published under the title: *Tibetta's World, High Jinks and Hard Times in the North County.* This is a new, revised edition. Why revise it? Because the previous cover and title misled many into thinking it was a children's book. It decidedly is not. I also felt compelled to rewrite and make additions to the original text. I am greatly indebted to my husband Wim who has, once again, edited, advised and supported me as I undertook this mad venture. And I cannot forget the Tuesday night gang who has encouraged and critiqued several parts of the book. Their suggestions have helped to make it a better story.

Great Camps and Characters

Barton Estate
    Seasonal Great Camp with several buildings on 29,000 acres
    Owners: Adam Barton and family
    Head caretaker: Stuart (Stu) Moore married to Sue Tower
    Assistant caretaker: Joe Morris married to Linda Morris

Camp Reedmor
    Large compound with a main building and several guest-cabins
    Owners: Byron and Prudence (Pru) Power
    Their children: Norman (Norm) and Winnie
    Head caretaker: Tuck Rising married to Britt Freier

The Greene River Hunt Club
    Remote seasonal hunting and vacation compound, off the grid
    Owners: Club members
    Head caretaker: Ace and Blanche Loneby
    Assistant caretaker: Slam
    Club president: Norton Smithers

The Raven's Nest
    Year-round Great Camp on 10,000 acres
    Owners: Bill Raven and his wife
    Children: Mark and Lila
    Head caretakers: Josh and Tripp Lively

The Sterling Camp
    Year-round home, a few other buildings on property
    Owner: Dr. Sterling Sears
    Caretaker: Big Moe

Characters

Tibetta (Tibby) Rising: daughter of Tuck

Addison Rising: architect, brother of Tuck

Justus Rising: owner of a clothing store, father of Tuck and Addison

Fawn Rising: wife of Justus, mother of Tuck and Addison

Bubbles Rising: wife of Addison

Aiken Bellows: father of Bubbles

Shelley (Shell) Taglong: sister and business partner of Britt

Rory and Eileen Taglong: parents of Britt and Shelley

Hood Slanter: owner of the Hood 'n' Wheel garage

Jane Slanter: wife of Hood

Katy Smith: classmate of Tibetta

Pat Smith: mother of Katy

Ma Rose: owner of the Hunters' Hub

Rod: brother of Ma Rose, city policeman

Sam Lively: local police officer and brother of Josh

Stalk: State Police Investigator

Tim Berson: owner of Robin Wood Lumber Company

Pitt and Rat: just Pitt and Rat

Part I

Missing

Chapter 1

A figure crouches against the wind and scopes out the scene below where a Great Camp sleeps under a light sheet of snow. Tucked snugly into the steep slope, its pitched roof conceals a vast estate, summer playground for wealthy urbanites. This two-storied structure looks out on a mountain-framed lake. The wide porch, viewing stand for aristocrats, stretches one end to the other. Panels of woven sticks line the railing, a touch of elegance on the massive bark-clad building: like lace on a dowager's gown.

At one end of this Great Camp, tall firs lean over, shielding it from threatening skies. A vast lawn spills down to the lake where snow-covered boulders line the shore and dark mouths yawn from under white overturned boats. Adirondack chairs, buried by winter, remind us that, come summer, warm days will bring the owners, their families and guests, all ready to enjoy the "good life". But for now, that coldest of all seasons is just setting in. The lake is frozen and still.

Our watcher on the hill, slightly swaying, shuffles down a steep path, circles to the camp's front, climbs slippery porch steps, and slides a key into the lock of a tall wooden door. Carved to look like a book, the door creaks open. The shadowy figure enters a chilly high-ceilinged room, searches for the keypad and with gloved fingers taps out a code, muting the alarms.

Inside, ghostly whispers fill the air. Massive furniture, covered by white sheets, sits solid and quiet. After lingering at the window to gaze out at the snowy land, the intruder sighs and turns away, tiptoeing through the cathedral-like room. Mounted on the walls, animal heads stare down, silent witnesses to this out-of-season activity. Shaky hands snatch at objects, popping them into a backpack: small statuette, silver spoons, antique vase and, for sure, more finds upstairs. A search of the bedrooms produces nothing. Annoyed, the thief tears through drawers finding only a couple of watches, gold cufflinks and – what is this? Buried under women's lingerie in the back of a bottom drawer: a locked flat metal box. No tools to open it now, but surely it is worth something, so into the pack it goes.

After a further search, the stranger treads quietly back downstairs, resets the alarm, locks the door and looks for the shortcut back to the road. But a fearsome winter gale has given rise to a classic North Country white-out. Billows of snow swirl through the air hiding from view the trees, lake, nearby cabins and bridge; landscape now evolved into a fantasy-scape. Wind drives the snow up, down and sideways, one minute blasting it to the ground, the next, blowing it clean away. Like a curtain sweeping across the stage, it hides the view. At times the path lies clear ahead; a second later it is gone. Which way back? Worries fly freely. *"Lost, so close and I'm lost –"*

Chapter 2

Light is starting to fade on a winter's afternoon when Britt drives up to Camp Reedmor. Her husband Tuck, its caretaker, finished with work, is waiting for her so they can take a walk together before returning home. After a quick hug he looks down at her feet and says, "I don't get it, Britt, wearing those high heeled boots? How are you going to walk with me in those spiky things? You look armed – or footed – to do battle."

"I have them on because I've just come from running errands in town, picking up the mail, buying food for entertaining."

"Entertaining? You don't need to "entertain" friends. Just invite them over for talk and fun. Anyway, what's with those stiletto heels? Was the meat still alive? Did you have to spear it first?"

"Listen Tuck, I don't relish being seen at the grocery store in shit-kicking country boots."

"Fashion in this town? Wearing fancy boots and that fur coat won't impress the locals. They don't give a damn. All right, let's skip the walk."

"So where's Tibetta"

"I left her playing in the kids' bedroom upstairs. Come on. You've got to see this: bunk beds like horse-pulled sleighs, raccoons carved into the rafters, a miniature log cabin set in one corner – replica of one of Addison's guest-cabins, stained glass windows with pictures of Goldilocks and the three bears – "

"Daddy, Daddy, come see what I found." calls a faint distant voice.

"Damn. Where is she? Oh my God. She's out on the ice. How'd she get out there? Oh God! Oh my God! Tibby, Tibby come back!"

"Daddy, come here – I can see right through the ice – they're fishies and a turkle swimming in the grass and a mermaid and trees. Daddy – "

"Tibby," Tuck yells, as he runs outside, "Tibby, come back right now. That ice can't hold you. Get back here!"

"But Daddy, come look," the young child persists.

"Come on Baby, don't stand, just crawl towards us. Now! Do you hear me? Right now. Just crawl this way –"

"Okay." Tibetta, turns and begins sliding along the wind-swept clear black ice but the going is slow. She stands and takes two steps. With a crack, the ice gives way.

"Daddy, help, help!"

"Oh my God, she's in!"

5

In seconds, Britt, pulls off her boots, races to the shoreline and starts to inch out on the ice.

"No, Britt. Stop! It won't hold you." Backing up, she grabs a branch and pushes it out to Tibetta who grabs it.

"Hold on Tibby, we'll pull you out," yells Tuck while grasping the branch with Britt. Together they pull. They watch as Tibetta, in her pink, soggy snowsuit, grabs the branch. They pull and she begins to slide forward, but the ice edge starts to break apart and she falls back into the water.

"Hang on, keep kicking!" Tuck yells at his five-year-old who just months ago had learned to swim. He runs to the boathouse.

"Where're you going?" screams Britt.

"Getting a ladder," he calls as he dashes around the building to lift it off the wall.

"Keep kicking your feet! Daddy's coming." Tibetta's pale face, pink hood pulled tight, peaks out in terror. Her hands in matching pink mittens try desperately to gain a hold on the slippery ice. Tuck runs back with the ladder, slides it carefully onto the ice, but before he can do more, Britt is down on hands and knees, crawling its length. Holding on with one hand, she reaches with the other, grabs Tibetta's arm and tugs her aboard. With the extra weight, the ladder starts to break through the ice.

"Don't move, hang on, I'll pull you both out," Tuck hollers. Feet dug in and arms straining, he manages to drag the heavily loaded ladder onto the shore. Then Tuck scoops up his soaking-wet child and makes a beeline for the truck. Britt, boots in hand, runs beside him. Inside the cab, Tuck strips off Tibetta's wet clothes while Britt wraps her fur coat around the shivering child, hugging her tightly. They speed for home, the sickly heater doing little to help. Tibetta, burrowed deep in the fur, thinks, *I miss my Gram but being inside this coat is sort of like snuggling in my Gram's lap.*

Chapter 3

Later that evening, Tuck returns to the frozen lake, staying well away from the boathouse bubbler where Tibetta fell through earlier that day. *Those bubblers – folks don't realize how weak the ice nearby,* he reflects. He skis out on a thin layer of snow now covering the ice. His healing leg is still recovering from the accident but he can manage an easy cross-country outing. His boards squeak as he glides forward over the frozen lake, talking to him as skis do when it gets below the big 0. He coasts quietly along, alone but not lonely, as he lays down double straight tracks: trail of a man in his element.

Night-ice booms, the sound rolling like thunder across the lake as dormant waters awake to seep up through web-like cracks in the surface. The night sky salts the earth with the light of millions of stars – *Out here in the wilderness – no urban light sullies the virgin snow – out here the semi-dark comfort of a winter's night.* Worries slide from his shoulders to fall in the snow: Britt's discontent, Tibetta's situation, his future. The crisp winter air cooling his head helps him stay more alert than emotional. Lack of focus can spell doom. Animals see clearly at night but Tuck must take care as he moves ahead in the dark. A bone-breaking fall, a drop through thin ice – such moments will pitch the skier to his death. His thoughts turn to the animal world where mice, skittering under the snow, live but short lives before the fox pounces; weary deer stagger as they fall in agony to clawing coyotes and squirrels are at constant risk from barred owl attacks, wing patterns in the snow marking the drama. *Accepting that kind of order must bring a certain reassurance,* reflects Tuck, *until one's own moment comes. People, on the other hand, tend to brood. That's probably why we screw up all the time. My soul's locked in my body like a prisoner in a cell. I wish I could get outside it, see the world with a more open mind.*

Tuck glides on across the ice, nostrils frozen half shut, mouth open, white breath blowing ahead. As he skis further away from Camp Reedmor, he wonders, *can we ever really distance ourselves* from *the job that feeds us, family crisis, loss, deceit?*

"I try," he whispers to himself. In the quiet, he takes stock of things, thinks more clearly under the boundless sky, remembers how, after breaking his leg skiing, Britt agreed to marry him, move temporarily to Meltmor while he took a job and worked on getting back into shape. Once healed and back in the groove, plans were for him to return to the international ski circuit, Britt accompanying him when she could. As long as they lived in Meltmor, he and Britt would keep Tibetta with them. Once they started traveling, she would return to her grandparents. *Is this really what I want?* He asks himself.

A barred owl calls: "Who, who who, whoo – just who are you-u-u?" Who is he indeed? At six feet, steely-muscled and trim, he appears to be a back-country kind of guy. From under his dark wool cap, a brown ponytail drops down the back of his Carhartt jacket, a match for his newly sprouted and now frosted moustache and short beard. His face is lean; his eyes dart about, constantly searching. Always alert, he finds full rest only in the dark of night.

Tuck ponders over the camp owner, his boss Byron, who loves it here in the Adirondacks but works long hours in the stress-filled publishing world. *Eleven months in the city for a few weeks in the North – hard work all year to provide his high-maintenance wife Pru – Mrs. Power to her caretakers – a few weeks in a Great Camp – I'm lucky, love it here but that camp – what is it? Inherited wealth? Undeserved luxury? Fine craftsmanship?*

He feels as if he's floating across the lake – *aahh, how beautiful the night – how right things seem out here. But, it's growing late, got to get home and maybe – or maybe not – talk to Britt of our future. Is this the moment? How long will she put up with me? She's so unpredictable, or is it me?* Still undecided, he follows his trail back to the Camp, his truck and the drive to his small home in town.

Chapter 4

In the village, in the back room of Tuck and Britt's drafty log house, Tibetta snuggles once more into the depths of Britt's fur coat which is now laid over her bed. She tries to fight sleep until Daddy comes back. *I wish I was home with Daddy and Grandpa and Gram. Why did he have to bring Bee here? Gram told me to be a good girl for a little while and Daddy will take Bee away and I can go home to Gram and Grandpa again. I liked when my daddy came to see just me.*

In the front room a rusty stove sizzles, throwing scant heat into the small, low-ceilinged room with its yellow-stained plaster walls. Britt, a stylish young woman, looks out of place sitting on a frayed, plaid cushion covering the seat of an even shabbier captain's chair. Brilliant red curtains gently sway back and forth in front of the poorly sealed windows. Used to city streets where bright fluorescent bulbs fend off the lurking dark, she finds the encroaching night threatening, tries to close it out. She is uneasy surrounded by the unfamiliar. And who is not? – be it city streets or wild northern woods? – hence her addition of urban curtains to the rustic interior.

Britt pulls her chair closer to the stove. Of medium height, she wears her hair short, accentuating her high cheeks and gray-blue eyes. Her mouth is small, her lips pursed shut. A blue, alpaca robe is tied tightly around her slim waist in an effort to stave off the chill. She is reading Conrad's *Heart of Darkness*, a book Tuck recommended. It's a rerun. She remembers plowing through the story in high school when all such undertakings were but fleeting assignments. Now it has morphed into something surprisingly applicable to man's state of affairs. In her thirties now, youth's halo of self-absorption having thinned ever so slightly, she is beginning to sense how much suffering stretches across the planet.

A year ago, she had sat by the bedside of her godson while he underwent chemo; had watched him struggle and eventually die. The injustice of it all, captured so well by Conrad's character, Kurtz, shouting, "The horror, the horror" hits home. Her mind wanders off the page as she reflects on how each perpetually struggles, in effect, to shield his or her own candle's light from blowing out in the dark. Recently these thoughts, like stealth missiles, had begun to invade her implacable sense of success. *I had such ambitions. How did I end up with a disabled athlete and his illegitimate daughter? I won't let myself ever again get so close to a child – the pain. And now I am in this honky-tonk town with Tuck's small-minded parents – my friends would laugh if they could see me now.*

Ah, she catches herself. *How easily I judge. I am too much like my parents: too critical. I shouldn't be so down on everyone, including Tuck. I do love him but this is not the life I expected. It's funny how folks think I'm cheerful but I only put it on. Like clothes, it shields me from prying.*

Half-finished thoughts, like dangling participles, circle in her head. She listens for sounds from the back room where Tibetta sleeps wrapped in innocence. *A link to one of Tuck's European trips, a love-child from a crazy fling, his not mine. I can be a good stepmother but I'm not going to be gaga over her like everyone else is. She's sort of cute except, unfortunately, she inherited a little too much of her Uncle Addison's angular features and less of Tuck's good looks.*

Lord – almost midnight. Britt gets up from her chair, goes to the window, parts the curtains and peers out. *Nothing. Where is he? Hope he's okay – so excited to bring me up North – now rarely stays home, like tonight – wish he'd do something I want for a change – band at the Town Trough could have been fun – would have loved to go – tells me he likes bluegrass but now he won't go at all. Why? – should have gone there by myself – worry when he wanders off like that – hard to understand.*

An engine grinds to a halt outside, footsteps approach. Britt stiffens, then relaxes as Tuck pushes open the door, steps inside, pauses, discards his boots and limps across the floor in sock feet. His mustache and beard are frozen, his poorly heated truck offering little heat. Britt looks up, anxious. He returns the look with the same uncertainty.

"Where were you?"

"Same place," he answers, "out on the ice. It was beautiful. Forgive me?"

"How can you take a chance walking on ice that was so thin this morning it even broke under Tibetta's weight?"

"The ice was thin because she was close to the boathouse bubbler."

"Okay but another thing, tonight was our chance to do something different, hear the 'Rippin' Rapids'. Your mother was supposed to babysit. Why wouldn't you go? You're always boasting of the great local bands up here."

"I do love those bands but I go to listen, not to wildly fling about the floor. You always try to drag me into dancing and if I don't, you dance by yourself. It's embarrassing."

"What's wrong with that?"

"It's just that most chicks up here don't do that kind of thing. When you go out on the floor, everyone's smirking. I don't like it."

"Then let them. What a cold place this is. Where is the fun in sitting hunkered down while the beat of music is coursing through my blood? I'm not dead yet. Why didn't you at least let me know where you were?"

Shrugging out of his bulky jacket, Tuck replies, "Guess I was upset that you wouldn't come along with me. My mother would have stayed with Tibby. I wanted you to see the stars lighting the winter sky, an awesome Adirondack night. Anyway, I'm just glad you're here. I was worried."

"Where did you think I'd be?"

"Maybe gone. This town annoys you so much, I'm sometimes afraid you'll up and leave. But, tonight, I had to get away myself, calm down, order my thoughts."

"You know, I want us to make it. I do love you." After a pause, she continues, "Are you still annoyed about my crawling out on that ladder, pulling Tibetta from the water?"

"Maybe, though I don't see it quite the same way. It was more my fault. A man shouldn't put his wife at risk like that."

"Listen, I was only trying to get to her as fast as possible. Anyway, you should stop thinking of me as a delicate city girl. You know, I'm used to doing for myself, not in a country way but a city way. My only thought was of Tibetta."

"Yeah, you're right. But it just didn't feel good having you get to her before I did," comments Tuck. He steps away from the stove toward the small, cold back room. For a tall man, his tread, even with a limp, is surprisingly soft. As he quietly opens the door, light from the front room falls across blonde scraggly hair splayed over the pillow. Sticking out from under Britt's fur coat are a tiny turned-up nose and one pajama clad arm wrapped around her new kitty, Snickles. He leans down, kisses and gently strokes his daughter's dream-filled head. Pulling the door shut, Tuck returns to the front room, plunks himself into an old rocker, stares at Britt, then timidly smiles. "Why is she sleeping under your silly fur? What happened to the blanket Addison gave her?"

"Oh, that? She's been wearing it all evening, dragging around on the floor picking up dust and wood chips. She insisted on taking it to bed with her. I know you don't like that 'furry fashion-rag' but how could I take it from her after such a traumatic day?"

He smiles. "Sure, that was nice of you. Can we just be okay now?"

Britt gets up, walks across the room to him. He wraps her arms around her and she presses her face against his powerful chest. After a minute of silence, she says "This is the way I really want it to be, not fighting but like this." Suddenly she looks up, "I forgot to tell you, Addison called. He sounded pretty upset. Asked you to call him back no matter what time you got in."

"Well, I'm sure he didn't mean this late. I'll call first thing tomorrow – though it makes me wonder. Did he hint what it was about?"

"He says very little to me. Sometimes I think he resents me. I don't know why." The truth? She feels locked out of this brother-to-brother relationship as much as she feels locked out of the community. At times it's like living in a different realm from everyone else, separated by a glass wall through which she can look but not pass. *Just because I wasn't born here, is that a reason to be against me? After all, this is still America, at least I thought it was, but the locals act like I'm a foreigner living here by the grace of their generosity. They don't realize that Britt Freier is a famous name in fashion.*

Tuck, his arm around Britt, leads her away from self-pity to something more sensual. "Tonight we have better things to do than phoning." They retreat to the refuge of bed and rewards far more satisfying than the fallout from interminable daily worries, happily oblivious of what awaits them in the morning.

Chapter 5

The next day, before breakfast but not before his coffee, Tuck dials his brother.

"Addison, it's me, sorry I got in too late to call last night. What's up?"

"God knows. Listen to this Tuck. I get a call yesterday from that psychiatrist at the rehab center, Dr. Kammer. He asks me where Bubbles went. Me? 'How am I supposed to know?' I told him. 'Don't get smart with me,' he says, 'Why didn't you bring her back at five?' I didn't know what he was talking about and told him so in no uncertain terms. Then he gets real puffy. Turns out someone, claiming to be me, picked her up by car around nine o'clock yesterday morning and never brought her back. The staff even claims they saw me. I don't know what the hell it's about." His words shoot through the line like machine gun bullets. Grimacing, Tuck holds the phone away from his ear. Addison continues to fire away.

"Why does that Dr. Kammer even think I would take her home again after working so hard to get Bubbles to sign herself in? What's he thinking – it's a joy to live with a drug addict?"

Tuck pulls at his beard while searching for something to say.

"God! That's strange. You hardly need this. What can I do?"

"I don't know. This Kammer guy seems like such a cold fish. I can't talk to him, can't stand his voice. Do me a favor. Don't say anything about how much I've complained about Bubbles. Don't need to give anyone more fodder to chew on. Until she got hooked she was a sweet person but after that she was a real trial to live with. Despite our pending divorce, I thought maybe getting her into rehab might help get her life back. Something weird's going on. I just don't get it. Kammer phoned my in-laws. Now they're in an uproar. Her father called and accused me of taking Bubbles out of the center so I wouldn't have to pay the bills. He was shouting at me, telling me he found out how expensive that place was. Who does he think urged her to go there in the first place? But here's the thing. He called the police."

"This phone's no place to talk. I'm coming down tomorrow. You around?"

"Sure. I can't go anywhere until this gets cleared up. God knows what will happen next."

Tuck hangs up, turns and stares at Britt. "I'm taking Tibby over to my parents. I'll be back before I go to work." Britt senses more to come.

"Tibetta, go get your snowsuit, time to go to Grandma's," she calls.

"Oh goodie!"

Britt is disturbed by Tibetta's enthusiasm for her grandparents. After all, *I have tried to be fair to her, I really have. But, I do need space to do my work – can't have her around all the time.*

A few minutes later, Tuck boosts his rosy, snowsuit-bundled daughter into the cab, then fires up his battered truck. It bucks and shudders its way across town to his parents' house. Tibetta adores her grandparents. She has lived with them the last five years while Tuck was on the racing circuit.

"How's PT coming, Tuck?" his mother asks, "How much longer before you're racing again? A World Cup skier shouldn't stay away too long. Someone else may grab your glory."

"Mother, it's not about the glory anymore," he replies, wishing he was as bundled up as his daughter, the better to ward off the assault.

"Not about glory? What are you talking about? Why, we were so proud of you winning medals in World Cup racing. The papers were spilling over with excitement. What about the town parade in your honor and all the TV appearances? Aren't you at all grateful?"

At this moment, a distinguished looking white-haired gentleman wearing neatly pressed khakis, a white shirt and black bowtie, enters the room. This is Tuck's father, Justus. "Son, a broken leg does heal. Lost your nerve? Afraid of the giant slalom? You need to work on getting back that old fire again. By the way, did you hear that your brother won the Green Design Architectural Award for his latest commercial building?"

"That's great. I do know about it but not the details. I want to hear more but right now I have to go to work."

"Work? You call caretaking work?" asks his mother. "Yesterday, my friend Esprit led our group in a séance. Not all of us received messages but Esprit did, telling her that you, Tuck, will become well known again and yet unknown at the same time. Don't know how that's going to happen if you don't work harder at PT."

Tuck flees; tired of static about what seems to matter more and more to everyone else but less and less to him. Where's the blame? Things he found important in the past were now losing their meaning. *How to share this with Britt? After all, when I first met her in the city, I was a ski champ with media-enhanced fame. I don't think Britt saw through that to the unsure guy inside. If I tell her now, will she still stay with me?* Doubts shimmer in his head like mirages on a desert.

He returns home to tell Britt of his call to Addison. Britt responds, "Bubbles probably ran away and maybe it's for the better. Some families seem to have bad genes and there's not much to do about that." She catches herself, *Oh Lord, there I go again.*

"I'm thinking I should go down to New York in the morning. Talking on the phone doesn't do it for me. I can't really sense his mood unless I'm right there with him. When I'm on the phone, I worry that my words will drop out the other end onto the floor instead of into his ear. You were planning to take the train down tomorrow anyway, why not change your plans and go down together in the truck? I'll spend the night at Addison's, and then drive back. You can stay and finish out the week at your sister's."

Once a month, Britt routinely travels to the city and works with her sister Shelley in their designer dress shop on 57th Street. They are partners in a small boutique for the well-heeled. Shelley is the business woman, Britt the designer who sketches out and creates the high-end dresses. Their customers are upper echelon Park Avenue residents.

"Your truck? You think it will make it that far?"

"I'm going to try. It's cheaper than both of us taking the train. What's the worst that can happen? If we break down, we'll take off the plates and leave it for some urban vultures to steal."

Tuck leaves for his job; Britt sits at her computer to dream up some new designs. The day passes, Tuck working at Camp Reedmor and Britt working from home. Their jobs are sometimes satisfying, sometimes not. Discontent stirs below the surface, erupting at times into bursts of irritation. How difficult to discern the true roots of discontent.

Chapter 6

The day dawns sunny for the trip to the city. Tuck turns to Britt, "I see you're ready to wow those city folks. Love ya honey. I'm proud of your success but you do look a bit like a space alien who fell into the paint pot."

"There you go again with that country humor. You think you're pretty funny, don't you?" she sighs. Packed and ready to go, they load the pickup, climb in and settle down for the long six-hour drive.

"Need your sunglasses?" asks Britt.

"Guess I'd better not; won't be able to see warning lights on the dashboard – and flash they likely will. How I'd love one trip which didn't include breakdown worries."

The road meanders south through deep gorges with magnificent mountains rising on either side. Their progress is slowed by a tourist-laden car creeping ahead of them.

"Mountain-peeper traffic. What a pain," Britt sighs.

"Yeah," says Tuck, "but tourism feeds our economy. I'm not sorry to see them peering out their fishbowl windows, thrilled by their so-called close encounters with the scary wilderness." In fact, Tuck enjoys the slower pace as he's not anxious to get to the city with its artificial shady canyons sunk deep amidst towering cement skyscrapers. Tuck and Britt, tripping between two cultures, relish the ride, enjoy being together, a welcome occasion to talk without interruption. In a rare mood, Britt opens up, admits her dress of the day is not very comfortable but customers expect her to model her own fashions.

"It amazes me," declares Tuck, "that seemingly intelligent woman discard perfectly good clothes – only to go out and spend hard earned dollars on more new outfits – all because some remote designer decrees it. Dumb! Of course, it keeps thrift shops stocked and your boutique thriving. Don't tell your sister I said that, she's got enough doubts about me already."

A long silence follows. Then Tuck reaches over, his eyes still on the road, his right hand seeking hers – but to no avail. "I'm sorry, that wasn't very nice of me was it?"

Still no comment from Britt whose hands remain tightly clasped in her lap. A few minutes later she asks, "Why are you always down on my work? What I do is helping us survive. Doesn't that matter?" In spite of what she says, his words stream deep within her.

"Now I've made you mad. Honey, I don't really mean it. You have amazing talents."

"If you mean that, then why don't you stop bugging me about the fashion world?"

"It's a deal. I will. I really just wanted to have a peaceful trip." They drive on for another half-hour, Tuck sunk deep in thought. *Shouldn't feel this way but I'm nervous about seeing Addison – not sure how much I'm willing to help him again – there's so much at stake. How can someone as rational as Addison cave to his wife's craziness, craziness which I fear may end up affecting the rest of us as well?*

Britt flips on the radio. From a seventies station comes Barbara Streisand singing "People who need people are the luckiest people in the world."

"God, if I ever heard a stupid song, that's it," explodes Tuck. "Figures my mother loves it but I don't know why needing other people should be considered lucky. If people would just think for themselves, the world would be a better place. I once heard a description of such people, the kind that always need to be led in a group – sheeple."

"I suppose you prefer Sinatra's 'I Did it My Way?'" responds Britt with an edge of amusement.

"No, not that either. It's not so important I do things my own way; it's more important I do what makes sense. If someone else has a better idea, I'm not opposed to taking it."

"Good, I'll remember that," she replies, leaning forward to shut off the music oozing from the dashboard. Tuck and Britt now settle more comfortably into the privacy of their journey. During one of the silences, Tuck drifts back, as he often does, to a certain moment last fall when he stood next to a waterfall at Byron's Camp. He was struck by the way flotsam, carried along by the current, swept over the rocks and dropped into a whirlpool where it got stuck, going round and round. *Am I also stuck? – travel – skiing – fame – emptiness?* He had grown up surrounded by athletes training for the Winter Olympics. Skiing had come easily and though he was naturally shy, once out on the slopes, there was no slowing him down. He became a highly competitive athlete, skiing his way to championship after championship. It was all so easy until, in Austria, he smashed his leg. It had been, he realized, a rather thoughtless lifestyle. He hadn't given much consideration to why he did what he did or what else he might do. He had grown addicted to hearing spectators urge him on yelling, "Tuck, Tuck, you've got the luck." It was like a drug, instantly gratifying – a dead end in the long run.

Is this all there is? Could there be something more meaningful out there? His older brother Addison, organized and a natural mathematician, had actually accomplished something lasting when he became an architect – but his brother had had different problems to deal with. *I helped him once but can I do it again? Will this all lead to breaking secrets? And Britt – sexy and lovely, how long will she wait for me to recover?*

Meanwhile, on her side of the seat, Britt wonders, *How long can I keep it up – spending one week a month working in the city?* Britt's design work provides the bulk of their earnings. *I'm stuck in the middle – never quite here, never quite there – just have to hold out until he recovers – nice when we're part of the international scene again – when it's the two of us without the distractions of family – Tibetta's sweet but I'm not the motherly type – besides, Meltmor is so provincial.*

Wallowing in the luxury of contemplation, they are surprised at reaching the city so soon. Her sister Shelley is glad to have her back at A Thread Ahead Boutique. Britt gets right to work in the second floor studio. Tacking one of her designs to the wall, she refers to it often as she drapes layers of brightly patterned material over a mannequin.

"Your work is beautiful," she says to the fabric artist who is working along with her.

"Our customers will love these," Shelley bursts out, sloshing in excitement as she pages through the new sketches. She is a wispy anorexic type woman with a massive dark hairdo cemented in place, giving her a slightly top-heavy appearance. Under this coiffure helmet, piercing blue eyes and an aquiline nose demand she be taken seriously, appearances to the contrary. Shelley brings Britt up to date on the business, her part of the partnership. "Do you think you'll have something for our seamstresses by the end of the week?" she asks. "If so, we can have the outfits ready for the Paris show with plenty of time for unexpected delays."

"For sure," says Britt as she thinks, *I hope so because a week away from Tuck is long enough – though I do enjoy the cultural life here – a break from the country bumpkin world – once we start traveling it will be easier to take off and come back to work with Shell – won't have to worry about Tibetta – she'll be with her grandparents – Tuck will be busy skiing.*

"How's the mother thing going?" asks Shell with a broad grin.

"What can I say? It's going – hopefully going away as soon as Tuck's leg heals," sighs Britt.

Chapter 7

Tuck arrives at his brother's place, only to find he's out. Strange – *he seemed pretty happy I was coming. Addison is usually as reliable as a rock.* Tuck takes a walk, planning to check back in an hour. Three hours later, after walking by the apartment for the umpteenth time, he looks up to finally see his brother's lights lit against the evening dusk. *What gives?* He wonders.

Tuck, buzzed upstairs, walks into his brother's white-walled condo where a starkly furnished sitting area faces a picture window looking out on thousands of other windows, city version of a star-lit night. With amazement, he studies his brother's frightening transformation. Addison is no longer the well-put-together, confident guy in colored shirt and pressed suit who generously welcomed you into his home. Dark half-moons now hang from under black eyes; he is unshaven, wears a wrinkled plaid shirt half in, half out of his pants, bare feet shoved into a pair of old sneakers. You would never guess this man has a closet overflowing with the latest fashions. He hardly appears the kind of occupant to live in such an immaculate condo. Still, he welcomes Tuck with a bear hug and brings him a cup of coffee before plunging into the problem at hand.

"So, I told you my father-in-law, good old Aiken, reported Bubbles as missing to the police. The staff claims they saw me pick her up. Knowing how he blames me for everything else, for sure he blames me for this too. Nice to have the family's trust."

"But, why did they think it was you that picked her up?"

"First of all, the front desk receptionist said that Bubbles told her I was there to take her out and second, she said she looked out the window and saw me waiting out on the sidewalk. That's why she gave her a day pass to leave."

"So, it sounds like they recognized you alright."

"Yeah, that's what they said but it's not true and they can't prove it."

"So what happened today? You look like bad, man."

"So, I'm just out of bed today, couldn't be later than eight, getting dressed to go to the corner deli for some coffee when the buzzer goes off. I start for the speaker to see who it is when there's a God-awful banging on the door. And who's out there? The police. Demand I come with them to headquarters; barely give me time to throw on some clothes. And that's where I've been for the last 9 hours. Called my lawyer; he came down. They treated me like a god-damned kidnapper. When I finally lost my cool, they accused me of acting guilty. My lawyer verified I had been at a meeting with a friend on the day in question. However, that meeting didn't start until 10:00 and Bubbles was picked up at 9:00 in the morning so that didn't help much. They couldn't pin anything on me so they finally sent me home – warned me not to go far, they may need me again. I've had it – ready to drop."

"Did you tell them *everything?*"

"Everything they asked – and that includes the life insurance policy I carry on her. Lucky they didn't think to ask me more." A long silence ensues.

"Have you eaten anything?" murmurs Tuck.

"Couldn't then, can't now – could use a whiskey though." Tuck walks over to a black liquor cabinet, complete with icemaker, glasses and a good stock of bottles. Pouring a stiff Scotch for his brother, he hands it to him, then walks into the kitchen and opens the refrigerator. An enormous something buzzes out over his head.

"My God! There's a fly in your fridge!"

"Oh," is all his brother responds in a weary voice, "Hey, why aren't you having a Scotch?"

"I'm supposed to be in training – been advised to cut down on alcohol," Tuck explains, "Sometimes I rebel, sometimes, like now, I do as I'm told. He takes a swig of OJ straight from the container and screws up his face. "Whew! What was that just slimed down my throat?"

"Oh man, you didn't drink the OJ did you?" exclaims Addison, suddenly alert.

"Damn straight I did but I don't think it's OJ. What is it?"

"Oh God! It was OJ weeks ago. Throw that stuff out or they'll be hitting me with murder charges in addition to kidnapping."

Tuck gives Addison a long hard look, then says, "Addison, brother of mine, we can't let all this get to you or we'll really be in a mess. Drink and unwind if you can. Doesn't sound like anyone's going to bother you for a while now."

"The thing is, it's not just me. Though I'm divorcing her, I still care what happens to Bubbles. In fact I'm paying for the fancy rehab – wonderful it if works and she gets back to being the girl she once was but – I'm not taking her back, too much has happened." Addison rambles on, "I keep trying to think of people who could have helped her escape the clinic's clutches, but I'm coming up blank. Did she run away or did something happen to her? I'm as mystified as anyone. Nobody believes that of course."

20

"So, who are her friends, who does she hang out with?"

"Hell, I don't know. She never brings them home. As you know, it all started when that Village gallery picked up her art work. She has talent, that's for sure. The reviewers rave about her. At first it was exciting but it was also the start of her troubles. That artsy-fartsy crowd she hangs out with – a bunch of groupies. I tried to pull her away but she got more and more defensive. She spends a lot of time with them but won't tell me much because she knows I'm down on the whole thing. She produces fewer and fewer paintings now."

"How does she manage to pay a bag man?"

"Oh – no problem. Her high and mighty parents have been slipping her a bit of 'mad' money for some time. I tried to tell them she was blowing it on drugs. They exploded at me for even suggesting that their perfect daughter could have a serious addiction. Wish they'd seen her all lit up – that would have knocked some sense into them – but of course, who wants to really hear the truth about anything? – especially when her old man was a kind of addict himself – had a little problem with gambling. I never understood how they ended up in such a lousy neighborhood until long after we were married."

"Is it possible that her habit was starting to cost more than she could pay?"

"Yeah, in fact she told me so. That's what made her finally see she was addicted."

"So – maybe her dealer picked her up?"

"Yeah, thought of that too. But, I have no idea who that is or how to find him."

"Let's give Dad a call. Sometimes he has good ideas. He's the one who believes that honest living wins out in the end," says Tuck.

"Right. And I'm the one who's starting to believe if you don't go looking for trouble; it'll come looking for you."

"Oh hell. Buck up dude. This isn't like you. Eventually we'll figure out what happened – then look back and wonder why we were so worried." Tuck is wise but not always right.

Addison rings their parents; his mother answers. "Addison, how are you? I've missed you so much. What's going on? I'm so glad your brother is there. You two don't have a chance to get together very often."

"True Mother. Hey, is dad there?"

"Sure, hold on. Is something the matter?"

Justus comes on the phone. "Son, what's going on?" Addison lays out the whole story.

"Oh no!" shrieks his mother.

"Damn it Mother, are you still on the phone? I didn't want you to hear all this."

"Well why shouldn't I? Aren't we all one big family? Aren't your problems mine as much as yours?"

"No, Mother, not to be cruel, but they are not."

"Oh I knew something like this would happen with that woman. She's always been strange. I told you not to marry her. I told you birds of a feather stick together and you see I was right. You marry those kinds of people and what do you get? Trouble. They never change."

Addison knew from experience that "those kind of people" referred to any folks who struggled to make a living – the kind his mother was convinced just didn't really want to earn a decent wage. "Mother, this is not the time for one of your rants."

"Fawn," says Justus, "would you please hang up? I need to talk to Addison alone."

"Well, I never! I care too you know. I'll have to talk to Esprit and see what she says about it."

"God help us," groans Addison.

"She's off now," says Justus. "I don't know what to say except keep telling the truth and everything will be okay. I'm sure this is all a misunderstanding and she'll show up in good shape. She probably just needed a break from the demands of drug rehab. That's the way I figure it. Hang in there son. I'm here for you if I can help."

Addison hangs up. "He means well but – but just keep telling the truth? If Dad only knew. If the truth comes out, it will make things worse." He walks over to the window and gazes out, hardly taking in the million dollar view. Tuck says nothing. After a couple of minutes, Addison turns around and strides across the room to the liquor cabinet. "I need another drink," he says, "then let's pack it in. I'm pretty ragged. Thanks for coming. I can't believe all this, just when I thought Bubbles was taken care of, my career launched – Boom! I'm hit by a tidal wave."

Another hour goes by; Tuck and Addison worries wash back and forth. Wondering what to tell, what not, the weary brothers finally crash for the night, utterly exhausted by the possible unraveling of their carefully planned lives.

Chapter 8

Tuck tramps into the house, happy to be home again. The unceasing roar of traffic coupled with the incessant blowing of horns, the shadowy city streets laid down between tall buildings and all the herds of people make him crazy. Snow from his boots trails across the floor but Britt isn't home so it doesn't matter. What does matter is warming the house for Tibby who needs to be picked up in an hour. He fires up the woodstove, plugs in the coffee pot, shrugs into a heavy sweater and exhales in relief. Twenty minutes later, coffee in hand, he picks up a book by Thoreau, "on loan" from Reedmor. He often peruses the camp's bookshelves, curious to know what Byron thinks worth reading. His collection serves as a personal guide and lending library for Tuck, one of the hidden benefits of his job. He opens to "Walking," a piece that moved him deeply when first finding it. He reads it again,

"I wish to speak a word for nature, for absolute freedom and wildness as contrasted with a freedom and culture merely civil, to regard man as an inhabitant, or a part and parcel of Nature, rather than a member of society. I wish to make an extreme statement, if so I may make an emphatic one, for there are enough champions of civilization: the minister and the school committee and every one of you will take care of that."

Powerful words. He lays the book down, stares into space and dreams, savoring a few quiet moments before going to retrieve Tibetta from his mother. Suddenly he notices a red flashing light on the phone. One message is okay; several spell trouble. He takes a sip of coffee, heaves himself out of the chair and warily approaches the phone, watching carefully as if it might jump up and attack. Depressing a button, he winces when his mother's voice emerges.

"We're waiting for you. Are you home yet? Pick up if you're home. What time are you coming over? Tibetta keeps asking when you'll be here, not that she doesn't love her grandma and grandpa, oh yes she does, I'll tell you that. She has a lot of fun with us. Just ask her. But, she does seem to miss you even though we took her shopping, played games and let her stay up late. But that's kids for you. Anyway, what I really want say is – actually I'm going to wait until you get here. You're not going to believe what just happened! You want to stay for supper? Call us."

An earlier message from his mother plays: "Tuck, you home yet?" and then again, from his father, "Tuck, pick up if you're home. We've got something to tell you."

Chapter 9

"Hey Tibby baby," Tuck exclaims, as his daughter races to leap into his arms. "Where'd you get that new coat? Steal it from someone? Fits pretty well. You look like a tame white bunny. What happened to my little wild brown-jacketed rabbit?"

"No-o-o- Daddy, Gram bought this for me. I'd never take someone else's coat. Then they'd be cold."

"Oh she's been spoiling you again. I can see that. Did you thank your grandma and grandpa for all the nice things they did for you – did you?"

"Of course she did. Now don't go teasing her Tuck. She's just a little girl. You might hurt her feelings."

"He doesn't really mean it, Gram, he's my daddy."

"Here, come sit on my lap," murmurs Tuck as he settles down gingerly on a fragile antique sofa tenuously supported by four impossibly slender legs.

"Now, Mother, what's all this you wanted to tell me?"

"I'll let your dad tell it. What I do want to say is that I talked to Esprit about you and she says – "

"Mother. No offense but this is none of her business – I really don't want to hear what she has to say. Just then, Tuck's father enters the room.

"Hey son. Do I ever have a story to tell!"

" So I hear. What happened?"

"I was headed home from a meeting last night, when I spotted a car oddly parked just down the road from the Way Way Yonder Pub. For good measure, I decided I'd turn onto the side lane behind the building and check things out – saw someone slinking along the back wall. Had my cell phone with me so I dialed the police. By the time the cops arrived, the 'slinker' had broken the window, entered the dark cafe and was busy with a tire jack separating the cash drawer from the register. Damning evidence. It was a case of 'cuff 'n stuff.' The man was hauled off to jail. The car was towed to Hood Slanter's."

"Wow, that's exciting. You actually stopped a burglary. Were you a little nervous – afraid the guy might see you and all before the cops got there?"

"I was. I don't mind admitting it. But, I just tried to do what a good citizen should. No more, no less."

"Dad, you get the prize. I'm impressed." After a few more minutes of chatter, Tuck declares they have to go, not stay for supper because he has things to do.

"If you're not staying to eat, make sure you feed Tibetta a well balanced meal."

"Yes, Mother, as always."

And the two set off for home. "What's for supper Daddy?"

"Well, how about road-kill skunk topped with blood gravy?"

"Yuck."

"So, have you ever tried it? How do you know it's yucky?"

Arriving home, Tuck unpacks their bags and wanders into the kitchen to see what he can find. Not much. He has forgotten to buy groceries. After scrounging around, he smiles to himself and comes up with the perfect "balanced supper" – peanut butter (*protein*) on whole grain toast (*fiber and carbs*) covered with chocolate sauce (*dessert*). Ah! An idea hits when he sees a jar of marshmallow fluff in the back of the cupboard. He applies it in a straight line down the middle of the chocolate (*skunk stripe*). Not able to stop himself, he slathers catsup on top (*vegetable, blood*). "Come and get it. Supper's ready."

Tibetta climbs on a chair, stares at her plate and bursts into high-pitched giggles. She loves when her daddy jokes with her. Tuck breaks into a broad grin. They eat, but only after Tibetta scrapes the "blood" off her food.

The next morning, after taking Tibetta to her grandma, Tuck heads out to the camp where he starts a fire in his shop stove, then walks outside to split and stack more wood. Byron likes the comfort of a fire on the occasional winter weekend when he retreats to the country. Tuck reflects that whoever said firewood warms you twice, once to stack, once to burn, failed to understand what's involved. *Trees need to be felled, trimmed, loaded into my truck, brought to the shop, sawed into short pieces – then split and stacked. Lots of hours building up a sweat.*

After chopping for a while, he stops and moves into his shop. There, an antique guide boat and Old Town Canoe rest on saw horses. Tuck gets to work patching them up. Hours pass before he is interrupted by a knock, the door flings open and a shout of "Mornin Tuck" booms out. Fellow caretaker, Stuart Moore, tramps in. Discarding thick gloves and a canvas jacket, he brushes the snow off, tosses them on a nearby stack of wood, stamps his boots and claps his hands together. "Man is it cold out," he says," you've really got the good life: heat, nice shop, quiet."

"Well, it was until you got here." Tuck smiles at his stocky friend whose black curly hair escapes from under his woolen cap. A weathered face belies his relatively young years. "What's up Stu?"

"Oh, just needed a change from the bloody camp. These owners, they take the cake. Last weekend they were bent out of shape about someone stealing food from their kitchen – all over me about it. Turns out it was their visiting nephews stocking up for a sleepover. How come you have so little wood left to split? I have three times as much to do."

"Been working at it all fall. What've you been doing?"

"Running round filling an endless stream of orders from Mr. Barton – no time to get anything else done. The man's got no mercy."

"Come on, Stu, you don't have it so bad. You've got a job and housing. Count yourself lucky."

"Yeah, true, but that's only part of it. The stove in my shop smokes all the time – can't stay inside long enough to get anything done. Thought I'd come over here a bit and take a break."

"Try talking to the Bartons about buying a new one?"

"Why bother – they'll just tell me to fix the damned thing."

"You don't know that – can't hurt to try. Of course, then, you'd have to stay in the shop and work longer," smiles Tuck.

"Take a hike! What kind of friend are you? – laughing at my problems – making out I have it easy!"

Tuck stops what he's doing, retrieves a battered tin pot, dumps coffee grinds in the water and sets it boiling on the stove – gives an extra a kick. "Think we both need a break; make the best of small pleasures."

"Yeah, I need that. Sometimes problems chase me around like coyotes after a deer. I want to do it just right but seems like there's not time enough to get things done the way they should be done. That's when I just shut down for a while."

"Oh well, despite your bellyaching, the Bartons seem pretty happy with you. You worry too much." Coffee ready, they fill mugs and settle down on a lumber pile to indulge in a little backwoods gossip. Camps may be remote but news flies around the lake faster than a missile.

"Heard one of The Hunt Club members insists on a fire in the fireplace every time he visits in the summer. Ace had to install air conditioning to get it cold enough so the extra heat didn't drive everyone outside." Tuck laughs as Ace continues.

"A downstate family bought the next camp over – closed off a trail maintained for years so neighbors could hike up the mountain. City folk – it's all about themselves, not anyone else! It really sucks."

"Does seem like the 'times they are a' changing,'" agrees Tuck.

"I hear your Pa caught a robber red-handed."

"That he did."

"Who's the guy?"

"Don't know. Don't think it was anyone from around here."

"Seems he had a rental car."

"You know more than I do." They chat for awhile. A half-hour later, Stu's store of news is exhausted.

"Well, I've told you everything I know. Guess it's time to go. Thanks for the coffee." As with many people, it never occurs to him that anyone else might have something to say. When he's through talking, he's through.

That evening, Tuck's coach calls for the umpteenth time. With Tibetta asleep and Britt away, Tuck decides to pick up the phone and finally tell it like it is. "PT just isn't going that well."

"That's what I've been hearing from the PT therapists. They keep me up-to-date. I've assured them you have what it takes. But, you don't sound like your old self. What gives?"

"Look, I'm not sure. This break from downhill has given me time to think – to wonder what I want out of life. The support from you and the team – it's great, but – I'm beginning to wonder if there isn't something more out there. Oh, I don't know – I'm trying to work it out." Sometimes it's good to spill the words dammed up in our heads, sometimes it's not.

"Hey, we've been banking on you for months, paying for PT, keeping your name in lights. You owe us more than this. You're our best hope for the team. Buck up man. You're in a funk. Snap out of it. Get on the slopes and see what you can do. Look, I'll come up there. We've got to get you back in training."

The next couple of days, a busy routine helps Britt's absence go by quickly. Tuck puts in a couple of six-hour days at the camp, leaves to work out for two hours at PT, picks Tibetta up at his parents', stops for groceries, goes home, does laundry, cooks, and makes time to play slap jack with Tibetta before bedtime. After that, he drops into bed, sliding into dark unconsciousness, when the weary often float blindly with the stream, never pausing to wonder how rough the rapids ahead.

Chapter 10

Tuck greets Britt with open arms, giving her a big hug. "Britt, moon and sun, how I've missed you. You light up my days – and nights." She smiles over his shoulder.

"You mean you missed someone to cook, shop and do laundry?"

"Come on, that's unfair. Of course, yes, I did miss that, but so much has changed since we got hitched. You've warmed things up, and not just for me. Tibby is even coming around – seems to be taking to you. In fact, since you pulled her out of the lake, she's come around a lot."

"Well, now that I'm back, you can start getting on the slopes. Is there enough snow in the mountains yet? Are the trails open?"

"Opened early this year. Yes, I need to be out there. Coach is coming up tomorrow."

"Oh honey, I'm so excited. You'll be skiing downhill again. Lots of folks are asking when you'll get back on the circuit." Britt, her face buried in Tuck's neck, does not see him biting his lip.

"Let's call it a day," he says, anxious to change the subject. They shuffle off to bed, bodies entwined, dreams divergent.

The next morning finds the slalom star digging out his skis, loading his truck and heading for the mountain. On arriving at the lodge, he is greeted with welcoming cheers.

"Tuck. You're back!"

"Make those boards fly!"

"Burn up the mountain!"

"Show the world!"

"Melt the snow. Go Meltmor!" He had hoped to return unnoticed. However, appreciative of the good will, he puts on a smile for the sake of his fans. After a ride to the summit, discharged from the lift, he pauses to gaze at the rime-encrusted firs and layers of white peaks floating into a cold blue sky. This is his landscape, his home, his love. He would linger longer but voices of other skiers, who followed him to the summit, are pummeling the quiet.

"Let's see you do it!"

"Let's go Tuck!"

"Tuck, Tuck, you have the luck!" He pushes off on this, his first descent since his accident. Slowly crossing back and forth, he tests his injured leg – and his resolve. The old thrill of skiing returns as he gracefully rides his boards, leaning to one side, then the other. His coach has arrived to watch and advise. The next hour is spent testing, testing, each time gaining speed, each time gaining confidence. One hour is the limit ordered by his therapists.

"Good start. Now I want to see you push a little harder," his coach says. Tuck stops, shoulders his boards and heads for his truck.

That evening, settled by the stove, he's surprised to see Britt pick up a picture book and read Tibetta a bedtime story. *Leave this to hit the circuit again?* His thoughts are interrupted by the intrusive ring of the phone. "Let's let the machine pick up," but Britt is already dislodging Tibetta from her lap as she reaches to answer it.

"What – they let him go? How can that be? I thought he was caught in the act." Tuck hears the distant crackle of his mother's words streaming through the line. After a couple of minutes, Britt hangs up and relates the news. "It seems the thief has been let go. He claimed his car had run out of gas, his cell phone was dead and, being too frigid a night to remain outside, he broke in to the Way Way Yonder Pub to call for help. The only phone available was a pay phone, the other apparently bolted up behind the kitchen door. Not having any change, he was busting the cash drawer open to extract a couple of quarters. It all sounded farfetched but when Hood checked out the car next day, turned out it was indeed out of gas. So – they let him go."

"That's odd," comments Tuck, "Think I'll stop by and talk to Hood. He hears a lot of gossip. Maybe he knows something because, as far as I can see, this doesn't add up."

Chapter 11

"Hey Hood," Tuck calls for the fourth time, squatting down to peer under yet another car. Finally an answer,

"That you Tuck? Out in a minute. Just doin' one more check of this here car. Police asked me to."

"So, what gives?" Tuck asks, as Hood, on a wooden creeper, rolls out from his hiding place.

"Naa much," replies the scarecrow of a mechanic, his once green overalls covered in black grease, even his glasses smudged. It's a wonder he can see anything at all.

"Is this the car they brought in yesterday from the pub?"

"Yeah, but don't ask me nothin' about nothin'. The driver guys seems okay to me. Just a misunderstandin' is all. Your pa was tryin' to do right – just made a mistake."

"How's that, Hood?"

"Well, turns out this guy Buzz Takher really was out of gas. He's city – probably just spooked what with bein' stuck out by himself on a dark country road."

"Huh, you, the village skeptic, you buy that? How come you're all heart this morning?"

" I'm just sayin' Hood replies while wiping his hands on a rag that is even oilier than his hands. "Hey, let's talk about somethin' else, can we? I'm tired of everyone askin' questions. It's just not that interestin'. Like, let's talk about you. Back on your skis yet?"

"I am." Tuck gives a tight-lipped grin and continues, "Hey, let's talk about something else, can we? I'm tired of everyone asking questions. It's just not that interesting. Like, let's talk about you. How's business? Lots of folks breaking down these days? That always makes you happy." They rattle on, neither one getting much out of the other. Coolness settles between them. The rumor mill grinds to a halt at the *Hood 'n' Wheel Garage,* the stream of gossip oddly dammed up.

"Guess I'll move on. See you later Hood."

Across the street, Pitt, Meltmor's valiant vagrant, back straight as a stick, approaches along the sidewalk, his tailored suit exuding an odor that ensures no one approach too close. "Things happening, things happening," he calls out to anyone passing on the other side. A rat, wearing a tiny plaid jacket, scrupulously clean from incessantly licking himself, perches on his shoulder. Rat, unlike his companion, is not a native but rather an elegant import: a gray-brown wood rat with delicate white feet and stomach. His fur-covered tail hangs down Pitt's back, mixing with his traveling companion's raggedy gray hair so it's hard to know which is which. "Rat speak, story squeak," he calls out. "Listen to Rat, lock up the cat." The strange pair is as much a part of the local scene as the modest shops and houses lining the streets.

The next couple of days fly by. Outdoor work fills Tuck's hours: splitting and stacking wood, repairing boats, clearing the drive of fallen branches. On the third day, a car pulls up to the shop. It looks like the one Hood had been lying under a few days earlier. Out steps a stocky, dark seersucker suit topped off with a low-slung, gray fedora. "What the – ?" mumbles Tuck, stepping outside to see the guy better.

"'Lo," says a pasty face with dark, crew cut hair. "Got a minute? I've somethin' to say you'll find pretty important." *Surely not from you*, thinks Tuck. "How's 'bout we go in that thar shed? See smoke comin' out, must be warmer in there – in fact most anythin' would be warmer than this frickin' place."

"Don't think so. This isn't my place to invite strangers in."

"Oh? Me thinks it's enough yer place that we go inside. Don't mess with me buddy. Ya betta listen to what I gotta say." *Something's wrong*. Tuck neither likes what he sees nor what he hears. He especially doesn't like this guy threatening him; he stands his ground.

"Here, you tell me here, right here if it's so important. I'm sure the cold won't freeze your mouth," says Tuck as he plants his feet apart, blocks the path and glowers at the stranger.

"Okay smart ass, listen up. That little Tibetta, I knows all about her – like she's no child of yours. Of course, most people don't rightly know that. Think she's yours, huh? Well, guess what? I used to hang out with har mama, Bubbles. You thinks Addison's har fatha? Well, guess what – he ain't. She's my little girl and I's layin' claim to her hea and now." Tuck shudders, suddenly feels shaky, needs to sit but never in front of this bastard. Never – never.

Thoughts flash through Tuck's head. *How does this creep know so much? What does he know? How the hell did this all get out? Who else knows? Is he bluffing me? What do I do now? Could it be he really is the dad?* He stalls for time – got to say something.

"Nice try, mister but it's just not so. What are you trying to do?"

"I's not tryin' anything. I's just tellin' you I's her fatha. Cute little tyke with her curly hair and smiley face. I's ready to lay claim to her – take her to the city, toughen her up a bit, teach her what's it takes to make it in the real world."

"Wait a minute. If you know Bubbles so well, then you obviously know where she is right now. Where is she?"

"That simperin' dame. The one who gave away her own kid? She's missin'? Her husband can't keep tabs on her, huh? He oughter know. Why don' you ask him where she gone to?"

Tuck's rage boils up, scorching him with intensity new to this gentle man. "Listen, get the hell out of my sight. We don't need your kind around here. I'll never share my baby with a degenerate like you. So scram."

"Rattled is ya? Don't take it so hard. There's a way outta this for both of us – I mean I'd like raisin' Tibetta, got no problem with DNA testin' to prove she's mine. Courts take that kind a thing pretty serious like. But, this maybe yer lucky day – turns out, fer now, I's right strapped for cash. So how about yous and me make ourselves a little deal?"

For the first time in his life, Tuck is trapped by fear. His carefully held secret is secret no more. Six years ago, Addison had confided to Tuck that Bubbles, pregnant and wallowing in drugs and depression, had begged to sign the unborn child over to an adoption agency. Addison, horrified, had told his brother about it. After some soul searching, Tuck had offered to step in and help his brother out. To prevent the merciless parceling out of the baby to strangers, to save his brother from despair, to keep the child in the family, he had agreed to claim her as his own. The story would be that she was the result of an affair in Europe. Now she has become more precious to him than he could have ever imagined. *Hell, nobody's taking her away from me now, especially not this creep standing here.*

So Tuck becomes the victim of blackmail. He can't be sure Tibetta is really Addison's child, nor, most likely, can Addison be so sure. It was but an assumption. Tuck does know that the marriage with the addicted Bubbles had been effectively over long before their baby was born. Pay this character, who he's sure now is the same Buzz Takher caught by his father, send a monthly payment to a mailbox in New Jersey, and the truth would lie dormant. It's too much for Tuck. Should the whole story come out, the consequence would be horrendous: Tibetta's grief, Britt maybe leaving when she learns she's been lied to, his brother's shame, his parents' despair, his own heartbreak if he were to lose his daughter. He can't see his way out of it. *All this because I tried to do the right thing. Wasn't that what Dad always taught us?* Somewhere in the mix, however, Tuck had overlooked the fact that, inevitably, what lies dormant will one day emerge.

The blackmailer, assured of payments, takes off down the road. Tuck is shattered. He recalls the day he met Britt in the city at a cocktail party given by his brother to celebrate Tuck's extraordinary world cup achievements. Something set her apart from the other blindly adoring fans. Was it her looks, her success in the world of fashion, a certain flair or something deeper? He's no longer sure. What a popular couple they were then – she, a strikingly handsome, fashion designer, he a popular, though injured ski champ. They hit it off right away. However, now that he's living back in the Adirondacks, new thoughts creep out of the woods and into his skull – like maybe there's more to life than pleasing the crowds. Maybe he's getting tired of the sports world, starting to enjoy the freedom, the hours of privacy that caretaking gives him, the chance to get out into the wilderness. Will Britt still love him through all these this? Now, just as he dreams of going in new directions, he is sideswiped by this creep demanding his take.

How to come up with the money without Britt knowing? They are barely making it as it is. Their small home had been bought with his earnings from the ski circuit. He still has a little tucked away but it's dwindling fast. Despair overwhelms him. The choice is clear, he must take action, protect Tibetta. But why now, why just as he is dreaming of a different kind of life – of permanently settling down – getting away from racing – seeking a new path, having a family – why does this have to happen now? Tuck vows action. But what action? How long will his savings last with this added expense?

Chapter 12

"That small town whippersnapper, he's got to go," rails Pru Power, as she settles into a chair by the fireplace in their ten-room penthouse. Her ring-laden fingers clasp a cocktail, her sexy, long legs extend out beneath the hem of an elegant, wool mini-skirt. "I told you his fame couldn't last. Look at his background. Who are his parents anyway? Common riffraff, nobody you ever heard of."

"What right do we have to call other people names?" says Byron. "Maybe we're merely luckier than some."

"Lucky? Nonsense. The cream rises to the top. If those Meltmor people worked a little harder instead of expecting handouts, attend a decent church, not a Catholic one either, dress a little better and watch their Ps and Qs, they wouldn't find life too bad. It's laziness that leads to such depravity. You can't trust a one of them. They don't know silver from stainless, gourmet from fast food – and I've never heard such English."

"Well, aren't we being a tad judgmental?"

"I'm only telling it like it is. That guy Chuck was way over his head, breezing around Europe – wallowing in fame. If he hadn't been so cocky, he wouldn't have crashed while skiing – serves him right. His brother did an okay job designing our guest cabins but that doesn't mean the rest of the family rates. I had a bad feeling the moment you took Chuck on as caretaker."

"Not Chuck, Tuck. And I think you're all wrong about him. We've been through three head caretakers now, trying to find the right man. After the last one quit, you know very well I had to find someone in a hurry. We were lucky Tuck came along. Personally, I like him. He's done a good job."

Byron, gray-haired and slim but with a once handsome face beginning to sag, leans back against the mantelpiece, elbows resting behind him, long slender hands dangling down. He remains silent, gazing at the young wife, once considered a prize catch. He had not understood at the time that Pru, twenty years younger, had grown up in a different era, one that would leave large gaps between the two of them.

"This is how I see it," continues Byron, "My father, and his father before him, always had caretakers. They trusted them implicitly. That trust was rewarded with loyalty. It worked for everyone. Most of these

Adirondack caretakers have great pride in doing their jobs well. Not only are they skilled in plumbing, painting, carpentry and electrical work, but they look ahead, spot potential problems we might never see coming. They know more about our camps than we owners have any idea of. In fact, nowadays, a lot of caretakers have college degrees in forestry, environmental studies and such. They would no more bite the hand that feeds them than you would lift a finger against the hostess at the Mayor's tea. Until something goes wrong, I choose to follow in the path of my family. I can't imagine a caretaker ripping off his boss. It doesn't make sense. Besides, even if you think these folks are so lowly, don't you believe in the American dream, that a person can rise through the ranks and improve his situation?"

"Ha!" Pru responds, "You know very well that's only a slogan used to keep the peasants in hand, give them some hope. Besides which, those who trust are those who get used. In this day and age you better look out for yourself, get the other guy before he gets you. Those brought up low class, remain low class. They don't get it; never understand they could get rich if they tried harder. Birds of a feather and all that –"

"Oh, so now rich defines a person's character? Guess that means some of our well-heeled madams rate high in your book, because a lot of them are doing very nicely: vacations in the islands, comfortable apartments, snazzy cars."

"Of course I'm not talking about them. No woman should sell her body just to get those things."

"But isn't that what a lot of wives do? Marry the right guy, sleep with him and they've bought themselves a ticket to the good life. Most don't give a damn about the sucker's happiness. No better than madams if you ask me."

"That's outrageous," explodes Pru. "Now you've gone too far. You with your pathetic excuse for lovemaking. You with your weird artsy friends. How dare you blame wives who put up with the likes of you. You're not half a man. There, I've said it."

"You have indeed. It's too stuffy here for me."

"What's that supposed to mean? I suppose you're too good for the social life around here?"

"On the contrary, I'm not up to it at all. In fact, think I'll pack my bag and leave for a while – need some fresh air."

"What a deserter. Abandoning me to go hang out with that depraved gaggle of writers you admire so much."

"What do you care? You have your culture-monger friends."

36

Byron heads to their bedroom, returning in a few minutes with a small overnight bag. "I'm going now; we can talk more another day."

"I don't think so. There is nothing more to say, in fact hasn't been for some years. I've already talked to a lawyer about divorce. Now is as good a time to tell you as any."

Byron takes a long hard look at the manikin he has lived beside for twelve years. She is indeed gorgeous. But, good heavens, why wouldn't she be? God knows he's paid enough for her body to be shaped by plastic surgeons, personal iron-muscled trainers, chemical pushers at high-end salons and fancy chefs who prepare starvation sized meals. How often he has slipped out to take his children for some hearty food at the nearby burger shop.

She returns his hard stare until, without another word, Byron grabs his hat and coat (Madison Avenue armor) and storms out the door for a night in a hotel.

The next day, the work at Brass Belle Publishing demands all his attention. But precisely at five o'clock, unlike other days, he surprises everyone by leaving his office and joining the hurried exodus of employees. Byron, once through the revolving door and on the street, is engulfed by a wave of emotion. It hits like a tsunami, tumultuous and full of the detritus of his failed marriage. Habit sets him walking toward his car but worry blocks his path. Changing direction, Byron strolls, somewhat in a daze, toward the promised serenity of a nearby park. The weather is pleasingly miserable; no chance of running into acquaintances, plenty of time to walk alone on the dark wet path which, like a snake, twists and turns its way into the woods. He follows, knowing it will bring him to his special retreat, an isolated bench by a bubbling brook. This time, however, he fails to reach his destination. Distracted, he ends up walking in circles, one moment sheltered by dark trees, a few minutes later exposed in the open again. He thinks on his life, how burdensome it is, joy gone – Pru doesn't attract him – did she ever or did he just do the expected when he married her? Her family, owners of a famous department store chain with an outstanding book collection – he an esteemed editor. A match made in Heaven? No, a match made by two eager sets of parents. But his kids, his kids mean the world to him. Memories of their rousing card games together, reading books out loud, swimming in the cold Cedar Bluff Lake. *Give them up? Share them with Pru? I get them Monday through Friday, she gets them on weekends. The holidays will be alternated. You keep most of their toys, I pay for private school, you take Winnie to ballet except on holidays when I take them, and Norm has karate on Wednesdays and sometimes on Saturdays in which case, who takes him then? One year I get to keep them on their birthdays, next year you do, unless you are cruising in the Caribbean when Norm's birthday rolls around in which case the following two years you get Norm for his birthday but not Winnie. Christ. Is this what we have to look forward to? Raising the kids as if they were small servants, there to fill parental needs? This will never do.* Byron walks on, seeing little around him, too much happening inside his head. Finally, he comes up with a plan, one he believes will ensure they remain living in one house: separate bedrooms, share the kids, keep up appearances but each lead their own life. Will Pru go along with it?

Chapter 13

Tuck, at work in the Camp's shop, hears the muffled sound of tires in the snow. Walking outside, he sees a Land Rover parked in the drive. Byron is heading his way, calling out "Greetings. Guess winter's moving in. Cold enough."

"Yah, that's so."

"I've got to talk to you. We've got trouble." *Not again,* Tuck thinks to himself, *like my brother said, if you don't find trouble first, it'll track you down.*

"What's going on?"

"We were up here two days ago, picking up a couple of things Mrs. Power wanted. Come inside the camp and I'll show you what we found." *This isn't good – what have I missed?* Byron unlocks the great, carved door to enter a gloomy interior. Thankfully, all looks okay.

"Notice anything different?"

"Can't say that I do."

"I'm not surprised. It's probably not the kind of thing you'd notice but several small valuable items are missing. For instance, a German porcelain figurine on this side table, a handmade lace tablecloth from Belgium here, and on that shelf," he says, pointing across the room, "an intricate woodcarving from France: a man with a basket of truffles, a pig at his side."

"Un-oh, I do remember that, now that you mention it."

"There's more. This way," Byron indicates as they climb the stairs, enter the master bedroom and are confronted by the sickening chaos of a ransacked suite. Everywhere, from bedroom to dressing room to bathroom, clothes, shoes, books and toiletries have been ripped from drawers and flung in a muddle on the floor.

"I'll be damned!" exclaims Tuck. "You've been robbed and I missed it. What did they take?"

"In addition to several smaller items, Mrs. Power says they got a metal box full of valuables."

"Damn. Were they worth a lot? Wish I'd known stuff like that was here."

"That makes two of us. I didn't know either. Funny thing, she says she can't remember exactly what she put in the box."

"This is bad."

"It's worse than bad. The police have been called. Officer named Sam Lively's handling the case. It looks like an inside job, and it looks bad for you. Sam was planning to talk to you. Heard from him yet?"

"Nope."

"You will. I hate to tell you but Mrs. Power insists you be fired, thinks you did it. You know she's pretty set in her ways – I've failed at tempering her. She puts the blame squarely on you. Also because the marionettes in the kids' rooms have been taken out of their boxes, one of them left with the strings tangled. And paper, crayons and a child's scarf left on the floor."

A long silence follows. After all, what is there to say? Clearly Tuck has been negligent, but to accuse him of actually stealing? He is devastated.

"Come on Tuck, say something. You know I don't believe you did this. What do you think could have happened?"

"Well, it's my fault for not finding this mess first. Part of it is my doing. That's my little girl's scarf. I had Tibby out here for a couple of hours on Friday. No one else was free to take her. I left her in the great room with her crayons and paper, told her to wait here while I shoveled snow off the back roof. Normally she draws for a half-hour at a clip. But this time she must have gotten bored and found her way to your kids' room. She doesn't have many toys at home so I guess the marionettes were tempting. I usually check to make sure everything's in order before I leave. But, that day Tibby wandered outside and was excited to discover black ice she could see right through. She knows better than to walk on it but she forgot and in her amazement, crawled out and fell in. The only thing on my mind was getting her out, home and warm. That's why I forgot to do the usual walk-through. I should never have left her alone, that was wrong and my fault. I didn't realize she'd be tempted to play with somebody else's stuff. She knows better."

After a moment of quiet, Tuck suddenly bursts out, "Bad as this looks, I didn't steal from you. I wouldn't dream of it. I wasn't raised that way. Caretaking's not what I'd planned to do with my life, but I try to give it my best. I'd never betray you. And now this, just as I was beginning to enjoy the work."

A long silence ensues. Byron breaks it by asking, "Your little girl okay after falling in?"

"Yah, she's fine. If she hadn't been, don't think I could have gone on."

"That I can understand. One other thing, Tuck, you got careless and dropped something on the porch. Lucky I found it and not my wife. Here," he says, reaching into his pocket and pulling out a small notepad which he thrusts into Tuck's hand. Tuck looks down at the familiar words scattered on the first page:

"Alone, high above the lake, turbulent winds split the doves' wings – falling, falling into the wave swept lake, sinking out of sight. Waters subside, a glassy calm – are those drowned doves or reflections from above?"

How did I get so careless? What else was in here? I'll have to check it out later. "I'm sorry. I seem to be screwing up everywhere – I'll get my things and be moving on. Thanks for the job. I'm truly sorry for all the trouble."

"Wait. Not so fast. You've indeed screwed up as you put it, but stay on a few more days while I think this through. I have to contend with Mrs. Power and then I'll make a decision."

Tuck drives away, followed by Byron. The long dirt road leads to the macadam on which Tuck is driving toward town when he realizes that Byron's car is not behind him. Turning around and heading back, he finds his boss half-way down the icy drive, his car resting on its side in the ditch. Byron is stranded, his cell phone battery run down. He is sitting on a snow bank clasping his shoulder. Familiar with sports injuries, Tuck wastes no time removing his own jacket, pulling off his wool shirt and using it to tightly bind Byron's arm to his chest.

"Thanks Tuck. I'm surprised you came back for me after what's just happened."

"I'm not a monster, in spite of what Mrs. Power thinks."

The two of them, Byron with some difficulty, clamber into Tuck's truck for the drive to the hospital where an ER technician takes an X-ray and finds no break. The doctor speculates it's a torn rotator cuff and puts the arm in a sling, strapping it once again firmly against his chest. Byron, worried about his car, is informed that Hood has pulled it out and towed it to the hospital. "How much is the bill?"

"Nothing. It's just what we do around here when someone's in trouble."

Byron needs to return to the city but is unable to drive. Tuck offers to take him there and take the train back home in the morning. For the first 45 minutes of the drive, Byron is in some pain. Then the pills kick in. Liberated by drugs, Tuck's boss slides into a restless slumber. Occasional mumbles emerge in an audio haze – "enough spin – losing spin – steady –" are his last words before sliding into a peaceful silence for the remainder of the trip.

That night, after delivering Byron into the not so friendly arms of Mrs. Power, he is back again on his brother's sofa. Addison, though still under suspicion in Bubble's disappearance, has gotten a better handle on himself. He is shaved and neatly dressed. The apartment is in pristine order: chairs neatly lined up around the table, pictures symmetrically arranged, everything square and shipshape in the rather sterile black-and-white interior.

They talk for a while and then Addison says, "I'm plagued by insomnia. Sometimes at night I get a real hollow feeling – like I'm empty – feel like something's missing in my life but don't know what. Nights bring battles with the clock, turning every half-hour to see the time, looking forward to morning so I can get up and put another exhausting night behind me. Days bring me blissful work and distraction, everything else fading into a fog until night comes. Then it starts all over again."

"So, beside Bubbles, what else is going on?" asks Tuck.

"Lots. Let me count them up. Number one, of course, is that Bubbles is still missing. Number two: her family, the Bellows, has a detective following me, convinced I did her in. And three: the police interrogated me again because with an insurance policy on her, I am suspect. Four: her psychiatrist, Dr. Kammer says he's bound by professional oath not to reveal what he and Bubbles discussed. Five: publicity about her disappearance has appeared in the papers and it's affecting my business. Six: I had to hire an expensive lawyer to protect myself against accusations."

"Accusers," says Tuck, "seems they're everywhere." *With all his worries, I sure can't lay any more in his path – like telling him about that bastard s blackmailing me.* Tuck was planning to ask for help with payments but clearly that is now out of the question. Instead, he shares with Addison how he too has been accused – accused of stealing. "I'm concerned the media-driven pack hounding my ski-life will find out and go wild with the info." I must say," Tuck bursts out, "we've sure got one thing in common: we're both going downhill fast."

"Yeah, but downhill fast for you means something different than for me. For you, it's a winner."

"Only if I'm headed in the right direction," responds Tuck.

"What's that mean?"

"I don't know. Right now I'm skiing along a ridge. One side is sunny, the other dark. Not sure which slope I'm going to descend."

"Not going to share more with me?"

"Not right now. I have to work out some things for myself first. Brother, what did we do to deserve all this?"

"Reminds me of one of Rat's frequent proclamations," continues Tuck, "Human race, sad disgrace – laugh in its face." Maybe they're right, maybe that's the answer." On that note, Tuck joins his brother with a shot of Jack Daniels.

"Thought you weren't supposed to drink, what with training and all?"

"That's so, but right now I could care less. The guys at home are always trying to get me to nip into their Jack Daniels. Mostly I've resisted but here? Now? I need a break."

To lighten the mood, Addison chimes in "Hey, somebody told me recently why Jack Daniels is so popular up your way – 'cause the square bottles don't roll round on the truck floor. That true?"

"Guess it's as good a reason as any," Tuck replies, as the brothers finally let loose a bit and chuckle over nothing in particular, just the absurdities of life. Eventually they turn to lighter topics, wishing, for one night, to stave off the clouds of trouble blowing their way. Next morning, Tuck is up early to catch a notoriously halting and unreliable train, the only choice he has to carry him back home. "Home to what?" he wonders.

Chapter 14

Tuck, Britt and Tibetta rise at their usual hour: 6:00 AM. After a breakfast of oatmeal with wild blueberries picked and frozen last summer, Tuck says his goodbyes, drops kisses on both Britt and Tibby and heads out to work – only he doesn't. Instead, he stops off at the Hunters' Hub for a second breakfast. It's his favorite diner despite the sticky sugar bowls and flies cruising around the red and chrome-edged tables. The small crowded room, a counter and stools separating customers from the kitchen, is the domain of Ma Rose, an enterprising woman. Years earlier, her logger husband was stolen away by a falling tree. She did the only thing she could think of – opened the Hunters' Hub and cooked, no longer for her husband, but this time for the entire community. There's not much choice on the menu. It doesn't really matter as all her grease laden food tastes about the same. But what the Hub lacks in quality is more than made up for by low prices and a friendly atmosphere. The big-bosomed, gray-haired, broad-faced owner rules her flock with kindness and good cheer, treating all her customers like family. She takes equal interest in each and every one.

"Why you sitting way back here in the corner son?" she booms out to Tuck.

"Don't much feel like listening to Sam shooting his mouth off. Need some breathing space this morning."

His thoughts drift back to the humiliation of being hauled down to the police station, Sam interrogating him about the break-in. "Okay Tuck, you're in trouble now. You're the guy with the key so everything points to you. We know you're facing hard times – being off the ski circuit. What you do, blow all your winnings? Your Pa must sure be proud of you. From big-time champ to loser. Didn't take you long. Your only chance of getting a lighter sentence? 'Fess up now."

"Listen, I know it looks bad, but I know nothing about what happened. Didn't you find any fingerprints?"

"No, but that doesn't matter. This was an inside job. You're the only one around here knows the security code," he replied, standing in front of Tuck who is sitting in a plastic chair. Sam, uniform stretched tightly over his chest, hand resting casually on his gun, leans over to glare in his face. Intimidation.

Tuck is jerked back to the present when Ma Rose says, "Sam? Haven't you heard? Guess Sam won't be in for a few days. Hey Ace! Tell Tuck what happened, he don't know yet."

Ace, his massive body overflowing a counter stool, is all too pleased to bellow out a story which, with each telling, has grown more elaborate.

"Blanche had to prepare a big lunch at the camp today so she couldn't make it to town for her sister's baby shower. Gave me a present to deliver instead. It's a doll made of a plastic jug with balloon head, arms and legs. She dressed it up in baby clothes and a bonnet. My truck wouldn't start so I took her old Ford. She had a pile of clothes on the front seat destined for the Laundromat so I plunked her gift down on top. I was driving into town when along comes our mighty lawman. He passes me in that big ole SUV, trolling the opposite way on the lookout for some poor sucker he could ticket. Suddenly, in the mirror, I see him wheel around, turn on the siren and fly up my rear. I pull over, open my window. I'd been smoking and the smoke goes pourin' out. I begin to make out his face as the air cleared. Real polite like I say, 'What s'matter Sam, you that desperate for a cigarette?'"

"Sam puffs out his chest smart like and fires back, 'What you doing with your baby in the front seat? Get him in that car seat in the back – right now! Some father you are!' So," here Ace breaks out in guffaws. The other customers, men ready to head out to work, have heard the story three times already and know what's coming. They echo his merriment. "So, I says, 'Now Sam. I know you're no dumb cop but if you say so,' and then I grab the doll by its arm and sling it into the car seat in the back. 'That better?' I say."

"'Out' screams Sam, 'Out of that truck on the double. You're not fit to be a father. Now you've done it. What a parent you are!' Man, was he ever mad. I was near splitting my sides trying not to laugh when our hero threw open the back door to save the stupid doll. Hot damn, was he ever rippin' when he found it was a plastic jug. He slammed that door so hard Hood may have to replace the hinges – comes flying over to me, pushed me down spread eagled on the hood, frisked me, God knows why, maybe looking for a cigarette, and reamed me out good. 'Don't ever do that again.'

'Do what Sam?' I says.

'Mess with the law', he replies.

'What I do wrong? Got out courteous like you asked me to. I tried to do what you asked.'

'You sassed me, calling me a dumb cock, and I'm writing you up.'

'Hey! Wait a minute. I never said that, I said you're no dumb *cop.*' But he wasn't buying it – steam risin' out from under his cap. He was gonna make me pay – somehow. And you know what, that ticket was well worth it. You won't see him in here eating eggs for a while; he's got enough all over his face."

By this time the Hub is in an uproar, men leaning back in their frail chairs, hooting and hollering, tears rolling down their reddened faces. Ma Rose smiles, letting them have their fun – then tries to put an end to it.

"Come on guys, he was just trying to do his job. Give the guy a break, will ya?" It's hard to quiet the room, but eventually they settle back down. "And the next time he's in here, I don't want anyone giving him a bad time either." Ma Rose, aware of laughter's sharp edge, is the only person in Meltmor who has some control over this crew. "Okay to laugh at folks but don't hold their screw-ups against them. We've all had them. Be glad Sam's on the job. He's done this town a few good turns." Tuck smiles in spite of himself, and does some reflecting on his own dark moments; no doubt others do as well.

The door suddenly swings open. Pitt strolls in and plunks himself down at the counter. The burly guys slide away, moving down a seat or two. "What's the matter – afraid of a rodent? The breakfast special for me, small one for him," he orders.

"Now Pitt, you know I don't like you bringing that wood rat in here, even if he is an endangered species. Ain't sanitary," admonishes Ma Rose.

"You let me in, Rat's cleaner than I am, licking himself all the time – that's more than I do. Besides, who else gives you such good tips? Rat roars, truth opens doors."

Tuck, used to this craziness, goes back to brooding: *How in the world am I going to pay that bloody blackmailer? How long will my savings last? How do I hide the payments from Britt? What next if I lose my job for stealing?* Worry creases his face. He pays Ma, who pauses a minute and gives him a worried look, then he drives home where the welcome silence of an empty house is waiting. Tibby and Britt have gone shopping, leaving him the privacy needed to call Byron.

"Byron? It's Tuck. What do you want me to do? Stay or go?"

"Listen Tuck, this is a bit of a mess but I don't want to lose you. Go to work as usual but watch yourself. No bringing your daughter out to camp. I've still got to work Mrs. Power around. She's gung-ho on seeing you fired but I'll try to straighten it all out. Hang with me on this one."

After two breakfasts and the phone call, Tuck is ready to start working. He drives out to the deserted camp where winter chores await.

He's relieved that he still has a job but realizes he's not out of the woods yet. The phrase takes on added meaning. The night before, a fierce wind storm, the kind most folks don't associate with the North Country but with which old-timers are all too familiar, has dropped two trees in the driveway. Tuck starts clearing them away, the chainsaw ripping through the trunks with a deafening roar. Suddenly, aware that Josh, caretaker for the Raven's Nest is standing by, he cuts the motor. Josh has a medium build topped with a round face, wide open eyes, black tent-shaped eyebrows and a stiff straight-up hair cut, all of which makes him look a bit like a perpetually surprised clown.

"Come to see if you need help," says Josh in the abrupt post-roar stillness. "Heard the wind come through last night – jumped the Raven properties but looked like you might have taken a hit. Any more damage?"

"Yeah. Knocked a hole through the pantry roof. Haven't gotten to that yet."

"I'll go take a look if you want me to – while you're finishing up here." The pantry roof, sagging under a felled pine, has suffered a puncture wound from the stab of a rogue branch. Josh makes his way into the house and through the dark low-ceilinged empty kitchen to the pantry door on the far side. Swinging this open he is sideswiped by a flying object hurtling inches above his head. A mess of shattered jars have liberally disgorged their contents over the shelves and floor: white flour, brown flour, sugar, honey and all kinds of other mystery foods. *Oh no, squirrels.*

A half-hour later, Tuck joins Josh to do battle with the foes who had invaded through the roof. Armed with brooms, they bat and lunge at the terrorists who slyly manage to elude their efforts. Battle cries ring out as they leap about in combat with what appears to be an endless supply of airborne invaders. "Watch it on your right, incoming." and "Right behind you, lift-off." When the action is over and the enemy vanquished, having retreated back through the open roof, the pantry is in far worse shape than an hour earlier: two windows smashed, more jars shattered, their contents added to the various colored spillages on the floor which, by now, no longer lie in pools but are tracked everywhere. The battle won, the war lost.

"That was great. Better than a hot night of pool," says Josh.

"A lot like racquetball," guffaws Tuck.

"Racquetball? What the hell is that?"

"It's a game Addison plays in the city. Two people with racquets hit a ball back and forth off four walls in an enclosed room. The ball comes at you every which way – like these squirrels. Sorry Addison wasn't here, he would have loved it."

"When did you say the Powers would be back?" asks Josh.

"Next week, of course. Damned if these things don't always happen at the last minute." Such are the problems of caretakers.

"Too bad but I have to get back to the Ravens now. Thanks for the game." A lot of cleanup lies ahead, no time for physical therapy today. He calls and cancels his appointment, then lets Britt know not to wait with supper. Repairs begin.

Hours later, the branch removed, the mess cleaned, the windows boarded up and the roof patched with tarps, Tuck decides to take a walk along the snowy shore trail, clear his head before heading home. The wind has died down, the sun is lying low, lighting the mountains with a copper glow. The stillness is welcome after his frantic day. Suddenly the Sears Camp looms up ahead. Lost in reverie, he had walked further than planned. Tuck has an urge to stop by and see his older friend, Moe, the caretaker there.

"Sounds like a crazy afternoon," says Moe.

"Yeah, it was. Funny thing though, I didn't mind. For several hours my head was free of worries. Then, as I was ready to go home, like lightning, worries flashed back. Got anything to drink around here?" The two men settle into drinking their beers. Moe stays with one while Tuck continues to his second, third and yet another. Tuck talks, Moe listens.

"Really nice there's no one around telling me not to drink. Seems like I belong to everyone except me – they're constantly telling me what I should and shouldn't do." Moe stays silent.

"At least, at the camp, I'm free to daydream, make my own decisions. Don't mind the hard work either. It feels good." Moe tosses another beer to Tuck who pops the top, throws back his head, letting the coolness slide down his throat. He rambles on for a while, words tumbling out, sometimes a bit incoherently. "Thanks for letting me spill my guts, you're sort of like the trusted uncle I never had."

"No problem."

"Guess I better start home. I'll sure pay for this. Wish me luck."

"Luck," says Moe. He walks Tuck back down the trail.

"Hey, what are you doing?" mumbles Tuck, whose usually shifting glance is locked in a stare directly at his feet.

"Making sure you get back to Reedmor. You're in no shape to walk this trail alone."

"I know these woods like back a my hand," slurs Tuck, "be fine – don't need a guide."

"Normally no. Now? You're beyond sober. Can't afford to lose a good caretaker – hard to replace."

The complement is not lost on Tuck. Once they reach Reedmor, Moe takes the keys, starts Tuck's truck and drives him home. Britt, amazed that Moe took such care of her husband, gratefully gives him a ride back to the Sears Camp.

"Don't be too hard on the guy," Moe cautions, "He's a good man, needs to work through some stuff."

Moe thinks back to his own younger days when, still filled with idealism, he was hired by a bank to work in their mortgage department. When he saw the bank pushing mortgages on folks who couldn't afford the payments, he voiced his concerns. The bank voiced its concerns as well. He was fired. Married and in need of a job, he quickly accepted one as a desk clerk at a four-star resort. He was instructed to tell African Americans that the rooms were full, even if they had reserved them by phone and arrived expecting to spend their holidays there. This didn't sit well with Moe. A couple of other experiences in the working world taught him that speaking up for what was right meant only trouble. Brought up on the golden rule, he discovered it doesn't apply where money is involved. Even in divorce, he'd lost everything to his ex who in her miniskirt and high heels easily deceived the judge into believing in Moe's cruelty. *Hard times lie around every bend – what advice can I give Tuck, poor bastard? None. I've no answers at all.*

Tuck is physically spent, emotionally quieter. Is it the beer or having a sympathetic friend hear him out? He munches down a plate of warmed over food, then, feeling a little better, lifts Tibetta onto his lap to hear about her day. She tells him all about the pink dress that Bee, as she calls Britt, is making for her and how they went out sliding together that afternoon and that Bee made her wear a silly helmet. Tuck hardly responds. Britt, feeling a bit sorry for Tibetta, tries to balance the mood by joining in the conversation with, "Boy, did you go down that hill fast, bet you weren't even scared. And how cute you will look in that dress. A real little lady. Show Daddy the picture you drew, the one of the owl. Lot of talent there."

"Okay, Tibby, it's late, time for bed," says Tuck. "Go get yourself a bedtime story." Tibetta rushes into her room, returns with a book, goes over to Britt, hands it to her and climbs in her lap. After the story, Tuck and Britt put her to bed, kissing her off to sweet dreams.

"How come she goes to you for a story?" asks Tuck, once they have left the room. He is glad to see his daughter growing closer to Britt but a bit resentful all the same.

"I think it's because, well, it's like you're not here with us, not listening. You're off somewhere else. Like, why didn't you come right home after work? You're drinking again. Oh Tuck, what's the matter with you?"

"I don't know Britt, I just needed to see Moe. He's such a good guy to talk with, like an uncle might be."

"Big Moe? I've never heard that guy say two words."

"That's true, come to think of it. Guess that's why guys like to talk to him. He listens."

"Maybe that's the same thing Tibetta needs from you," responds Britt who is equally amazed that his own child went to her instead of Tuck. *Admonished again and rightly so. I don't do a very good job of walling off problems from my family. Like, where do I go from here? Caretaking suits me but won't be enough to pay blackmail every month; I'm truly trapped.*

The past casts a long shadow he can't shake off. The only time he finds peace is at night.

Chapter 15

Tuck hires Slam, a goodhearted, hard working, devoutly alcoholic carpenter who sometimes takes extra jobs to augment his earnings. Help is needed to get the Power's camp back in pre-windstorm order. Slam, who acquired his name through a predilection for drinking, driving and colliding with other cars, has long since had his license revoked. He needs to bum rides from folks to get around. Nevertheless, stocky, scruffy and always looking for a ride, Slam is likeable and fun. When it comes to women, however, personality doesn't do it. The ladies think him cute but, to his utter frustration, he gets no further. "Don't know what I do wrong. I just can't connect with them," he says. "I find a gal as difficult to grab as a slippery fish," which description no doubt has not helped his chances. Slam has dated more women than most, but second-dated none.

"Maybe if you weren't so sloshed when you date a chick, you'd be able to carry on some kind of conversation with her," says Tuck.

"Could be but I git so damned panicked around women, I gotta have a little something to prop me up."

"It also doesn't help if you insist on showing a date your infected toe."

"How'd you hear about that?"

"She told me. I think you need some tutoring in romance."

"Lowdown scoundrel of a woman, making fun of me. I was just trying to give her a good time."

"Think we should get Wayne Roy to help, he sure knows how to hit on them, even the frigid ones seem to melt in his grasp," replies Tuck.

Slam, when sober, is a skilled carpenter. It helps him find offseason jobs when money is tight. Slam and Tuck work well together. They enjoy each other's company.

During the summer, Ace and Blanche hire Slam to work at the Greene River Hunt Club, helping to maintain the many historic cabins that comprise the compound. Something always needs fixing, from window screens to rotten sills, roofs to stairs. Slam, as well as Ace and Blanche, live on the property from early spring through late fall. The camp serves members and their families who travel from the city to breathe in cool mountain air, luxuriate in the beauty of the Adirondacks and occasionally do a little hunting. Residing at this remote lakeside establishment, without electricity (or off-the-grid as they say) and far from town, is a perfect setup for Slam who has a nose for bars and can't pass them by without stopping to visit. As for Ace and Blanche, they love being out in the wilderness, enjoy the isolation, the wildlife and lakeside living. Accommodations aren't bad either. They have their own cabin with living area, kitchen, a bedroom for themselves and one for the baby. Slam stays in a wing off the main lodge.

"Sometimes it gets sort a quiet out at the Hunt Camp," Slams tells Tuck, "so I fill the time building model bridges – always liked bridges, the way they leap over space pulling folks together."

"Are they copies of real bridges or do you design them yourself?"

"On no, they're all copies. Tried to make a replica of the Brooklyn Bridge but that was too hard. They're mostly modeled after local ones. If folks were more alert, they'd pay more attention to these constructions."

"Made many?"

"Yeah, quite a few. Some are copies of bridges that are falling apart. This way, I can sort of save them."

A week later the Power's camp is back in order, though it's a given that Mrs. Power will find something to complain about. That worries Tuck as does the fact that in the long run, she may persuade Byron to fire him. Anxiety is taking its toll. *Who could have had access to a key and the security code to break into the camp? How am I to earn enough to pay the blackmailer? Will I have to return to racing?*

Camp back in order, Tuck returns to PT. "We're trying to help you get back in tip-top shape but you need to show us you're ready to go to the edge. Where is that fire, Tuck?" says his coach. Tuck doesn't know. He tells himself to push harder, leave his options open but something is missing.

One night, as he and Britt sit by the fire talking, she reverts to the subject of drinking. "You know PT will go faster once you stop. And, by the way, how long do you think until you are racing again? You always made it sound so exciting. I can't wait until you're ready and we leave Meltmor – get back with our crowd, travel in Europe. I'm getting tired of ten-foot snow piles, the roar of sleep-disrupting plows, the worry of hitting deer, pedestrians and the sometimes drunken snowmobilers on winter roads. How much longer?"

Our crowd? What's that supposed to mean? wonders Tuck. He also begins to wonder just why Britt married him. He recalls her father's doubts. 'I want a man who can support my girl in style. I'm not sure you're the one. Be well aware she's used to the good life. What happens when you're no longer at the top of your game, shoved aside by up and coming younger athletes?' It was not a good family start. Rory Taglong had nailed the very same worry Tuck had tried to suppress. The result had been an enigmatic response to his future father-in-law.

'The same thing that'll happen when the climate warms and all the snow melts. We try to adjust,' he had answered. Britt waits patiently until Tuck comes out of his drift.

"Britt, I don't know. I do love you. I see Blanche and Stu's baby and wish the same for us, children and many good years ahead." It was an evasive reply.

"I love you too," Britt murmurs, despite her uneasiness.

"Britt, I haven't told you this before because I didn't want you to worry but I guess it's time to explain why I've been so preoccupied." *At least this excuse will do for now,* thinks Tuck. "You said you are willing to listen so here goes. Remember the break-in at the Camp? Well, Mrs. Power accused me of doing it and wanted me fired immediately. Byron is sure I had nothing to do with it. He has managed to let me keep the job on a temporary basis. He likes the way I work. However, I don't yet know the outcome. All this time I've been waiting for the other shoe to drop, for Mrs. Power to press charges."

"Oh Tuck," cries Britt. Untangling bare feet from under her, she rises from the chair and walks over to kneel beside him, wrapping her arms around his waist.

"Why didn't you tell me sooner? No wonder you've been so preoccupied. What an unfriendly place this is – people making crazy accusations."

"The accusations don't come from here; they come from the city queen with all her airs. Folks here are supportive," he says while thinking to himself, *except for Sam's belittling interrogation.*

"That's even more reason to get out of this town."

"I guess you're right," he replies, "but I'll be sorry to leave Tibby with my parents again. Now that I've had more time with her, the idea of leaving to travel tears me up more than ever."

"I get that. I had someone leave me once – a child, my godchild. He left for good though – died of cancer. It was awful. At least with Tibetta, the goodbye is only for a while. We can come back between trips and be here with her again. There *is* something special about her."

If you only knew how special, you would be shocked. How in the world can I keep all this secret? Ponders Tuck

Chapter 16

In recent years, digital networks have put news before our eyes in record time. For a long time before this, however, Meltmor had a different but equally effective system. Here, without help from the electronic age, news travels like static electricity, sparks jumping from one person to the next whenever the atmosphere is highly charged – and there is no place more highly charged than in the Hunters' Hub. Ma Rose hears that Sam is finally fed up with the constant ribbing and teasing of his cronies. He's ready to move to the city. "There," he says to any bothering to listen, "the law gets the respect it deserves." It just happens that Ma's brother is visiting her right now, and it also happens that he is a retired New York cop. Could he talk to one of her customers and give him a little advice and support? Sure, he'd be glad to. And so, Sam and Ma's brother Rod, a flabby faced character with dyed black hair, sit down for coffee at the Hunters' Hub.

Rod doesn't lack for words; they flow freely and without pause for a good half-hour. From this discourse, Sam gathers a few nuggets such as: "I loved my job. Violence was my pump. Never got enough of it. My best friend was my gun. Look at all the scars: knife wounds in my belly, bullet holes in my chest, razor slashes on my arms. Yes, it got the adrenalin going. Meltmor is boring, you should move to the city. Crime and mayhem constant – great fun. Proud to say that when I retired, I earned an award for never killing anyone. No, I wounded them pretty bad but never put 'em down."

When the cascade of words seems to momentarily dry up, Sam interjects, "So what do you do now that you're retired?"

"Go to the OTB, drink, smoke. Don't none of that bother me. I'm tough and strong as a steel beam." After another hour of warlike declarations, Rod says, "I have to go – need a cigarette. My dear sister Rose has given in to all that sissy stuff about not smoking inside." Rod pushes away from the table, stands up and, one leg dragging, limps out of the Hub. Ma Rose comes over to Sam's table where he is finishing up his umpteenth cup of coffee.

"Why's he limping?" Sam asks, "Wounded on the job?"

"Nope." says Ma, "Had a stroke – heart attack too."

Two days later, Sam and his older brother Josh, under gray snow-laden clouds, layers of wool guarding them against a frigid wind, hunker down in canvas chairs far out on the ice covered lake. They nurse cans of beer while staring across the ice waiting for the tip-up flags to spring into life, alerting them to a fish strike.

"So why now, why after all these years are you suddenly interested in ice fishing?" asks Josh, "not that I'm not happy to have you here but it does seems a bit weird."

"I don't know – guess I wondered why you do this. I mean, we could be sitting by a nice warm fire right now. Seems like that might be a better way to spend an afternoon than freezing our butts off out here."

"Maybe."

"So, what's this all about?"

"Sam, just sit here a while and see how it feels."

"Right now it feels damned cold."

"Yup."

"Why not just buy the fish? Save yourself the trouble?"

It's not the same."

"You know, I really came out here to tell you I've been thinking about leaving, going down to the city."

"Heard that."

"But yesterday I talked to this guy Rod, retired cop, brother of Ma Rose. Now I'm not so sure anymore. Pay's better but I don't think I like the tradeoff. Trouble is, I'm really sick of the guys around here getting on my case. I don't deserve it."

"That's so."

"So now I'm stuck between a rock and a hard place. Don't know where to turn."

"You're putting yourself there, you know?"

"You think I'm to blame? Get real."

"Not saying that. Just that you take yourself too seriously. Do that and the guys go for you like wolves after a hare."

"What do you know about it? You've always been the hit of the crowd."

"Not always. Remember grade school, how they called me monkey boy 'cause my arms hung so low and my feet were so big? I've been there."

"Yeah, but you never minded. I even called you that. You just laughed about it."

"That's right, because I finally figured how to make you guys stop. Started joking about it myself – took all the fun away. Laugh at yourself before the others do. That's my motto. If you'd told about the doll before anyone else did, the guys would've laughed but with you not at you. If you think 'cause you're a cop you have to be more virtuous, I'm telling you right now, that pisses folks off. Lighten up, Sam."

"Yeah, right, as if you're so bloody cheerful all the time – a freakin' optimist. It's not that easy in my situation."

"A jokester does not an optimist make. Optimists lack imagination, I don't. I just do the best with the hand I'm dealt – more like an opportunist."

"Yeah, but what've you got to worry about? Caretaker of a large estate, seven guys working for you plus all the summer help you hire. Free run of the place to hunt and fish. Your life is a piece of cake compared to mine."

"True, it's not bad but it's not what I'd planned. When I graduated with a forestry degree, I thought I'd have my pick of national parks: government job, great perks, chance to share my knowledge, but we were in a downturn and there weren't any jobs, so I found this and took it instead. Now I'm glad I did but back then, fresh out of school, life brought me down a peg or two, bit of a slap across the face for a young whipper-snapper right out of college. Listen, you think when the Raven's guests arrive and treat me like an ignoramus, you think that's fun? Believe me, it's a pain in the butt but I try to laugh it off. Eventually, after I've had them out on a couple of fishing trips, they start to change their tune. I grant you, law enforcement can be serious business. But, even then, I bet there's plenty of ridicuous stuff to laugh about. "

"I'll think about it. I'm not eager to move down to the city after talking to that guy."

"Sam, give yourself a break. Get outside. Enjoy the fabulous wilderness. There's more to life than busting your ass on the job. Keep it up and you'll end up like that Rod guy, nothing to live for but his work. He sounds like a real 'has-been'. It's the spin you put on your top that makes life worth living. "

"Geeze, when did you get so philosophical? Never knew you thought about this stuff."

"You never asked. Guess I got this way from sitting out here on days like this, the beauty, the solitude."

"Yeah, it's sort of nice. Haven't sat around like this since I was a snot-nosed kid." There is little talk after that, both worn out by having uttered far more than the usual banter. To Josh's amazement, Sam stays on the ice with him until dark. They catch a few fish, jaw a little but mostly sit, each drifting about in his own thoughts.

"Funny how you think about the comforts of home when you're out in the cold, and the beauty of outdoors when you're inside and warm," comments Sam.

"The contrast sharpens the experience," replies Josh.

When it's time to leave, Josh offers a rare invitation, "If you decide to stay here, we'll go out on snowshoes and tramp around the estate. You'll be amazed. In the summer, it's even better for seeing it all: acres of private woods, mountains, trails and ponds to explore. One pond even has rare heritage trout. Electronic gates in the feeder brooks keep other fish from getting in to contaminate the line. You'll also understand what a big job it is to maintain everything. I've got over fifteen buildings and lean-tos to worry about as well. It's not the easy work you think but it doesn't keep me from having fun." Josh waves Sam on his way, then shakes his head and laughs. "Only time will tell," he says to himself.

A couple of days later, Sam stops by the Hub for a dripping greasy hamburger like only Ma can make. "Got something for you to see," says Ma Rose. "It's in the backroom."

"What's the problem?"

"Oh Sam, not everything has to be a problem. You may be feeling low right now but at any moment your boat could start riding high. Come, take a look." Over in the corner of the pantry, stuffed among a jumble of obscenely oversized jars of mayonnaise, olive oil and red sauce, is a large cardboard box.

"Look inside." Sam approaches with trepidation, peering cautiously over the edge only to find it filled with tip-ups, a bait bucket and folded chair.

"What's this?" he asks.

"The guys got it for you. Heard you were out fishing with your brother. Thought they'd help you get started."

"What guys?"

"You know, the crew that hangs out here and gives you a hard time." Sam just found a lot more to chew on than his lunch.

Chapter 17

Meanwhile, far from town and without a wisp of sound, Tuck and his buddy Tim Berson, the 35-year-old, dark-haired handsome owner of Robin Wood Lumber Company, glide through the silent forest, leaving behind a single twin ski track and frozen breath-puffs hanging in the air. Tuck is distracted: *Buzz, damn his ass.* He shakes his head, trying to clear it. But, he can't stop hearing Buzz, more buzzing, until it grows louder and with a whoosh, two snowmobiles go buzzing past. *Now I know I'm obsessed – got to get my mind off that guy, think about something else.*

"Good timber in here," says Tuck.

"It's good alright. You can't beat trees for keeping the environment healthy."

"Wow, never thought I'd hear that kind of left-wing tree-hugger talk from you," laughs Tuck, "Don't tell me you've actually stooped to doing some green reading?"

"Thanks pal, nothing like a friend to put you in a box. Yeah, actually I have – that and talking around some. I'm thinking about going into sustainable wood products, buying from guys who carry the SFI certification, Sustainable Forestry Initiative. Healthy forests, healthy air and all that."

"Proud to know ya, man. Not worried about your bottom line?"

"Yeah, you've got a point. That's why I haven't made a final decision. If I carry more expensive products I run the risk of losing some of my customers. I don't know. But, till now I've just been running a business. If I make this change, I'll be running a business and doing something meaningful. I like the idea. I've even thought about dredging old logs off lake bottoms, a growing industry – offering those instead of rainforest wood. Tons of virgin timber lie under water and well preserved. If the wood can be safely retrieved, I'm in."

"Cool but could be risky. Maybe this is your chance though. The damned dollar shouldn't always dictate. If you do go that route, I could talk to Byron and Addison about it. The concept fits right in with Addison's green sustainable buildings. They might like the idea enough to promote it with prospective camp builders who go for the latest trend – and this sounds like it might become the 'in' thing to do. These Great Camp owners know each other and word gets around."

Tuck thinks how he too would like to change the direction of his career. He's practicing on the slopes again; Coach helping him regain his race-winning form. It's slow going. If he had his druthers, he would prefer to escape the rule of money, leave the ski circuit altogether, but with blackmail hanging over him, he sees little chance for that. Tim and Tuck share a special camaraderie, both often struggling with ideas outside the realm of convention.

"Speaking of going your own way," offers Tuck, "did I ever tell you how I really broke my leg in Austria? It's something I'm not supposed to share per instructions. This is what really happened. It was a stormy morning. Our coaches had told us to wait hitting the slopes until later. I was tired of hanging out with the guys, had an urge to get away by myself and decided to ski alone despite the weather. When I got to the mountain, snow was blasting horizontally across the slopes. A bit risky to go up. I talked to the lift operator, told him I was by myself and I'd check in again when I got back down to the bottom. Would he please make sure I had returned should the weather get worse and they closed down the lift. He was okay with that so I rode to the top and started my descent. By that time, it was a whiteout – I could hardly see my own feet but I was on my own and that felt good. Then, I lost the trail, flew over a cliff, landed in a heap and broke my goddamn leg. I lay there a long time. One of my teammates finally realized I was missing and remembered seeing me leave the lodge with skis over my shoulder. They sent out the ski patrol and found me flopped in the snow, slowly freezing to death. Later, when the operator was asked why he didn't alert anyone, he was full of remorse. 'That was Tuck Rising? Wow. If I'd known that, I would have done something. I thought it was just some dumb tourist.' Says a lot for humanity doesn't it?"

"Interesting. You never were cut out for the group scene. Let me guess. The coach thought it would make better press if they claimed you hurt yourself during training?"

"Yup, something like that. It's not supposed to get around but it's nice to finally tell someone what happened. I don't do well packing too many deceptions," *and I already carry enough,* thinks Tuck.

"Not deceptions, man, 'miss-spokes' they're called these days. In the eyes of the public, miss-spokes are okay, lies are not." This brings a good laugh and lands them back in the present. They fall silent, enjoy skiing under the arch of snow-laden firs, the boughs creating a cathedral ceiling overhead. "This place feels sort of sacred doesn't it? If folks are looking for God, they ought to come out here 'stead of creeping down church aisles."

Two more hours of skiing brings these friends the enjoyment of bright sunshine while yellowed leaves, torn from beech trees, flutter about like winter butterflies. A snowshoe hare explodes from a snowdrift and a deer herd, sheltering under hemlocks, stands quietly staring. After their outing, the two men return to Tim's truck. They are surprised to see a "For Sale" sign taped to the driver side window with a note from a prospective buyer stuck under the wiper blade. "Damned if the guys aren't messing with me again, they never give up," Tim says, the two laughing at the antics of some pal of Tim's who just couldn't resist posting the sign, "and, I can't believe someone actually wants this old rust bucket. If he's that crazy, I may just call him up and sell." They hop in the truck and head home. Tim drops Tuck at his parents' house for a visit. He finds Justus lounging in an overstuffed chair, the room lit neither by sunshine nor lamplight, as if his mood had called in the shadows.

"Hey Dad, you feeling down?"

"Why do you ask me that?"

"Because it's so dark in here you could mine the gloom with a shovel. Are you worrying about the opening of SuperPig?"

"Son, that's not the way we taught you to treat newcomers here in Meltmor. You may not like box stores but at least be courteous and call this one by its right name, SuperBig."

"Okay, Okay, Dad, but I'm concerned about your business – worried that this SuperBig invader plans to hog all the Outdoors and Inn's clothing customers. I've heard some of these box stores move in, lower prices to grab all the customers, then raise them when the competition is pushed out."

"You don't build customer loyalty over so many years for nothing. I've treated folks well; they'll do the same for me. That's how it works, that's how it always will. No worry there," his father protests.

"Dad, it's not about good management anymore, it's about cheap gratification. Times are not what they used to be."

"Don't worry son. I realize you mean well but I've been around the block a few times, I know of what I speak. No, it's not my business that depresses me so much as the news I see on TV, reports of increasing cruelty, misery and poverty the world over." Suddenly light floods the room as Fawn, a plumpish woman with permed blonde hair and apple cheeks, comes in and flips the switch.

"It's like a morgue in here." she complains. "You can hardly see each other." Then, picking up on the discussion, the last few words of which she overheard, she adds, "Anyway, there's no reason to be so somber. My friend, Esprit, sees into a future the rest of us don't even begin to understand. Esprit says the world is moving toward a great coming together. Poor people just need to work harder if they don't want to be poor. We need to help them think positive and try harder and Esprit's Girls, that's what she calls us, are going to help them do it. She's showing us how to reach out with love to women in other countries – explain our lifestyle – show them our culture of prosperity and justice so they can make it happen in their own countries. And we won't stop there, if they don't change their ways, Esprit assures us that America stands ready and willing to help them do it with whatever force is needed. I'm so honored to be part of it all."

"I hope Mother's kidding," Tuck murmurs to his father.

"I'm afraid she's not" replies Justus.

Aware they are whispering, Fawn continues, "You think I'm silly but just wait, you'll see I'm not. I'm off to my group right now as a matter of fact. Esprit is a powerful medium, she channels strength to her girls. Only yesterday, we lit candles, turned the lights low and sat around her table, levitated it too. If that isn't proof the spirit was there, I don't know what is. Esprit says bumps in the road are just there to test our faith. If we believe hard enough everything will be fine." With that, Fawn flings a wool coat over her flowered dress and marches out the door, her boots clacking down the hall.

"Dad, I think you've provided too well for mother. She's going crazy from boredom. You've got to do something."

"She wasn't so involved with this nut until you came back with Britt and took Tibetta away from her. I guess she's only looking for a cause. I wish I could provide her with a better one but she won't listen to me. In fact, I found out this Esprit is sharper than you'd think. I was looking up background information on the SuperBig," (*so he is worried*, reflects Tuck) when I came across the catalog store from which Esprit insists her followers order all their so called spiritual clothes. Guess what? A little sleuthing and I discovered her family owns the company that sells them. Pretty clever. Whenever I suggest that your mother find some different friends, she replies that she won't be so easily misled by nonbelievers. She is forever quoting Esprit who tells her, 'Be careful about hanging out with women who refuse to join us. Birds of a feather stick together, link up with nonbelievers and you'll be marked.' Fawn hangs on her every word."

"You know what? I think between your absorption with the news and fixation on the store, Mother feels lonely and doesn't know where to turn. It's easier for her to follow a leader than struggle along by herself."

"Son, I know you're concerned and mean well but she does have me, you know. There is no good reason for her to chase off after that tropical bird Esprit."

"Maybe you don't open up to her about your concerns? Everyone knows you're fairly down and Mother told me she's worried. Right now she's grappling for something to believe in – and Esprit is it."

"Okay, let's stop with all this nonsense. Maybe it's time to start worrying more about your own career and leave mine to me. Looks like your future path is murky right now. What are you planning to do about your future?"

"Sorry, no harm meant – I'm doing my best, Dad, though it never quite seems like enough."

"Talk to your brother. He's made a respectable place for himself in society. I think you could use some sound advice from him." *Yeah, if you only knew. He's the very cause of much of*

my trouble, Tuck reflects.

Chapter 18

Tuck's days fall into a pattern: at the camp by six, work until two, then off to physical therapy, followed by ski practice a couple of times a week. Afterward, he stops by the tidy, white clapboard-sided house where Tibetta stays with his parents after her day at kindergarten. Picking her up, he drives home, his bouncy daughter chatting about her day and trying to show him her drawings. These are cherished moments for Tuck: timeless space together.

Some days, while at work, he takes a break to go raid the camp's library. Tuck is discovering the great joy of reading. *It would be nice if there were more time for this indulgence,* he reflects. He enjoys learning how people in other places and other ages wrestled with problems similar to those faced today; how predictable the repetition of historical events; how circular our lives. He is appalled at how little mankind learns from history. In school, it was repeatedly pounded into his head that history was important. But force is not always the best way to deliver a message. Sometimes the hammer breaks the nail. *We're repeaters, for better or worse.* At times, he catches himself standing and staring. *It's happening again, daydreaming.* With an effort, he wills himself back to the job at hand. *If I don't pick up the pace, get something done, Byron will be back on my case as he was when he reminded me, "Keep your mind on your work or I'll have my wife complaining again."*

To clear his swirling brain, Tuck imagines tossing his thoughts into a river where they are swept downstream, caught in a quiet pool and retrieved later. It helps him refocus on the tasks at hand. One of those chores, splitting and stacking wood, provides a kind of worker's meditation. Turmoil washes away and the hours pass quickly.

Driving back from physical therapy one afternoon, he suddenly remembers that Tibetta is spending the night at his parents' home so doesn't need to be picked up. This gives him a little extra time. On impulse, he stops and parks at the Hub for a quick coffee. Officer Sam is the only one there. *Guess I ought to sit with him. Can't very well avoid it.*

"Sam, what gives?"

"Not much I guess except of course the fishing gear you guys got me. That was real nice."

"Hope you use it. Won't do much good in the box, not many fish inside there."

Sam laughs. "Some truth in that, for sure."

"Hey Sam. Don't let all the ribbing get to you. We can be rough at times."

"Got that right. I've been thinking of moving away from this abusive town. My brother Josh says he keeps wolves, like you guys, away by laughing at himself before you do. Never realized he had wolves to worry about."

"Huh. Guess we all do. I once read somewhere about using humor as a trick to deny misery."

"Sort of like my brother does – it's not so easy."

This guy is too serious, same as me, Tuck realizes with some surprise. "Well," says Tuck, "Now you know how I felt when you went after me for the Power's robbery. You were the wolf then."

"Just doing my job, never really thought you had anything to do with it but you know orders are orders. They tell you to give someone a hard time, that's what I gotta do."

"Well Sam, I've got to be getting back to the missus. Do what Ma Rose does, slather on the oil, keeps bad stuff from sticking to you."

"Right, and I'd need so much, they'd be calling me grease ball next – well, see ya."

That evening Tuck and Britt get ready to head out for a party with other caretakers. "Dress warmly, we're going to have a bonfire on the ice."

"Outside?"

"I've yet to see a bonfire inside, that might be interesting – or not. Yup, outside. It'll be fun. You'll see."

"Good Lord. Don't know when I'll ever get used to this life."

"Don't know either. Look, it's not what you bargained for but I'm still hoping something will change your outlook."

Pitt and Rat have a different take on hope: "When hope assumes, trouble looms."

"You I love but some of these people you hang out with are really crude. They seem, I don't know, sort of thoughtless – have a weird sense of humor," Britt says.

"You'll get used to it. They're not bad folks." Tuck goes outside to start the truck and warm it up. In a few minutes, Britt joins him.

"I put more logs on the fire so the house will be good and warm when we return from this crazy arctic excursion," announces Britt as a way of letting him know once more how she feels about the evening.

On arriving at Cedar Bluff Lake, they tramp a short distance out on the ice to join friends gathered round a blazing fire, some standing, some sitting on sleds or pieces of firewood. A crystal clear starry sky arches over this glowing scene of merriment. "Hey Tuck, Britt. Keg's over on the sled," indicates Stu with a thumb pointed back over his shoulder. "What a night huh?"

Tuck moves toward the keg, catches Britt's frown, changes direction. "Got anything else here? Britt doesn't drink beer."

Nice cover Tuck, my darling, you're a quick thinker. You've ducked the ridicule of these oafs who think if you don't drink, you're not macho, thinks Britt. Tuck locates a few stray soda cans knocking about in an oversized box out in the dark beyond the reach of firelight. Grabbing a couple for the two of them, he holds his mittened hand over the soda labels and heads back to Britt. The crowd consists mostly of caretakers, so, as one might expect, the talk revolves around their work. "I got to fill the Raven's ice house soon. Anyone interested in helping me with that?" asks Josh.

"What do they need the ice for, don't they have a freezer?" asks Britt.

"Sure, but they get a kick out of giving their summer guests cocktails cooled with ice right out of the lake. Of course, it would be lake ice anyway as all their drinking water comes from the lake as well."

"So," says Big Moe with a smile, "why not just make it in their freezer and load it into the ice house? – be easier."

"Now there's an idea. But they might get suspicious if they found their ice house stacked full of tiny 1-inch cubes. Anyway, they like it done for tradition's sake and harvesting can be sort of fun. Who's in?" Several voices answer.

"Great, I'll call you when I'm ready. Thanks."

"Wish the Bartons would drink lake water. They have a well. Everything pumped from that is treated with ultraviolet but still they don't trust it. I haul in gallons of bottled water for their use," says Stu.

"Aw stop bellyaching" Josh pipes up. "We all do that. It's one of the easiest parts of the job – that and emptying mouse traps."

Ace, a heavy but muscular, large man ambles over to Tuck and Britt who are standing slightly apart from the group. "You seem a bit somber these days," he says.

"Guess so. There's been a robbery at the Power's Camp and Mrs. Power accuses me of doing it. Being under suspicion feels like a punch in the gut."

"What does Byron think?" Ace asks, a deep creased frown filling his forehead.

"He doesn't believe I had anything to do with it but you know how it goes, his wife is from a younger generation of city folk. They distrust everybody. Of course, I do have some guilt in the matter because they noticed the missing items before I did. That's not so good but I can't do much about it now."

"Listen, never told anyone before but I've screwed up too – guess we all do sometimes. I think these owners don't know the half of what we go through to keep their camps running smoothly. But, I wouldn't trade caretaking, the freedom, the outdoor life, for a million dollars – well, maybe for a million. Anyway, it was last spring. I was supposed to replace one of the cabins' brown shingled roofs with a new green one – get it all done by Memorial Day. Heavy rain was predicted the next week so we had to put on speed to do it. We took a few risks we probably shouldn't have. I put in a rush order for the shingles. Slam met the delivery truck at the landing, the driver helped him load them into the work boat and, gunwales barely above water, he managed to haul 'em back up to the club without swamping. I was pretty ticked when I saw that boat. Didn't want him to take that much risk but you know Slam, always trying to please. Anyway, we were doing our best to get done before the weather turned. Blanche here," he said, as he put his arm around her broad shoulders, "Blanche, God Bless her, is fearless about a lot of things, heights being one. Next thing I know she's up there with us nailing down the roof. We worked like the wind. Suddenly a thunder storm came barreling down the lake. We held our positions till the last shingles were nailed in place, then practically slid down the ladder in our haste to get out of there. In the nick of time too. Lightning hit a nearby tree and we bolted for shelter. Man, were we ever proud of the job we'd done. Having heard the weather was bad, Norton Smithers – he's the club president – had called and asked if there was any damage, 'Did we get tarps over the roof in time, were there any leaks?'

"'Not a bit,' I told him, 'we managed to finish up just before the storm broke.' He arrived the next day along with several families, took one look at the roof and exploded.

"'What the hell? Ace, the roof's the wrong color.'

"And then I suddenly remembered he'd ordered green. In my rush to get the do the job, I'd ordered the same color brown again. What to do? Well, Norton is no spring chicken so I said, 'Oh Sir, I remember you distinctly telling me brown. I thought at the time how nice green would look but as you had said brown, I did exactly what you wanted.'

"'Brown? I didn't tell you brown.'

"'With all due respect sir, I distinctly remember, you saying so and to be sure I got the color right, I made up a rhyme, go to town, order brown.'

"'Really? Can't believe I told you that but as you seem sure of yourself I must have. How could I make such a mistake? Guess my wife is right, I am getting old.'

"I looked at his white hair, creased face and bent frame, smiled friendly like and said, 'Old? You sir? Not you. You're as young and spry as anyone I know.'

"'Thanks Ace,' he answered, 'I guess I must have been confused. Brown will have to do. I'll tell the club I forgot what we'd decided on. They'll probably be okay with that but my wife won't. I'll have to listen to her carry on about it. She doesn't think quite the same about me as you do. She's tells me I look well along in years. Women. They simply have surgery whenever something droops. She's got more stitching in her than my granny's quilt.'"

Tuck laughs long and hard. "Love it. That does make me feel better."

"I'm just telling you all this so you'll feel better but don't be passing it around – might ruin my reputation."

For the rest of the evening, stories spread through the group like fire through dry grass – one account touching off another, many hitting on the subject of nudity. Caretakers, often treated as if invisible, are witnesses to a lot of sunbathing in the buff. But, duty bound, they never confess to seeing anything.

"Family squabbles too; we hear a lot we don't admit to. Guess money doesn't protect a person from everything; these people are still all too human," says Ace.

"Yeah, but it's a lot more fun to fight with your wife if you don't have to worry about money as well," responds Stu, "wish they'd share a little more of it with me."

"They do, says Tuck," You guys get hung up on all the wealth but those owners provide us with a good living, and their acreage keeps wilderness and hunting grounds from development. Here's to a long and healthy future for Adirondack Great Camps."

"Got a point Tuck, we'll drink to that," chime in several others as they lift their beers to the starlit sky and toss them off in thirsty gulps.

"But I do wonder just how some of them make their money and how dirty it is," pipes up Stu again.

"Guess a lot of it's tainted by Wall Street and banking shenanigans but at least the dough is recycled here in the Adirondacks, kind of

Robin Hood style," responds Sue Tower who, despite her padded winter jacket and snow pants, is a noticeably slender and elegant woman.

Drinking and good cheer take over, except for Britt. She is cold in her lovely but inadequate jacket. No matter how close she huddles to the fire, her near side is too hot and the other side freezing. Slowly the crowd thins. Britt and Tuck, one of the last couples on the ice, finally leave as well. He walks her back across the ice to the truck where he turns on the poor excuse for a heater and tries to thaw her out. "I think I'll never warm up again."

"Sorry Hon. You really need to dress for the weather up here. I tried to tell you it would be cold. How about we stop at Stewarts for hot coffee to warm you up a bit? Then I'll do the rest after we're home in bed."

"Sounds good. I don't get why you all like to go to a party bundled up like Eskimos. I was just trying to look nice for you Tuck," Britt says.

"And you did Honey. You were the best looking woman there. You always are. After all, you didn't get last year's Urban Fashion award for nothing but I was worried you'd be too cold – and you were."

After a long silence during which Britt snuggles close to Tuck, she says, "Tuck? Could Ace have been fired for lying about that roof?"

Just then they pull into Stewart's, go inside for coffee and to sit where it is warm for a bit before going home. Picking up the conversation again, Tuck continues.

"Yes, he could've been fired. He shouldn't have lied but caretakers take pride in doing things right. Ace is pretty macho, guess he couldn't bring himself to 'fess up to the Club members. In the scope of the universe, how important is it really that one of the club's rental cabins has a brown roof instead of green – I mean, does it truly matter? Ace's father and grandfather were caretakers there many years before he came along. The family has always been highly regarded. In fact, The Hunt Club members all pitched in and bought Ace and Blanche a sizeable trailer home so they'd have some place to go in the winter. Those two are essential to the smooth operation of the Hunt Club. Members know they're lucky to have Ace as well as Blanche who cooks their meals. They would have been miffed but that's about it. In fact, I even wonder if he did fool Norton. He's a good man and possibly even more wily than Ace. He might very well have understood that Ace's pride was at stake."

After coffee, they climb back in the truck and head for home.

"I find the caretakers' sense of humor, like Ace's story, as dumb as a bucket of rocks. And it's hard for me to join the conversation. When I try, people listen politely, turn away and ignore me. I feel locked out," Britt says.

"Well, you do have to watch what you say – like complaining about guys leaving their trucks idling when they make a stop somewhere. That's just what guys do up here. You can't mess with it."

"But – but – but you told me you care about pollution and the environment and that you would help Tim find customers for his sustainable wood. Why is that okay and what I say is not?"

"Well – there's a little more to it than that. For instance, how about all those guys who arrive by pontoon planes for the weekend? What about the gas they're using? That should be mentioned as well. I guess it's the way you say it and, I don't know if I should tell you this, but it's partly because you're new around here. Maybe better to do more listening for a while. Do that before you make suggestions and eventually you'll see them come around. You can't ramrod ideas through. Folks need time."

"You know what? I can't wait till we're traveling again. There's a cold wind blowing through this place."

"I'm so sorry you feel like that. What do you want me to do?"

"Just keep working at PT so we can leave as soon as – "

"Whoa, what's going on here?" Approaching their house, they are stopped by a road block and a crowd in the street. Sam breaks away, walks over to the truck, pushes back his cap, wipes his sleeve across his face, then leaning down to peer inside, says, "I wish I didn't have to tell you this but your house is on fire and it's pretty bad."

Chapter 19

Roaring, snapping and cracking, their modest home is bellowing furiously, vertical rivers of flame lapping at the night sky. Tuck's arms wrap around Britt, whose face is buried in his jacket. He watches the fire without expression. Hoses crisscross in all directions, the street runs with water, in spots slicking over with ice. Fire trucks parked at crazy angles litter the area. Crowds of firemen and onlookers gather in small groups, there being little else left to do. Tuck and Britt stand to the side, by themselves for the most part. Their friends, unsure what to say, leave them some space. Justus arrives, jacket over pajamas. Walking up to Tuck and Britt, he puts his arms around them and says, "Ma's waiting at home for you. The spare room is ready. Tibetta is asleep and knows nothing. Britt, you want to come home with me? Watching only makes it worse."

"Thanks but I need to stay here for now. I want to find out what happened."

Stu approaches, his wet fire jacket and pants starting to crackle over with ice, "Ace and I did our best; we managed to save the cat but little else. Sue has him at the house for you. There's a small pile of stuff in the back of my truck but the flames drove us back and we couldn't do much. Put your laptop on the front seat. Hope it's okay. Don't think it got wet."

Britt lifts her head and stares at Stu. His face is flushed and smoke smudged, his eyebrows and hair singed, his arm bandaged. "Thank you, thank you," she manages to blurt out through tears. "What happened to your arm?"

"Just a little burn is all. It'll be okay in no time."

Tuck nods, "Where's Ace? Is he okay?"

"Yeah, he's fine. Couple of burns on his hand but nothing serious. I think he's over by my truck right now."

"Come on Britt, we might as well see what's left of our lives." There in the bed of the truck was a small collection of knickknacks with a lone slightly blackened teddy bear sitting on top. Tears flow freely; the two of them stand embracing and weeping, momentarily away in their own world.

The next morning finds the family sitting around the Risings' breakfast table, stunned. Tibetta has been told what happened, is rocked and snuggled while she clutches her fire-singed bear and sobs. Fawn, aware that distraction is needed, offers to take Tibetta to visit at Sue's house where her cat, Snickles, must remain for the time being, the grandparents' house being too pristine to allow pet hair to sully the white carpeting. After that, a shopping trip to buy new clothes is proposed. "But I want my old ones, cries Tibetta, "and baby doll and Chunky and my toys."

"I know love," says Fawn," but think what fun it will be to have all new ones."

Tibetta continues to sob; the rest of the family sits wordless. Fawn finally persuades Tibetta to follow her upstairs where she washes and dresses her in yesterday's clothes. With soft wet cheeks, Tibetta kisses everyone goodbye and then, not unwillingly, takes grandma's hand and the two of them leave.

"Hang on to Smokey the Bear," Tuck calls after her, "He needs a lot of hugging from you after what he's been through."

Britt, deep circles under her eyes, sips at a cup of coffee; eating is out of the question. Justus and Tuck talk about what to do first. Britt listens for a while before commenting, "No matter what we do, life will never again be the same," putting into words the only thing that is certain after such a disaster.

She is astonished that Stu and Ace had realized how vitally important her laptop was – her entire design business on it and stupidly not backed up in weeks. They had risked their lives to save it – that and Snickles and Tibetta's bear. Amazing. Something else to think about.

Tuck tries to rally into action. Where to begin? How to collect their meager fire insurance? How did the fire start? What do they need to do first? Finally it hits them: everything needs to be done first. Well, first they need to go buy some clothes, but Justus insists they go to his store and take whatever they need. Unfortunately, his store doesn't carry underwear, something only available in Mapburg, fifty miles away. Credit cards, social security numbers, birth certificates, and Britt's driver's license: everything must be replaced. How to find time for all this? It would be easier to go back to the familiar routine of work. How I wish we could. Maybe it's just a bad dream. *Why do we have to deal with all this? Why us? Why? Why? Why? How fast things can change.*

The following weeks are consumed with chores. Each day they remember more things they had lost and more things in need of replacing. Hours fly by, filled with endless chores: businesses and agencies to contact, forms to fill out, their own jobs to keep up with, extra attention for Tibetta and continuous shopping, always more shopping. Amazing how many things we put our hands on in a day:

toothbrush, soap, skin lotion, nailbrush, deodorant, hair brush, pens, paper, toys, shoes, socks, aspirin – a lot of aspirin – band aids, scissors, keys, the list is endless; everything needs to be replaced. Money gets tighter and tighter. It is a fulltime load of work piled onto days already filled with their jobs. Tuck is exhausted. Britt is exhausted. Tibetta is bewildered.

As often as they think of things they need, they also remember those things which can never be replaced: Silver Cups won in races, awards for fashion designs, a special doll, photographs, clothes, pictures: everything connecting them to their past, those cherished things – gone forever, all up in smoke.

Britt tries to be brave but breaks down weeping far too often for her liking. Tuck? Tuck sometimes breaks down as well. So much gone. The house, a ramshackle place but nevertheless their private space, purchased at low cost from an elderly aunt who had moved to a nursing home. At one point, Tuck says to Britt, "Honey, you lost all your drawings. That must be terrible for you. With your talent though, hopefully you'll be able to reproduce them."

"It's not *my* drawings I'm sad about, it's Tibby's. She will never again be five years old. We've lost all her pictures – her first precious attempts at artwork."

Tuck's eyes flicker, trying not to break down, not because of the fire but because, at this unexpected moment, he is rewarded with something he had been wishing for: Britt's growing attachment to his daughter, even calling her Tibby for the first time. *Crazy – finding joy at a time like this,* Tuck thinks, *just crazy.*

A few days later, meager savings fast dwindling, Tuck and Britt get astonishing news: friends are planning a fundraiser for them at Tim's shop: local musicians to play, food to be served and dollars to be raised. Meanwhile, Fawn, in a timorous voice, vainly tries to insist they remain living with Justus and her. However, Tuck and Britt, married but a few months, want a place of their own. Not until this moment does Tuck tell his wife that a caretaker's cabin had always been available at the Power's Camp.

"Why didn't you tell me before? Why did we live in that dilapidated house when we could have been in a tight warm cabin?"

"I guess it felt too close to my work. I need to keep a little distance and I wanted something of our own, something I could work on remodeling. You can't do that when someone else owns your place. Anyway, for now, Byron says we are welcome to move there and, at this point, it will give us more privacy than living with my parents.

There doesn't seem to be much for rent around here. What do you want to do?"

"Want to do? I want to go back to the way things were – oops, there I go again feeling sorry for myself. Okay. Your parents have been wonderful this last week but I don't feel comfortable around your mother. I know she tries. It's just that they are so different from us. Let's go live in the cabin."

"Great. That's what I want too. We won't have much in the way of furniture and stuff. You may have to rough it for a while. Think you can manage?"

"Sure. It will challenge my creativity," Britt says with a glimmer of a smile. When Tuck's parents hear their decision, Fawn begins to wail. "Why leave here when we can provide everything you need? I'll do all the cooking. You'll have your own fancy bedroom. I'll take care of Tibetta and we will all be one big, happy, cozy family."

And Tibetta is devastated at moving away from her grandparents again, leaving her special bedroom with Disney characters on the curtains, a Donald Duck rug and her Cinderella bedspread. She tries not to cry but tears stream down her cheeks. She softly hiccups and sobs. Tuck is heartbroken. Britt feels slightly guilty about taking Tibetta away, and hurt that she does not want to come with them. But, that 'one big cozy family' is the tipping point. Offering many thanks for all his parents' help, they stick with their plans and before a week has passed, move with Tibetta into the caretaker cabin. Snickles is back with them which helps comfort Tibetta. Their meager belongings consist of sleeping bags on the floor, plastic garden chairs around a large wooden spool which serves as a table, a few forks and knives and a couple of pans for cooking. Tough as this is for her, worse is yet to come. Inspectors have found the cause of the fire. The report is out. Tuck wants to protect Britt from it but doesn't know how. Some things just have to be faced.

Chapter 20

"Hon, they found the cause of the fire. It's not good. Better sit down while I tell you. The stove door was left partly open and a log rolled out onto the floor." Britt's eyes open wide, staring at Tuck, willing him to take those words back. Suddenly she leans forward over the spool-table, drops her head on folded arms and is absolutely still. Tuck walks over and, this time, it is he who kneels down to put his arms around her.

"It's not your fault, its mine. I never should have brought you up North. Life is too tough. You aren't used to woodstoves and all the ways of North Country life. I am so sorry."

Remembering back to the night of the party, Britt is horrified. Before leaving the house, she had put a log in the stove, left the door cracked open to create more draft, then forgotten to close it again.

"How terrible. The whole town will know. How can I ever show my face again?"

"Don't torture yourself over this. We will manage. In fact, there's actually an upside to this," Tuck says, trying to ease the pain, "Whenever something burns around here, the first thought is of Adirondack lightning."

"How could anyone think that? It's winter."

"No, not that kind of lightning. Adirondack lightning's what they call it when a building's burned for insurance. Happens all the time. At least we don't have to worry about nasty accusations. It's clear that we are the victims of an accident." But Britt is beyond consolation. Tears flow like lava, streaking her face and leaving it hot and flushed. They hear a truck pull up outside their cabin.

Josh and Stu knock and then enter. "Got some stuff for you, want to come take a look?" Britt does not. She wants to hide. Mortified, she starts for the bedroom but Tuck grabs her hand and pulls her with him outside. To spare her embarrassment, the guys avoid looking at her tear-streaked face, addressing Tuck instead. In the back of the truck, lashed down beside Josh's ever present canoe, is a double mattress, box springs, an easy chair and a youth bed.

"The Ravens sent these over. Want 'em?"And so begins an outpouring of generosity. Britt, deeply humiliated, can't understand why anyone would want to help a blunderer like herself. Several camp owners send checks and town folks drop by with donations, everything from cooking pans to clothes. A fundraiser is planned for the following week. The last thing in the world she wants is to face all those people who know that, because of her carelessness, the house burned down.

"These folks are going all out for us, the best thing we can do is attend and graciously accept," Tuck reminds her.

"You're right, Sweetie, I am being selfish. But how can you ever forgive me for what I've done?"

"I already have, because I love you and because of something I once heard Pitt and Rat say, 'Admit mistakes, access grace.' My fault as well as yours. Who of us has not made our own mistakes?"

Tim's combination storefront/warehouse has been cleared for the fundraising party but Britt is surprised by what still remains ready for instant use: two canoes, a bike and snowboard hang on the walls. A large motorcycle leans on its stand in the corner. *I never saw a business set up like this before. In the city it would be considered very unprofessional but up here, nobody finds it strange.*

The sound of instruments being tuned comes from the back room where Tim, hidden behind piles of lumber, has installed a recording studio. Soon the players join the rest of the crowd and lively notes of bluegrass swell the room, vibrating the floor and filling the space with foot-stomping music. Britt is surprised to see Tim leaning over a guitar, his fingers flying over the strings. Even Blanche, despite her cumbersome bulk and large calloused hands, is delicately strumming a banjo. Slam, most fittingly, bangs away at the drums. The music sails forth with an intensity she has never before heard. Other guitar, banjo and mandolin players join in from time to time, several of them Britt recognizes as caretakers and local shop owners.

"I can't believe how many of these people are musicians. I had no idea."

"Music is a big part of life up here, lots of talent in these mountains." Tibetta is there and before long everyone is delighted to see her, along with other kids, dancing in front of the band, arms and legs flung in all directions. Big Moe leans his large frame against the back wall, some of his wiry gray hair captured in a ponytail, the rest sticking out in a wild array which continues down into sideburns. A long beard and moustache hide most of his handsomely-aged face. He observes the action, like a man peering out from a duck blind. A slim blonde in a tight mini skirt, young enough to be Moe's daughter, is swaying back and forth to the music, trying to attract his attention. She's a lively number who is hoping, in vain, that Moe will dance with her.

Esprit has come and is much in evidence, thanking everyone for being there, as if she were the reason for their attendance. Other than that, she is doing little to help. Hood Slanter and his wife, Jane, Stu,

Josh Lively's spunky wife Tripp and Ma Rose stand behind tables stretched along one wall. They are serving up plates from heaps of home cooked food spread out before them. The lofty building seems crowded with more people than could possibly live in Meltmor. And, that is the case, many having come from their caretaker cabins at the Great Camps situated far from the town's humble streets.

Stu, recalling his recent run-in at camp, is surprised when Mr. Barton hands him an envelope to give to Tuck. Inside is a $500 check. He thinks back to the morning when he had received a tongue lashing from Adam Barton. He wonders if there is a connection. The Bartons had been up for a rare winter overnight.

"You're late to work. I've been looking for you for over an hour. The stove quit working and we were reduced to cold cereal for breakfast."

"Sorry sir, I overslept, was up most of the night fighting a fire at the Power's caretaker's home."

"That's all well and good but you need to decide if you want to be a caretaker or a fireman? You can't be both," Barton had barked. Stu, exhausted and with a natural inclination to feel put upon, let his mouth get the better of him. He felt he didn't deserve this treatment.

"I am both. And that's the way it's got to be. We survive around here by helping each other when trouble strikes. You won't find me late again – unless there's another fire. I'll start your stove now so you can get a bite of hot food." He suspects Adam never told his family about the incident.

Tripp brings two heaping plates of food over to Britt and Tuck. "The food isn't very hot anymore but you should try it," she says, laughing merrily as she passes the plates to the two dazed honorees of the festivities. Not hungry in the least, they nevertheless make a valiant effort to shovel in the lasagna, salad and slice of homemade bread. Britt looks at Tuck, her eyes starting to flood. He leans over and, to be heard midst all the noise, cups his hand around her ear, "It's amazing isn't it?"

She turns to him and doing the same asks miserably, "Don't they know this is all my fault?"

"Sure they do, but that doesn't mean they don't care. Remember – they know how tough life can be. Hon?" he says turning her face up so he can look down into her eyes, "Ease up, give yourself a break, move on."

Suddenly the room grows quiet as Blanche begins to talk. "I figured it was time the caretakers have their own song so I wrote one. I'll start with the chorus, join in if you like." In a husky voice, she belts out the words.

She starts with the chorus.

Caretaker, camp keeper, guardian unsung
Keep your nose clean and hold your tongue
Wood to be split, logs to be stacked
Trust you carry like a pack on your back
Your job is to please; your job is to serve
It takes a good heart and steady nerves

A tree falls on camp, the roof springs a leak
Best fix things fast, folks coming next week.
Out in the garden, the deer fence is down,
The flowers need water, they're all turning brown.
(chorus)

Repair me those docks, mend me those stairs
Defend the camp from wandering bears
Folks coming tomorrow? Have no doubt
The plumbing will crack, the pipes start to spout
(chorus)

Guests want to fish but can't paddle a boat
It's your job to help and keep them afloat
A fisherman's cast lands a hook in your face,
You barely wince, just smile with good grace.
(chorus)

Missus wants thyme in her soup tonight
There's none to be had but you'll buy some alright
Set off in the boat, its only three miles
Then hop in your car and drive a while
(A few voices join in for the chorus)

Thyme clutched in hand, you're back in two hours
To cook up that soup for folks to devour
Now, where is the family, where did they go?
Why out to dinner with Sir Reginald Snow.

Now the whole room is singing and clapping hands to the chorus.

May Great Camp owners continue to thrive
They pay the wages that help us survive
Most are kind, some are not
We take 'em as they come, 'cause that's our lot.

After a thundering applause and appreciative yodels, the band takes a break and heads over to the food and beer. Esprit, wearing a wide-brimmed straw hat and full length, tight chartreuse dress, walks up front and grabs the microphone. "Everybody, your attention please. Because this is such a stressful time for us all but Britt especially, I'm happy to announce that, as of today, I am making her an honorary member of Esprit's Girls. I'm offering her a free membership in my classes where she can join our séances and I will teach her the wisdom to deal with her problems."

A scattered polite clapping is heard; a few mouths are hanging open, a couple of hands shield comments addressed to neighbors. "Is she for real?" Says Britt out the side of her mouth as she gives Esprit a big forced smile.

"Nice grinning babe. Good God, she's even more out there than I thought. She's crazy. But, don't worry, no one expects you to go – except my mother."

A strong odor suddenly surrounds them. Pitt sidles up to Tuck, the implacable wood rat perched on his shoulder, and hands him an envelope, "What the heck, take the check; Rat vowed, don't be proud." And he fades into the night.

"Who in the world?" asks Britt.

"Town character," says Tuck, "Most think him crazy. Me? I think he's crazy like a fox. Look at this, a hundred dollars. He's rumored to have money hoarded away, must be true. Can't believe he did that. Strange, really nice. Pitt is as much an endangered species as his rat."

A half-hour later, the band kicks into high gear, tunes flowing till midnight. Britt gets numerous hugs along with sympathy and offers to help with meals and babysitting.

Late that night, back at the cabin, Tuck carries a sleeping Tibetta to her new bed, tucks her in with her bear, then sits down with Britt over a cup of coffee. Both are astounded at the outpouring of support. "Still feel locked out?"

"I guess I have some thinking to do, or re-thinking. You know that song Blanche wrote? The way she sang it moved me a lot – made me see caretaking in a new light. Suddenly, I was so proud of you, proud that we are a part of all this." *Gosh, I'm starting to feel like I belong here – just as Tuck's getting close to returning to the ski circuit. Best I not say anything,* Britt thinks to herself. "I realized for the first time what a huge responsibility you guys carry, how much camp owners depend on their caretakers. You have to be real diplomats." Tuck feels a certain weight lift off his chest. *Maybe she's beginning to see there's more to me than a ski champ – maybe –*

Over the next weeks, Britt tries to sort it all out. *The songs I heard coming out of these mountains, amazing – beautiful. Never heard anything like that before. Hope I hear more.*

Often flashbacks of the fire, their losses, the struggle to put their lives back in order, her role in it all, drops her into a vale of tears. Dressed sometimes in new clothes from the family store, sometimes in donated ones, Britt feels she has lost a piece of her identity.

"You haven't at all," responds Tuck, "in fact, because you wear those clothes with such style and grace, it shows our neighbors how grateful you are for their generosity."

"You think so?"

"I do. Shows people you're not stuck up, shows them you're one of them."

"Is that what they thought of me?"

"Some, not everyone, but now I think people are beginning to see the real you, starting to understand why I love you so much."

The overwhelming generosity of so many people, some Britt hardly knows, helps the young Rising family get through the dark days. They are encircled by kindness. Tuck is extremely grateful but less surprised than Britt, for this is his hometown. He knows how folks come together to support one another. But Britt? It's new to her. She is beginning to see things differently. Torn between gratitude and sadness, Tuck and Britt grow closer, take turns lifting each other spirits. Frequently, they cling together, and when Tibetta is there, extend that embrace to include the elfin child. But shadows still linger, stretching out across this struggling family.

Tuck can't forget he must find some way to deal with Buzz. How to do that remains a cloud over his days. Britt is unsure how she feels about leaving: part of her is ready, part wants to stay.

Chapter 21

Byron calls Pru from his office. "How about meeting me at Winston's for dinner tonight? We need to talk. I have something that may interest you. Can you make it for seven?" By 7:30 they're nursing drinks and staring at each other around flickering candles, the romantic glow of which is wasted on this couple.

"So, what do you have to say that could possibly interest me at this point?" she says, her cold eyes raking him over as if confronting a snake.

"It's like this. Norm and Winnie are important to me."

"That's news. Mostly you act like this family lives in a foreign country."

"Look, I'm sorry things have turned out like this. I know you're disappointed in me. However, I hate to make the kids suffer for our problems. I've done some thinking," he says while reflecting to himself, *she's right, they do seem to live in a different world from mine.*

"About time."

"Listen, how would you feel about our donating a pediatric wing to the hospital in Meltmor? It's a poor town and they could use one, as we learned with Norm's appendicitis attack. It would be a natural thing for us to do and it could be dedicated in your name, the Prudence Power Pediatric Pavilion. Has a nice ring to it, don't you think?"

"Well, the idea has some appeal but I'm sure, knowing you, there's a catch? I smell a rat. What's your nefarious scheme?"

Pru's lawyer, May Raine, was already drawing up divorce papers and, rather unprofessionally, had declared "Get rid of the bum, we'll nail him for all he's worth."

"Simple. I want to keep our marriage intact, in appearance at least, if not in fact. You go your way I go mine, but we live in the same house so I get to see the kids."

A long silence follows. The waiter returns, Byron orders another round of martinis. Pru clutches her glass a little tighter and looks down at the table, her long blonde hair sliding forward to curtain her face. Byron sits. The restaurant, excessively warm, feels suffocating. He remains quiet, however, determined to wait her out. The second round of cocktails arrives. Still no word.

Finally, without looking up, she says, "Since when did you start wanting to see the kids so much? You've hardly been home long enough for them to know you're their father."

"I know that. Fallen into the trap of so many, letting the job take possession of my life. It's the thought of losing what little contact I have that makes me realize I'm missing out. I don't want things to go on like this."

"You sure are missing out, been missing for years. I need to think about all this. Part of me wants to say yes, not for you, mind, not for you but for the kids. I don't really want them to be without a father in their lives. Mean as you think I am, I do care." *And that pavilion, my name only? I could go for that. After all, he's the one who gets all the recognition. I'm tired of being the good wife in the background. I deserve better.*

A stilted conversation accompanies their dinner but in the end, a plan is worked out; no one to know their arrangement, both free to live as they see fit. Byron consoles himself with the thought that, *our setup will differ little from those arranged marriages, often loveless, which for centuries were considered not only practical but highly acceptable.*

"Good," says Byron, "I'll get on it right away. I imagine this will make doctors in Meltmor pretty happy."

And I will finally get the recognition I'm due, thinks Pru. Byron, reflecting on the situation, says to himself, *two disillusioned people linked by cash and kids. Suspect a lot of our friends live this charade as well. If they can do it, why not us?*

Meanwhile, up north in Meltmor, another man struggles to justify his action but this time of a different sort."Back 'er up, more, more," says the dump master, that indispensable character who is part of the North Country scene and frequently a source of the latest news. "Whoa, stop."

Hood jumps out of his truck.

"Need a little help shovin' this ole junk out of here."

"Sure thing, but why are you getting rid of your cook stove? Still looks good enough."

"Not good enough for ma Jane. I've done gone and bought her a new one. She's fought with this here monster long enough. This baby's not only faulty, it's durn right dangerous."

"So, you come into money or something?"

"Nope. Just had a good year. Seems as if everyone needin' truck repairs lately."

The stove disposed of, Hood Slanter rolls off down the road, calling back "Thanks for helpin'." Hood smiles to himself as he thinks back to the moment he told his wife what he'd done. 'Jumping juniper!' How are we going to afford such a thing?" said Jane when he first told her what he'd ordered.

"Business been pretty good a late and I know you've been wantin' a new stove for all that Meals to Go cookin' you do. Seen you strugglin' for years with that tiny oven and only two workin' burners and I says to myself many times, if ever I get a little extra, it's goin' for a new stove for ma Janie." *And why shouldn't I be able to give my wife somethin' special like everyone else does?* Hood tries to reason out the rightness of his action, a mental activity rare to this poorly paid mechanic. *The big boys in government takes bribes; Wall Street fat cats help themselves off the top. Nobody finds nothin' wrong with that. So, what's the harm of me acceptin' a lousy thousand dollars? So what if a guy pays me for sayin' that gas tank was empty? Big deal. I's not doin' nothin' anyone else's not doin. I mean, is it so wrong to take care of my wife – she who gives so much time to helpin' others? Still though, probably best not to tell her how I came by the goods. What harm's a little lyin' anyways?*

Later, Tuck arrives at the Slanter's home to help Hood unload and carry a new stove into the kitchen. Jane is thrilled. "Think I'll call it 'Cookie.' Stop by later Tuck. I want 'Cookie's' first meal to be for you and your family – should be ready 'bout 5:30."

Driving back to the camp, Tuck plans his afternoon. *Got to do a camp walk-through today, check for power outages, water and gas leaks. Ought to go down into the basement, empty and reset all those snap-traps. Checking for mice is like checking for leaks: both water and critters seep through cracks in pipes and basement walls.*

That afternoon, Tuck leaves camp to go get Tibetta when, on rounding a bend in the driveway, he comes upon a large balsam fir fallen across the road. He slams on the brakes, backs up, takes the dirt road leading to their caretaker cabin with its own driveway out to the main road.

Britt, can you pick up Tibby this afternoon, and also stop and buy an outdoor thermometer? I've got to clear a big old tree out of the road."

"Of all the things we need right away, why a thermometer?"

"I don't know – somehow it annoys me not to know the temperature outside when I get up in the morning. Makes it harder to plan my day."

"Strange. It would never occur to me to wonder about that."

"It's a country thing, because we're outside so much. Oh, and I almost forgot. Could you also stop by Jane's house? She has something to give us." Tuck heads off to his shop for the chainsaw.

Britt drives into town to her in-laws' house. She is truly grateful that they care for Tibetta in the afternoons after kindergarten. It allows her time to carry on her design work as well as countless other tasks related to the loss of their home. *Still, I find Fawn hard to take and she's none too fond of me either.* After picking Tibetta up and admiring her drawings, Britt drives over to Jane's home where a trampled snowy walkway leads up to a paint-peeled house with shutters hanging at crazy angles. A broken window pane is stopped up with an old rag. There is a bell but ringing it several times brings no response. As her knocks are not heard either, she finally pushes the warped door open and, with Tibetta trailing along, walks into a cold front room, calling "Jane, are you here? Tuck couldn't make it so I came instead."

"Oh Britt. Hi cutie," says Jane to Tibetta. "I just finished fixing beef stew and potatoes for your family. I do hope you like it. And there's an apple pie for dessert. Come look at my new stove. I wanted your family to have the first meal made on it. After all you've been through; I thought this would give you a couple of nights off from cooking."

Jane, a slender, stoop-shouldered woman stands beside the shiny new stainless steel stove. It dazzles in contrast to the worn linoleum floor, chipped enamel refrigerator and old tin sink. Pushing her straggly hair back off her sweat covered brow, she says, "Now I can cook more meals for the Meals to Go service." She is dressed in a blue housedress covered by a patched, full length faded gingham apron, freshly washed and pressed.

"How often do you do that?" asks Britt in amazement. It would never have occurred to her to do such a thing.

"Twice a week if I can. We have so much and so many have so little, I feel real bad for them."

"Meals to Go? I didn't know Meltmor had one of those organizations. Didn't think there was enough money in this town to support such a thing."

"I guess there isn't but not all the donations come from town folk. It's supposed to be secret but I know for a fact that at least two of the anonymous contributors are Bill Raven and Byron Power. There may be others too." Just then the door opens and in staggers Hood, clearly half in the bag. Jane rushes to explain. "Hood doesn't usually drink like this but he had to have a tooth pulled without Novocain so he got good and liquored up before going." Hood totters past on his way to the bedroom.

"Is he allergic to Novocain?"

"No. It's just that Novocain's too darn expensive."

Britt turns to leave, thanks Jane profusely, then walks out, her heels tapping noisily across the bare floor. Opening the car's back door, she sets the basket of food on the seat and buckles Tibetta in.

"Tibby, we've just seen an angel."

"Who? You mean Jane? She can't be an angel. Angels have wings."

"Only pretend angels. Real angels are in disguise. You've just seen one." *Gosh,* Britt thinks to herself, *I've never thought of doing something like cooking for the food pantry. Here I've been wondering how to thank everyone. The best way might be to pass on the kindness – volunteer somewhere. At least I'd feel better about accepting so much charity. But, what in the world can I do?*

Chapter 22

An afternoon snowshoeing on Cedar Bluff Lake gives Tuck space to think. His options seem to be irrevocably defined by his past. Just as he's ready to change course, wham, life slams him back in his tracks. *How much easier to do the expected – except I just don't want to anymore – don't feel competitive enough. Doesn't matter though, guess I'll have to return to racing. It earns the cash I need and satisfies the family. Britt, at least, will be happy. She's looking forward to leaving Meltmor, doing some traveling. Parents will be proud. Buzz will get his dough and I will once more be a prize pawn in the chess game of hardcore sports.* Tuck's future seems to lie solidly before him – solid like a closed door.

My parents have been great, raising Tibby while I was away, but this time leaving her will be harder than ever. There is so much we're beginning to share. I love her curiosity, love teaching her to think for herself, to explore things off the beaten path. Maybe though, it's just as well if I'm not around too much. Why teach her independence when it makes life that much harder? Break with convention; go your own way and before long, society's wardens show up to herd you back on track. What's better, the seed dropping in the midst of fellow trees, there to sprout and ensure those woods live on, or the seed that blows far away to start a new forest, perhaps a better one? Which course will my Tibby follow? I wonder where she'll take root?

He tramps slowly back to the truck, off to work, then to physical therapy and lastly, to the mountain. Arriving at the slopes, he finds his coach waiting. "Let's see what you can do, Tuck. The team doctor thinks in a couple of months you'll be ready to try some racing again. A lot of people are counting on you. We even got an offer from Zapper Ski Clothes – all you need to knock 'em dead on the course. You can't beat that."

And so Tuck pushes hard for the next couple of hours but his leg hurts and he fails to feel the old rush kick in. He tucks and shoots the track but his gaze wanders to the distant mountains rather than to the moguls speeding toward him. Cheers of "Let's go, let's go," follow him down the hill.

When he reaches the bottom, his coach following closely behind says, "It's a start, but we've got hard work ahead to get you in shape – get your old fire back."

That evening Tuck decides. *Tomorrow, I'm tossing it all to the winds. I'll take Tibby for the day – ski together, finish up with a walk in the woods. A whole day only for us.* He drives home, stopping first to pick her up from his mother's.

"Britt is off visiting with her parents so it's just Tibby and me. Tomorrow, I'm keeping her home," he tells them.

"But she has kindergarten tomorrow. You can't take her out of that."

"Oh yes I can, watch me."

"But you'll set a bad example. She'll start thinking it's okay to skip out. She'll think she can drop out and go play any old time."

"That's true. Maybe not such a bad idea."

"Oh Tuck, what are you saying?"

"Just kidding Mother, don't worry. It's only this once."

And so the next day finds Tibetta and Tuck out on the kiddy slope. No longer roped to Tuck, Tibetta is skiing freely on her own. She, like so many children, still short and close to the ground, is unfazed by the risk of falling. She skis with abandon, giggling as she flies down the slopes. Tuck watches with delight. Later, after a day of sunshine and fun, comes another big surprise.

"Can I stay up late tonight?" his daughter asks.

"Better than that. How would you like to go for a walk with me?"

"In the dark? That's scary."

"That my little urchin is why I want to take you for a walk tonight – the dark is only scary when you don't know what's out there."

An hour later finds them driving through the shadowy mountains, a bright full moon riding low on the horizon. "Daddy, look how the moon is bouncing around. It's playing peek-a-boo with us." Tuck is about to explain how the twisting road makes the moon appear to move about, then thinks better of it. *Why not let her see it her own way – isn't that the joy of childhood? Why take it from her?*

A few minutes later, he pulls to the side of the road. They get out of the truck, pull on mittens and are soon trudging along a hard packed trail, a couple of inches of new snow muffling their steps. The moon has now risen well above the mountains. Tonight, the large white disc is moving high in the sky – flung up there for the benefit of this father-child duo – for them and them alone. They are drawn by its magic.

Snow-covered hemlocks stand protectively guarding the narrow track, their branches brushed briefly aside to let pass the tall man who, bending over slightly, reaches down to hold his child's small hand in a reassuring firm grasp. In her white jacket and cap, she bounces along keeping pace with her dad's footsteps. In fact she makes him think a bit of a snowshoe hare. Moonlight cascades through the woods inking long skinny shadows behind each tree. They tramp in silence, Tibetta clinging to Tuck. Suddenly, a terrifying scream bursts from the top of the trees. Tibetta's eyes pop wide open. With one swift leap she springs into her dad's arms.

Smiling, he snuggles her to his chest and whispers "Shhh Cutie, that's a barred owl. Nothing to be afraid of. In fact, it's a scream few people ever hear. It only happens when the owl first starts his nighttime hooting. I think it might be his way of demanding that forest animals pay attention. Let's be real quiet and listen a minute; we'll probably get serenaded with owl's softer voice. See? There's nothing to be afraid of. Listen."

"Are other people afraid of that scream?"

"Probably would be if they heard it but few do because few go walking in the dark. Folks have lit up the world with lights, maybe out of fear. Sort of silly isn't it? When it's so pretty out here? In fact, let's answer. Maybe he'll talk back to us."

With that, Tuck, sounding more like the owl than the owl himself, begins hooting "Who, who, who whoooo, who, who, who, whoooo are you-all –" It isn't long before his call is returned.

"Daddy, Daddy, the owl is talking to us; he must like us. Daddy, how do you know it's a daddy and not a mommy owl?"

"Good question. I don't; could be a mommy up there talking to us. Now let's leave him alone so he – she can hunt. You okay now? If you get down and walk you might see something interesting on the path"

"All I see are holes in the snow."

"Who do you think made those? See how straight they are – in a line ahead of us? That's a fox. See how the tracks look crisp and fresh. If we are real quiet and walk on a bit, we might see him – her. Sometimes it's hard to tell if it's a daddy or mommy in the lead."

"But I don't want to get close, it might eat us."

"Who teaches you such foolishness?" And so Tuck explains about foxes. Tibetta reassured, the two walk on, her dad encouraging her to listen rather than talk. For a long ten minutes, amazing feat for a young child, they proceed in silence. Suddenly Tuck spots the fox with his bushy tail ambling along up ahead. He quietly points the animal out to Tibetta. She is a little nervous but excited at the same time.

"Daddy, you know what? I was afraid to come out here. I thought it was dark and I couldn't see anything but I can see a lot."

"Sometimes we need to go meet the things that scare us. Then they don't scare us nearly so much." Suddenly there is a loud crack. Tibetta jumped but this time not into Tuck's arms. "That was a tree snapping from the cold," he tells her. "Loud wasn't it?"

"Yeah, but I'm not afraid anymore." They come out into a clearing and look up at the brilliant velvet sky filled with stars. "The moon has lots of babies, I wonder how she takes care of them all?" says Tibetta. Tuck smiles and turns to lead her to the truck.

"I have no idea but I do know one baby whose bedtime passed a long time ago."

"I'm not a baby. I can stay up way later than this." But as they walk, Tibetta moves slower and slower, frequently bumping into his leg.

"How would you like a horsey ride back to the truck?" he asks, swinging her up over his head and down onto his shoulders. "Should the horse walk or trot?"

"I want the horsey to run." exclaims the happy child.

"I can't do that yet, this horse has a bad leg. How about a trot?" And so they return the way they came, a delighted child holding her dad's ponytail "reins" as she bounces along on the shoulders of a limping, happy horse. Tuck tries to hold on as well, hold on to this defining moment, feel it fully, cherish it for the future. But, his mind keeps leaping forward to the time when he will be far away. It breaks his heart. *Hold on to this moment,* he tells himself repeatedly, *seize it while I can.*

Tibetta is asleep by the time Tuck's truck pulls into the driveway. He carries her to the bedroom and pulls Britt's fur coat over his daughter. Suddenly, the future intrudes again. *I would much prefer to tuck her into bed each night than tuck myself down some distant course. But, do I have a choice? I think not.*

Chapter 23

A recent snowfall requires that Tuck plow the dirt road leading to the Power's camp and the smaller roads to the caretaker cabin and his workshop. He is just finished and getting out of his truck when Byron pulls up.

"Hello Byron, what brings you up here this time of year?"

"Couple of things. First, I've worked it out with the wife. You can keep the job until you're ready to go back to racing. Please, give me at least a two months notice before then. The second thing is, I feel like doing a little manual labor for a change. Thought I could do some work around here. Must admit I don't know exactly what it is that needs to be done in the winter – or the summer for that matter – but there must be chores you could use an extra hand with?"

"Sure. There's shoveling to do but mostly all that's left is clearing the kitchen roof at the back of the camp. I'm planning to refinish the rowboat so that needs to be scraped down. Is that the kind of thing you mean?"

"It is. I'll do some scraping if you show me where to start." Tuck takes him inside his shop, throws another log on the fire and sets Byron to working on the guide boat. The roof needs to be shoveled but Tuck, thinking he'd best stay close by, instead busies himself taking apart the chainsaw, cleaning and re-oiling it. He had heard that camp owners sometimes like to "get their hands dirty" helping with camp chores, a break from their professional lives, an opportunity to get to know the caretakers better. Often the desires of inexperienced volunteers are more trouble than help. But, Tuck needn't have worried, the scraping doesn't last long.

Barely twenty minutes pass before Byron straightens up, his hand on his hip, and gives a groan. "I've got to stop a minute. My back is stiff and my wrists are killing me. Never realized this was so tiring. Mind if I sit in your rocker?"

"Not my rocker, it's yours. Go ahead. Want some coffee? I'll put the pot on."

"How long does it take you to scrape down a boat like that?"

"Don't know, never timed it. I do it in bits and pieces when nothing else is happening."

"If you were working for big business, you would be timed and know exactly how long the job should take."

"Guess that's why I'm not. Efficiency is good for the bottom line but it's dehumanizing. I doubt if they calculate into that formula the time it takes to go to the bathroom, stop and help a friend whose truck slides off the driveway or rescue a neighbor's kid who falls down and skins his knee."

"True. The goal of efficient business is to keep employees away from those kinds of distractions, shield them from anything that interferes with making money."

"I don't know. I think I work along at a good clip here but I wouldn't want to be cut off from what's happening around me. Isn't that sort of sterile"?

"Can be. Guess that's why I come up to camp whenever I can get away. Never feel walled-in here. I love this place: the woodlands, streaming sunsets, birds singing their spring return, waves of mountains – brings me peace. So, you working on other boats this winter?"

"Most of your boats are in pretty decent shape. I finished repairs on the canoe and that's looking good. One other canoe needs the gunwales sanded and oiled but that's about it."

"How's this kind of life compare to the ski circuit? What's that like?"

"It's okay I guess. I'm under a lot of pressure to get back in shape and race again. I'm feeling a bit boxed in – wishing I could find a way out. My parents, coach, teammates, fans – they'd all be annoyed if they knew."

"Sorry to hear that. Things with your family getting any better since the fire?"

"Thanks to you for offering the caretaker cabin, we're slowly rebuilding our lives – trying to return to normal, especially for the sake of Tibby. You don't realize at first how much you lose when something like this happens. Seems like every day we find more things that need replacing: from spoons to bank forms. We're getting along though."

"Do you ever slow down, relax a bit?"

"Not anymore, what with the job, recovering from the fire, skiing and physical therapy. I used to do a fair amount of reading but lately I haven't so much."

"What kind of books?"

"Oh, let's see: *Moby Dick, Walden, Main Street,*" Tuck pauses as he tries to remember. "I read the *Third Wave* a little while ago, also *The Lonely Crowd* – like Hemmingway, especially *The Old Man and the Sea*. Recently I read some of Russell Banks's work – stuff like that."

"Really? Interesting. Those happen to be some of my favorites as well."

Not surprising, Tuck chuckles to himself, *because those are all books I borrowed from your library.*

"You know, I keep thinking back to the notebook you dropped on the porch. I read a couple of pages in it. Do much writing like that?"

"Yeah. A little, nothing to speak of – helps me get my thoughts straight."

"Hmmm. Would you allow me to see to see a bit more of it sometime? I'm curious. Would you mind?"*Mind? Mind having someone from one of the most prominent publishing companies on the East Coast take a look at my scribbles? He'll laugh his head off but why the hell not? Isn't life about taking chances? Isn't that how I got ahead in racing?*

"Guess I wouldn't mind but don't expect much. They're just ramblings. As a matter of fact, all my writing's right here in the shop. It's one of the few things I keep private. Good thing too. I would have been sorry to lose them in the fire. Anyway, as long as you asked, guess I don't mind showing you."

Tuck walks over to a small desk: a board laid across two file cabinets. Here he keeps track of camp expenses, purchase warranties, subcontractors' names and addresses, garden catalogs, inventories and the Power's guests' names and preferences, such as which guest likes to be taken fishing in the early mornings and which will absolutely not eat venison. From the back of a bottom drawer, he pulls out a scuffed up manila folder, thumbs through it, removes a few sheets and hands the rest to Byron.

"I've never shared these with anyone. Writing works as a sort of escape valve for me, a way to let off steam." The next hour passes, neither of them saying much. The rocking chair creaks with the regularity of a clock. Tuck continues cleaning tools, Byron reads. Tuck, increasingly nervous as the moments go by, wonders why he let himself be talked into sharing his innermost thoughts. Byron eventually stops rocking and sits staring ahead, a pale willowy figure outsized by the large wooden chair. His neat LL Bean outfit is marred by flakes of paint; his gray hair dusted the color of the boat. He looks like anything but a high-powered executive.

"From your notes here, you sound ambivalent about success as a ski champ. Should think you'd be resting on your laurels at this point – not sweating the pros and cons. You really flail into the downside of fame. What got you going on that subject?"

"Well, partly because when I race, I feel like a hurtling billboard. I realize there's a tradeoff – their sponsorship for my advertising, but it's starting to bug me. When I ski, I've got sports brand graffiti all over my body: company names on my helmet, shirt, ski pants, boots, gloves. I feel like a commercial cannonball shooting down the slope. Even standing still, the skis have to face out to the camera so the company name is evident. Sometimes I wonder if the real me still exists inside all the flash. It's like my body's possessed by corporate America. They own me."

"Wow. It's obviously a real problem for you! Nevertheless, you've survived nicely on all the sponsorships and, no doubt, accumulated a good stock of clothes and equipment as well."

"I had. Now, it's all gone, zilch – up in smoke except for a few dollars I've managed to put away. That's got me thinking too."

"Interesting. It confirms what I suspected. You've got more going on under that cap than you let on," Byron comments. "How would you feel about letting me take this folder with me so I can look at it when I have more time? I'll get it back to you when I return." *Let him carry away my innermost ravings? Am I crazy? That's more than I bargained for.* Despite reservations, he finally agrees.

"Sure. I guess so. I'd rather no one else sees it though."

"They won't. I'll bring it back next time I'm up this way." Byron tries a little more scraping but it doesn't last long. He takes a walk on the plowed roads, enjoying the cold nostril-burning air. A half hour later, after saying goodbye, he climbs into the Land Rover and departs up the road, tires spinning as he disappears in a dust-up of snow. *Gone. Poof. Did something just happen?* thinks Tuck, or *am I dreaming?*

The following week, he receives a call on his cell. "Hello Tuck. This is Byron. Got a minute to talk?" *Oh Lord,* Tuck sighs to himself, *now what?*

"Sure. I'm good."

"It's a bit awkward doing this over the phone. The office is busy and I can't get up there for a while but I did want to get back to you. I've finished reading your notes. Your ramblings are compelling. I like the way you put things in perspective, surprising for an unschooled writer like yourself. Needs a good deal of editing, of course, but I could work with that. Did you ever think of tightening up these ideas and writing articles?"

Tuck's jaw drops. He hits his chin with his fist and closes his mouth again. *Holy Cow!*

"I guess deep down I've wondered about it, but I wouldn't know where to begin."

"Well, I do. That's my job. You're on to something: the large role of advertisers in our lives has resulted in Joe Q. Public's obsession with image and fame. Illusion over reality. When pop stars get more recognition than the man who gives microloans to third world countries, something's amiss. Our views are similar."

"I'm not so good at expressing what I mean though."

"You're wrong. You're not bad. I'm in the book business but have plenty of friends who are magazine publishers. What if you work on one of these ideas, the one you know most about, say, sports stars? Flesh it out. Give it to me when you're finished and I'll see if I can edit it into something publishable." Tuck is astounded.

"Do you really think we could make something of this? I've got to tell you, I find it all a bit farfetched."

"Skeptical? I'm not surprised. It's part of your makeup. But don't let doubt hold you captive. Give me an answer, you interested or not? I'm not going to offer a lot of hand holding. Either you go for the proposition and do it, or forget the whole thing right here and now."

"Gosh, yah, I mean, sure, I could try."

"It's got to be more than 'I'll try'. Either you commit to it or not."

"Alright then, I'll do it."

"Good enough."

"Keep it to 1200 words. Make sentences short and concise. Pick up a book on composition and look it over. Writing is a lonely occupation; sure you're up to it?"

"Life is a lonely occupation. Yes."

"I'll make copies of your work and put them in the mail. That way you can start right away. Why don't you get back to me in three weeks. Do you think that will give you enough time to turn one of your pieces into an article?"

"I'll do my best but let me ask you; if an article gets published, would I get paid?"

"Yes. Not a lot but with enough articles it can add up. Give you a little nest egg."

"Okay. I'm in." Tuck hangs up and begins to mull over the possibilities. *Maybe this can help pay off the blackmail. Wonder how much I could make? Problem is Britt would want to know where all the money was going – that could be a problem. Of course, if she doesn't know I'm doing this, she wouldn't get involved. Wonder how I can keep it from her?* Suddenly he's back on the phone, dialing Byron's work number. The secretary picks up.

"Mr. Power's office. Who's calling please?"

"Is Mr. Power in? This is his caretaker, Tuck Rising."

"I'm sorry, he's not available. Would you like to leave a message?" she asks, like a robotic parrot on autopilot.

"Ah, yes. Please tell him that – that – please tell him, ah, that I would appreciate it if he would not use my name regarding our recent discussion."

"Yes Mr. Rising. I will give Mr. Power the message. I'm sure he'll get back to you should he have time."

"Thanks." After hanging up, he thinks about his name: Rising – bread – heat – balloons – the sun – fog – hope –

Chapter 24

Britt wakes with a start, frozen with fear by the sight of a figure crouched in the corner of their bedroom, silhouetted by a flashlight. She reaches for Tuck only to find his side of the bed empty. *I knew we should lock the house at night,* she is thinking when Tuck, hearing her move, says, "Hon, you awake? I'm sorry; I was trying not to disturb you."

"Disturb me. You scared me to death. What on earth are you doing?"

"It's crazy I know, but my best ideas seem to come at night. I had to get up and jot them down so I wouldn't forget them."

"Ideas? In the middle of the night? You're supposed to be sleeping."

"True, but for some reason, my brain seems to function best in the dark; figured if I used a flashlight it wouldn't wake you."

"Like what kind of ideas?" *Snagged. How do I explain without giving away that I'm writing?*

"Oh, things I need to do at the camp, things we need to buy, agencies we still need to contact about the fire, forms that need filling out, stuff like that. There's always something else we have forgotten."

"Now Sweetie, you've got to put that stuff aside and get some sleep. One thing for sure, worry never leaves, sort of like a dog sleeping by the bedside, he's always there when you get up, demanding immediate attention. That's why I like cats better."

"You're pretty articulate yourself," says Tuck as he wraps her in his arms, passion sweeping all ideas out of his head, hers too, as they apply their creativity in new ways to intertwine their hungry bodies.

The next morning finds them eating breakfast at the spool-table. Tibetta is snuggling a purring Snickles but crying again, remembering a favorite doll lost to her forever. "Is my doll in Heaven?"

"Yes, your doll's in Heaven along with your other animals. They're all happy up there but they do miss you, the same as you miss them." Tibetta's tears cause Britt to choke up as well. *Will my grief never subside?* she wonders. *One moment I'm fine, the next, I feel as brittle as glass.* Britt thinks again of all they have lost, indulging in a bit of self-pity. *There's simply too much to do, too many obligations, too much to remember.* Suddenly thoughts turn to Jane: Jane with so little education, so few possessions, always smiling and giving so much. *If she can show such resilience, surely I can too.* Her thoughts are interrupted by Tuck, "The ice harvest at the Ravens is this afternoon but I can't make it.

Coach wants me on the slopes. I think you should go though and take Tibby. It's a fun event."

"Go alone? I hardly know these people and I'm definitely not comfortable with them."

"That's exactly why you should go. Get to know them better. It might get your mind off all our troubles. Besides, if not for yourself, do it for Tibby. There will be kids there she can play with."

"Okay," sighs Britt, "I guess so but how will I get there? It's a long walk over the ice, too long for Tibby. You'll have the truck."

"No problem. I'll get someone to pick you up. Think they're starting about noon."

At 11:45, a rusty, dented pickup stops in front of the house. Britt and Tibetta go out to meet the driver. "Hi. I'm Sue Tower. Remember me? I'm taking you to the ice harvest. Squeeze in the front, it's a tight fit but at least warm enough, though I must say we are lucky with the weather. Supposed to get up to 32°. Great day. The Ravens are away in Switzerland. Too bad, they usually enjoy this event." Britt is surprised to see this elegant looking woman driving an old rusty pickup truck. *It doesn't fit – she seems out of place*, she thinks, still under the influence of her past culture.

Arriving at the Raven's Nest, they find a swarm of men and women out on the solidly frozen Cedar Bluff Lake. One man is pulling a gasoline-powered saw along behind him as he follows marked grid lines. An arc of ice-dust soars up from the spinning blade; the sun reflecting off the crystals forms a sparkling rainbow. Others are operating 5-foot manual ice saws which look like two-man loggers' saws except there are handles on one end only. They're making final cuts to free the blocks that will be pushed over to the polers.

Tibetta, dressed in a navy-blue snowsuit, walks slowly out on the ice, close to where other children are playing. Hesitant to join them, she uses a stick found on shore to draw pictures in the snow. Occasionally she glances up at the other kids. An older girl dashes over, grabs her by the hand and shouts, "Come on, we're playing tag." Tibetta's face cracks into a smile and she is off and running.

A couple of women are poling blocks down a long black channel of open water, at the end of which men are wrestling the heavy ice onto a conveyor belt rising to a truck bed. Though they work in a protected cove, Britt can hear, not too far away, the sound of water rushing over a dam. Stu bellows at the kids, "Get the hell away from there, don't want to see you near the cutting area and stay back from the dam where the ice is weak. We don't need you falling into the water." In an aside, he grumbles, "I sure don't want to freeze my butt off jumping in after some dumb rug-rat."

"Oh stop it already," someone exclaims with a grin on his face, "Be good for you – might clean off your crust."

Tibetta, frightened by his yelling, starts walking off the ice but the other kids, unfazed by Stu, continue to run around. She waits a minute to see what will happen. When nothing more does, she returns to join them again.

Britt is wondering what role she can play in this scene when Sue comes over and says, "Here, I'll show you how to pole the blocks down the channel." A wooden pole with a hook on the end is placed in her hands and a quick explanation follows. "We just hook the blocks like train cars and push them along. Try not to splash water on the ice; it makes it more slippery to stand on."

Britt starts poling and, concentrating on her work, is caught up in the moment. For the first time, thoughts of the fire, losses and disappointments are totally erased. It's just the pole, the ice and water.

"Keep 'em coming there Britt," she hears someone call. A few minutes later, "Hold it – hold on. We have to wait for the truck to come back." She is happy to rest for a minute. Looking around, she sees the truck is up by the ice house, the guys sliding the blocks off on to a chute which disappears down inside. Josh walks over to her.

"Let's see what you've got on your feet?" Britt looks down at her cowboy boots. "I mean the soles on those boots." She picks up one foot, starts to lose her balance and grabs at the arm offered by Josh. "Thought so. Leather is the wrong thing for walking on ice, way too slippery. Tuck should never have let you come out dressed like that. You need to be careful standing near the edge. Next time, tell that negligent husband of yours to get you some rubber soled footwear."

"Okay," says Britt, torn between defending Tuck who had given her good, but slightly too small winter boots, and admitting that she refused to wear them. She is slowly becoming aware that nothing goes unnoticed here, including her safety.

"Truck's back, let's get those blocks moving." Britt and the other women resume work. A few minutes later Sue is at her side.

"Want me to take over a while?" Britt is greatly relieved but at the same time envies this woman who looks so delicate but is apparently not. Britt's back is killing her but she's reluctant to complain. "If you want something else to do, they could use some help cooking the dogs and burgers. The grill's set up on the shore beyond the truck." *That was thoughtful, must have realized I needed a break. I wonder how these others keep going. It's hard work.* Britt, reassured to see Tibetta and the kids now playing safely on the land, walks over to join the others setting up tables. "Don't grill 'em to death Ace. Remember this is good all-American beef, not Hunt Club porcupine."

"Ah, you're a bunch of softies. I eat porcupines just for the pleasure of spitting out the quills." This is followed by laughter and a few good natured insults. One by one, others lay down their tools and stop to eat. "These city folk, they have no idea what we go through to provide them with cocktail ice."

"Right about that but, on the up side," chimes in Ace, "they put a lot of trust in us to get the job done right, no micromanaging here. How many folks can say that about their employers?" Josh laughs out loud.

"They have to trust us, they don't understand the half of what's involved. Myself, I think this is awesome. I wouldn't want them to know what a blast it is."

"You guys are lucky in a lot of ways," adds Tripp, "free run of the estates – hunting and fishing whenever you want and no boss much of the time. How much better can it get?"

And from Josh, "Yeah, that's the truth. What's more, I got to admit, I work for good people."

"Well, it could be a little better for me 'cause I'm not my own boss, Stu is," comments Joe, one of the caretakers who works for him at the Bartons.

This sets off more laughter until Stu retorts, "You wouldn't trade your job either. I've tried to fire you a dozen times but you've been coming back for 10 years – must not be all that bad."

Good friends all, the jabs roll off backs like water off a slicker. "Dessert's ready," announces Blanche. They swarm over to the table and stare in admiration. A large pan-sized cookie, covered with white frosting, a cut out in the middle and grid lines throughout: her version of an ice cutting field. Surrounding the plate are plastic toy trucks with piles of white frosted cookies cut to look like ice blocks.

"Fantastic!" "Amazing!" " Brilliant." are the enthused comments. "Someone got a camera? We need a photo. Blanche, what a chef. What an idea."

A half-hour later, the cookie-trucks empty, hearty appetites satisfied, they flow back to work. Britt, somewhat rested, sees a pole lying on the ice and picks it up, ready again to join the line along the channel. A sense of wellbeing warms her like a patch of sun. *This isn't half bad; I never expected to have fun out here today.*

"I'll be damned," exclaims Ace who is loading ice onto the truck, "there's something frozen into this block." Everyone stops to take a look. It is indeed. A pick is brought over and a red wool mitten is dug out. "Strange – wonder how that got there?" Not five minutes later, after resuming work, another mitten shows up.

"Anyone lose his mittens?" asks Josh. "Better check your hands and see if they're covered," he jokes. The kids come running over to see what's happening and immediately start clamoring for the mittens. "Okay, okay, back off. As I found these mittens, I decide who gets them and I'm awarding this prize to the newest member of our team, Tibetta Rising."

At the end of the day, the ice house filled, Josh thanks everyone and they all head for home. Sue takes Britt and Tibetta back to their cabin. Along the way she says, "I hear you're a fashion designer. Who designs your fabrics?"

"Oh, a few different artists depending on what I'm creating. Color is especially important to me. Why do you ask?"

"Because I'm interested in fabrics and yarns myself. I experiment a lot with dyeing wool and knitting sweaters with it. My colors are more earthy than brilliant."

"How interesting. I didn't know. Do you sell somewhere?"

"No. I only work in small quantities. My dyes come from mushrooms."

"Mushrooms?"

"Yes, I'm a mycologist, I study fungi."

"I never heard of such a thing. Where do you find mushrooms, surely not around here?"

"Oh yes, on the estate."

"Which estate?"

"The Bartons."

"Do they give you permission?"

"Don't need it when your husband is the caretaker."

"Stu is your husband? Wow! You have a different last name like I do. Mine is Freier. Lot of people around here don't know that.

"I kept mine because I once wrote a mushroom identification guide under my maiden name, so I've held on to it." *I'll be darned – she wrote a book? I never would have guessed. Just goes to show, never assume.*

"Someday could you show me something about your dyes?"

"Love to. Once spring comes and the rains wet things up, I'll take you on a mushroom hunt."

That night, back at the cabin, Tuck asks Tibetta how her day went. Trying to keep her eyes open but barely able to eat, she mumbles back. "It was fun Daddy, we ran around, played tag, ate cookies and I got a new pair of mittens."

"Sounds good. Now, it's time for bed, pumpkin seed," says Tuck.

"But I'm not tired." Tuck sweeps her up, carries her to her room and she is asleep before he closes the door.

"How'd it go today?" Tuck now asks Britt.

"You know, I didn't think I'd like it, but everyone was so nice. I had a good time, even helped with the ice. A change from the hard driving fashion world." – *and I'm getting more and more attached to these people. Can't let myself do that, we'll be leaving soon,* Britt thinks with a touch of regret. "I didn't realize that Sue was married to Stu Moore. Seems strange. He's such a complainer and backwoods kind of guy and she seems so upbeat and sophisticated."

"Don't be misled by his whining. Stu is highly skilled. I've been told he's one of the best caretakers in the area. Sue's no dummy either. She understands there's more to him than most people know."

"How was your day?" asks Britt.

"Okay I guess. I'm doing my best. Coach is shooting videos so we can review them and work on my form. I'm trying but it doesn't seem to come as easily as it did." He thinks back to his coach's words, 'Thought you'd be further along by now. Hope that accident didn't leave you too fearful to go all out. I don't see you pushing like you used to.' *He's right, I don't have the same drive anymore – got to find it back – got to make this work. What's our future if I don't?*

Chapter 25

Tuck clicks on the morning news, lights the workshop stove and, coffee in hand, settles down at the computer to do some writing, a routine which, for some time now, he has managed to conceal from Britt who thinks he is working on boat repairs. A few minutes later another click shuts off the radio but not the thread of gloomy reports which continue to play through his head. Tuck's thoughts, like his constantly shifting gaze, rove from one subject to another. *Amazing how little we care what arms sales do to the world – can't imagine living in Yemen, Iraq, Afghanistan – never knowing when a bomb will hurtle threw your roof or the front door be kicked in, your wife, your kids, yourself, eradicated like a nest of ants. How do folks live with such terror? Violence begets violence –*

A flash of brilliant light jolts Tuck out of his reverie, returns him to his surroundings. Through the window, he gazes upon layers of fiery red clouds lit by the rising sun. *Red, for many the color of war – for us, the color of sunrise, an autumn tree, the mark on a blackbird's wing.*

After two hours, he shuts down the computer and turns to the job of caretaking. Fortunately for him, winter is a slower time of year. Work is done at a more reasonable pace: maintaining and repairing the 1920s buildings, keeping the roads plowed and the flat roofs snow free. In the large shed, an endless pile of wood is always waiting to be split and stacked, and of course, each of the ten buildings gets a walk-through at least once a week. Byron had asked him to knock down a small shed that was on its way to falling anyway. The job completed a couple of days ago, he is moving salvageable boards into storage when his cell phone rings, "Hey, it's me, Addison. I'm on my way up to check out a piece of land for one of my clients, you around this afternoon?"

"Sure, but not till after five. I've got ski practice and PT but I'll be home by then." The day passes quickly, Tuck returns home just before five. He is distracted as is often the case these days, torn between daily responsibilities and writing endeavors. *Can't forget to pick up milk, eggs and toilet paper – stop by for Tibetta – coach wants me to bring a different pair of skis – wonder how to write about the pitfalls of fame? – should I call my article 'delusions of grandeur'? – now where did I put the ice scraper? – got to still do my leg stretches – did we mail in the form for a new car title? – the cabin's wood box needs filling – oops, there goes Snickles, must have sneaked out when I opened the door – better catch him before a fox does – do sports stars ever stop enjoying their sport? I'm late with Buzz's payment this month – Damn it all, how am I going to do all this?*

At five, Addison arrives. Tibetta, excited to see her uncle, climbs onto his lap and begins checking his pockets. "What are you looking for little girl?" he teases. She giggles and with a squeal of delight, finally locates a soft plush frog hidden in a jacket pocket. "Well," he says, "Didn't know he was there. That guy must have jumped in at the store. I guess he was looking for someone to take care of him."

Tibetta slides off his lap, runs to her room and returns with Smokey the Bear clutched in her arms. "Meet Mr. Froggie," introducing the two, "now you have a friend to play with and you won't be lonely anymore." Then Tibetta runs to the woodstove and pulls a pair of red mittens off the drying rack. "Look Uncle Addie, look at my new mittens." Uncle Addie looks, then takes them from Tibetta and studies them closely. He looks again at Tibetta and gently asks, "Where'd you get these?"

"Uncle Josh gave them to me. Aren't they pretty?"

"Uncle Josh?" asks Addison, staring at his brother. Tuck fills him in on the story of the mittens.

"What's so interesting?"

"Huh. I don't know. It's strange, Bubbles used to have ones just like these but no doubt there are thousands of similar ones out there. Just made me think of her for a moment." A long awkward silence follows before Tuck hauls himself off the sofa to get beer for the three of them. Addison moves to a bench close by the stove and, looking around, compliments Tuck and Britt on how quickly they are turning the cabin into a home.

"Don't know how you stay so upbeat. Can't imagine losing everything like you have."

"We didn't lose everything, only a lot of things. We still have each other and Tibby, Thank God."

"You also have a lot of courage."

"Trying," says Britt, "It's been tough."

"And she's tough," says Tuck, looking at Britt, "You've been a trooper – managing better than I have." Turning back to his brother, "So how about you. How's it going?"

"Getting by, but I can't stop thinking about Bubbles. How can a person just disappear off the map like that? The police have no clues. They've run out of leads – suspect she ran away. That doesn't sit well with me, nor does it with her parents. They never stop hounding me, convinced I have something to do with it – leave messages on my phone, send threatening notes. I've even seen them standing on the street watching to see who comes and goes in my building. I don't blame them in a way but they're barking up the wrong tree."

"Damn I'm sorry," says Tuck. "Life can be screwy."

"You've plenty of your own bad times but at least you have a family, unlike me. I've got to admit I've made a few mistakes in the past. They've come back to haunt me."

Britt breaks in, "But Addison, you're famous. Two weeks ago I saw one of your 'green' houses in *The New York Times*. You make your parents proud. I can hardly see what you have to regret, unless you mean marrying Bubbles."

I don't regret that. She was a looker in her day, an artist and a good woman. It could have worked out but it didn't. Shit happens.

After drinking a beer or two, the brothers head over to see their parents. Fawn greets Addison with a big hug, Justus smiles, gives him a lengthy hand shake. After a few polite enquiries about Bubbles, a daughter-in-law of whom they were hardly fond, Justus changes the conversation to the less personal and begins, "I've been listening to the news. What's the matter with those foreigners? Here we are helping the Pakistanis and they show their gratitude by asking us to leave – just because we hit a few civilian homes – a little collateral damage – they get all bent out of shape. Problems everywhere you look. Even in this fine country we have poor people choosing welfare over work and loafers opting for unemployment over jobs. They should be ashamed. I don't know what the world is coming to. Guess it shouldn't bother me but sometimes it gets me down. I must say we're grateful you're not like that, Addison, You've worked hard, made us proud."

"Dad, you're lucky in a way," says Tuck, trying to resist responding to his father's unjust criticism, "Just think – all that bad news compressed onto a small flat screen – a virtual reality. Turn off the tube and banish despair from your life. One push of the button and poof, peace. Just like that."

"Son, that's downright cynical. Problem is, that's exactly what people are doing: watch the six o'clock news then shut it off and forget the bad stuff as if it isn't happening. No one is doing much to change things. Of course it's not so simple but you know that. By the way, Tuck, you weren't doing too badly yourself until the accident. How's the PT going anyway? Making progress with the skiing?"

"Doing my best Dad but it's slow going."

"Put your shoulder to the task. You need to show a little gumption. Word around town is you've been drinking again. Thought you were supposed to be done with that stuff."

"Not only that," pipes up Fawn, "but it might interfere with Britt getting pregnant."

"Now Mother, where in the world did you get that idea?"

"Well, Esprit said —"

"Stop with Esprit." roars Justus. "You told me yourself that you were starting to have doubts about her. She knows nothing about babies, never had any herself though I'm sure that doesn't stop her from giving advice."

Fawn, intimidated by her husband, shrinks down in her chair. The brothers, feeling sorry for their mother, change the subject to the latest news around Meltmor. They report that Sam has taken up fishing; that the Hub's heating system froze up when the temperature dropped to −40°. It closed the place down for half-a-day bringing a full stop to the rounds of gossip; that Inky Washburn hit a deer and smashed her hood; that someone opened a tea room on Main Street.

"Don't see that working," says Justus. "What kind of man wants to have tea after a long day of work?"

"True," says Tuck, "and real men don't eat quiche. Everyone knows that." Justus, unsure how to take his comment, lets it pass. The small talk continues until Addison leaves for the city and Tuck drives back to the cabin.

"More trouble," says Britt as he enters. "Mrs. Power was here and was she ever furious. Wanted to know why you tore down the shed. Said it was going to be a play center for the kids. She said for you to get up to the house as soon as you get in. Got Tibby all upset hearing her blast off like that. I finally calmed her down, read her a story and got her to sleep. She has no right to come barging in here like that."

"Nice work. You read Mrs. Power a story? That must have been interesting."

"Oh Tuck, this isn't funny. You should have heard her."

"Don't worry, I'll get my chance. That's why I never wanted to live in the caretaker cabin. It's too close to work; we're always at the owners' beck and call, day and night. What's she doing here anyway? She never told me she was coming. I didn't turn up the heat for her."

"She's here to pick up some photos. Are you going up there?"

"I'm going. I may have a few choice words for her as well."

"Don't get fired, Sweetie, we need this home right now."

"Right. That's exactly why I don't like living here. I need a home that's not part of my job."

Tuck heads for the main camp. As he walks, he cools down, starts to think of what is at stake. By the time he knocks on the door, he decides to play it smooth. A furious woman opens the door, beginning a verbal attack that nearly blows him off the porch.

"How dare you take things in your own hands around here. Who do you think you are? I've had enough of your highhanded arrogance. Why am I surprised? I know what you are, where you come from." A score of accusations roll off her well-practiced tongue. "Who are you to tear down that shed? I planned to convert it to a place for the kids, wired so they could use their computers, listen to music, play video games, have something to do while they're up here in this godforsaken land. Now you've destroyed it. You'll pay for this."

"Sorry, I didn't know," he manages to say when there is a pause in her rant, "but Byron did tell me to remove the shed."

"There you go again," Mrs. Power shouts. "It's Mr. Power to you. And he's not your only boss, I am too. You should have checked with me as well."

When Tuck gets home, he is steaming. "She's just like invasive loosestrife around the lake: tall, gorgeous and causes everything around it to wither and disappear." Dialing his cell, he reaches Byron at a restaurant where he's finishing his dinner. "Mr. Power, I need one boss, I can't work like this," he says, and then mentions the other things Byron's wife had said.

"Tuck, not to worry. I'll have it out with Mrs. Power. From here on, I'm the one in charge, no one else. Sorry about all this. You take orders from me and me only. You did exactly what I asked. Thanks. And by the way, it's Mrs. Power when speaking to her, but just Byron for me."

Tuck hangs up. "I'm going for a short walk. Need to calm down a bit."

"That's fine, but it's getting dark outside, better take a flashlight."

"It's not really dark – just seems that way when we're inside looking out. All we can see from here are reflections of ourselves. Outside, eyes adjust and see things more clearly."

Chapter 26

It must be spring. Cleanup teams are picking up the debris which has lately emerged from under the last remnants of Meltmor's dirty snow. Large roller-brush trucks sweep the sand-covered streets; volunteers collect soggy trash left by careless folks; paddlers drag tires out of the river.

Another sign of the change in weather is the annual report from backcountry hikers who tell of seeing a scary character carrying a rat and camping out in the lean-tos. The locals nod and explain, "That's Pitt. Guess he's moved outdoors again. You'll see him around town – comes in to buy meals at the Hub, new clothes at the Outdoors and Inn. Where he gets all his money is a mystery." Equally odd is the fact that he winters in the basement of the Presbyterian Church, guest of the gracious congregation. "Here he comes now," one of the cleanup crew observes. Pitt, looking like he recently emerged from under a log, comes striding along with Rat on his shoulder.

"Pitt rumblin', Rat tumblin', town jumblin'."

"Shut up Rat." grumbles another, knowing it safe to address Rat but not the volatile man who carries him around, "Stop scarin' folks with your crazy talk."

At the Great Camps, the countdown is on, snow melting fast. Caretakers must get things ready by Memorial Day, or more often by July 4th, when families return to take possession of their camps. Docks need to be reset, leaves raked, bird feeders and bird houses erected, fences repaired, garden soil turned, trails cleared of winter windfall, gutters cleaned, water systems turned on, boats launched, motors tuned up, road wash-outs filled – it seems impossible to get it all done in time. Despite that, Tuck is smiling irrepressibly, is even buoyant.

"You sure seem happy," comments Britt. "Must be PT's going well."

Byron had visited to announce that after editing Tuck's article, he had managed to get it published in *Humanity*, a respectable journal published by one of his colleagues. *Secrets. Wish I didn't have so many. Wish I could share this with Britt. Just thinking about it makes it hard to stop grinning.* As Byron promised, it was issued under the name Charles Rover, the pay to be forwarded to a post office box set up by Tuck. It would help towards paying off Buzz. Byron brought him a copy of the journal. He was as pleased as Tuck with the results of their mutual endeavor.

"Thanks for pushing me into this," says Tuck, "of course, some of the pay should go to you as well. I don't get why you won't take your share."

"I don't need the money and clearly you do. But I also get satisfaction out of helping with this. It offers a nice alternative to my usual routine. I'm somewhat fed up with the publishing world – get little joy from my job. I chose the field because I love good literature. It's rarely about that anymore. The days of genius editors like Maxwell Perkins are past. Today it's about marketing and sales; companies driven by smart-ass suits who care only about profit. The world of entertainment determines my company's picks : 'how-to' books, movie star biographies, 'tell-all' celebrity drivel, slam-bam action stories, murder and sex. We rarely meet the needs of the thoughtful reader."

Tuck is flattered by Byron's sharing this with him but wonders why.

Byron goes on, "I like how your work digs into the motivation behind the scenes, unmasks the image, calls it 'the great trickster' that it is. So, did you enjoy working on this?"

"Yup. To my amazement time seems to fly when I'm writing."

"I'm hoping you'll stay with it – set out on a new path." Their talk is interrupted by the arrival of Addison, up for the weekend again. Conversation ensues with discussions about camps, woodlots and estate acreage.

"Never walked much on your land," says Addison to Byron.

"Come on then, I'll take you out on a couple of trails."

After they depart, Tuck works a few more hours before knocking off for supper. Britt has driven to town and picked up Tibetta. Later, Addison returns to join them. They have just finished eating when an inebriated Tim shows up with Ace and Blanche.

"Didn't want you guys to get too lonely way out of town like you are." *Hardly*, thinks Tuck. *Got the lonely part right*, reflects Britt. As there are too few chairs to go around, they all settle on the floor. Ace and Blanche talk about readying the Greene River Hunt Club for the season.

"I was wondering," asks Britt of Blanche, "how you manage to cook for everyone with the baby to take care of and all?"

"Oh, that's easy. She gets passed around from guest to guest. They love her. It's like she has ten or more grandparents. Sometimes I even set her infant seat right in the middle of the big dining table, makes a great centerpiece. Members love it and she's happy as a loon. Leaves me free to cook and serve."

"How does she know loons are happy?" murmurs Tibetta who is snuggled in Tuck's lap and fighting sleep.

"Good question. How do you know?"

"Ah," says Blanche, "because I hear them laughing early mornings when they fly from lake to lake. You've got to get up early to hear those 6 o'clock loons." That's good enough for Tibetta who soon drifts off to sleep. Blanche keeps talking, "A lot of people don't realize what caretaking life is all about. Some day, when I have time, I'd like to write more songs about it – when I have time. I wonder when that will ever be."

"Next winter when we're back in the trailer," says Ace, "I'm going to work on remodeling our kitchen. Once I'm finished, it will be a lot easier and faster to prepare meals, give Blanche more time to compose. I'm going to add counter space, put in a new refrigerator and replace the hotplate with a stove."

"What about a microwave?" says Britt. "That would save Blanche lots of time."

"Nope. Not putting in anything more recent than the fifties. That's the last time either of us understood the technology. These newfangled contraptions sure cause a lotta grief."

Tim chimes in, "Like the ABS system in my truck, locking and unlocking with a mind of its own. Going down a steep icy hill the other day, it unlocked at the last second and shot me right out into the main road. Lucky nothing was coming. I disconnected it after that."

"Yeah," says Tuck, "and now they build trucks with a system that locks all the doors the minute you step out of them. Computer geeks – know nothing of life in the real world, just life on a screen – but it doesn't stop them from programming ridiculous add-ons – taking control out of our hands – like Big Brother, pretending to know what's best for everyone. "

"That sure doesn't fly in the North Country because you guys here know everything already," laughs Britt, only half in jest. Conversation turns to which caretakers prefer the solitary nature of winter work and which prefer the more communal summer atmosphere when owners' families and guests flood the premises. Tim is in rare form and, forgetting his promise to Tuck, bursts out with "Well, we know where Tuck stands on this one. I mean, look what he was up to when he broke his leg."

"And what was that?" asks Britt.

In his inebriated state, Tim forgets his promise not to tell what happened and spills the whole story to the delight of Ace and Blanche but not Tuck. Addison, already aware of it, stays silent.

After their friends depart, Addison crashes on the sofa; Tuck and Britt go to bed where Britt begins in an irritated whisper, "Why didn't you tell me the truth about your accident? Why all the secrecy? Why does Tim drink so much? When are you going to stop drinking? When will we travel again?" They have a lengthy confab which stretches well past midnight, leaving them both exhausted. *It always seems to go like this,* thinks Tuck, *no sooner do I see my way out of a hole, than boom, something pushes me back down again.*

The next day, after work, Tuck tells Britt he needs some space and is going camping for a night. She is upset. "Who're you going with? Are you mad at me?"

"Not at all, though I think you're pretty mad at me right now. I need to be alone, figure out some stuff, find myself back. Wilderness is where I do it best."

"Okay. Don't get lost while you're out 'finding yourself'."

"You forget. I'm from here. It's city folk that don't know where they're going, not locals."

Chapter 27

Tuck's backcountry sojourn brings clarity to a jumble of possibilities. Maybe I do share something with city folk. After all, I've been as uncertain which path to choose as some urbanites are about which woods trail to follow. But now, should circumstances allow, I know what I want to do. Circumstances allow.

Two days later, a call from Byron marks the moment. Yes, *Humanity* is getting positive feedback on the article. "Now, here's the exciting news. The journal has proposed we do a series. Take the same approach we did to examining sports world champions and apply it to other fields. It would be called the 'The Paradox of Success.' I'll help with topics, research and editing, you work on the presentation. For me, it's a nice change from book editing. The pay wouldn't be much at first because you, aka Charles Rover, are a first time writer – still, it's a big coup."

"This is amazing. Once can be a fluke, not sure I can keep it up. I'll do it though, if you're ready to gamble on me."

"It's a deal, I am. One thing though. I've shared a lot with you – you going to tell me why you want your name kept out of this?"

"Some day but not now. I need to continue these articles as Charles Rover." Tuck begins to sense some kind of need in Byron, a desire to get closer. *Don't quite get it, but for now this may work – help solve my blackmail problem.* "Watch out, though, writing is lonely work," continues Byron. "It can cost you friends and health."

"As I said before, I don't mind being alone. Caretakers are used to that. Besides, we're not a lonely lot, only solitary." Tuck flashes to other ideas related to image. *Patriotism and religion are images of virtue but are actually prejudices that can lead to intolerance or worse – creating a bad image of others seeks to justify man's inhumanity to man – image – image – too often obscures the truth –* Tuck's self image is shifting like the wind blowing leaves, ideas swirl around him in a whirl. *I think it's time to share my decision with Britt but I'm afraid. Will she leave me? Is it all over already? And Tibby beginning to warm up to Britt, what will it do to her if Britt leaves? I'm such a misfit, why can't I just go along to get along?*

Later that night, after Tibetta is tucked in her sleeping bag and safely off to dreamland, after the dishes are washed and the stove packed with logs, Tuck and Britt finally settle down on the floor sitting close to one another, basking in the light of the fire. They sip their coffee while sharing a calm moment – the calm before the storm.

"Hon, I love you. We have our troubles but I always believed we'd get through them together. You've been a rock putting up with me, coping after the fire, caring for Tibby, making work trips to the city. Whatever happens from here on, I want you to know I'm grateful for all we've had together." Britt tenses. *Where is this leading?* she wonders, *something's wrong.*

"You know I've been distracted but I've never told you the real reason why. I wasn't sure myself. Now I am. It's like this. I've decided the race circuit is not for me. I don't want it – can't face it anymore – need to quit." There is a long silence. "Britt, say something. I've been dreading this moment. Don't just sit like that. What are you thinking?"

"What do you want me to say? I'm shocked, learning I'm no longer married to the ski champ I thought you were," she answers, torn between relief and despair.

"You're right. I've failed you."

"I didn't say that."

"I've said it for you, you don't need to."

"Then don't. I can speak for myself."

"So – speak. Talk to me. This breaks me up as well as you."

"Okay. Why? Why are you quitting something you're so damn good at?"

"Couple of reasons. First, I want us, not my parents, to raise Tibby. But, there's something else. With all the suffering, all the corruption in the world, spending my time winning medals begins to seem frivolous. I need something more meaningful." Another long silence.

"Like what kind of meaningful? Are you planning to save the world? What makes you think you can do that when no one else ever has?"

"Listen, I know I can't but at least I want to feel like I'm trying. What can I do? Don't know yet. I'm still searching. For now, I need to keep the caretaker job – keep money coming in." *Wish I could tell Britt about the blackmail, about my writing, about so many other things.*

"And what do you expect from me?"

"That's up to you. You and Tibby mean more than you can know. Tibby is coming to love you like the mother she never had. My dream is for us all to stay together, make a life here in Meltmor. But I know that isn't something you want. You've been putting up with this place because you thought it temporary. Don't think it's fair to tie you down to rural life, you're all city." Britt gets up, walks to the fridge and, unusual for her, offers Tuck a beer.

"Want one?"

And rare for Tuck, he replies, "Not really."

Britt sits down at the table and begins, "You don't know me as well as you think. Maybe you've been too tied up with your own problems. You're not the only one to love others, I do too: you and Tibby. I didn't want it to happen, tried not to get attached to the little munchkin but I am. Hard to stay here? Maybe, but I've come to feel a little better about Meltmor. Hard to see you quit skiing? Yes. But, I meant it when we took those vows, 'for better or for worse.' This is starting to sound like the 'worse' part but let's see what happens. I'm so afraid you won't find something meaningful but you deserve the chance to try. Must admit, the town isn't half as bad as I thought. I'm even beginning to connect. People have been good to us, to me, even become friends, but whether I can make a life for myself here is something else." Tuck leans over and wraps his arms around her.

"Oh babe, you're amazing."

"I love you Tuck, that's the only reason I would even consider giving this a try, that and the fact that I've gotten so attached to Tibby. But, I've also got a career and my own needs. I'll have to see if I can make it all fit." They sit in silence for a while. Then Tuck starts talking.

"You asked me before why I never told you how my ski accident really happened. I guess Tim spilled the beans but he didn't tell you why I did what I did. The accident was something the coach wanted covered up, said it would reflect badly on him if it got out that I had not stuck with the team, taken off on my own and screwed up while messing around when I shouldn't have been. But I really needed to get away from it all. Whatever coach suggests, we're expected to do. He's sort of a guru; he decides, we follow. That kind of group mentality was starting to bother me, a weight pulling me down."

"So – you rebelled? Took off on your own?"

"Yeah, I did. It felt good too."

"Seems to be a habit of yours." *Is that what's going to happen to our marriage? One day he'll suddenly take off on his own? What kind of a life can I have if I'm worried about that all the time? Maybe I should take off first, save myself the suspense.* "Is this how it's going to be with caretaking too? One day you just walk away?"

"No, that's different. There, I'm my own boss most of the time, free to do things the way I think best. And you know? It's not such a bad deal. A lot of caretakers have degrees, could get fancier jobs but prefer what they're doing – like being outdoors so much, the physical work, the wilderness. It's not always easy though – takes a lot of diplomacy to work around peoples' moods. We have to close our eyes to things we shouldn't see – not talk back, though it's tempting." Tuck and Britt, each grappling with the change of plans, put in a night of fitful sleep.

The next evening, after attention focused on their jobs has given some relief, they drive to Tuck's parents to announce his decision, get it over with as soon as possible. On hearing the news, Fawn bursts into tears. "Not going back to skiing? Meltmor is so proud of you. You have put it on the map. And this is your thanks?"

"Mother," Tuck reminds her, "I thought you liked our living nearby." Then the real truth emerges.

"I do, I do. But I thought you were going back to skiing and Tibby would live with us again. Now, she will only visit here, after all we've done for her, never again live with us." And Fawn continues to weep uncontrollably.

"This is grave news indeed," responds Justus. "It's not enough you have an illegitimate child, now you're a quitter. You owe this family something. You need to learn some discipline, get a little steel in that backbone of yours. I've been worried about something like this happening. Certainly does reflect badly on the family."

"Sorry to disappoint you but there it is."

"And what do you think of all this, Britt?"

"I'm going along with whatever Tuck decides – for now. He's struggling to work it all out, I'm sure he will."

"Spoken like a loyal wife but I don't share your confidence. Tuck, I think, jobs being scarce, your best bet is the army. There's always a need for good soldiers to defend our country. It would give you some direction – and it would surely make us all proud."

"I appreciate your concern but I don't think that's something I want to do. I realize that war is the voice of the country these days but I'm not part of that chorus. I'll take the ring of peace over the thunder of war any day."

"No guts. That's what I was afraid of. The military is precisely what you do need." Justus shoots back. Fawn weeps even harder,

"Please, please everyone, please stop fighting," begs Fawn.

"Exactly," agrees Tuck as, his own feelings unleashed, he sounds off with, "What a bloody militaristic country we live in. We're so in love with violence that when we can't dig up real battles we reenact the old ones. I'd like to see someone reenact the signing of a peace treaty for a change." Justus's face turns deep red, his scowl ferocious. He is at a loss for words.

Coming to the rescue, Fawn finally recovers enough to say, "Let's everyone calm down and not get so angry. Your dad has been under quite a strain lately which makes this doubly hard on him. The SuperBig is trying to buy out his inventory, put him out of business."

"Fawn, that has absolutely nothing to do with this conversation. Anyway, I wouldn't accept the paltry offer those guys made. I've run a quality store for years, have good loyal customers. Honesty and sound business practices always pay off. I'm not worried about the SuperBig. I'll be fine. You'll see."

As further conversation doesn't bring them beyond a "wait and see" future, Britt and Tuck depart, carrying his sleeping daughter. Tibetta has heard the news. She won't be going back to live with her grandparents. She is a little disappointed but, *it's Okay 'cuz' my daddy will be home with me every night and I sort of like Bee now.*

Live in the moment. I still have a wife, a daughter and a job – at least for now. But this "wait and see" is hard to live with, reflects Tuck. The best way, no doubt. It is better not to see into the future

Chapter 28

The weather has turned, a defining moment in the North Country: lake ice is out. With the reappearance of open water, hopes rise. Folks dare to believe that spring might actually return. On a particularly warm day, Pitt strides through town, jacket flapping open, huge sideburns and gray hair flying, Rat on his shoulder perpetually washing his whiskers. "What lies in the dark, rises with the sun. Thus speaks Rat." Pedestrians part way as they see the duo coming, crossing the street to leave them sole rulers of the slush filled sidewalk.

"At least he's cheerful this morning," comments Ma Rose as Pitt saunters past the Hub, its door open bidding the warm air enter.

At the police station, news is not so cheerful. Josh has reported that a body was found in the lake near the Raven's Nest. Local police call for assistance from the State Police who send Investigator Stalk and the forensic identification unit.

Arriving at the Raven's Nest, they are met by a visibly upset Tripp. She directs them to the lake where Josh is waiting. "I was down here checking to see if debris had washed up against the dam. All that rain and snowmelt brought a rise in the lake. I was looking down into the water when I noticed what looked like long grass washing back and forth. Suddenly I realized it wasn't grass but someone's hair."

The corpse is dragged to shore where it is confirmed to be a woman, fairly well preserved due to the cold water. She is dressed in a heavy jacket and boots.

"I may have seen her before. I'm not sure and can't remember where it could have been." comments Josh.

"I wonder how long she's been in the water. She's in fairly good condition, except that she's dead," comments one observant officer.

"That's a bit of a drawback," wryly responds another. "I'm thinking she might have been swimming under the ice a while."

"Let's have a bit of respect here," demands Investigator Stalk. Turning to Josh he asks, "Where are the Ravens? Do they know about this?"

"Not yet. They're on vacation. Want me to call them?"

"No. We'll take care of that but we'll need their number. If you would get it for me now, I'd appreciate it." Josh, pale and shaky, is grateful for an excuse to leave the horrific sight of the corpse. He walks off toward the house. The officers, practiced at sending onlookers away, begin their work. After taking measurements and several photographs, they carefully examine the body and surroundings. Sam removes a bulging backpack from the woman's back. "This thing weighs a ton," he announces, "What's a little woman like this doing carrying rocks?"

"Bag it," orders Investigator Stalk. Emptying her pockets, the officers find little else than a balled up handkerchief and remnants of a lipstick. Nothing seemingly significant but everything handled with gloves and saved for later inspection. Arrangements are made to transfer the body for autopsy.

It's not long before Byron receives a call from the police. "Sir, we've recovered your stolen property. We think all of it."

"Good work. Where'd you find it?"

"It's grim, sir. A body washed up against the dam near the Raven's property. Caretaker found it. It's a woman, your things in her backpack." Stalk describes the findings.

"That's rather ghastly. Any idea who she is – was?"

"Not at this point. We'd like you to come up, identify your belongings and see if you can help us figure that out."

"You mean I'd have to view the body? Not sure I have the stomach for it."

"Yes, we'd like you to do that. So far, we haven't found any identification. We're also checking missing persons' reports but you might be able to speed things up."

"I understand. I can't leave here until 5:00 PM. That should get me there by about 10:30 or 11 tonight."

"Fine, come to the station first thing tomorrow morning. I'll meet you there at eight."

By late that afternoon, the police narrow down the missing person list to two possibilities, either of whom might be a match. One is Bubbles Rising. They call Addison first because the other woman, from the West Coast, is a less likely possibility. By eight the next morning Byron arrives, as does Addison, deep circles under his eyes after a sleepless night. Both men are brought to the back room, offered coffee and seats at a long coffee-stained table in a linoleum-floored, dingy-walled room.

"Welcome gentlemen," says Investigator Stalk in a polite but officious voice. "We've made a couple of discoveries since we talked to you last night. First, balled up inside the woman's handkerchief we found a key. Here it is." He produces the key sealed inside a small plastic bag. "This look familiar to either of you?" The two men lean forward.

"Can't be sure," says Byron, "but I think it could be the key to my camp."

Addison adds, "I used to have a key to your camp too, from the days when I was working on the cabins, but haven't seen it for so long, I can't remember what it looks like."

Addressing Addison, Stalk says, "Addison, we'll need confirmation. Would you please try to find that key when you return home," says Stalk. "Let us know if you do? Now, the second thing we found –"

"Excuse me officer, but you told me this body might be my wife. Could I see her before we go on. I can't focus on any of this until I know," exclaims Addison in a trembling voice.

Already fairly certain of Bubbles identity, the detective has looked into her background and learned a few things. "I believe that would be your soon to be ex-wife?" responds Stalk.

"That's correct. If you're implying by that, that it doesn't matter to me, you're very wrong. I still care what happens to her."

"All right then. I'll have Sam drive you over to the morgue. We can come back and continue this conversation afterwards."

Addison is taken in first. His worst nightmare. There she lies, not a runaway as he had hoped, but the dead, shriveled, waxy looking body of his emaciated wife. Feeling sick and faint, he staggers from the morgue to the outer waiting room where Byron catches him as he starts to sway. "Easy man," he says, helping him to a chair. "It was your wife?"

Addison can only nod. His body is convulsed by a great shudder as he leans forward, elbows on his knees, arms shaking, tears flowing. It is some time before he is able to talk. "Whatever was she doing up here? How did she die? She didn't deserve to end like this."

When able to walk again, he shuffles out to the police car. Sam is waiting to drive them back to the station. Sam's demeanor is professional but the expression on his rigid face betrays the conviction that his passengers are involved in something nefarious.

The police, informed that a man fitting Addison's description had picked Bubbles up at the Institution, are somewhat skeptical of his reaction. True, a witness had placed him at a restaurant near the time she had been picked up at the clinic, but the witness was a friend having an early morning coffee with him, and friends, with the best intentions, have been known to lie. It had been a busy morning and nobody else could remember for certain that those were the two sitting at the back table. Bubbles's parents, the Bellows, had never stopped nagging the police, certain that Addison had had something to do with her disappearance.

"I have another question for you," continues Stalk as if the last horrific scene had not interrupted their conversation, "Did you ever bring Bubbles up to the Power's Camp?"

Addison, lifts his head, stares straight at Stalk but appears to be looking right through him. His reply is barely above a whisper.

"Yes. I brought her to see the two guest cabins I designed. Byron said it would be okay to do that. I showed her all around."

"Did you go inside the main camp?" He nods his head. "How did you get the key?"

"I already told you," Addison replied with some annoyance, "I had one from when I was overseeing construction of the cabins."

"Why did you need to go into the main house if you were constructing separate cabins?"

"Part of the cabins replicate the inside of the main camp – had to check that the details were right."

"Did you know the security code?"Addison takes a deep breath, gives a long sigh and brings his focus back again to Investigator Stalk, as if he'd just discovered him sitting there.

"Of course."

"Did your wife know that code?"

"No. I had it written down and hidden with the key."

"Why did your wife want to see the place?"

"She'd never seen an Adirondack Great Camp – knew I admired them – wanted to see one for herself."

"Did you notice if she took particular interest in anything special while there?"

"No. She was amazed, amazed at the size, the architecture, the setting and all."

"One last thing. Do you want us to notify her parents or will you do that?"

"I think it best you do. They're pretty hostile toward me."

"Okay. That's all for now. You can leave but don't leave the city except to come up here. You'll be hearing from us again." Addison, pale and wobbly, rises to go. Byron gets up as well.

"Not you," says Stalk. "We have more to discuss."

"Excuse me but this man has had quite a shock, I'd like to help him to his car. I'll come right back." Once outside, Byron suggests that Addison wait for him so they can go for a bite of food and steady themselves before driving back to New York.

Returning to the station, Byron listens to Stalk as he continues, "You recognize everything in the pack? Is there anything missing?"

"Not that I'm aware of."

"Good. The next question, what's inside the steel box and where is the key?"

"This may sound strange, but the box belongs to my wife and I don't know what's inside. She has the key. She told me she kept a few pieces of jewelry in there but I really can't say."

"As this incident involves loss of life, we are going to have to open the box, either with a key or by force. That's up to your wife. Please call her and let us know the answer."

"I'm going home tonight. I'll talk to her and call in the morning."

"Good enough. Now, one other thing. How much do you know about this architect?"

"I know he's done some excellent work for me at Camp Reedmor. He came highly recommended. He's one of the best. His specialty is sustainable building and Adirondack- style design. In fact, he originally came from right here in Meltmor."

"Really? That must be the Rising son that moved away years ago. Has he got a brother Tuck?"

"Yes he does, he's a good caretaker, works for me at my camp."

"I know that. Tuck is well known around here, kind of a folk hero. Didn't realize it was the same family. Huh – interesting. One other thing. Did you know Addison still had a key?"

"Don't know that I did but it wouldn't have mattered anyway. I trust him."

"Well, that will be all for now. Thank you for your cooperation. I'll be in touch."

Outside, Byron finds Addison walking near his car. "You okay to drive?" he asks.

"I'm okay."

"You want to go see your family while you're here?"

"No, I can't deal with them right now. I just want to get back to the city."

"Right. Then why don't you follow me? It's only five miles to the Chadwick in Cliff Rock. We could stop there for lunch and drinks. You look like you could use a little something, and so can I for that matter."

Addison, thankful for his understanding, feels utterly dazed. Byron, driving slowly ahead via a back road, watches the rearview mirror, keeping an eye on Addison's driving. At the Chadwick they stop for a couple of hours, after which, somewhat restored, Addison comes out of his fog and appears alert enough to safely continue to the city.

Back at the police station, a call was made to the Bellows informing them of the tragedy. After the first shock, there was an explosion from the other end of the line. "This is exactly what we feared. This is proof that Addison is the murderer. He must have taken her up there and drowned her. She would have no other reason to go to Meltmor. We want her body sent to us immediately." Offering his sympathy but no further information, the detective tells them an autopsy must first be performed. He will be back in touch as soon as that is complete.

That evening, Byron reports the day's events to Pru who says, "I think it's just as well she died, she's no great loss to anyone, don't you agree?"

Byron does not, but what's the point of arguing. "Investigator Stalk wants to know if you will send a key to the box or should they force it open? What's in it anyway?" As a solid ice wall now splits his marriage down the middle, it comes as no surprise that Pru changes her story to tell him that it isn't jewelry in the box but something else.

When Addison reaches home, he calls his brother. "Should have stopped in to tell you but I wasn't up to it earlier." He tells him what happened. "I can't find the key or code I used to keep in my desk either. I'm going to have to call the police and let them know." Tuck listens in amazement.

"Want me to come down? I can leave tonight if you like."

"No, not yet. What I would like is for you to tell the parents in the morning. I'm not in the mood to hear their reaction."

Early the next day Sam gets a call from Byron. He takes the message for Investigator Stalk. "My wife says to go ahead and bust that box open. It will save me another trip up there with the key."

"So, are you going to tell us what's inside or make us discover it for ourselves?"

"This is a bit awkward for me but I'll tell you alright. The box contains at least ten if not fifteen thousand dollars. What I can't tell you, and what she won't tell *me*, is what she was saving it for. We may never know. Don't think you'll get a straight answer from her, even under interrogation. She's a tough one."

In his line of work Sam knows a lot about the domestic battlefield. *Yet another reminder why never to give in to temptation and fall into the bottomless marriage pit*, he reminds himself.

That same morning, before Tuck gets to him, Justus picks up the paper on his way to what was to be a routine day of work. Not. The headlines come at him like an attack missile. "Body found in Cedar Bluff Lake, wife of architect Rising." He changes direction, rushing back to the house to tell Fawn and call Addison. "The nerve, the

120

outrageous nerve. How insulting to find this out from the paper. Why haven't we been called? We should be the first to hear this, not the last." At that moment, Tuck arrives to explain.

"So," Fawn reacts, "sorry for Bubbles but Addison was getting rid of her anyway so it's perhaps no major loss." Tuck, appalled but not surprised, deals with his parents as best he can. Justus insists on calling Addison immediately but there is no answer. His fury might have caused him to self-implode if he had known that a jacket lay over his son's answering machine, hiding from view the red blinking light of a phone whose ringer had been turned off.

Later that afternoon, the metal box is forced open, its contents confirmed. Two days later the autopsy report reveals that Bubbles had drowned. There was no outward evidence of foul play. Stalk decides to phone the clinic where Bubbles was being treated. He finally gets through to her psychiatrist Dr. Kammer.

"It would be helpful if you tell us anything Bubbles said that might cast a light on what happened to her."

"Doctor-client discussions are absolutely private. I can't do that."

"Even when the patient is deceased?"

"Yes, even so."

"Are there circumstances that would allow you to make an exception?"

"I can't think of any offhand. Doctor-client communications are strictly confidential. You say there is no evidence of foul play?"

"Not quite. I said there was no immediate evidence of foul play. It's still possible that someone drowned her. We don't know enough at this point. We think she might have said something to you that could help us figure this out."

"Sorry. I don't see how I can help you." Dr. Kammer answers before hanging up.

The body is ready to be released. Investigator Stalk calls the Bellows who declare she must be sent to their town undertaker. "That creep Addison is a vicious murderer. He was trying to divorce her, planning to collect on her insurance. We will fight to the death not to let him bury her – and he better not show up at her funeral either."

"I don't think there will be any problem with that," replied Stalk evenhandedly, "He anticipated your feelings and told us if that is what you want, he will go along with it."

"There. You see, guilty as charged," answered Aiken Bellows.

121

Chapter 29

"No one should die so young. Still, whatever was she up to? I don't know what to think," says Britt on hearing the news. "I guess I never understood what your brother saw in her, but a thief? It doesn't seem to fit."

"Doesn't make sense to me either," agrees Tuck, "Like what was she doing up here anyway? How did she get here? The one thing I am sure of, my parents' reaction is over the top."

"What happens now?" asks Britt.

"Nothing for the moment. Guess we have to wait and see. In the meantime, we try to go on as usual."

"In that case, let's follow George W. Bush's advice to the American people: when things become overwhelming, go shopping," says Britt.

"I'll go because we need to replace a lot of things, not because of that man's trivial mind. Ever done the yard sale crawl?"

"Don't tell me we're going to look at other people's junk? I thought we had some insurance money, plus, we still have money from that incredible fundraiser."

"Yeah, we have a few more dollars but not nearly enough to cover all our needs. Besides, you can find some good things this way. It's sort of a game to see what kind of deals you can get."

"How humiliating. Do you really want to be seen rummaging through other people's throwaways?"

"Around here it's considered good fun. You'll be amazed who you meet doing the same thing. Just give it a try. If you don't like it, we'll go somewhere else."

Reluctantly, Britt agrees to go. They scoop up Tibby, stop in town for a newspaper listing the yard sale locations, and they're off. At the first house, amidst an expanse of clothing-filled tables spread across the front yard, they meet Sue Tower and Stu Moore.

"So glad we ran into you," says Sue. "I was meaning to call you. I'm offering a guided mushroom walk tomorrow; the announcement was in the paper but I don't know if you saw it. Britt, would you like to come?" Britt, remembering her conversation with Sue about using mushrooms for dyeing fabrics, agrees to go, but has concerns about the forecast.

"It's supposed to rain tomorrow though."

"Oh, that's even better. Mushroom weather."

"You mean you'll still go?"

"Absolutely. Meet us at 10:00 AM at the Otter River trailhead. Can you bring her Tuck?" Stu and Sue leave, followed by Tuck and Britt who, finding little else than well-worn baby clothes, also move on. "I must say, I hardly find this appealing."

At the next stop, Tibetta hops out of the car and heads for piles of plastic toys. Picking up one after another, she asks over and over, "Can I have this?" Repeatedly the answer is no.

"Plastic, a plague on the world. How arrogant to saturate people's houses with this monstrous stuff that will never decay," comments Tuck, clearly annoyed by the attraction it holds for Tibetta. Britt sighs. Tibetta gets cranky. Finally he gives in and lets her get Mr. Potato Head. Prices on toys are cheap. *With good reason*, reflects Tuck, *nobody can knows how to get rid of the stuff.* He hands Tibetta the nickels and dimes which easily cover the price of the hideous plastic potato. She even has some change left over. Her collection has begun to grow: a box of colored pencils, a pad of paper, a porcelain dog. Hopping back in the car, Tibetta is bursting with excitement.

"Look what I got. It's a real Mr. Potato Head. I always, always, always wanted one of these." She has trouble opening the box so Britt reaches into the back seat to help.

"That's because this is brand new. The box is still sealed. Wow, are you a lucky girl." Tuck rolls his eyes. Tibetta checks out all the pieces. Then opens the pencil box, pulls out a dark green color and in no time is busy drawing on her new sketch pad. She draws a round face full of lines and a turned down mouth.

"Guess who that is?" she giggles. "That's daddy looking at my plastic toys. It makes his face all crinkly." Britt grins, even Tuck breaks out in a smile. The third stop looks a little more interesting. Britt spies a table full of household goods. "I'll be darned," she says, "if this isn't a Le Creuset roasting pan. In the catalogs it costs ten times as much. I've always wanted one of these."

"Grab it and hold on to it then," says Tuck. "Lots of people out here looking and that kind of thing goes fast."

Further searching produces another Le Creuset pot and a large serving spoon with a hand carved wooden handle. Handing these over to Tuck, she asks, "Isn't that the owner of the Pine Tree Gift Shoppe over there? Why would she be here?" "I told you. Everyone does this. I just saw Blanche too. Good thing you grabbed those pots 'fore she saw them." Britt steps over to pay.

"Say, didn't your house burn down last winter?"

"Yes, it did. I am so glad to find these pans. They're exactly what I want. How much?"

123

"Nothing. Take them. I wouldn't charge anyone who's been through what you have. Glad you can use them."

"Oh, thank you very much. That's so nice." Ace appears around the corner with a collection of tools in a wooden box.

"Wow. Great find," admires Tuck.

"Yup, I thought so too. Can you use them?"

"Of course not. You found them first."

"What? You replaced all your tools already?"

"No, not yet but sooner or later I'll get there."

"How about sooner? I picked these up for you. I have enough already. Shall I put them in your truck? Looks like you've got your hands full."

At another stop, while checking over the goods at a multi-family sale, they were startled by a piercing scream. A woman, clearly a tourist, dressed in pastel shorts, plastic sandals and a halter top, is hightailing it out of the yard with her nattily dressed husband loyally running behind. Customers surge forward to see what happened. It seems someone had left a partially filled pizza box sitting on a table. As the woman approached, a large white-footed rat scurried out from under the lid, running in the direction of the garage. In hot pursuit, a couple of men follow it to – Pitt, napping in an old armchair; price $4. Rat leaps onto his boot and runs up his leg, taking refuge on Pitt's shoulder. Pitt opens his eyes, turns his head, smiles and mumbles, "Run stupid Rat, run, learn where you belong and where you don't."

"That's it Pitt, out of here. You lost me a potential customer. Tourists need to be welcomed, not scared out of their wits by dangerous Adirondack beasts," remonstrates the owner of the place. Everyone has a good laugh as the New Jersey car is seen speeding off down the road.

After two hours, Tibbetta is complaining she's tired and Tuck calls a halt. "Already?" asks Britt, a new convert to this North Country mania, "We've just started." On the way home, the bed of the truck carrying, among other things, a chair, a cupboard, two paddles (but no boat) and a wicker hamper, Tuck looks over at Britt, smiles and asks, "What do you say? Not a bad haul for a couple of hours work, huh?"

Britt glances back at him, "Okay, okay. I didn't know. Guess I'm turning into a real scrounger."

"Not a bad trait in my book."

The next day, rain pours down. "I don't think I want to go out in such miserable weather," declares Britt.

"Oh come on. It will be fun. Listen, you can wear my slicker and rain hat. What do you have for boots?" With pride, Britt hauls a pair of elegant bright red rubber shoes from under the bed.

"Babe, they'll be fine for the first five minutes. After that, you'll find them filling up with mud, sticks and water. We need to get you a good pair of tall neoprene rain boots."

"Don't bother, these will work fine."

Tuck drives her to the trailhead with a promise to pick her up at noon after he meets with his coach and team to tell them he is through.

"Noon? I have to stay out in this till noon?"

"That's how long the walk lasts. I'll take you home now or pick you up later. Your call."

Britt looks around in amazement. Over ten people, men and women, young and old, are standing in the downpour, baskets over their arms, faces half-hidden under soggy, drooping hats. "This is crazy but if they can do it, so can I."

The walk begins and despite misgivings, Britt finds herself caught up in the excitement of looking for the earthy delicate fruits which lurk under leaves and sneak their way up dead tree trunks. The hunt, to her surprise, is actually quite addicting. Time passes quickly. Noon comes along, and with it, Tuck and Tibetta to pick her up.

"How was it?"

"Odd, just plain odd. But, sort of interesting. Sue showed me a gorgeous sweater she had on under her raincoat, all yellows and oranges made with mushroom dyes. I usually prefer bright colors but there was something enticing about those earthy tones. I was quite taken with them. Did you know mushrooms can be used to dye wool and silk?"

"Nope."

"She invited me out to their place to see which mushrooms she uses for colors. It might have possibilities for a new line of clothing. A friend of hers is coming along to show us the plants she uses for dyeing wool."

"Feet wet?"

"Do you have to ask?"

The following Friday, Sue picks Britt up for a walk at the Barton Estate where she and Stu live. On reaching the property, Sue punches in a security code that opens a steel gate disguised with stick work to appear less formidable than it is. The gate keeper, working in his nearby garden, gives a friendly wave. They go a considerable distance along the road before Britt asks, "How big are these grounds anyway?"

"Twenty-nine thousand acres," answers Sue. Britt is astounded. It sounds like a western ranch not an eastern mountain camp. Not wanting to appear more ignorant than she already feels, she nods her head as if this confirms what she had suspected.

Sue pulls into the drive by their caretaker home, a moderate-sized dark green-shingled, two-story building. Linda Morris, parked in the driveway, is waiting for them. Just then, the front door opens and Stu steps out.

"I'm going to the office for a while, got a lot of families coming up this week, need to make out the schedule for who stays where and when. The Bartons have guests at the Trillium Cabin this week and they've reserved the Mud Pond lean-to for a picnic today. You may want to avoid those areas," he says, adding, "Morning Linda, Britt."

After Stu drives off, Sue invites the women inside. "I need to pick up a couple of collecting baskets and my field guide." Linda and Britt follow her up the steps. The interior is inviting and cozy. Landscape watercolors adorn the pine walls, overstuffed chairs crowd the living room. In the middle of the cheerful yellow-painted kitchen, an old wooden-legged, tin-topped table is weighed down with papers, bills, a check book, a catsup bottle, leftover breakfast plates, sugar bowl and half-filled coffee mugs sporting "Barton Estate" in gold letters on the sides.

"Nice home," comments Britt.

"Yes, we're very lucky, plenty big with three bedrooms, dining room and two bathrooms. Only problem: it's all cut up into small spaces. I wish we could knock out some walls and open it up, but we're not allowed, it's not ours to change." Returning to the car, Sue drives them another four miles, passing several turnoffs along the way.

"Are we still on the estate?" asks Britt.

"We are. There are some eight miles of roads through here. You would know if we were getting to the property line. It's cleared for easy patrolling. Soon we'll pass a lovely birch-lined 10-acre pond. It's a favorite fishing spot for many of the families who visit. We're headed for a large boggy area right beyond that. It has a wooden walkway across it – great place for finding mushrooms. From there we'll follow the trail to the horse meadows so Linda can show us some of the field plants she uses for her wool dyes."

The next three hours are an eye opener for Britt. She would never have dreamed that so many interesting colors could be made from native plants and mushrooms. "Did you go to school for all this?" she asks the others.

"I have a Masters in biology but I've studied mushrooms on my own for years now," Sue answers. "I'm addicted, not to smoking them but to learning about them," Sue laughs.

"And I got started when we began raising sheep," says Linda, "so I could have my own wool for knitting. Then, I thought, why not use the plants around our place as well, make my own dyes? Hey, there's my man."

"Joe, meet Britt."

Joe, out clearing the trail, stops, wipes at his sweat-soaked face and talks to the women for a few minutes before they continue on with their field trip. "What's he doing out here?"says Britt, forgetting she had met him before.

"He works for Stu, he and about ten others. It takes a lot of caretakers to maintain twenty-four buildings, six lean-tos, the grounds, roads, trails and boundary line."

"I can imagine," says Britt, but she can't really. "Is this the biggest estate around here?"

"One of the biggest but there are a few others of similar size."Not 20 minutes later they meet a couple walking in the rain. Stepping to the side of the path, Sue greets them with "good morning," waits for them to pass before continuing.

"Funny, they looked like Bill and Marianne Morris, the national news anchors," comments Britt.

"No they didn't look like them at all," laughs Sue, "that is them. They come up here fairly often but don't say anything about it to anyone."

After the walk, Sue invites Britt and Linda to her house for a bowl of comfort food: vegetable soup made of the last of the frozen vegetables from the previous year's garden. After lunch, she drives Britt home. "I can't thank you enough, Sue, I'll be thinking about how to use some of these natural dyes in fashion design."

That evening, sitting at supper with the family, Britt eagerly shares her day. "Why didn't you take me? I would have had fun," pouts Tibetta, surprising them by her wish to do something with Britt alone.

"Another time, cutie. This was an adults-only day." Turning to Tuck, she continues "I felt sort of stupid out there, not realizing there were so many Great Camps here and how incredibly big they are. Who owns them and why don't we ever hear about their guests, like Bill and Marianne Morris? Oops, I wasn't supposed to say I'd seen them."

"That's okay this time. It won't go beyond these walls. You don't hear of these folks because, as you know by now, many of the owners are not only wealthy but famous. They come here to escape their highly public lives – often bringing guests who also want a break from notoriety. They don't want to be disturbed. Caretakers and town folks understand that and protect their privacy."

"It was interesting today to see Sue and Linda move so easily through the woods. You'd think they were on a sidewalk the way they maneuver around the logs and rocks – sort of like deer. It felt like they were part of the woods."

Tuck is delighted something has gone well today, because for him, it has not. "Oh Sweetie," she says, "how selfish. I forgot to ask how your meeting went with the team and coach."

"I knew, when I told my coach I was quitting, that this confab was to pressure me into changing my mind. First they tried flattery to persuade me to stay on. When that didn't work, they changed tactics and got nasty – gave me hell – said I was breaking my contract, letting down my teammates, had wasted the coach's time, that it would probably result in their getting sued by my sponsors. It was not pretty. But a decision was finally made to excuse my desertion by claiming my broken leg was not healing properly and I'd never again be a topnotch racer. That would sound more acceptable to everyone, and might get them out from under potential lawsuits. Of course my teammates will never forgive me for this. The last comment I heard someone mumble as I left the room was 'Tuck, you suck.'"

"How miserable. I'm so sorry."

"Well, yes and no. In a way it was bad but something else happened which cast a new light on things. The more they pushed me to stay on, the more I realized their concern was not so much for me but rather for their own careers. To the extent that my being there increases the team's chances of winning more championships, they care. Beyond that, I don't think they do. I can't say I blame them but realizing this makes it, morally speaking, easier for me. I just don't feel I belong there anymore."

Chapter 30

Britt drives to town to the hardware store. Tuck has asked her to pick up work gloves and some kind of 'weird stuff' he insists on flushing down the pipes, a kind of medicine for the septic tank he explained. *Country life sure is peculiar.* While searching through the aisles, she runs into Linda Morris who asks her, "Did you hear the Bartons are putting their place up for sale?"

"I had no idea. It's such a gorgeous place, why would they do that? Can't afford it anymore?" Linda's husband Joe, overhearing their conversation, emerges from the paint aisle and joins in.

"I think it has more to do with what today's owners find entertaining. Used to be the Barton's parents and grandparents would come up here to fish, hunt, and hike the mountains. This next generation is more interested in laptops, Walkmans, TV, movies and occasionally a boat ride and waterskiing. If they hike at all, it's to tone up their anorexic bodies, not to enjoy the woods. In fact, most of them would rather go inside to their health club than get outside in the fresh air. They come here for a few days at a time, get bored and return to the city. Just don't enjoy it like their parents did."

"What happens to you if they sell?"

"Don't know. Only time will tell."

"That's rough. Work's so hard to find these days and all."

"It's okay. We're used to scrounging for a living. It's a way of life around here. We'll find something," replies Joe. *How can they be so complacent?* wonders Britt. *I'd be worried stiff if my future was that uncertain. In fact, I am worried stiff.* A few minutes later, while Britt stands in line to pay, Esprit in miniskirt and halter top splashed with oversized flowers, comes up behind her.

"Been to the SuperBig yet?" she asks.

"Not yet."

"Oh, you've got to get over there. Is it ever fun! They have all kinds of inexpensive clothes, shoes, house wares, nick-knacks, paint, tools – everything you could ever want."

"I'm not so sure," says Britt, "but thanks for telling me about it."

"Not so sure? Not so sure of what? Don't tell me you're like Fawn, worried about your father-in-law's business? He'll be fine and if he isn't, then he can find something else to sell. After all, the SuperBig has aisles and aisles of towels, sheets, blankets, dresses, jackets, toys, statuettes, paper goods, gifts. It's amazing."

"I'm not sure I want to see aisles and aisles of all that stuff made with slave labor," responds Britt, "Sounds a little depressing."

"You're just spoiled; lucky you have so much you don't need those things." Suddenly Esprit stops, realizing what a gaff she has made. "I mean, don't you need all these things after the fire and all?"

"I guess so," replies Britt, as the tears well up. *Oh no, here I go again. Not in front of Esprit! Just can't seem to get past the crying jags.*

Esprit, noticing the tears, pounces like a cat.

"I've already invited you to attend my class for free. I'll teach you how to handle tragedy, teach you living skills and give you a spiritual tune up. You need to get past that fire. I'll expect you at nine tomorrow morning."

"Thanks Esprit, but I have to work in the morning. I won't be able to make it."

"Work? Nonsense. This class is more important. You can work later. I'll see you there." *Some people never give up,* thinks Britt. To her relief, she's next in line. Don, owner of the family hardware store, greets her by name, asks how things are going and adds up her meager purchases.

On the way home, she considers the plight of her father-in-law. He's putting a good face on it but she's heard that his business is slowing down, crazed customers rushing to the big box store. Only occasionally has she heard anyone comment on the SuperBig's lack of the personal service that Justus offers. When asked to contribute to the local food pantry, the SuperBig's management said they would check with headquarters. That was the last anyone ever heard about that. Officer Sam Lively, to her surprise, was one of the few who openly voiced an opinion. "It's important to stand by your neighbors in a small struggling town like Meltmor and Justus donates to local causes. Won't see the new store doing that," he was heard to say.

That night, Britt tells Tuck about her day. Then, suddenly changing the subject, she blurts out, "Does anyone ever ask you about Addison and Bubbles?"

"Rarely," he answers.

"No one ever mentions it to me either. Don't you think that is strange? Doesn't anyone care?"

"Yup. Seems odd. You know what? I think it's because Bubbles was found with that pack of stolen goods. Folks get real uncomfortable when someone does something they don't understand. They prefer people in neat little boxes, all wrapped up nice and tidy. She slid out of hers and got lost. We are supposed to be embarrassed about that. My parents are humiliated – convinced it will tarnish their reputation. They'd be happy if her name was never mentioned again. To me, that's rather selfish. After all, it's not about them. It's about the tragedy for Addison and Bubbles." *In a way, I feel a real kinship with Bubbles,* thinks Tuck, *I don't know what happened to her but she seemed to be trying to change direction. God knows I'm trying to do the same but folks don't like that. Sometimes my past feels like a heavy tail pulling me over backwards. Wonder if Rat ever has that problem?* Tuck wonders what made him suddenly think of Rat; associating himself with Rat makes him smile.

"What are you thinking with that smirk on your face?" asks his observant wife.

"I'm thinking of you and how beautiful you are, beautifully dressed or, better yet, beautifully undressed – more my style."

He grabs a dangling foot, pulls off her sock and begins kissing her instep –

At six o'clock the next morning, Tuck is up and out of the house. Byron's and his articles are moderately successful. At least they inspire letters to the editor: some pro, many con. Controversy creates readership; the publishers are pleased. Tuck is astonished at his own accomplishments but also at the irony: here I am excited about all this, and yet, unable to share it with the person who would be most happy for me. He thinks back to a recent call from Byron. "Would you be interested in trying something a little more ambitious, like coauthoring a book together? Don't answer me now, just hear me out. On reviewing the articles we've completed, it strikes me that we could write a book about the various aspects of winning: what winning means, its psychological effects, the social fallout and what it says about our culture. There are endless fields of application: art, music, sports, business, politics, etc. Look, you come from a working class background whereas I have the privilege of living, to a great extent, off a trust fund. This disparity would give our work a broader perspective. Together we could do something interesting."

The idea intrigues Tuck but he's still unsure why Byron takes such an interest in him. Tuck steals away to his workshop, enjoying a little quiet time to mull over possible approaches to such a book. *Dark world events seem to hang on the fringes of my thoughts – like the echoes of a nightmare – not quite remembered but haunting my day – a darkened peripheral vision. Maybe the key to where to begin lies somewhere in this realm – like what pulls our strings, makes us perform as we do –*

131

pushes us to try to excel over everyone else. Britt could help me with this. After all, she has won her share of awards and fame in the fashion world. Then he remembers. In order to keep paying blackmail and to maintain his commitment of secrecy to Addison, he will have to keep Britt in the dark about it all.

Back at the Outdoors and Inn Clothing Store, Justus is facing the worst thing he has ever had to do; lay off a longtime, faithful employee. "Fred, this pains me more than you can imagine, an unforgivable strike against my conscience. I've got bad news."

"It's okay Justus, I know. I've seen it coming for some time now. You're letting me go, aren't you?"

"Fred, it's terrible. You've been a sterling and loyal employee for twenty years. This is something I never dreamed I would do but – but, my back's against the wall. The big guys are driving me out of business. We don't get the traffic we used to."

And I thought my loyalty to Justus would always be rewarded, thinks Fred, while out loud he says, "You're a good man Justus, I know you've tried to avoid this but the times they are a changin', that's for sure."

"Get yourself over to the unemployment office and sign up. I'll keep you on for another week but that's it. I can't do more. I'm so sorry."

"So am I but not half as sorry as the little woman's going to be when she hears this. Hell's bells. This will really fire up her boiler. Not sure I want to face her with this news. Think I'll brace myself with a nip or two before going home tonight."

"If you want to go sign up right now, go ahead. I'll mind the store until you get back."

"Thanks. Guess I best do that. It's humiliating though. Hate to be seen over there. It's not a line I've ever stood in before. You know what folks will say."

Walking along to the unemployment office, Fred cuts a wide swath around Pitt who is napping on a sidewalk bench. Rat, however, is sitting on his shoulder, wide awake with beady eyes watching him pass. Rat hisses at him as he passes, "Fate turns, men balk, victims walk."

Fred is not the only one aware of the hard times hitting Justus's store. Fawn is too. Just as their household budget has grown smaller and smaller, so too has Justus's self-assurance. It pains Fawn to watch him pull away from her and, as each day passes, become more morose. Insomnia plagues her. She tosses and turns at night wondering what she can do to help. Exhausted, Fawn finds it hard to keep up with housework, shopping and cooking. She wants to talk with Justus but he holds her off, too proud to admit that he is in financial trouble. Typically, as often happens when men lose confidence, he shoves away the very person who cares most about him. Finally, Fawn comes up with a plan. *I'll find a job.* The idea terrifies her, having never done such a thing. *I wonder what I can do.* Then she remembers that Dr. Sears is looking for a house cleaner. Moe, remembering she had her own house cleaner, had asked if she could recommend someone. She didn't let on that they no longer could afford to keep someone on. It hadn't occurred to her at the time to apply for the position herself – *but why not? I'll request it be kept a secret. No one must know. Justus, especially, would be mortified at my sinking so low. This way I could slip the extra earnings into my household budget without his even realizing.*

A phone call to Moe and she was hired with the promise that neither he nor Dr. Sterling Sears would tell anyone about it. *Sears Camp is remote. No one will see me out there, and neither Moe nor Dr. Sears are much for talking so Justus and others need never know what I'm up to.*

Then she began to get cold feet. Did she have the nerve to do this? Afraid she might back out, she had made the call before really thinking it through. *Now I'm committed. Good. No second thoughts, I can't get out of it. This way I can help and Justus can retain some of his pride. I wonder what Esprit would say if she knew. I wish I could tell her, but I wouldn't dare. She probably wouldn't approve anyway as she never approves of anything I do. But, she is the expert in all things spiritual and what do I know?*

Part II

A Year Later

Chapter 31

Now that Tibby is six, she belongs in a good private school," Justus declares. "We'll help pay for it."

"We really appreciate that," responds Tuck, "but we can't afford it, even with your help, nor is it something I want for her. She is better off in public school with her friends."

"Are you crazy? What kind of education is that for a bright child? And think of the family reputation."

"What reputation? Addison and I went to public school. Wasn't a problem then. What's changed?"

"What's changed is our position in the community. We are a well regarded family. It's been a long hard struggle to reach this point, something you apparently don't appreciate. It's a social position we should not so quickly throw to the winds," explains Justus.

"I don't see why social position has to dictate where Tibby goes to school. Dad, what you've earned is far more important than social position, it's respect, and not for your status in the community but for who you are and what you've accomplished. I don't think you will lose that if Tibby goes to public school."

"Then you haven't learned much. Such things do make a difference, in fact are extremely important."

"Okay. So we don't agree. What bothers me is my fear that if she goes there, she'll start thinking she's better than public school kids. I know. I remember private school kids looking down on Addison and me when we walked home in the afternoons. And, we couldn't attend their dances either. I don't want Tibby to grow up thinking that way."

"For Pete's sake Tuck. You never used to complain about that."

"You didn't allow complaining."

"You might want to be careful about not passing your own prejudices on to your daughter."

"That's not what I'm trying to do. I just don't want, nor can we afford, to put her in private school and –"

"Besides," interrupts Justus in a huff, "Tibby *is* better than other kids. It's time you started caring a little more about the feelings of your family. You've already rocked the boat by having an illegitimate daughter, who by the way, we have welcomed for your sake, and cared for while you were on the ski circuit. Don't you think you owe us something now? For instance, have you given more thought to joining up with the military? It will give you the discipline you need plus security, and an honorable living."

"Look, it's like this. I'm sorry to disappoint you but as I said before, I prefer the persuasion of peace over the power of force. The military is not for me." Fawn breaks in, afraid rumblings of a disagreement are going to ignite into full-blown battle.

"Esprit says that families which argue need to practice more spiritual work together to regain their balance."

"No offense Mother, but aren't those the words of a divorced woman who abandoned her kids?" says Tuck in an effort to defuse a tense situation.

"Divorced three times." adds Justus, unexpectedly breaking into a grin, "and made a fortune suing her exes."

"That's true but Esprit says we must learn to forgive one another – and she is considered a leader in the field of psychic outreach. We need to listen to the advice she channels from her guru. She teaches a wisdom skills class that might help us," responds Fawn, courageously persevering in her attempt to be taken seriously.

"Done," says Justus. "Consider Esprit heard, from her mouth to your lips to our ears. That's plenty enough for me."

Tuck thinks it a good time to flee. Tibetta, bored with the adult talk, runs ahead and jumps in the truck. Fawn comes to the door with Tuck, detains him by laying her hand on his arm and saying, "Don't be too hard on your father. He doesn't want you to know but he's losing customers. The business is shaky."

"Thanks for telling me. I'll keep that in mind."

Arriving home, Tuck relates his conversation to Britt who bursts out laughing at the absurd notions held by her in-laws. Then, without warning, she breaks down in tears.

"Oh no, what is it? Did I do something wrong? I thought we had decided on this already. You said you agreed."

"Yes, I guess I did," she mumbles between sobs, "It's just that everything seems so hard: your parents never happy with us, losing all our stuff in the fire, decisions about Tibby's school, exhausting trips to the city and then, on top of that, country life requires so much extra effort – stoking the woodstove, 8-mile drives to town in a cold, drafty truck, mud and snow covered roads, mouse invasions, power outages, internet failures, frozen water pipes – guess I'm tired. And then, I planned to volunteer in the community but find it hard to find time to do it."

Tuck, having no answer, takes her in his arms, hugs her tight and leaning down, presses his cheek against hers. Britt, seeking comfort, nestles down inside his embrace. But her thoughts are not stilled, worries fill her head. *I do hope this was the right choice, marrying Tuck and following him to Meltmor. Sometimes I still wonder.*

"Hey, you know our house burning down was a kind of gift to the community."

"How in the world do you come up with that now?" asks Britt, lifting up her tear stained face.

"Look at it this way. We helped a lot of people change their ways, made their lives safer – like a few friends told me that because of what happened to us they went right out and bought smoke alarms. Another person said he gathered up his important documents and put them in a safe deposit box. And that's not all. I've heard several folks started backing up their laptops for the first time ever, then gave the backup to their neighbors for safe keeping."

"How do you come up with these things, Sweetie?" She is silent for a moment, then trying to smile, continues "Gee, if you think of it that way I guess you could say our fire sent up smoke signals warning people to be careful. That stretches the upside but I'll take it. There doesn't seem to be much else right now."

"Yes there is," says Tuck, lifting her off her feet and twirling around, "we all have each other. What can matter more than that?"

"You're right, I know. I do need reminders of the good things we have. I love you. You and Tibby seem to handle all this better than I do."

"I think Tibby does. Me? I guess I'm like so many men, pretending to more courage than I feel, trying to give the impression I can handle everything."

But in fact, for Tuck, some things *are* going well, so well that he tends to forget what a struggle it is for his wife. He rises early each day, starts the cabin's woodstove, then stepping out into the cool, crisp, smoke-filled air of a gray dawn, shuffles through the leaves on the walk to his nearby workshop. There, after starting another woodstove, he sits down at his laptop, tapping away at the keyboard for a couple of hours before beginning work on chores. Tuck is astonished that the article series is going so well. It inspires him to make an attempt at starting the book Byron suggested.

His research and writing lead him on a path of constant learning and new ways of thinking. But, it's like living in two places at once: his creative world and the real world. The intensity he once focused on skiing has now shifted to the written word. He collaborates closely with Byron by email. Nobody else realizes what a double life he leads.

I love writing –it's becoming a passion. I wish I could let Britt in on the new direction I'm taking. She's wondering why caretaking is enough for me. And then, there are my parents. They can't believe I actually like caretaking. It's tough sometimes but only for six months, the rest of the year's more like a part-time job. It takes more skills than I have at the moment – got to master those – so much time into skiing – missed out learning things caretakers should know: hunting, knowing the flora and fauna, practicing sustainable forestry, repairing electrical wiring and who knows what else. It's a wonder Byron keeps me on but I'm getting there. I wonder if these camp owners have any idea what it takes to be a good caretaker.

Autumn

It's the season of 'putting-away: boats, docks, porch furniture, window screens, planters, bird houses, bikes, summer clothes and thoughts of lazing under a hot summer sun. The countdown begins. Before snow flies, driveway edges are staked to guide the plow, deadened flowers are pulled, firewood is stacked, outdoor paint jobs are finished.

"Whoa," we call to the sun god, "Where are you going with all those warm, green-blue days?"

"Not all endings are sad," he replies, "I have brought an end to attack bugs. Is it not joyous to be free from slapping and scratching?"

Days are earthy: the smell of decay rises; green leaves turn to glowing reds, browns and yellows as chlorophyll drains away. Snow waits around the bend. Quiet fills the air. On morning walks, we avoid crunching frozen pools so as not to break the brittle silence of a gray dawn.

Chapter 32

Tuck turns to the tasks at hand. An early snow is predicted and he has yet to line the long dirt road with markers. He finds a few leftover stakes from last year but needs more. Some he makes from scrap wood; others, he cuts from young beech saplings, stripping the branches and giving them a pointed end. The ground is starting to freeze. They need to go in right away. Finished by lunchtime, he realizes they are not visible enough – need bright colored flags to keep the plow truck on track. What to use? He hits on an idea.

Five hours later, Britt takes the truck and heads out to pick up Tibby. Eyes popping from her head, she exclaims out loud. "Good Lord. He didn't. Please, don't anyone come visit until I get back home and make him fix this." On returning 45 minutes later, she bursts into the house.

"Tuck. How dare you."

"What?" he asks, all innocence.

"My red panties. You flagged the road with them."

"Oh that," he smiles. "Well, I needed red and you told me your sister gave you that stuff and you hated it. Anyway, in the interest of recycling, waste not, want not."

Tibby begins giggling. "Daddy, is that really what those red flags are? You put Britt's panties on those sticks? I have some red panties, can we use those too?"

"Now there you go. Use Tibby's if you must but absolutely not mine."

"Come on, Britt. It's all in good fun. Besides, I cut them up so no one can tell what they are." Just then, hearing the roar of an engine, they look outside to see a truck parked in the drive and Josh practically falling out of it with laughter.

"Hot Damn. Fantastic!" he shouts as he sees Tuck appear in the door. "Britt, she's awesome. High fashion comes to the woods. Wait till I tell Tripp. This can become a trend. If you dare to do it, I'll bet Tripp will too. Britt, you city girl, you've got style."

"Too late now," says Tuck, "I think we may have started something."

"We? You, you madman. He knows exactly what's hanging out there."

And so begins the rage of staking out drives with brilliant red panties. Fortunately the more conservative camp owners are absent during the winter. Those camp owners who stay year round soon get over the shock and cave in to the fun of it. And Britt? She caves too. Of all her accomplishments, this particular event brings her more North Country fame than anything else has. Justly or not, she gets credit for her daring and whacky creativity.

"Well knock my socks off," she says to Tuck. "North Country folks have a strange sense of humor."

Chapter 33

"I stopped off at the Hood 'n' Wheel to order those studded snow tires" reports Britt, "but the place was all locked up. Do you think something happened to Hood or Jane? I've never seen him closed on a week day before."

"Yup," laughs Tuck. "Something's happened alright. Deer season. Hood's family depends on venison. He won't open again till he bags his limit. Too bad for anyone whose car breaks down. They'll have to cool their heels until he comes out of the woods. Hunting's sacred in these parts."

"Hunting. A cruel sport," responds Britt.

"Not really. Think about it. I agree it should hardly be called a 'sport' unless we arm the deer as well. But, for many around here, it's a necessity – allows them to stock up on a good healthy supply of meat."

"But it's so uncivilized, shooting those beautiful elegant animals in cold blood."

"What's kinder, letting critters live free and wild before shooting them, or factory farming – cattle and pigs all crammed together in filthy pens, animals mooing and moaning in panic, their bodies filled with fake food and antibiotics? I can taste the fear in that kind of meat. I'll take venison any day over that."

"I never thought of it like that before."

"Ever eaten venison?"

"Nope. Don't know that I want to. Let me guess – you're going out hunting."

"Yup. I have to confess though, despite my country roots, I don't have any hunting skills, sort of turns me off to shoot those big brown-eyed, gentle bounders. Think I've got a lot of learning to do."

"Then why in the world do it?"

"A couple of reasons. First, caretakers are expected to take guests out hunting *and* make sure they go home with a deer. Second, if I can't kill my own food, why is it okay to let others do it for me?"

"Well, you've got something there. I never thought of it quite that way."

With deer season comes an influx of armed outsiders with buck-fever. Locals prudently retreat to the safety of their homes. The visitors insist they come to enjoy the delights of the woods as much as the excitement of hunting. Odd though, they don't seem to show up other times of year when killing is forbidden. But, not to be unfair, hunters make a big contribution to the North Country economy: buying supplies like booze, lots of booze, guns, ammunition, brand new 'rustic' hunting clothes, large egg and bacon breakfasts and comfy sleeping quarters. "Byron has guests coming to camp Reedmor who want to go out hunting," Tuck tells Britt, "bit of a problem for me, of course, so I asked Big Moe if he'd take them out, let me trail along and begin learning the ropes. He's a good man, said he'd be glad to. Guests are coming tomorrow."

"Seems like an odd thing to expect of caretakers" says Britt.

"Not really. It's all part of the job. Byron is forgiving of me not having the skills. He checked with Dr. Sears to see if he'd lend us Moe's services, for pay, of course."

"I hope you don't plan to bring home any dead animals."

"Would you prefer live ones? Seriously though, if I can shoot a deer, it'll save us a lot of money and be healthier than that store-bought excuse for protein."

Two days later, at 5:00 AM, three yawning guests, outfitted with their spanking new L.L.Bean hunting clothes, orange caps and guns, incongruously pile into a Volvo sedan and follow Tuck over the long, bumpy, dirt road leading to Sterling Sears's camp.

"Remote enough," says one of them.

"I hear Sterling lives here year 'round," says another, "can't imagine what he does for entertainment. Pretty solitary life if you ask me." Arriving at the camp, they find Big Moe and Sterling waiting in the drive. Sterling greets them, "Welcome gentlemen." He's a bit of a recluse, not much for family or guests. At one time he was heard to explain: "I like people well enough – as long as I don't have to be friends with them." Sterling Sears is as frugal with words as is his caretaker, Moe.

So, after a little, in fact *very* little small talk, Moe asks, "You all ready to go?"

"Ready to go. We'll get our stuff out of the trunk."

Just then a car pulls into the driveway and parks. The group stops what they're doing to see who it is. "Holy smoke." exclaims Tuck as his mother steps out. He walks over to her and asks, "Mother, what are you doing here?"

"I might ask the same," she replies.

"I'm going hunting. You planning to join us?" he grins.

"Oh no. Truth is, I didn't think I'd see guests out here. I didn't want you or anyone to find out about this but now it's too late," she sighs. An irreverent thought flashes through Tuck's mind: *is my mother having an affair with Dr. Sears? How outrageous of me,* he admonishes himself, unable, like most sons, to imagine his mother sleeping with anyone at all. "Now that you're here, I guess I can't keep it from you. I've started housecleaning for Dr. Sears."

"You? House cleaning? I can't believe it." Somehow that seemed even more unlikely than an affair. *My mother, the sheltered lady of a successful businessman, the woman who looks down on working women has taken a cleaning job?*

"I'm so sorry. I was trying to keep it a secret. I don't want to disgrace the family."

"Be with you guys in a minute," Tuck calls to the others as he starts walking toward the camp with his mother, his arm protectively around her shoulder. "Mother, it's no disgrace to work for a living. In fact, I'm impressed. Does dad know?"

"No, that was one of the conditions I insisted on before taking this job. Nobody is to know. Your father would be humiliated if he found out. He's so proud."

"So, why are you doing this?"

"Because, though he won't admit it, the business is losing a lot of customers. We've had to cut way back on our budget. SuperBig offered to buy him out but he refused. Please don't let him know what I'm doing."

Tuck leans over. Gives her a big hug and says, "Mother, you are the best. It's our secret." *Except for Britt. She'll be as amazed as I am. Wonder why Moe's wife's no longer cleaning the place?* He returns to the guys loading up their packs.

"Grab your gear. Everyone bring food and water? We may be out there a while," calls Moe.

"We're all set but with that pack basket on your back you look like you plan to be gone for a week." comments one of the guests.

"Got that right. This is wilderness – take it seriously. We need to be ready for emergencies: weather, accidents – accidents which mean spending the night in the cold," responds Moe.

"Hey, that doesn't sound too reassuring."

"On the contrary," he replies, "this hulking pack should reassure you completely, it's an outback version of insurance." The day is cloudy and cold with a light snow starting to fall, good for tracking. Their boots crunch the leaves as they set off into the woods, not especially quietly. After an hour, Moe stops near a herd path and everyone hunkers down to wait. "Tuck and I will go out and drive the deer in your direction. Stay alert. They'll be coming along this runway."

Cramped from sitting still for nearly an hour, the hunters are beginning to shift about and whisper. Suddenly one of them holds up his hand. They all freeze and listen. A half-minute later, they too hear the dry rustle of disturbed leaves. The designated hunter, slowly lifts his gun, slips the safety and waits. Patience is rewarded. A buck appears, pauses and stretches his head forward to better see. Boom! The magnificent creature rears up, runs a couple of steps and drops. "By God, I got him." exclaims the possessor of his new "trophy".

It's cause for celebration, but the enthusiasm fades somewhat after cutting a sapling, stringing up the deer and struggling to carry it back to camp along a trail that seems far longer than the same one they had hiked that morning.

This trip marks the start of Tuck's apprenticeship. The first lesson comes when one of the men casually approaches a downed deer. Moe, responsible for everyone's safety, jumps to restrain him. "Don't go near. Let me finish him off, make sure he's really dead; a wounded deer is a dangerous animal."

"Like wounded men," mumbles Tuck under his breath. But perhaps the most important lesson learned is not so much about deer behavior as that of overeager hunters. Hikers are sometimes mistaken for big game. When that happens, the hunter is often excused on the grounds that the victim was "acting like a deer." One of a guide's many jobs is to make sure such accidents never occur. The day is deemed a success by the visitors who return back to Camp Reedmor where Byron awaits them.

That night, Tuck tells Britt about his hunting adventure and also the news of his father's failing business. But the most amazing tidbit is that his mother is cleaning Dr. Sear's camp. "Mothers do show up in the strangest places," he concludes.

"Some do," agrees Britt. "I never would have imagined your mother taking a job. Gives me new insight on her. Funny, I've been thinking lately – people are sort of like wells, we know their position but not their depth. Sure seems to apply to her."

"Guess it takes a good dowser to know that," replies Tuck.

"A dowser?"

"You know, one of those people who walks the land carrying a forked stick that dips down when passing over ground water. A good dowser can also read the pressure and the depth."

"Surely you don't believe that stuff?"

"Surely I do. It works. Lots of people site their wells that way. Why it works no one seems to know. Same as why some can see beneath another person's façade, sense his innermost feelings, while others cannot."

Enough talk for both. They are off to bed where the wildness of Tuck's hunting is applied to a less murderous activity.

The following evening, a group of hunters assembles, this time at the Greene River Hunt Club. Blanche has her hands full cooking supper for ten members, who arrive without their wives, for an annual hunting outing, often a raucous one. On the first night, all but two indulge in card playing and Scotch drinking until late in the evening.

"How're you going to get up at five tomorrow and even see straight?" asked one of the abstainers, a man by the name of Reginald Hartford.

"We'll be fine. Why don't you join us?"

"Thanks but I'm turning in early."

Next morning, just shy of 5:00 AM, Stu and Tuck pull up to the Greene River Hunt Club, there to help guide the hunters for a day. "What you doing with the shovel, Ace?" Stu asks. "Oh nothing much, smoothing down the ground a bit." No way is he going to confess that his job includes shoveling up dog poop. His buddies would tease him unmercifully for months to come. Such is the country culture and such is the life, at times, of caretaking.

Five o'clock, the agreed departure time for the hunters, finds Ace, Stu and Tuck standing and waiting, along with two early risers, Reginald Hartford and his brother George. They wait and wait. "Getting light. Better take these two gentlemen and start," says Ace to Stu, "I'll stay till the other guys show up."

To no one's surprise, the morning is well along before the rest of the party is ready, having first wolfed down Blanche's pancakes, bacon, eggs, toast and coffee while pumping up their self proclaimed reputations as skilled hunters. After indulging in such a gargantuan meal, the guys, more weighed down than energized, stumble out the door to be met by a formidable sight. Hanging head down from the rack are two handsome bucks: one 4-point and one 2-point, a spike horn. "Wow. Who shot those beauties?"

Needless to say, Reginald and George, smirking a bit, are more than happy to claim their trophies. The rest of the group tries valiantly to suppress their irritation. The result? That evening, by 10:00 PM, lights are off in the cabins and the main camp is eerily quiet. Does it help? Some. The next morning, Ace and Stu lead a hunting group. Moe comes over to assist a couple of the other men. Tuck tags along still anxious to learn more. Two deer are taken. The men are vindicated. So, it's back to cards and martinis, except for the Hartford brothers who, after an evening coffee, read their books a while before heading off to bed.

"Culture vultures, those guys. Don't know how to loosen up and have fun," complains Tank, one of the members who, already three sheets to the wind, can be counted on never to stray from the herd.

"Ah, leave them be, different strokes for different folks," rejoins another. Not all the hunters are novices. Some, like the Hartfords, actually teach Tuck a few things. As deer have a highly developed sense of smell, they should be approached from downwind. With only a slight breeze, however, wind direction can be hard to figure. George shows Tuck a trick: pick up puffball mushrooms along the trail. Squeeze one and it emits a fine spore dust, revealing the direction of the slightest stir of air. Eager to learn, Tuck soon figures out which men have most to teach him. It's the quiet guys, the brothers.

Realizing this will be their last chance to hunt before departing, Ace's group opts to stay out late on Saturday afternoon. Outdoorsmen, used to spending time in the woods, are adept at taking a break and sitting down wherever they happen to be. Not so with these men, or sports as they are called in Adirondack tradition. They insist on first finding a lean-to. When they finally do, they are dismayed that someone's sleeping bag, clothes and cooking pots are stowed in a corner. However, lean-to etiquette dictates that space be shared with whomever shows up. So the sportsmen, glad to rest their weary legs, plunk themselves down, open their packs, pull out lunch and thermoses of coffee. Suddenly a crazy looking, raggedy old man holding antler-like branches above his head, leaps deer-like around the corner. "Oh my God." exclaims one of the hunters as they collectively scramble to their feet, knocking over the thermoses in their rush to escape the lean-to. Ace never moves; *Wimps*, he says to himself.

"Ha. Scared you did I? If I'd really been a deer you would have missed the shot of a lifetime. In fact, that deer would've gone after you faster than a rat's wink."

"Ah Pitt, don't go terrifying our guests like that. You know it's not real hospitable," says Ace.

"Just having a little fun. No harm done. You can come on back, gentlemen, and clean up the crumbs. I'll sit quiet like and wait. What I need, if you would be so kind, is help transporting my gear out of here. The approaching cold weather begins to chill my bones. Time for me to move into town, go to church, lay low for the winter."

Startled by the British accent pouring out of this wild man, the men listen in amazement. Then, somewhat embarrassed by their reactions, sidle back to the lean-to, heads lowered but casting wary glances toward Pitt. Sandwiches are finished in uneasy silence.

"As long as we're ready to head out, if you don't mind," says Ace, "you could each take a small load and help Pitt get his stuff back to my truck."

As one man leans over and grabs a small cloth bundle, Rat leaps out and runs up his arm. "Son of a bitch." explodes the guy, madly shaking his extremity so that Rat goes flying, "What the hell is that?"

"That, my dear fellow, is my buddy Rat, best friend man ever had. Doesn't lust, swear, lie, deceive, or get violent. Better company than I believe any of you can lay claim to. Up on my shoulder, Rat," Pitt says, "Survey the world from your lofty seat. Hear Rat's advice, 'Overlook much, squeak little.'"

Just before dark, Ace brings the dumbfounded group back to the club without a deer but with a story to tell, so bizarre that it nearly makes up for the loss. However, a couple of men are still not content. "When my grandfather used to come up here," one said, "they brought a buck-truck around so those who didn't get their deer could buy one off the driver. What happened to that?"

"Guess some traditions just got to go. Rangers keep close tabs on hunters these days. They don't look so favorably on that kind of stuff."

"Doesn't bother me too much," says another empty handed hunter, "My wife doesn't eat meat anyway."

"You should tell her what George Carlin said," responds his colleague, "'If God didn't want us to eat animals, he shouldn't have made them out of meat.'"

By the time the hunt club members are ready to leave, only two men are still without deer. Though, of the deer taken, one isn't good for much. It was Tank's, one of the guests. His aim had been poor; he wounded but failed to kill the animal. Stu, armed only with a pistol, asked to borrow Tank's rifle so he could go after the deer and complete the kill. The blustering Tank refused to share his firearm but was glad enough to let Stu save him the work of tracking. Bad move. Stuart Moore, not one to gracefully accept insult, followed the stricken deer for an hour before finally putting it out of its misery, nor did he stop there. Angry that he was refused the use of Tank's gun, and because tracking the deer had been such hard work, Stu lingered long enough to put a few more holes in the poor carcass, insuring that not an inch of edible venison was left. "That'll show the bastard," he announced to the surrounding woods. "Sometimes these city slickers really piss me off."

After the hunters leave, Tuck returns to Camp Reedmor. He exercises a caretaker's option to hunt on the Great Camp property. Heading out early, he practices tracking through the light snow. The first deer he follows is a proud beauty which he lingers to admire for so long it finally bounds away. A little while later, catching up with a second, he lifts his rifle, pauses a split second, then fires, bringing down the beautiful creature with one merciful, possibly lucky shot. Standing there, alone in the woods, he savors the full import of this defining moment: grateful for the gift of the deer; aware of things changing, of providing for his family, of earning his place as a caretaker.

So concludes the deer season, a brief few weeks when folks pursue their luckless victims. But, hold on a minute. Listen to what Rat says, "We all be hunters – words and laws our ammo. Beware."

Britt learns to eat venison.

Winter

It rarely snows all at once in the Northern Adirondacks. Instead, flurries, almost too fine to notice, dance through the sunless sky, dropping delicate flakes upon trees, rocks and the backs of shadowy deer. Finally there comes a morning when, looking out the window, we suddenly notice an old stump is buried under a white fluffy quilt. Two days later, a big moss-covered boulder sinks out of sight; the only clue to its existence: evergreen ferns rising off its top. Rarely does a big storm arrive to strike with fury. Instead, as change often does, winter sneaks up slowly, unnoticed at first. Later, looking back, we try to remember exactly when it all began.

One frigid morning, rising early, we see the woods have been touched by a fairy wand, the forest dressed in lace and crystal, sunshine slanting through the trees lights a bejeweled dawn. The air swirls with sparkles. Frost feathers creep up the windows. Trees snap in the cold. The woodstove dawdles at its task of warming. Chickadees, finches, and nuthatches flock to the feeders, there to fight for lifesaving food. Owl perches nearby, awaiting his chance to snatch breakfast from this flock of gourmet morsels. In this season, empty feeders bespeak empty intentions; betrayal of feathered friends.

On Cedar Bluff Lake, huddled on the wind-swept ice, dark furry muskrats gather around a spring hole, each dining on tasty plants dragged from the lake bottom: their communal pantry. In the distance two deer stand on the ice stretching high to nibble at overarching cedars, out of reach in the summer, lifesaving food in the winter. White, all is white – color of cold – land of the rugged.

Chapter 34

"Hi Jane. Just stopped by to see what I can do to help the food pantry. I've been meaning to get back to you but somehow time got away from me."

"Hi Britt. That's okay – know you've had your hands full since losing your home. Wouldn't expect you to be helping right now."

Jane looks closely at Britt, sees her starting to tear up. "I'm sorry. I shouldn't have said that – not nice of me."

Britt, trying to laugh through her tears, responds, "Not your fault, Jane. It was months ago, time I get over it – sometimes though, I just start crying all over again – "

"Sure Britt. We can't be brave all the time."

"But you are," says Britt, pleased that her self-imposed social barriers are beginning to fall. She is truly impressed by this hardworking but underappreciated woman.

"Me? I didn't lose my house."

"Yes but – " *How do I tell her I think her life so utterly depressing I wonder how she stays cheerful?* ponders Britt as she grapples for the right words. "Yes but I'm sure you could use more things for yourself instead of giving so much away."

"Isn't that what God wants us to do, help others?" replies Jane. Britt, lacking so much as a stick of religious inclination, doesn't know how to respond but thinks, *who am I to question this woman's motives? If it helps her cope, so be it. We don't all have to do things for the same reason.*

Britt continues, "I'm here to find out what I can do. Don't have a lot of time and I'm not much of a cook but if you have some recipes, I'll try to make a casserole or two for the food pantry."

"That's nice," says Jane as she walks over to a kitchen shelf stacked high with mechanics' magazines, cookbooks and newspapers. The whole mess starts sliding down on to the kitchen floor. "Oh well, easier to sort them this way," says Jane as she kneels down to sift through the pile. Finding what she wants, she stands up again, her knees dusty. Clutched in her hands are a couple of recipes torn from magazines: one for a macaroni and cheese dish, another for apple pie. "You can borrow these, copy them down and return them next time you're in town."

"Thanks so much, I'll do that."

Britt leaves Jane's tumbledown house. She drives to her in-laws' green-shuttered pristine white home, set back in a spacious front yard at the other side of town. Every day, at three o'clock, Tibetta walks to her grandparents from her public school on the same block. To their surprise, she loves school and soon acquires a reputation for making her classmates laugh, sometimes too often for her teacher's liking. She stays at grandpa and grandma's until Tuck or Britt comes to pick her up. At the moment, she is out in the yard with the neighbor kids trying to build a snowman out of the scant three inches of snow that fell the night before. "Hi Bee, look what we're making," she calls, running over to Britt who squats down to give her a hug; then Tibetta runs back to her friends instead of going inside as she would have done if Daddy was picking her up. After admiring the leaning, leaf-studded snowman, Britt goes indoors.

"Hi Britt. Justus is down at the store." Fawn sits poring over a clothes catalog. "You caught me. Please don't say anything."

"Say anything about what?"

"About me looking at this catalog. I do try to buy my clothes from his store but Justus does all the ordering and he doesn't always understand what a woman my age is looking for. Don't ever tell him I said that."

"Don't worry, I won't. But tell me. Just what is it you're looking for?"

"I'm not exactly sure but older women's clothes are so dark and dowdy. And, they still make them with low necklines and short sleeves. I can't wear styles like those. My skin isn't smooth like it used to be."

Britt is surprised her mother-in-law is confiding in her. She even starts to feel a little sorry for Fawn – the woman whose simpering attitude can be so irritating and who is so quick to find fault with Tuck and herself.

"I don't think you look old. You don't look a day over forty," objects Britt, stretching the truth a wee bit.

"Well, I can't look my best if all I find are short dresses that show off my knees, not my best feature. Wait till you get as old as me. You'll see. Everything is designed for the young and gorgeous – that's where the money is," she adds in a thinly disguised allusion to Britt's boutique.

"I can see it must be a problem. Have you found anything you like in the catalog?"

"No. As we age, people lose interest in us."

"Surely that's not true," Britt says with a certain pang of guilt because, on afterthought, she realizes that all too often, that's exactly how it is. She starts to see Fawn in a different light, a light that brings out a more sympathetic view of this insecure, overly dominated, rather lonely woman. *How sad she feels this way about herself and her looks. I wish I could compliment her on the courage she has shown by finding herself a job – but I'm not supposed to know about that.* "So, you're looking for a dress with a high neck, long sleeves, falls below the knees and is colorful. Is that it?"

"Yes. That sort of sums it up. It's so annoying to see nothing but underfed skinny models promoting dresses that look like they're glued onto their bony frames."

"I have an idea. How about letting me design a dress for you? I'll sketch something that accentuates your best features, and let you take a look at it. Once you're satisfied, I'll send it to my sister Shelley and she can have it made up at our boutique. How about it?"

"That is very nice of you but I could never afford such a thing."

"I'm not looking for pay. It will be a thank you for all the time you've spent taking care of Tibby."

"That's very nice but I can't accept. Justus would take it as an insult and Esprit says we shouldn't accept gifts but purchase things ourselves."

Britt tries to suppress her rising irritation. How can any woman be so 'constitutionally superior to reason,' as the author Wilkie Collins once put it? But, she's clearly not the only one; Esprit has a class full of them. Britt is tempted to drop the whole thing but, remembers she's trying not to be so critical and reconsiders. *If I want to learn tolerance, this is as good a time to start as any.*

"I know what we can do. Christmas is coming. Why don't I make this your present? We won't tell Justus what we're doing, and you'd best not mention it to Esprit either. I'll sketch out the dress and show it to you when no one's around. Then, once we have what you want, I'll have it made and surprise you at Christmas. Nobody can find anything wrong with that." Fawn's eyes open wide with admiration.

"But isn't that kind of sneaky?" she objects, at the same time hoping to find a way around her scruples.

"Yes, kind of sneaky. What's wrong with that? Haven't you ever done anything sneaky before?" she asks, curious how Fawn will answer that one.

"But it's not right to be sneaky."

"Sometimes, when others box us in, sneaky is the only way out. Do you really want to live in a box, a smart woman like you?"

Fawn can't believe her ears. *No one has ever considered me smart before. It feels sort of good. Think I'll do this, after all, I mean, like she says, why should everyone else tell me what to do all the time?* Before

Britt leaves, Fawn asks, "Heard anything more about that woman Bubbles, what happened to her? Not that I care. She had it coming."

Oh no, just when I was warming up to her she has to go and spoil it. Controlling her annoyance, Britt says she thinks the investigation continues but no one knows much yet.

The temperature plummets and snow begins to fall as Britt and Tibetta drive home. Britt is feeling unaccountably relaxed and happy. *Did I drink less coffee today or is it something else?* They arrive at the cabin to find it warm and cozy, Tuck having built a roaring fire. "Something smells good," Tibetta exclaims. "What are you cooking Daddy?"

"Venison, my little woods rabbit."

"Daddy, when you shoot a deer, how can you be sure it's not one of Santa's?"

Tuck pauses a minute before replying, "Oh, that's easy. Santa's deer wear green holly with red berries in their antlers. I'd never shoot anything red and green. In fact, that's why hunters wear red. Everyone knows red means Christmas and they'd never shoot at it." Britt looks at Tuck in amazement.

"You know the most incredible things," she says. Tibetta runs off to her room. Britt takes advantage of her absence to ask, "By the way, speaking of Christmas, don't you think we should ask Addison to join us this year? He's down about Bubbles. The holidays are not a time to be alone, especially with his kind of worries. Do they still think he had something to do with it?"

"His friend has vouched for his whereabouts but he's never been completely cleared either. The nurses still claim they saw him pick Bubbles up at the clinic."

"What do you think happened?"

"I have no idea. The only thing I know is that, self-confident, efficient and businesslike as my brother appears, underneath he's gentle and vulnerable. This whole thing is breaking him apart. He could never hurt anyone – never."

"Then let's invite him for the holidays. Tibby will love it too. She's crazy about him."

"You are the best. I'll do that."

"If you think I'm the best, how about we drop Tibby off at your parents for a couple of hours and go hear the Rippin' Rapids? They're playing at the Town Trough tonight."

"Sure. It's a good band. I'd like to hear them too – as long as you don't try to make me dance or worse, start dancing by yourself."

"It's a deal. You'll go?"

"I'll go. It's time we do something for you. I'll call my parents about Tibby. Let's head out in about an hour. That band should warm us up on a cold night like this."

By eight o'clock, Tuck and Britt are seated at a small table with Stu and Sue who unexpectedly showed up. Most people know each other except for one man sitting in the corner, a pockmarked face accentuated by a black bristly crew cut. His stocky physique is straining the seams of a gray shirt open at the collar and shiny worn dark pants. Though he is sitting in the shadows, everyone is acutely aware of his presence. Tuck stares hard at the man, his eyes turn to slits. He has a difficult time hiding his feelings. "You look worried, you think he might be a detective or something?" says Britt.

"Nah, he's probably a lonely out-of-town visitor."

"Maybe, it being the Christmas season and all, we should invite him to join us?"

"Absolutely not," Tuck shoots back. *Why is the bastard here?* he broods, *could be a problem.* Tuck, distracted, stops talking and occasionally casts dark looks at the stranger. After a few minutes, the man pays his bill, gets up and saunters out. Visibly relieved, Tuck once more joins the conversation.

"Hey, there's Wayne Roy," says Sue. "the stuffed shirt who owns a place way out on Cedar Bluff Lake, what's he doing here?"

"You don't know? He's been in here before. Watch him, you'll see."

Before long, Wayne gets up, wanders over to the bar and settles himself on a stool next to two women. After a few minutes, he attempts to strike up conversation. They turn icy stares in his direction but, not put off by their frigid demeanor, he continues his efforts. The tension seems to dissipate and before long, Wayne Roy is seen grabbing one woman's leg with a firm grasp. She makes a halfhearted attempt to shake him free but he is strong and continues to hold her in a steely grip.

"Lecher. He's on the prowl, looking for a lay again. The lake people would go ape-shit if they knew he did this, but they never come in here, consider it a dive. Funny how he's too upscale for the likes of us when around his friends but happy to hang out here when he's by himself and horny. Dumb ass."

The music kicks in, starts softly but soon warms up into foot-stomping high gear. Britt can sit still no longer. The beat stirs her soul and her feet. Noticing that Sue's foot is also madly tapping the floor, she leans over, raises her voice and says, "Let's go out there and dance together."

Sue looks back at her, pauses a minute before breaking into a grin.

"Yah, let's do it." Before the guys realize what's happening, the two of them are out swaying and gyrating around the dance floor together.

"Oh my God," says Stu, "Women dancing with women. What is Meltmor coming to?"

"Damned if I know," responds Tuck.

"I'm thinkin' your city girl is responsible for this."

"You may be right. I must say, it's damned embarrassing. Everyone's watching them."

"They don't seem to care, look at them go, laughing and wriggling. My God." The guys lower their eyes but Tuck and Stu are all too aware that others are waiting to see what they will do. Finally Stu says, "Okay. We've been had, can't let this go on any longer. Let's go out and break them up." And that's how, though Britt kept her promise not to dance alone nor ask Tuck to join her, the two couples ended up dancing the night away. It was a challenge, as Tuck's clodhoppers came down on Britt's dainty shoes as often as on the floor, but they managed and had fun to boot, so to speak.

At one point, looking toward the bar, they saw Wayne grab one of the somewhat inebriated women, swing her off her stool and arm firmly around her waist, lead her out the door. "He knows how to get what he wants, that's for sure. I should take lessons from him," says Stu.

"Don't need to, bonehead, you already get what you want, whenever and wherever," counters Sue.

It is late evening before they return to the truck. It is sitting at an odd slant. On coming closer, they see why. By the yellow light of a street lamp, Tuck can just make out slash marks in the tires on one side of his truck. *Jesus. That bastard – a day late with my payment and he screws me over.*

"Why would anyone do this? What's the point? Everyone knows this is your truck. It's almost as if someone is out to get you. Oh my God. This is really scary." says Britt, trembling by Tuck's side as he leans down to inspect the damage.

"Not to worry, it's just stupid vandalism," he says, hoping his words will reassure her. *Buzz is warning me. How much longer can I deal with this? My nerves are starting to get the better of me. Britt will pretend she's okay but I know this will only add to her fears about living in Meltmor.*

A truck comes down the street, slows and stops. Stu gets out. "What gives?" Tuck shows him the damage. Stu is shocked.

"Don't remember this ever happening around here before. Come on, we'll take you to pick up Tibetta and then give you a ride home. Hood can come out and get your truck in the morning. You better let the police know too." *Not*, thinks Tuck.

Later at home, Britt keeps talking about the tire slashing.

Tuck finally says, "Enough about that. I want to change the subject. You know, that was pretty sneaky what you did tonight?"

"Maybe."

"But I have to admit, it was fun. Don't think I've let myself go like that for a long time. You did warm up the night."

"So, is that such a bad thing?"

"Never. Just keep it up. I'm feeling wild." And wild they are for the next hour, helping to erase, but not entirely, the sight of the stranger in the corner.

Chapter 35

Christmas in the north: snow caps the mountains, piles around trees, drifts across the roads. Grownups battle slippery roads as they shop and party, struggle to stay within their budgets, resist fattening food, keep up with work and get enough sleep. For adults, it can be stressful, for kids, a blast. In Meltmor, light-festooned trees line the Main Street. Music blares from tinseled storefronts. Cloned Santas stand ringing bells for money at every corner which leads Tibetta, walking with her dad, to think the red-suited guy is following them.

Nostalgia for our youth brings happy memories, often plunging us back into childlike activities. Such is the case when the town plow, going a mite too fast, roars down a narrow side street, spraying snow up in an arc. Parked on this street is a dark green pickup, at least it is until the plow dumps six inches of snow over its top, then speeds away leaving silence in its wake. Slowly the doors on either side of the white blanketed truck push open. Josh slides out of the driver's side, his wife from the passenger's. "I'll be damned. Can you beat that? It's almost like he meant to bury us."

Pitt, perky-eared Rat in place, is passing by on his way to a hot, starchy meal at the Hunters' Hub. His crinkly face cracks into a broad, broken-toothed smile as he calls to Josh "For sure he did, that was Whacky Walt at the wheel, aiming right for you, he was, grinning too. Seemed full of Christmas cheer. Rat's advice: "Give him flack, throw it back."

"Now Josh, don't let him taunt you. We've got shovels," Tripp says, retrieving them from the bed of the truck, "let's act like good law abiding citizens for a change, dig ourselves out and head home. Remember, it's the season of peace."

"It was till that jerk came along. No good deed goes unpunished in my book of fun. Hey, look, he's turning around and coming back down the other side of the street."

Before she can protest, Josh is packing a sizeable snowball and, ready to throw it, crouches behind his truck. As the plow approaches, going slowly, the better for Walt to gloat, Josh jumps up and hurls his missile straight into the cab window. His aim is good: Walt's glasses go flying, shattering for a fare-thee-well and causing him to lose control of his vehicle. Freed from the restraint of its driver, the plow truck charges up the sidewalk at a good clip and crashes through the plate glass window of the Town Trough.

Fortunately, the customers, still sober enough to hear it coming, leap for cover. By the time the errant vehicle stops at the bar, it's the only customer in the room. The engine off and glass no longer falling, the unflappable owner, Babs, emerges from a backroom. Crunching over the debris, she walks up to the cab door and says, "Why Walt, I thought you weren't supposed to drink on the job. What you doing stopping at my bar in the middle of the day? Looks to me like you're breaking the rules and a lot of other stuff as well."

The police are summoned, reporters not far behind. Walt's face turns a furious purple; words keep sputtering out of his mouth. Oddly, nobody seems to have witnessed the accident, except for Pitt of course, who reports seeing a kid out throwing snowballs, which you might say is true. Josh and Tripp are safely back at home, enjoying a drink when Sam calls.

"Who me, brother of mine? I would never dream of doing such a thing," responds Josh after being questioned by Sam.

"Pitt is the only witness and he says you didn't do it either but Walt's sure it was you. There's a hell of a lot of damage. Looks like the town may get a mighty handsome bill for this one."

"Gee, that's awful. How's Walt, he didn't get hurt, did he?"

"Nope, only his pride. He mentioned your name several times in a not too favorable manner. It's my official duty to warn you – better watch your ass till this blows over."

When Josh hangs up, Tripp, stretched out on the sofa, pipes up, "You are incorrigibly childish. Now what?"

"Not to worry, nothing will happen. It's Christmas time. Not a season for revenge."

"And what was that you just did?" she replies, sitting up and smirking at him.

"Come on Tripp. You gotta laugh, it was a hoot. Just making a little fun. Think I'll suggest Babs serve a new drink at her bar, the 'Walt Whammy'. Has a nice ring to it, don't you think? You gotta wrangle a little fun out of life." With that, the two of them hold back no longer and guffaw loud and long.

So there it is; Christmas brings out the kid in us all. The season, stuffed with parties, caroling and a bit of rough play, passes quickly. The big day finally arrives. Addison arrives as well, having accepted Tuck's invitation. Santa finds his way to the cabin where Tibetta is sleeping, at least until 6:00 AM when she hauls everyone out of bed. It has been a tough time for this little girl. Addison has helped Santa to be generous with presents in hopes the loot will erase some of the memories of her losses. "Don't know that it works that way," comments Addison, "but it's the only thing I can think to do."

Britt's parents, Rory and Eileen Taglong, who see her only on the rare occasion when she carves out time from business trips, have decided to come up for Christmas. They are not crazy about staying in such a "hick town" but Britt promises to reserve a room for them in a "respectable" motel. Britt's sister, Shell, will not be there as she is going to Maryland to celebrate with friends. On Christmas day everyone gathers at Justus and Fawn's home for family fun. Tuck's elderly aunt from whom they had bought their now defunct house, is brought from the nursing home in a wheel chair. She has never been told about the fire. It is agreed that kindness dictates they keep it that way. "Why spoil her remaining years?" the family says. *For that matter, why spoil anyone's remaining years? More kindness might be a good thing. None know how much time is left on the clock,* reflects Tuck.

It's the season for giving carefully chosen presents, a good number of which miss the mark by a mile. Never mind, it's the thought that counts. Those most appreciated include an unwrapped present delivered unexpectedly into this gathering by Big Moe himself. Having courteously discarded his boots at the door, he treads, sock-footed, hesitantly across the white carpet as if it were broken glass not deep plush. A big man in a plaid, wool shirt and orange cap, he appears as out of place in this frilly, pastel-walled home as if he were a meteor crashed through the roof. "Brought something for Tibetta," Moe says, producing from behind his back a beautiful carved wooden ark which he made and meticulously painted. "Noah was the first one to understand the importance of biodiversity," he tells her, as the conservative Taglongs and Justus Risings stand rolling their eyes at the implication of his words. His message requires a little explaining to Tibetta; the finely crafted ark does not.

Tibetta, dressed in embroidered green overalls, plops down on the floor. She is immediately engrossed in removing the deck house and pulling out the lovely pairs of miniature carved animals hidden inside: skunks, mink, otters, beavers, fishers, bears, deer, foxes and a pair of enlarged mosquitoes – all Adirondack natives. Moe makes a fast exit, leaving Tuck and Addison gazing jealously after him.

Addison gives Tibetta a picture to hang in her room. It had been painted by Bubbles a few years earlier: a beautiful autumn landscape with hills of orange and gold, and a single large tree in the foreground, glowing red in the sunlight. Several eyes roll again. Never mind, it is for Tibetta's pleasure only and she seems happy enough with it.

A big hit is the dress that Britt gives to her mother-in-law. Fawn, the seemingly meek little wife, does an admirable job of acting surprised. After putting it on, she walks about the room modeling the bright yellow, delicately flowered outfit, delighting everyone except Justus who demands to know where it came from. "I made it for her," explains Britt, effectively putting a stop to any further comments from him.

Having lost her favorite doll in the fire, Tibetta had been repeatedly begging for a new one. Unbeknownst to one another, Britt and Tuck had each responded to her wish. Tibetta unwraps Britt's present first, a soft cloth doll with embroidered face, long, yellow wool hair and a white apron over a yellow, delicately flowered dress just like her Gram's. This brings forth squeals of delight. Then she opens Tuck's, a boy doll carved out of pine, scraggly lichen for hair attached to a dried bracket fungus head with a face drawn on the spongy side. Moveable legs and arms are connected with interlocking screw eyes. It is dressed in a glued together set of deerskin pants and shirt. "Oh Yeah," exclaims Tibetta, as the adults exchange pained looks, "now I have a daddy doll and a mommy doll, like daddy and – can I call you Mommy just like my doll?" she asks. Britt stares at Tuck in surprise then bends down and embraces Tibetta, tears welling up again.

"Oh Sweetie, you can, you can. I'd like that a lot." Tuck leans over and circles them both in his arms. *Maybe I'm finally going to have a normal family – in spite of fate.*

But what of the other presents? Britt gives Tuck a cassette player with headphones so he can listen while working outside. "Thank you so much love, how thoughtful," he says while thinking; *she still doesn't get it – the outdoors so full of birdsongs, wind singing in the trees, squirrels chattering, coyotes howling; why would I want to block that out?*

Tuck gives Britt a pair of heavy, well insulated Sorrel boots. These are larger and fit her feet perfectly. "Thank you Tuck, how lovely," and to herself; *I wouldn't be caught dead wearing these oversized clodhoppers. What is he thinking?*

With great aplomb, Justus presents his sons their presents, a book of American military history for Tuck: *will he never drop the subject?* – a photo book of Adirondack Great camps for Addison. And so a traditional North Country Christmas is celebrated at the Rising home. Similar to many such events, it is loaded with sentiment, good food, a bit of cynicism, occasional irritation and lots of hugs and kisses. Everyone returns home, happy, exhausted and more than ready to get back to normal.

The day after Christmas, however, brings more surprises. Byron calls early in the morning to announce he is on his way up, would Tuck please open the main house, turn up the heat and get it ready for him. "That's odd," Tuck comments to Britt. "Don't think he usually visits this time of year. He's coming alone, not bringing 'the wife', as he has taken to calling her. She doesn't like the cold and snow."

"I like Byron," says Britt, "but there's something different about him. I can't quite put my finger on it, but it's there for sure." Byron arrives around noon and comes right over to the cabin.

"Have something for Tibetta, she around?" Tibetta hears him from her room and comes running out to be presented with two gaily wrapped boxes. Inside, she finds king and queen marionettes dressed in royal blue and gold satin. They lie cushioned in white tissue paper. "Be careful not to tangle the strings," Byron warns kindly. Tuck and Britt are speechless. Tibetta lifts first one, then the other out of the box and begins walking them around the cabin. "I got to make them pick their feet up high so their clothes don't get too dusty," she quips as the adults break into laughter.

"Don't get too smart," comments Tuck, "or we'll set you to sweeping up around here." Later, Tuck stops up at the main camp to see if Byron needs anything. To his surprise, Addison is there, the two of them sitting by the fire having drinks. Addison stays only another ten minutes, then leaves. When Tuck asks Byron if he needs anything, he is taken off guard by his reply.

"As a matter of fact, there is. I mentioned working on a book together. You never got back to me about that. Have you thought about it at all?"

"Yes I have but you never brought it up again so I wasn't sure if you were serious or not. In fact, I have already been working on it for a while."

"Good. It's a big commitment. That's why I wanted you to take some time to think it over. It's going to take a lot of hard work."

"You have more faith in my writing than I do, though I must admit, I enjoy it. To my surprise, new ideas seem to keep on coming for both the articles and the book. There is definitely a crossover of themes. However, I have a concern. I'm going to need fulltime work to support my family and I'm not sure whether you plan to keep me on here permanently or not."

"No problem. I should have made that clear earlier. I forget how tough it is to make a living; never having had to worry too much about that. Seems like caretaking suits you well, combines with writing. How do you feel about it?"

"Got to admit, I'm liking it."

"In that case, it's time I give you a written contract and more secure position. You're doing a good job. By the way, how are you fixed for health insurance?"

"I'm not."

"Then we'll add health insurance for you and your family as part of the package. I'll draw up a contract and include two weeks' vacation but not during the warm weather when Reedmor is open. And, the cabin is yours to live in."

"That sounds good. Thank you so much. It takes a real worry off my back. I'll do my best for you." After a pause, Tuck says, "Can we go back to the subject of writing again? I'll work on a book but still want it to remain just between the two of us – no one else to know."

"Strange request, Tuck. You going to tell me why, or is that still a secret?"

"Guess it is, for the time being. Nothing personal though," says Tuck, wondering how he will ever get out from under the curse of blackmail.

The Taglongs, who had planned to return home on the day after Christmas, decide to stay longer. Having roundly condemned rural life, their decision seems odd. "More going on here than we thought," Britt's father announces. "Jazz pianist Curly Joe is playing on the 28th. Big name in the city. Have no idea what he's doing up here in a place like Meltmor but it's a chance to hear his work without paying the big bucks he costs at home. In the meantime, we spotted an art gallery that your mother wants to visit."

By that afternoon, snow begins to fall. There are the usual accompanying power outages and slippery road conditions. It might be seen as the best gift of the season. Nobody can travel: no visiting, no appointments, no work. Romantic candlelight glows in homes and motels. Landline phones are out of commission, effectively stopping all business calls. Except for emergency workers, tranquility settles over the town of Meltmor. Even the Taglongs find they enjoy the new experience of silence, broken only intermittently by the muffled sound of a snowplow passing. The storm, imposing a halt in daily activities, comes as a welcome relief after the frantic pace of the holidays. Peace now; turmoil later.

Spring

Early spring: a breath of warm air, slivers of green poking through tired snow, and hidden among last year's leaves are tiny woodland flowers: white, pink, and lavender: spring beauties, violets, hepaticas. Drippy green leaflets, mush underfoot as mud-spattered boots tramp along by gurgling creeks. Mornings fill with bird songs rewarding music-starved ears.

Somewhat later: ice out, loon calls, trout season. Bundles of green sprouting branches, propelled by muskrats, sail across the water. Black fly misery, bug nets, shimmering green hills, sun-filled blue sky. Occasional snow showers bury yellows, blues and pinks under a blanket of white denial.

Impatient we wait. Mud, sloppy and splashy, fills roads, trails and fields. March passes, April passes, May, June. Then boom, it comes. Three whole days of northern spring followed without pause by the rush of summer. Boots tossed aside, jackets abandoned, hats discarded and UPS men appear in shorts. Fawns, cubs, kits: a motley crew of babies hidden in the woods. Life renewing itself.

Chapter 36

Schools break for spring vacation. Families, who have the means, take their children and temporarily flee south to warmer, drier climes. Streets are empty, restaurants closed. Meltmor is mostly deserted. A few people, however, are happy to stay put. One of these, Sue Tower, welcomes this time of year for it marks the start of good mushroom weather. Britt is caught up by the enthusiasm of this new friend of hers. "Hey Sue, I know you're into dyeing knitting wool but you told me that silk also takes mushroom colors. Have you ever thought of dyeing silk scarves?"

"Not really, there's no demand for that kind of thing. Mostly people want warm, practical clothing, and besides, I don't know anything about working with silk."

"Well, I've been thinking about it. I have an idea. What if I showed you how to work with wax resist on the scarves? We could collaborate on the designs. I can order plain white silk, get things started by showing you how to create patterns. Would you be interested in using your dyes to do that?"

"Sounds like fun but, as I said, I don't think anyone around here would buy them."

"You're probably right, but – down in the city, customers at A Thread Ahead love to buy fashion accessories that are avant-garde, artistic and one-of-a-kind. If you're interested in the idea, I'll talk to my sister, Shell, and see what she thinks."

A week later, rain begins in earnest. The mountain snowpack starts to melt, adding massive volumes to the already prodigious amount of water rising everywhere. Creeks grow to brooks, brooks to rivers, rivers to torrents overflowing their banks. The rumble of crashing water is deafening; a warning to folks to get out of the way. Like other moms, when Mother Nature goes into action, there "ain't nothin' gonna stop her." Trees tilt sideways, sliding down into the water as river banks collapse; hillside trees topple as the ground becomes saturated, sometimes falling on highways. Boulders rumble along river channels, crushing all in their path; bridges, roads and houses wash downstream, some never to be found again. Mother Nature, agitated, is surprising us with new maneuvers.

River water seeps through the basement walls of the Presbyterian Church. Pitt and Rat scurry from their flooding winter digs and head for the high ground proclaiming, "Abandon ship. Mother's on the warpath."

If you can't start a war, then disaster's the next best way to unite a community – and unite Meltmor it does. The Coil River, deciding to uncoil, stretches straight out across a land tongue where several stores, St. Catherine's Church, the synagogue and a number of apartment buildings have safely stood for years. As water begins to rise, volunteers move sandbags to the site. As the water rises higher, they move furniture and possession to second floors. When even this is not enough, they move tenants to higher ground. The call goes out for help and scores of residents respond. Britt, on her way to the shed where sandbags are being filled, meets Jane. "I'm heading over there with cookies I made for everybody."

"Great idea," says Britt. *How come I didn't think of that? Here I am taking coffee to Tuck but forgetting everyone else.* When she arrives at the site, she finds not only strong young men, but teenagers, gray-haired men and a number of women all pitching in. Britt recognizes several caretakers and a few wives. Some drive front loaders, some fill sandbags, some operate trucks. It had never occurred to Britt that when a disaster strikes and volunteers are needed, she might do her part as well.

"Thanks Hon," says Tuck as Britt hands him a cup of coffee. "I sure can use this. What are you doing today?"

"I did have plans but think I'll change them. Jane made cookies for everyone but all I'm good for is mac 'n' cheese and apple pie. Baking is not my thing. Think they could use me here?"

"Do you want to stay? That would be super. I know they could. Talk to Heyward there, he's managing this whole thing."

And so Britt learns, along with others, to do a job she never suspected would be needed in this mountain town: sandbagging. Ladders are laid across sawhorses. Orange road cones, their tips cut off, hang down between the rungs. Some folks hold bags under the cones, while others shovel sand from a pile into tops of the cones. Bags filled, they are tied off, and swung off to the side where others stack them on pallets for transfer to the flood site.

Town factions dissolve as everyone rushes to help. Those who normally have little to do with one another now work cheerfully side-by-side, cracking jokes and telling stories. Even Mayor Heyward Sly, CEO of a local pharmaceutical company and under suspicion of influence peddling, becomes unassailable, having shown himself a highly efficient manager of this salvage operation. Pitt's Rat, eyelids lowered in disdain, murmurs, "No need to worry or be in a dither, got a first rate scoundrel to tame the river."

The Red Cross arrives and sets up emergency shelters. FEMA comes to offer flood victims low interest loans. In the heat of the moment, all appears to be running smoothly. Only later will the true impact be felt: loss of jobs when businesses wash away, relocation of buildings to safer ground, rebuilding of roads and bridges, farmlands flooded with toxins and taxes levied to pay for it all. Something has shifted; life-changing events are in the making.

Katy Smith, a classmate of Tibetta's, moves with her mother Pat to the armory shelter, their apartment and meager possessions destroyed by the raging flood. Katy is a quiet little girl. Shy and dressed in ill fitting clothes, she is easily overlooked. Tibetta had never noticed her until she heard about her apartment getting flooded.

One day, during school recess, Tibetta says to Katy, "It's awful to lose all your toys like that."

"How do you know? You've got everything you want. I don't like you." Katy replies.

"No I don't and anyway, our house burned down and I did too lose everything, just like you."

Katy's raised eyebrows disappear under her straight, dark bangs. "You did? You're just saying that."

"It's true – I did too."

"But I lost my bestest teddy bear ever," wails Katy.

"That's the only thing I didn't lose," says Tibetta, "but he got all smoky and smelly."

"See? You have your Teddy bear and I don't so you're luckier than me. Everybody's luckier than me."

That afternoon as Britt drives her home, Tibetta asks why Katy's mother doesn't buy her a new Teddy Bear.

"Her mother was already very poor. Now she has nothing left at all. She can't spend on things like that," explains Britt, "but, you know what? I think we can. What do you think if we go back into town and see if they have one at the Pine Tree Gift Shoppe?"

"But I thought we didn't have money for stuff like that?"

"Normally we don't, but sometimes you have to go ahead and do something because it's right, not because it's practical."

"Goodie. Are we going right now?"

"I'm turning around as we speak." And so they drive to the gift shop, find a lovely, way too expensive, teddy bear and pay for it with a credit card. "Oh Mommy, please, please, please, can I get one too? He's so cute."

"No Tib, this bear is for Katy. You'll see. When she's happy, you'll be happy." But, Tibetta wasn't so sure that seeing someone else happy was the same as having a brand new Teddy Bear.

The following morning at school, Tibetta finds Katy and says, "Come see what's in my locker." When she opens the door to show Mr. Bear sitting on the shelf, dressed in a red set of overalls, Katy bursts into tears.

"You're mean," she cries, "You're showing off."

"Don't cry silly" Tibetta utters impatiently, "I got him for you."

"For me? You got him for me? Can I have him?" Tibetta hands the bear to Katy, whose tears are running down her recently washed face as she looks out in surprise from under her bangs. Her long hair is carefully braided. She wears a dress too small and shoes too big.

Katy hugs the bear, then puts her arm around Tibetta, "You're my new bestest friend ever."

The teacher, coming over to see what's going on says, "Why Tibetta, what a nice thing to do. It's time for 'show and tell' so, Katy, why don't you bring your bear over and tell us all about it?" Secretly proud to be noticed for her good deed, Tibetta's face lights up with a smile.

A fund is established for flood victims. Not only does the Meltmor community donate generously, but several good sized anonymous gifts are received as well, generally assumed to come from some of the Great Camp owners. The Ravens bring two soloists up from the long-running Broadway musical, *Auntie Shame,* and put on a concert with all proceeds going to the town. Tuck and Britt help clean out water-damaged homes. The devastation is horrific, debris not only soggy but filthy, covered with mud and reeking of decay. Clothes, curtains, rugs, art work, photo albums, toys, books and furniture – possessions on which we all too readily hang our identities – earmarks of past lives now tossed upon the ever growing heaps of trash.

Back in the cabin one evening, after five days of helping, an exhausted Britt comments to Tuck, "You know, I used to think nothing could be as bad as our fire, but now I think that flooding is even worse. Owners go back to their damaged homes and have to see their stuff again but then throw it all out. Must be agonizing. At least a fire is quick and final; no looking back. And, most people have some fire insurance but practically no one has flood insurance. I must say, these Adirondackers are incredible. Their response to all this is 'It could have been worse, we'll manage.'"

Tuck is familiar with life in the sparsely populated wilderness: harsh climate, poor farming conditions and few well-paying jobs. "Guess that's because folks up here are used to hard times. God knows they've had more than their share. That thinking is what gets them through."

The phone rings at the cabin, Britt answers to hear Shelley exclaim, "Mushroom dyed scarves. Awesome. Let's work it." Britt calls Sue, who is delighted at the news. "I've already started collecting. It's a great year for mushrooming." She hangs up and tells Tuck about their plans.

"There you have it," he responds, "all that miserable rain turns out to have an upside – good for mushrooms."

And so the floods came, washing away a portion of the town as well as a degree of prejudice. The question remains, however, will the gains make up for the losses? Will the floods change people's lives and if so, how? Do we learn anything? Pitt does. He visits the Baptist Church, located on a hill, to ask if he can move to its digs next year and find a new winter home in that church's warm basement. His shoulder-percher concludes, "God warns: take to the high ground, climate's warming, floods abound."

Chapter 37

Tuck and Britt are having coffee at the Hub when Britt looks up and suddenly notices a familiar looking man sitting in the shadowy back of the room. "Who *is* that guy?" asks Britt, "He creeps me out."

"No idea," lies Tuck.

"He seems to show up a lot these days and he's always looking our way. Let's get out of here. I can't enjoy my coffee with him staring at us. Could there be a connection between this guy and your tires getting slashed? After all, he was around the night that happened."

"I doubt it. We shouldn't let bad luck make us paranoid. That was most likely some messed up teenagers out for thrills. But, if he makes you uncomfortable, we can leave."

They shove back their chairs, pay Ma Rose and head for the truck, leaving behind the city-suit with black shoes, a fedora pulled down to just above dark eyebrows guarding even darker staring eyes which follow them out the door.

"I need to stop at the Lakeside Marina – pick up parts for one of Byron's outboard motors. Mind if I do that before we head home?" Arriving at the marina, they see a crane lifting new pontoon boats off a flatbed. Walt is at the controls. On Saturdays, he takes on extra jobs operating heavy equipment.

"Morning Walt. Lot of boats out on the lake already. See Josh's truck is here; the Raven's new power boat arrive?"

"Week ago. He's taking it over to their camp as we speak." Tuck and Britt amble inside to look at engines and pick up parts. It takes a while as Cap, owner of the Lakeside Marina, is a generous man who shares everything, including all gossip which comes his way. Fact or fiction, he doesn't hold back, believing as he does, that it's not his place to censor news. They learn that the Raven's new boat was powerful but lacking in grace – that the Bartons have been in to order several pairs of flashy neon water skis even though they may not be at the camp much longer – that Ace will soon, thank God, rescue Slam from the bar life by hiring him again for seasonal work at the Greene River Hunt Club – that Ma Rose's arthritis is kicking up and slowing her down – that landlords are getting help from the town to repair their flooded buildings but the tenants aren't getting much help at all – and that Hood seems unusually cheerful lately. The stream of info-chatter is interrupted by a stranger entering the shop.

"I'm interested in buying a used truck, what have you got?"

"Sorry to say, much as I'd like to sell you one, I don't have any. Just boats."

"Sold out are you?"

"Not exactly, more like I've never carried trucks but I'll be happy to sell you a nice new pontoon boat. We've got lots of water around here, some 3,000 lakes and ponds in the Adirondack Park, last time anyone counted. Better way to travel than by road. Just curious though, what made you think I sell trucks?"

"The one on the roof out there. I thought it was an ad."

"On the roof? I've got a truck on the roof? Uh-oh." They all charge out the door to see. The pontoon boats are unloaded, the crane and Walt gone, the parking lot mostly empty. However, up on the flat-roofed building sits a familiar looking truck. "No Way. I'll be damned." exclaims Cap. "I do believe we're looking at Josh's wheels. What the hell did they do, sprout wings and fly up there?"

"Ha. I think Walt has won the next round of their skirmish. If that isn't the best." laughs Tuck.

"No shit. Pardon Britt. And what's more, Walt told me he was leaving for a week's vacation right after this job. How's Josh going to retrieve that baby?"

"He's not, I'm thinking, not for another week until Walt gets back."

"Weird sense of humor if you ask me," says Britt, "I don't see what's so funny."

"Hon, you should know by now, it's how folks entertain themselves around here. Livens things up a bit. You certainly can't call this a sleepy town."

A phone call to Josh informs him his truck is no longer available. With a "Goddamn it to Hell. I'll kill the asshole," he relegates Walt to one of the two common descriptions of guys in the North County: 'asshole' or 'an okay dude'.

"Now, now," says Tripp, irritating him beyond endurance, "remember what you told Sam, 'Laugh at yourself before the others do, takes the sting out of it.'"

"Yah, right. Son of a Bitch! This time he's gone too far. I've got to have that truck this week. In fact, I need that goddamned truck right now. What the hell am I supposed to do? Asshole!"

"Guess you'll have to thumb rides and keep laughing," Tripp responds as she makes a quick exit outside for a breath of fresh air. Just then the phone rings. "Hey Josh, heard you're in a bit of a bind. Glad to give you a ride till you get your truck back. That Walt, he sure is a hoot. Got you back and didn't even break the law doing it."

"Jesus Sam. This is no joking matter. Don't know what I'm going to do."

"Ah, well, as I said, I'll be glad to give you a ride whenever you need it."

"How about right now? I've got an order of grocery supplies I'm supposed to pick up for the Ravens this afternoon."

"No problem. I'll be out there in twenty minutes." Exactly as promised, twenty minutes later a police car pulls up to Josh's cabin.

"Goddamn. I'm not riding around in that. Why in blazes didn't you come in your own car?"

"Don't get picky now. I'm trying to help but I'm on duty. This puts me in some jeopardy as well, you realize. I'm not supposed to use this car for private business. In order to keep up appearances, I'm afraid you'll have to ride in the back." And that put the finishing touches on Josh's humiliation. For the next week, townsfolk were treated to the spectacle of Josh being transported around town like a dangerous criminal. His brother tried to console him with silky words, "Think of the fun you're giving everyone. Laughter, as you have told me so often, is good for the belly."

Tuck and Britt are at breakfast one morning when Byron calls. "I'm coming up for a week on May 12th. We're bringing ten guests so I'll need you to open Reedmor: the main camp and some of the guest cabins. I guess Cedar, Wintergreen and Fern will do it, the others you can open later. And put in a good supply of wood for their fireplaces. It's probably still cold at night and I want to make sure everyone is comfortable."

"Yes sir. How about groceries? You need me to pick those up as well?"

"I do. I'll email you a list. We'll be bringing our own chef, prep cook, butler, one maid and a chauffeur but you'll need to hire a couple of staff earlier than usual this year to get everything ready. Summer employees can be hired later once the kids are out of school."

Tuck hangs up and turns to Britt.

"Funny, they're coming much earlier than usual and bringing a bunch of guests. Wonder what's up?"

"So, why didn't you ask him? You seem to know him pretty well."

"Not my place to ask. You need a sixth sense to know when you can step over the line and when not. I am, after all, merely an employee or, as Mrs. Power would say, one of the servants. Forget my place in the scheme of things, and I can be terminated like a mouse in a trap. I'm trying to get a feel for all this."

"And you actually like this job?"

"I do. Caretaking jobs are hard to get. I'm darn lucky Addison persuaded Byron to give me a shot at it. You only get this work by word of mouth and recommendations. In fact, caretaking positions at these great camps are often passed from one generation to another so opening are few and far between. I must say it's a challenge to switch from the welcome solitude of winter to the frantic pace of summer. I should have more skills than I do but I'm getting there. Luckily I learned carpentry from the days when Dad worked on house repairs. My fishing skills aren't bad either. We did a lot of it as kids so I can take people out on the lakes okay. However, I have a ways to go when it comes to plumbing and hunting."

"Basically, your job is to make everything run smoothly so the Powers won't have to worry their delicate little heads about anything at all," quips Britt.

"Yup. Need to accept the rich man's privilege the way subjects do their king. But there is an upside. I have to manage others as well as do hands-on work, and I can be outdoors much of the time. I like the combination."

"I can see that; only I wish we didn't have to live right here. We're too readily available – expected to drop everything right away and do whatever is asked."

"Right. That's why I didn't accept the cabin offer when Byron first made it. Some owners require 'on-campus' living but luckily Byron does not. Look, let's make getting a place of our own a priority. I don't know how long it will take but planning will give us something to look forward to. You know," Tuck continues, "you can count yourself lucky in one way. Just a few years ago most caretakers' wives were expected to work at the camps right along with their husbands: cooking, cleaning, doing laundry. That's changing. Now women are starting to insist on choosing their own work. I like that. I like that you're so successful in the fashion world. I'm hugely proud of what you do."

"I never heard you say that before. You've changed."

"Yeah, I think I have. I desperately needed time away from racing to mull things over. The swirl in my head is starting to clear. I realize how much you've inspired me by the way you've handled the fire, my caretaking job, my parents. Finally I'm getting the life I needed." *Though not entirely,* Tuck thinks to himself. *There's still blackmail to deal with.* He quietly reflects on the trap he's in. *If I refuse payments, Buzz will get tested to prove his paternity. That guy would gladly lay claim to Tibby. I'll do whatever I have to so I can protect her, my little girl, my tussled blonde-haired darling, my elfin companion.*

"Why so silent Sweetie? Sometimes I feel you're drifting away from me. It's scary. What are you thinking?"

"About how much I love you and Tibby – how I hope you and I will have our own baby one of these days." It's Britt's turn to go silent. *Some things are what they are*, she thinks, reflecting ruefully on her own secrets.

"Now I'll ask you the same question, why so silent?"

"And I'll answer the same way." She says, "Just thinking how much I love you and Tibby."

I better get moving." Tuck pushes back from the table and grabs a last bite of toast before pulling on his jacket. "This sudden visit of the Powers means I'm going to have to hustle. I'll need to hire a couple of people for seasonal work. I wonder if Jane wants to do it? She used to work at these camps. I'm going to town and talk to her."

Tuck stops at Hood and Jane's house but she's not home. He drives to the garage to ask where she is and, to his despair, finds Hood talking to Buzz.

"Just getting my oil changed," Buzz announces smugly before stepping out of the garage. Tuck tells Hood he's looking for help at Camp Reedmor; does he think Jane would be interested? On leaving the shop, he finds Buzz lurking among the cars and makes a beeline in the opposite direction. It doesn't work. Buzz catches up with him. "What do you want? You're getting the pay you want. You got to stay away from me. Britt's starting to wonder about you."

"Is she now? Too bad. I's just remindin' you I's still around so don't get no funny ideas about duckin' out on our deal. By the way, I know yer struggling to make payments. I'se figured out how to get a bigger take and reduce what yous owes me. Better for both of us. I's heard like Josh and Tripp Lively are goin' outta town for a coupla days. Hear yer the fill-in. Here's a warnin to ya. If alarms go off at the Ravens and yous gets called, best take yer sweet time gettin over there to check em out."

Tuck stares hard at the fiend, then shoots out "I'll think about it."

"Well pardner, cause pardner you is, don't be thinkin' too hard. Not good for yer family's health."

"Not a finger on my family. This is between you and me, okay? I'm in. But if I catch you, I'm going to have to turn you in. Your realize that?"

"Like I said, you take yer sweet time gettin there and all. Got it"?

"Got it. You effing bastard."

"Now, now, easy does it pal," says Buzz as he strolls away, hands in his pockets and smiling.

Chapter 38

It's in his dream, no, it's real. *Yikes, the phone is ringing.* Tuck leans over the side of the bed and grabs the receiver "Hello?"

"This is the Shriek Alarm Company; we have an alarm going off at the Raven's Nest. This Tuck Rising?"

"Yes."

"We're told you're the man on call. Check it out. Call the police or fire department if needed. Let us know after." Security companies are used to false alarms coming in from these remote camps. Sometimes a squirrel, sometimes a branch through a window sets the systems going.

Britt rolls over, "What's the matter?"

"Alarms going off at the Ravens. Got to go check it out." Tuck swings his feet to the floor, stretches, then stands and walks over to a chair where he retrieves a pair of pants tossed over the arm rest. From the closet he pulls a clean shirt before heading to the bathroom. Ten minutes later, he returns fully dressed. Ambling into the kitchen, he opens the fridge door to grab a carton of milk and a cold pancake.

"Don't you think you better hurry?" calls Britt from the bedroom, hearing him banging around.

"Probably another false alarm," he answers. "I'm on my way." In the mudroom, he sits down and pulls on his work boots, carefully lacing them up to the second hooks from the top. *Better take my gun*, he remembers, returning to grab it from a locked case. Fully ready, he finally walks out to the truck, warms up the engine, then rumbles off down the road, leaving Britt wondering about such procrastination.

Arriving at the Ravens long dirt road, he follows it a quarter-mile before parking to walk the rest of the way. If later asked why, he can always explain he was trying to sneak up on any potential thief. Tuck pockets his flashlight, gets out of the truck and, his eyes adjusting to the dark, strolls quietly along the road, now slicked over by a late spring temperature drop which has turned the rain to ice. Not five minutes later, rounding a curve, he is startled to see headlights off to one side, shining at a crazy angle through the bare trees. *Huh. That's odd. What am I looking at?* Tuck walks closer and hears an engine running. He can barely discern through the flattened brush a tilted car facing away from him. Cautiously he walks closer, peering through the dark trying to make out what's happened. A few more steps and he comes upon the car which has rolled onto the passenger side and is resting against a tree, the driver's door ripped half off its hinges. No one appears to be around. He clambers up on the under carriage, reaches inside and turns off the engine. Silence. Somehow this has something to do with Buzz, but where did he go? "Hello, Hello, anyone around?" Tuck calls out. Then, spotting a dark heap back on the road, he returns to see what it is. *Oh God, it's a body. What the hell has Buzz done now?* Foul play. I've had enough. I'm through playing games. Got to call the police. He flicks on his flashlight to see a darkly clothed figure, the face covered by a facemask. Tuck leans down and lifting the person's head, peels off the mask. Startled he jumps back. It's Buzz.

Moving him aroused Buzz enough to moan, "Help me man, I's hurt."

"Guess you are," responds Tuck shakily.

"That you, Tuck? Do somethin'. Git help. I'm bleedin." And bleeding he is, the blood pumping from a gash in his neck. Tuck lowers the battered head back down on the road, stands up and stares down at him. *Guess I should apply pressure to that wound. Yes, guess I should.* He continues standing there, not moving. "Tuck man, hev a heart. Help me, I never really meant ta hurt ya. Help." His voice is weak, his strength oozing out in a dark puddle on the frozen ground. Tuck stands watching for several minutes. The blood starts to congeal in the frigid air. Long strangled by the bond of blackmail, Tuck now feels it melting, rising and floating away, like bad dreams vaporizing in the dark night. As Buzz grows colder, Tuck grows warmer, waves of relief flowing through him as the injured body stiffens on the ground. Buzz closes his eyes, his breath comes in rasps. Can't believe I'm watching this – not doing a thing – should be helping. A terrible rasping breath shudders out of the crumpled form, his chest stops heaving, the body is still. Quiet envelops them both; a heavy silence hangs above their heads. Instinctively, Tuck holds his own breath, waiting for Buzz to breathe again. He does not, Tuck does. Game over. Tuck looks up, stares into the night sky. Adirondack stars have never been brighter, the air never so clear. Like a night watchman, an owl calls out across the lake, another answers. "Who looks for you, who looks for you all?" *Nobody anymore, thinks Tuck with a sigh of relief* and he answers in a whisper, "All is well, all is well in the North Country tonight." *I should phone the police.* But he doesn't, not right away. *I need a little time – need to rest on this bridge of darkness, a moment of peace. Once I make the call, the outside world will come crashing in.* Finally he pulls out his cell phone, dials 911 and sets the scene in motion. The rest of the night is a blur of phone calls, sirens, flood lights, ambulances, flashbulbs, recovered loot, questions, reports, tow trucks: chaos shoving sanity deep into the darkness. It is an accident caused by skidding on black ice, a springtime danger locals know well, outsiders do not.

In the morning, before the newspaper is on the stands, talk of the event ripples through every area residence, diner and store. Loot has been recovered, some of it art work, the artists said to be of great renown. Names like Chagall, Leger, Tissot, Renoir and Vermeer are rolling awkwardly off the tongues of Meltmor's breakfast crowd. It seems the Ravens had a little-known museum room at the camp, with built-in humidity and heat control. An Ansel Adams photograph and a damaged Tiffany vase had also been found – heard of Tiffany and Adams but those other guys? A license in the thief's pocket had identified him as Buzz Takher. He'd been seen around town some but nobody knew much about him except that he'd been accused of stealing before. Justus had caught him red-handed but somehow he'd gotten off. Not in evidence that morning is Tuck, who, still shaken, is at home nursing his third cup of coffee while waiting for Britt to return from taking Tibetta to school.

When she gets back and the two of them are alone, he begins to fill her in on most, but not all, of the accident details. "Is it possible that he was the same stranger we kept seeing about town?" asks Britt.

"I think so, though it was hard to tell. He was badly messed up."

"Seemed like he was always staring at us. Gives me the shivers just thinking about it. You know, this is awful of me but in a way, if it's him, I'm glad he's gone." *Now there's something we agree whole heartedly about*, thinks Tuck, *though she doesn't have as much on her conscience as I do, standing there and letting him die like I did.*

"Natural reaction. I'm going to try to get some sleep now. I'll get up later and see if I can rescue some piece of this day. Jane wants to work at the camp this season and says she has a friend who might be interested. Got to get them on board and start readying the place for the Power's arrival. There's much to be done."

Britt goes back to work. She thinks about Fawn's reaction to the dress she had made her. Britt's act of kindness had brought the two closer together but Fawn was surprised to find that friends, jealous of her new outfit, were becoming more distant. "I've always been close to them but now I feel like they are jealous of me. It's coming between us," Fawn had said. It reminded Britt of advice she had given an acquaintance who, unable to afford something more elegant, was planning to wear a simple dress to a fancy party. "If you go looking respectable but not too flashy, all the women will love you. If you out-dress them they'll be critical." Remembering that gave Britt an idea.

What if I make similar dresses for other women in Meltmor? Wonder if they would also like colorful clothes with high necklines, long sleeves, dresses that flatter but don't look doughty.

With this thought, an idea takes shape. *Maybe I could open a shop here in Meltmor, an offshoot of A Thread Ahead Boutique.* Britt is excited. *I'll talk to my sister and see what she thinks.* She can't wait to tell Tuck. When he rolls out of bed later that day, she starts talking away. Finally she stops, "What do you think? Would you go along with this?"

"But why would you quit something you love in order to work with local folks?"

"I guess for the same reason you quit something I thought you loved."

"Fair enough. So – if you open a shop here, it must mean that you're starting to see this town as home."

"Maybe. Do you think my plan can work?"

"It's worth a try. I'm ready to go along with it. After all, you stuck with me when I jumped ship. I like your willingness to try a jump of your own."

That evening, Tuck drives to his parents' and picks up Tibetta. Anxious to change the subject after a half-hour of interrogation about the accident, he mentions Britt's idea to open a women's dress shop in Meltmor. "That's all well and good," says his father, "but being a woman and all, she best hire a consultant to advise her how to go about doing that. She does remember, I assume, that I sell women's clothes as well. Not that I'm worried about her stealing customers but it's not a very active market right now. I hear the same from the SuperBig. Women's clothes are not moving at the moment."

"You seem to forget that she already has a business in the city and a prosperous one at that. Britt and her sister are not some bimbos flailing around out there. Besides, what is this constant need to hire consultants? It's throwing good money away, if you ask me. Consultants brainwash everyone into suspending their own creative thinking. If the 'consultant industry' disappeared, folks might actually use their very own God given commonsense. Now wouldn't that be a hoot?"

"You have a thing or two to learn yet, my boy. For starters, what's with all the cynicism? Don't see you successfully roaring into the business world."

"Sorry Dad. Guess you're right. I know it is tough being in business these days," Tuck says backpedaling from his outburst as he remembers that his mother is working secretly to make up for his father's loss of income – and pride. *I'm beginning to feel bad for my old man. He's pretty vulnerable right now. Wonder if he knows that Fred, his long time right-hand man, got a job at the SuperPig?* Tuck hauls himself up out of his chair, saying, "Got to get this bunny back for supper," and he gallops out the door with Tibetta riding on his shoulders crying "Giddy up cow, faster, faster."

"Cow? Where'd you get that idea? Cow?"

"Hee, hee," she giggles delightedly, "Our teacher told us that cowbirds sit on cows so you're the cow, I'm the bird."

They drive toward home, Tibetta soon falling asleep. In the ensuing silence, Tuck's mind plays back over the day's events. The last 24 four hours have been packed like a barrel of live ammo. *When the dust settles, I wonder how we'll be.* He flashes back to the accident. *What kind of a guy am I to just stand there like that? Just who was Buzz anyway? Was he truly Tibby's dad? Even if he was, I could never let Tibby go, especially to a lowlife like that. Am I safe from more threats out of the past? I need a beer, sorry Britt, but right now I need a beer like a fish needs water. Turn me on, tune me in –*

Chapter 39

"You look great this morning," Moe says to Fawn as she gets out of the car in her new dress. "Aren't you worried about wearing that to clean in?"

She blushes, not used to such compliments. *I guess wearing this new dress does make a difference,* she thinks. "Oh, I'll cover it up with an apron."

Moe continues, "That Buzz guy, no family, no will. Police finished with his Cliff Rock apartment, need someone to go in, clean, pack up his things. Interested? Let me know when you stop back for your pay."

Fawn walks to the camp and begins the weekly cleaning. She had heard much about these second homes of the wealthy but until working here, had never been inside one. Once more, she pauses to look around at the polished cherry floors, the 20-foot wide fieldstone fireplace, benches set inside either end and topped by a long split log mantle. A palatial winding mahogany staircase, edged by fancy twig banisters, climbs to the second floor; tall birch bark panels break up the vertical plank walls; a rafter-filled ceiling supported by tall trees seeming to grow right out of the floor, hovers high above; lifelike salmon flip half off their glossy plaques and the stuffed heads of a 8-point buck and large black bear peer down at her. Two great blue herons hang from the ceiling as if flying in for a landing. The solid Mission furniture is dwarfed by the scale of the room. She especially loves the chandelier hanging over the 15-foot long maple table in the dining room. Made from a large cedar root, its tiny rootlets are intertwined with hundreds of miniature LED lights. *Gee, this is really something*, she marvels, *am I ever lucky to work here.*

She comes once a week to clean the great room, kitchen, dining area, Dr. Sears's bedroom and office. The tower room, lined with book shelves, is cleaned only on request. Dr. Sears has never met or spoken with her. If the tower needs cleaning, he makes sure he is absent. Three hours later, work done, she walks over to Moe's cabin. "I think I'd like to take that work cleaning Buzz's apartment, as long as Justus doesn't hear about it."

Suspect that's not the only thing I won't be telling Justus, thinks Moe. Fawn's got more to offer than she knows. Her hair is graying but she has a sweet smile and she's not a bad looker, especially in that dress.

"Great." I'll go now and call the police to let them know. After finishing the call, Moe says, "How about sitting for a minute, rest your feet. Would you like a cup of coffee?"

"It would be nice but I don't know that I should."

"And why not? Justus doesn't get home till late does he?"

"That's true. It's usually after eight and when he does walk in he's so tired and depressed he hardly notices me at all. I don't seem to be able to cheer him up."

"A good looker like you? He's lucky to have you."

"Oh, I don't know about that. By the way, where is your wife?"

"Gone."

"Is she away for long?"

"I'll say – left several weeks ago – not planning to return."

"I'm so sorry. I didn't realize. I shouldn't have said anything."

"Not to worry. I'm over it. She got lonely what with the isolation out here – said I didn't talk enough – don't talk much 'cause it's all been said before. Besides which, speaking to truth just brings trouble."

"You're funny," giggles Fawn, "She used to clean for Dr Sears didn't she? So that's why he needed me to come work for him.?"

"Something like that. You like the job?"

"Yes. You know, I've never done anything like this before. Actually makes me feel sort of good, like I have something to offer."

"You certainly do," he replies as his unspoken desires simmer.

"So – how's your son doing? He's a good guy."

"He's doing real well. Got a big name for himself down in the city. People like his designs and he's got lots of work lined up."

"Nice. Actually though, I meant how's Tuck?"

"Oh, okay I guess. He appreciated your taking the Power's guests out and teaching him some hunting skills."

"Like I said, a good guy. No worries there."

"You think so? But he threw over his skiing career for no reason at all."

"There's always a reason. We may not understand it, but there's always a reason."

"Oh. It's getting late, I think I better go. Thank you for the coffee."

"Watch out for the deer on the drive out. Take it slow."

A few days later Fawn drives to Cliff Rock and packs up and cleans out Buzz's apartment. She's nervous about the job but tries to reason with herself that there's nothing to be afraid of. Anyway, she and Justus need the extra money. She opens the closet door to begin putting Buzz's clothes in plastic bags. But, what is this? She spots a familiar looking coat. *Why, it makes me think of the one I gave Addison. My goodness, there's a hat here too which is also like the one I gave him.* That's strange. She takes the coat off the hanger, looks at the tag and sees it's from The Outdoors and Inn Clothing Store. Taking the narrow-brimmed gray fedora down from the shelf, she checks the inside rim to find the same label. *Addison's! Good Grief. Why are these clothes here? Oh, this is terrible. I must ask Justus or Esprit what to do. No, on second thought, I know what to do. I'm going to take the coat and hat home. After all, I gave it to Addison, not this guy, so I have the right to give it back to my son.*

She returns home and immediately calls to tell Addison of her discovery, "How do you think it ended up in that man's apartment?"

Trying to avoid setting off his mother's usual hysteria, he reins in his astonishment and, thinking fast, says, "I outgrew those clothes and gave them to Good Will. He must have found them there. I'll get Tuck to come over as soon as he can and take the clothes to the police."

"Oh no. We can't do that. Then Justus will find out I'm working. By the way, did you know that already? You don't seem very surprised by all this."

"Yes Mother. Tuck told me, secretly of course. He and I are tight. I would never have said anything."

After talking to his mother, Addison immediately dials Tuck and tells him the news. "That guy must have been the one who paraded as me at the clinic that day. I told Mother you would be right over, not to do anything until you get there. She can be arrested for withholding evidence if those clothes don't go to the police. Could you get over there and take the things to the station? Convince her that Justus doesn't have to know she was the one to find them."

"Sure thing. Fortunately I've got the new staff started so I can get away for an hour or two." Tuck hangs up, jumps in his truck and drives to town. Fawn shows him the coat which he carefully checks over. Crumpled deep in an inner pocket he finds a note with Bubbles's clinic address on it.

Tuck takes the coat, hat and note to the police. This sets him to wondering again about the mysterious demise of Bubbles. I feel like the ingredients of this enigma are finally all on the table. We're just missing the chef who knows how to put them together.

Two days later the police call Addison. "Looks like Buzz might have been the man impersonating you but we still don't know what his connection was with your wife. What we do know, however, is that he was a dealer who lived most of his life in New Jersey near the Lincoln

Tunnel. The investigator wants to try again to see Dr. Kammer's notes regarding his sessions with Bubbles. How do you feel about that?"

"Makes sense to me. I'm as anxious to understand this as you are. But you guys at least owe me an apology for what you've put me through." It is duly given.

The toxicology report won't be released for another five weeks. There remains a missing link in the series of events that led to her death. However, even as one link goes missing, new ones are forged: Yin and Yang. Bubbles's parents, the Bellows, are contacted by the police who tell them about the discovery of the coat, hat, and note. They, as well as Addison, agree that Dr. Kammer should be requested to open his records. This time a judge subpoenas Dr. Kammer for the information. The process can take a while so everyone is in for a wait.

Fawn continues to clean the Sears Camp every Wednesday. While Fawn is there working, Sterling Sears, the semiretired climatologist, prefers to hole up in the tower library reading and doing research. Moe, on the other hand, prefers to make himself available, often inviting Fawn for a cup of coffee after she finishes cleaning. One day, on leaving the main house, she sees Big Moe down on his hands and knees at the far side of the driveway. "Oh dear. Is something the matter?" she cries, running to his side.

"Not at all. Come over here. I want to show you something." Fawn joins him. "Here, hunker down, get a closer look." He points out white and yellow blossoms of Dutchman's breeches rising out of the leaf litter: first signs of spring. "Remind you of white and yellow trousers hanging on a line?"

"Why yes. I see what you mean. They're lovely. I never knew we had such flowers around here." Moe pulls out a magnifying glass the better to view the delicate small plants. Fawn leans in closer and losing her balance, is quickly steadied by Moe's arm around her shoulders. Righting herself again, she is nervously aware that he keeps his hold on her. *I should ask him to remove his arm but he might think I'm reading too much into this.*

"I love learning about the nature around us. Justus has no interest in this kind of thing. Wish he did. He's missing a lot." *That's for sure*, thinks Moe with satisfaction.

Several weeks later Josh calls Moe. "Bill and Julia Raven want to invite the local school children, first and second grades, to come to the Raven's Nest for a guided nature walk. Want their privately educated

185

children to meet some of the local public school kids. They asked if I knew anyone who could lead the trip. That would be you. Interested?"

"Sure – guess I can do it."

"Good. By the way, haven't seen your wife around for a while. How you all doing?"

"Left me back a ways."

"That's terrible."

"Not really – liked her cooking and wrestling her in bed but that was about it. I enjoy the solitude."

"No regrets?"

"Not a one. We weren't actually married anyway. I wouldn't commit to such lifelong imprisonment. This way I walk away a free man."

"Big Moe, if you aren't the damnedest dude I ever met."

A week later, Tibetta's first grade and the second grade classes celebrate the end of the school year with a field trip to the Ravens. Thirty children, four parents, two teachers and one grandfather, Justus. Tibetta had begged her beloved grandpa to come along. He decides to go, unable to resist her pleas. After many instructions, some repeated several times, Justus reluctantly turns the store over to Fawn and gets on the school bus along with the others. When they arrive at the Raven's Nest, Bill and Julia Raven, their children and Big Moe are there to greet them. Excited kids, bursting out of the bus, are finally corralled and follow behind Moe along a trail which meanders through the estate. After crossing a stone bridge, Moe leads them to the edge of a stream, pointing out bright yellow marsh marigolds springing from the water. "Indians used to cook these leaves, ate them like spinach. You all like spinach?"

He's answered with a chorus of yucks, "We hate spinach."

"Good, because if these leaves are eaten raw, they're poisonous. Never taste anything without an adult okay? Now, who can find the next flower?" A minute later, one of the children discovers a cluster of small white blossoms. "Good eye." exclaims Moe. "That's toothwort. Roots of this plant, ground up, can be used like pepper."

The walk continues, Moe helping the children search for tiny spring flowers and telling them how Indians used the plants for medicine and food. The kids find the hunt great fun, but only half pay attention to what Moe is saying. For Justus however, it's an eye opener. He's fascinated. Never before had he realized how many colorful blooms are scattered through the woods. Spring flowers are small and easily overlooked. For the first time he learns that spring consists of more than mud. The lively group troops on, finding star flowers, hepatica, wood sorrel, Jacks hidden in pulpits and more.

As they stroll along the path, parents hang back and talk amongst themselves. Justus, pretending to be somewhat bored, as if he's heard it all before, walks a little ahead trying to surreptitiously catch every word Moe is saying. *How does this guy know so much? Think I'll stop at the store and buy a book on this subject. Actually, I'd better order it online instead. Don't want anyone to see what I'm up to. They'd laugh themselves silly if they caught me, the respected business man, studying up on wildflowers. Of course, right now I should focus on the store, not sure how I can keep it going though damned if I'm going to let on to Fawn.* Suddenly words he heard Pitt utter yesterday come back to haunt him. *"Truth is dandy, lies are handy, choose your candy."*

Chapter 40

Dr. Sears is away at a conference in Banff, Canada when Fawn arrives to clean his camp. By one o'clock, she has not returned to Moe's cabin for their usual weekly get together. *Wonder where she is; think I'll go check.* He gives a call on entering the main lodge and hears a faint response from the kitchen. On entering, he finds Fawn lying on her back on the floor. Rushing to her side, he kneels down to find her eyes open but slightly unfocused. "What happened?" he asks.

"I'm not sure. I remember feeling faint. Next thing I found myself on the floor."

"Anything hurt?" asks Moe.

"Yes. The back of my head."

"You must have hit it when you went down. Can you get up?" Fawn rolls to one side and attempts to lift her head and shoulder but the effort is too much. With that, Big Moe, not only large but strong, slides his arms under her, lifting Fawn off the floor. He easily carries her through the main room, out the door and over to his cabin where he gently lowers her on to his bed. "Want me to take you to the doctor?" he asks.

"Oh Lord no. Don't do that. The doctor is apt to tell Justus and then he'll find out that I'm working. I'll be okay. I just forgot to eat breakfast in my hurry this morning. This happens sometimes. Think I need a little something to eat."

In the kitchen tucked into a corner of his two-room cabin, Moe puts tea water on to boil, slices two pieces of bread, pulls out an iron fry pan and scrambles a couple of eggs. Returning to the bed he tries to lift her into a sitting position. She doesn't weigh much but her breasts, large and warm, press against his chest, exciting him to get even closer. Lowering his head, he bends down and lets his lips brush hers – a kiss which she hesitantly returns.

"Oh my goodness," she says. "What are we doing?"

"I think you know very well," replies Moe. "I think you're as hungry as I am."

"I am. We should eat."

"That's not the hunger I meant. But, yes, you need some food." He props a pillow behind her back, then holding a cup of tea to her lips, steadies her hand as she takes a sip. "Now for some eggs."

After eating a goodly amount for someone who has just fainted, she proclaims, "I think I'm as good as new, head feels okay. Thank you for taking care of me."

"But I'm still hungry," he murmurs. With that, he lays her back down, stretches out by her side, and gently brushes her hair off her face.

"Aren't we too old for this?" Fawn murmurs even as she feels herself melting and trembling helplessly. The large hands of this gentle giant, work their way down the length of her body. There is no stopping now, both of them burning with desire. Piece by piece they remove each other's clothes until, skin to skin, they are completely engulfed in the act of love. Fawn, who is always pleasing others, finally allows her own desires to be met.

A few days later a light wind blows gently over the Northern lands, its wispy fingers stretch into quiet corners, stirring the air to awaken buried dreams. Maybe it's in the stars, or maybe it's the season, but everywhere it wanders, the soft spring breeze delivers a breath of promise. Even Rat, riding Pitt's shoulder, has shed his wintry mood and some think it is he who mutters, "Spring breezes follow winter freezes."

Word travels around town, "Rat's been seen without his wool jacket, must mean summer's coming." The Power's family and their guests come up for the weekend. Their arrival has sparked curiosity: "Mr. and Mrs. Power are scheduled to make an important announcement at the hospital."

On Saturday, regional dignitaries, sniffing the chance for publicity, show up at the hospital to rub elbows with the Powers in an attempt to promote the impression they are in some way connected to whatever is about to be announced. That afternoon, Byron takes the podium in front of a crowd of over 200 faces turned reverently in his direction. With a show of great respect, he introduces his glamorous wife to the eager crowd. Flipping her long blonde hair from her face, she steps forward, gives a broad carefully manufactured smile and breaks the welcome news. She will be funding the construction of the Prudence Power Pediatric Pavilion. This information is received with all the enthusiasm that any fame seeker could ever wish. The building will forever carry her name in true corporate graffiti style. Mrs. Power will take her place alongside others on the wide pedestal of notoriety. She graciously bows to her fans peering up from below. Addison Rising is the architect, designing a "green" building in accordance with the trend toward environmentally friendly construction.

The Power's entourage returns to the city on Sunday but Byron stays on. He has been visiting camp frequently, partly because he enjoys being away from the city and partly to help Tuck with their articles. Realizing they need a good deal of work time together, Tuck is nevertheless somewhat uncomfortable around Byron. Lately, their conversations have strayed off topic to discussions of rural life, the aftermath of the town flood, and then this: "Tuck, you happily married?" *Odd thing to be asking*, thinks Tuck.

"Happy as anyone I suppose."

"And that means?" pursued Byron.

"It means we have our good days and bad days, though fortunately a lot more good days. Women. You know how that goes."

"I certainly do." There is a long pause, then Byron resumes, "There are other options."

"What are you saying?" responds Tuck.

"I mean women aren't the only ones to give pleasure." It finally dawns on Tuck where this is going.

"I don't think there are any others for me. Britt is my everything, a bright moon in a dark sky."

"That's your answer?"

"That's it," Tuck responds, wondering if this spells the end of his caretaker job and publishing venture. But it takes more than one event to sabotage Byron's equanimity. He is enveloped in a blanket of wisdom; one broken strand changes neither his attitude nor appearance.

"Plainly spoken. So, let's get back to our work. I hope the coming years will bring you peace and harmony. It's more than most ever find." *And certainly more than I have ever enjoyed, except here at camp*, Byron reflects.

Discussion on that topic is never to rise between them again. In fact, it put to bed, though not in the way Byron had hoped, the underlying tension in their relationship. Byron and Tuck's alliance, now well defined, is back on track; the articles, the new book, and his caretaking job the only subjects of any further talk.

"By the way, you said we ought to think about publishing our book soon. I've changed my mind about something. I'd like to use my real name, Tuck Rising, as coauthor."

"What made you change so suddenly? Just curious."

"Can't rightly say but I'm ready. The article series though, I still want that to continue under my pseudonym."

"We can do that. I've thought of a title for the book. What do you think of this? *Victory on the Head of a Pin*?" Tuck liked it alright; it seemed to perfectly capture the manuscript's theme.

"Good. I'll get going on it." Several days later, Byron, his head bursting with ideas, launches another thought, a kite sent up to test the force of the wind and the strength of Tucks creativity. He asks Tuck to stop by the main house.

"Ever think of writing fiction?"

"No. Why?"

"Well, it seems to me you might do something rather interesting. I think we can target completion of our coauthored book for eight months from now. After that, you might consider a new direction. Nonfiction doesn't reach people on the same gut level as fiction."

"But, I thought you were looking for serious writing."

"I am. Make no mistake. Good fiction is serious. It share's the author's views on life and as such is very honest about its intent. Nonfiction, on the other hand, pretends to tell the truth but, in fact, is a selection of events based on the author's bias. Fiction carries more truth than nonfiction. Where it succeeds, it serves as one of man's greatest teachers."

"Never thought of it that way. Don't know that I'm up to such a challenge," responds Tuck.

"You are. You have insight and imagination. Your writing style will keep developing as long as you keep tapping away at the keyboard. Give it some thought. Fiction however, is very personal, not something to collaborate on. I'll edit but nothing more. You're going to have to walk this path alone."

"I'll think on it." After this conversation, Tuck feels the need to escape, retreat outside. He heads for a woods path leading to a black pool of water in a deep hollow behind a quarter-mile-away. Reaching the shore, he sits down on a log, stretches his long legs before him and leans back against the rough bark of a white pine. The branches above hum as a gentle breeze blows softly through the needles. The water is flat calm and, like a mirror displays a reverse image of the surrounding trees. He speculates on which is the better way to view the world, right side up or upside down?

After an hour of quiet, Tuck gets up and returns home to find Britt bursting with news and chatter. "The realtor has found the perfect space for me to set up a shop. I checked it out this morning and signed a lease. It's the place where Inky Washburn had her studio. Sales didn't go well there so she's moving to a larger storefront where she'll hook up with several other better known painters. She thinks the public will dare to buy her work when they see it displayed alongside established artists. I think she's right. People rarely trust their own judgment; depend instead on the approval of others. It's amazing how many folks won't even choose pictures for their walls without consulting interior decorators. Seems like they're more concerned with the image they project than the one they select. Why would you hire someone to tell you how to beautify your own home?"

"Hey Honey, slow down a minute. Congratulations. This is a big step forward. When can you take it over and what will it be called?"

"I have the name all picked out, 'Peak Colors'. I'll sell affordable dresses and slacks with easily adjustable waistlines. I plan to design handsome but practical clothes for older North Country women: the forgotten species. Everything will be made of easily washable, no-iron, brightly colored fabrics. Inky will be move out by next week and then I can start remodeling. So, do you think it will work?"

"I think I love your courage in taking this risk. Bucking expectations gives us wings. Bravo!" Tuck marvels to himself at the shift in Britt's attitude. *The women she once looked down on are now the ones she wants to please.*

A week later 100 people line up on the street to pass Inky's pictures along, hand to hand, bucket brigade style, from her old studio to the new. The police are on hand, purportedly to help at street crossings but in reality, to make sure that no one "accidentally" makes off with any paintings. "I love all my friends," states Inky emphatically, "but that doesn't mean I trust them. After all, many are misfits like myself and the way I figure, 'trust but verify.'"

Soon thereafter, contractors are hired to remodel Britt's shop, putting in a sewing room, an ironing room, an office and the storefront. The builders are skilled and dedicated but along with construction comes the inevitable amplified music blasting from the ever present radios. Sometimes, when Britt stops by to check progress, her ears burn with the sounds of hard rock; other times it's blue grass or folk, both of which she enjoys. Eventually she learns, before she is even out of her car, to recognize the workers by the type of music playing. One time she is shocked to hear Brahms soaring forth. That is the preference of a man known as "Professor James," an older, more sedate carpenter with formal musical training in his earlier days. It occurs to Britt how little employees' jobs reveal about who they really are.

Shelley is somewhat resentful that Britt wants to strike off on her own and spend less time in the city. Nevertheless, she agrees to loan money from A Thread Ahead to help get their new store up and running. In exchange for the favor, she counts on Britt continuing to design clothes for their city customers.

And what of Justus and his titanic struggle with the SuperBig? He is keeping the Outdoors and Inn Clothing Store open, but annoyed at the turn of things. His 'loyal' customers, with the exception of Sam and

Pitt, have been spotted slinking into the SuperBig. But, as so often happens, just as spirits start to sag, the sun shines on a new path, chasing away shadows and beckoning us to follow. Justus has been keeping his impulsive purchase hidden under the counter. Now with time on his hands, he brings out the wildflower book for a closer look. Here and there, he recognizes certain blossoms. He pages through the illustrations, amazed at how many can be found in the Adirondack region. *I wonder if any of these grow right around here. I've never noticed.* He begins closing the store earlier each day so he can escape to the woods in search of the elusive, colorful blossoms. His secret life brings him pleasure, though he would never admit to such unmanly behavior if confronted. *What would my friends think?*

And then one afternoon, Pitt cruises by at the moment when Justus is closing the store early and sneaking out the door. "No good liar, store needs buyer." *That Pitt is a pain but harmless though I do wish he'd throw the rat away.* "Cat's purring, luck stirring," he heard again.

Chapter 41

Tuck and Fawn are sharing a few rare and special 'mother-son' moments. "I remember when you and Addison were little and put on plays with the neighborhood children," Fawn says. "He was the director; the rest of you were the actors. They all did exactly what he told them, except for you. You insisted on doing everything your own way. That used to make him awful mad. I remember one time especially. Addison dressed you up as the big bad wolf. You crawled around on all fours with a gray bathroom rug thrown on your back and the elasticized toilet lid covering your head. Your ears were made of cardboard and your tail was a frayed piece of rope. You were supposed to be scary and chase Little Red Riding Hood but instead, you felt sorry for her. We all had a good laugh at the kind wolf who was trying to help the blanket clad 5-year-old Little Red Riding Hood find her way through the kitchen chair-woods."

"Huh. I don't remember that at all. I do remember," recalls Tuck, "that we used to sneak down to the river and race birch bark canoes on the rapids. Once Addison fell in and was swept downstream. I was scared and ran along the bank trying to reach him. He finally caught hold of a branch sticking out from the shore. When he managed to crawl up the bank, he was grinning ear to ear. First thing he said was, 'Promise not to tell our parents. They're always warning us of the dangers of currents but it was actually fun to be carried away like that.'"

"Goodness," responds Fawn, "How terrifying. It scares me even now to think about it. Surprising too. Addison usually did what he was told. It was you we worried about, with a mind of your own, always breaking the rules."

"Yup. But Addison broke plenty too. He was just sneakier, not as straightforward about it. Like the time he secretly bought a calculator and, against the teacher's instructions, used it to do his homework. You thought he was a genius to figure out the arithmetic so fast. I guess he was, come to think of it, because he learned how to do those problems on a calculator long before the other kids even knew what one was. Remember how he used to keep lists of numbers? – 7 bike trips to Cedar Bluff Lake, 10 swims in Cold Brook, 15 canoe trips to Snake Island and I think he climbed all the high peaks just so he could add 46 to his list. He's always been fascinated by numbers and technology, probably helped him become such a respected architect."

"The things we never knew about you two!" says Fawn. *And the things you still don't know*, thinks Tuck. "With all the lakes and rivers around here, I was always afraid of you both drowning. When the town flooded last month, it brought back my old fears."

"You aren't the only one. Those floods have made a lot of people more fearful. And it's time they should be; time to realize climate change is for real. We'd best prepare because, for sure, there's more to come. Tibby tells me her friend Katy has been having terrible nightmares about drowning ever since she lost her apartment."

"That's different, Katy's only a child. What does she know about anything? And how much of a home is an apartment anyway? By the way, I hear her mother has become a welfare queen. What chance will that poor child ever have?"

"Now wait a minute, before you go too far with this. The child obviously understands quite a bit or she wouldn't be so afraid. And, did you realize that Katy's mother worked at the Laundromat, that she lost her job because the Laundromat was destroyed by the flood as well? She managed to support the two of them quite nicely until fate turned the tide."

"But single mothers, they should be ashamed."

"Ashamed of what? Sleeping with a guy she thought loved her? Lots of very 'upright' people have taken that path. What's the sin? She did what many do. She wasn't the one to abandon the family, he was."

"You always see things differently. You know how to turn things around, get me doubting everything. After talking with you, I don't know what to think. You sound a little like Moe who says if we know a person's story, we'd be less judgmental. Not like Esprit who thinks that everyone simply needs to be straightened out." *Moe? Where did that come from? Since when did she start caring what Moe says?*

Their conversation is interrupted by Justus walking into the room. "Oh darling," says his mother, "I kept supper warming for you. You must be tired after working so hard. Come, sit down and I'll bring you your meal."

"Thanks. I am pretty hungry."

Glancing down at his father's feet, Tuck notices that his usually pristine shoes are muddy. *Now that's interesting. I wonder what he's been up to.* It's almost nine o'clock. Tuck is ready for home.

"I'm off now. Love you," he says as his father visibly cringes at the modern trend of putting sentiment into words.

During the drive home, Tuck is suddenly struck by an idea. Talk about play acting combined with Tibby's love of marionettes comes together in a burst of inspiration. What if I write a book about marionettes manipulated by those above until the day when the boy marionette's strings get tangled with the girl marionette and he cuts them both loose from their handlers. I could have fun with that – discovering life on their own terms. Maybe Byron is right. I'll have to give fiction a try but first, I've got to get our book finished.

Tuck arrives home and hears that Addison has called. "He wants to come up again for the weekend," reports Britt. "Seems to suddenly enjoy visiting us a lot. I think he's lonelier than he wants to admit."

The next morning, Britt drives Tibetta to school, afterwards stopping at the grocery store to pick up eggs and milk. As she prepares to pull out of the parking lot, a startling sight confronts her. There is her mother, in high heels and a pink pants suit, stepping out of a realtor's car across the street. Britt puts on the brakes and watches as the two of them walk up to a house with a 'For Sale' sign prominently displayed in the yard. "Good Grief. Am I seeing things? I guess it's true, mothers do show up in the strangest places." she exclaims out loud. Parking the car again, she hops out, strides across the street and catches up with her mother. She and the realtor are about to enter the house. "Mom, what are you doing up here?"

"Hi Britt. I was going to surprise you but as long as you caught me, I guess it's obvious. I'm looking for a vacation house."

"I thought you didn't like this town."

"We can talk about that later. This is my realtor, Bobbi. Bobbi, this is my daughter Britt. Bobbi still has a couple more places to show me. After that, why don't I meet you at Applebee's for a cup of coffee. We can talk then."

"We don't have an Applebee's."

"No? That's okay, a Starbucks or Dunkin Donuts is fine too."

"Don't have those either. How about the Hunter's Hub?"

"That hokey place? Don't you have any decent coffee shops around here?"

Bobbi breaks in. "We try to support our local businesses, keep the vulture chains away. That's part of the charm that attracts tourists to our area."

"I was trying to save you the extra drive but if you'd rather, why don't you come out to the cabin for a cup of coffee?" suggests Britt.

And that is what happens. Later that morning, sitting at the spool-table, Eileen Taglong explains to her daughter why she and her husband, Rory, came to have a change of heart. "It's like this. Last time we were here staying at the motel, remember that?"

"Of course Mom."

"Well, while we were here we met some other guests who told us about a play they had seen. Said it was really good. You all were busy that night, so we went alone to the Dragon Theatre. While there, we met a Mr. and Mrs. Raven, very important people, he is CEO of Crack and Wippett in the city. They told us a lot more about the area than you two ever did. Don't know if you realize it, but many famous people summer up here. So, we thought, why not us as well? So, that's how it happened. Dad couldn't come this time; he had an appointment with his broker so I said I would make a first tour of the area. Of course, this way we get to see more of you and that darling little Tibby. So, won't it be fun? We had planned to surprise you but, like I said, you caught me in the act."

"Don't worry Mom, you surprised me alright. Wait till Tuck hears this. He won't believe it. You always thought Meltmore was such a dorky town."

"We didn't realize a lot of things about it at first. Like the Ravens, they're from Philadelphia you know, they told us that the concert pianist, Marion Fingring, is playing in the Hotel Meltmor dining room next week. She's well known and has played Carnegie Hall. Imagine that. Who would have thought it?"

"I could have told you that but you wouldn't listen."

"Oh fiddlesticks. Of course I would have. But the Ravens, they are a very wealthy family. They run in different circles from Tuck and his family."

"Mom, I know very well who lives here but I think there are a lot better reasons to like the area than to hob-knob with Great Camp owners."

"Don't be so proud," admonishes her mother. "Anyway," she continues, undeterred, "I stopped at the local photo shop to see if I could find an aerial picture of the town. I want to show our friends back home just where we are buying but the shop was closed with a note taped to the door saying 'Be back soon.' I stopped back twice but it never did open – not soon, not later. What a way to run a business. I wanted to buy a photo. Not very smart of the shop owner. He could have made a good sale."

"That happens a lot around here. When you see a note on the door, check the weather. If it's warm and sunny, the owner is most likely out hiking or paddling. Their priorities differ a bit from the usual. I'm beginning to think they've got them right. You ought to see what happens when deer season comes around. A lot of employees up and disappear. Don't come back till they've bagged a buck. It's the custom of the country."

"Well, I never. But if that's the way they choose to live, that's their problem. No wonder they're all so poor."

"Since moving to Meltmor, I've begun to see things differently. I used to think big profit was the only goal but a lot of people up here – I think they're on to something different. They find joy in the place they live and the things they do more than the stuff they own. Closing work to go explore the outdoors keeps balance in their lives. Not such a bad idea. By the way, that makes me think of something else. While you're vacationing here, expect to run into Pitt, a crazy man with an unusual looking white-footed rat. He strolls around town during the day. Town folks often cross the street to avoid him. However, there's a strong suspicion that his, or it could be Rat's words, should be carefully heeded. In fact, it was something they said that got me thinking the way I do: 'Efficiency, deficiency. Joy is the ploy.'"

"Well, dear. You always seem to have a better answer. I'm used to it. Your father is the same way."

"Sorry Mom, I don't mean to be like that." *Now why couldn't I just keep quiet? Here I'm doing the same thing she does: not listening. They say 'like mother, like daughter.' I'd best watch myself.* Her mother continues talking, "I also notice several art galleries in the area. I'll have to check them out but I imagine it's only locals exhibiting so I'm not getting my hopes up." *And I'm not going to tell you that many of these local artists exhibit nationally and have considerable reputations. No, I'm not going there anymore, I'll simply listen,* Britt comments silently. *You'll have more fun finding out for yourself.*

"All I really want to say is welcome to the town," Britt tells her mother, "I'm so happy you want to buy a vacation house here. Tibby will have another grandma close by. She'll love that."

After visiting for an hour, Britt's mother gets up and leaves. No sooner is she off down the road then Blanche drives up, an ever present canoe riding on the roof of her car. "Who was that I just passed?"

"Believe it or not, that was my mother. She and my father have decided to buy a vacation home here."

"Wow. Did you know they were planning that?"

"Not a bit. Life is sure full of surprises. Looking at your canoe makes me think about all the paddling we do and how it sort of mimics the course of our lives. We float along like boats on a river. Sometimes it carries us crashing through rapids; sometimes it drops us into quiet lakes. Just when we think calm lies ahead, we go around a bend and new ventures open up. Guess I just rounded a bend. It's quite a ride."

"Hey. That's nice. Can I use that in a song sometime?"

"Sure."

"Problem is, I can't find time to write anymore music what with volunteering in town, cooking for the Hunt Club and taking care of the family, I don't seem to have a second left for myself."

"Guess you'll have to give something up."

"But I can't. I have to work and I love being there for my family. If I stop volunteering, people will think I'm selfish."

"Something has to give. I guess it depends how much you want to do something different. Me? I think you'd be selfish not to give music more time. A lot of people enjoy the songs you compose. That could be your contribution instead of volunteering."

"Goodness. I like it. How'd you come up with that?"

"Probably because I've been struggling with the same thing. I want to open a shop in Meltmor, in fact I am. But, it means less time for volunteering and less time spent with my sister at our city store. She's not happy about it though she's willing to help me do it. I've struggled with the conflict. Am I deserting her? Am I being selfish? In a way yes but in another way no. I think women up here need more choice in clothing. Our high-end customers at A Thread Ahead already have theirs." Britt suddenly flashes back to Tuck's comment about more affluent women throwing out perfectly good clothing in order to go after the latest fashions. "If I want to do something useful, then I've got to accept that other people, like my family, think me irrational. I can't worry about that. Maybe doing something irrational means we are more rational than those who are scared of public opinion. 'To be or not to be?' as a famous man once said."

"Wow. I love it. Let's Be!" exclaims Blanche, catching the mood. They both do a little jig around the spool-table. Clinking coffee cups together, they sing out "A toast. A toast. Here's to life on the river!"

Chapter 42

Addison arrives for a weekend at Tuck and Britt's cabin. Tibetta squeals with excitement when he picks her up, whirls her around, then plops her onto the slumping sofa. "Uh-oh, I forgot to bring a present for you," Uncle Addison announces.

"You didn't forget! You didn't! You're fooling." and Tibetta, her nest of curly blonde hair flying, begins jumping up and down and demanding "Empty your pockets, all your pockets." He makes a great production of going through his coat, his jacket and his pants pockets before finally pulling out a small bag. "Oh. Surprise, surprise. Look what I found." As soon as he hands it to her, she unties the top to pull out a tiny furry 'something' inside with a long nose and tail.

"What is it? He's got such a funny face and he's sort of covered with a shell. He's so cute," she says, clasping him in both her small hands, "Oh, Uncle Addie, I love him but I don't know what he is."

"That my pretty, is an armadillo. Normally he lives down south in Texas but he wanted to find out what life is like in the North. I told him, 'I know a little girl who will give you a good home.' He's probably the first armadillo to ever visit in the Adirondacks. Don't let your kitty get a hold of him."

"Look, he's got letters on his back. AB. What does that mean?"

"AB? AB? well," Addison says as he stalls for time, "AB is his name. AyeBee. Good name, don't you think?"

"AyeBee. Yes I like that. Hi AyeBee. You'll like living here. I'm going to take you to my room to meet my other animals."

"Hey, before you go, tell me how school is going."

"I like school mostly except when the teacher gets mad at me."

"Why would she ever be mad at you, angel girl?"

"Well, sometimes it gets boring so I try to make the other kids laugh. Once I put a rubber snake in one of the teacher's boots outside the classroom door. Boy did she jump when she went to pull them on. Everyone laughed so hard. It was really fun but I had to stay in for recess."

"You've clearly been around your dad's friends too much. Sounds like something they would do."

"Got that right," says Britt. "The humor here gets rough at times." After Tibetta leaves, Britt asks, "So what does AB actually stand for?"

"Do you really want to know? Not sure I should tell you. You might not understand."

"Oh give me a break. Is it the name of your Texas lover, Sweetheart?"

"If you must know, he's a mascot. I bought him at the Armadillo Bar near Washington Square. That's where I go to seek spiritual comfort when I'm feeling low. It's a kind of sacred refuge. I make a point of tithing there every week. Keeps the management happy – and me too." Tuck breaks into a grin which quickly disappears when he catches Britt scowling at him from across the room.

Forgetting her vow to be less critical, Britt says, "So why bother coming up here to escape your troubles if you can do the same thing by sloshing around at the bar?"

"Guess I miss seeing my niece – and you all of course. By the way, is Byron here yet? He wants to look over the new pavilion blueprints."

"He's here," says Tuck.

"I'll step up and see him then. Don't wait with supper, not sure when I'll be back."

After Addison leaves, Britt says, "Why does your brother have to get drunk all the time? Seems like a smart guy, what's his problem? And why is he always off to see Byron as soon as gets here?"

"Don't know," replies Tuck, suddenly seeing his brother in a whole new light. "Listen, don't be too hard on him, he's suffered enough already. He tells me Dr. Kammer has released the records to a judge who has gone over everything and blacked out information not relevant to the case. The edited records have now been given to the investigator who is trying to make some sense of it all. We should be hearing something soon."

"I'm sorry. There I go again, judging. It's so hard to shake old habits. I forget what an awful time he's had but his drinking thing sure scares me. I'm afraid he'll drag you into it."

"You don't have to worry about that. I may drink a beer or two but I won't go overboard. I've got my sights set on something new; can't afford to lose time on a hangover. I'm excited about it but right now my plans are still a bit shadowy. I've got to work them out a little more before telling you the details. As soon as I'm ready, you'll be the first to know."

"Hey, that's not fair. Can't you give me a hint?"

"Just trying to put a little suspense in your life. You've often complained this is such a sleepy place."

"Yes I have, but you know what? I was the one who was sleepy. I'm beginning to see we can have a good life here. After our house fire, I was amazed at how kind people were to us, except for the tire slasher. But, of course, a good life here depends on whether *you* find something that turns you on, the way racing used to."

"I think it's happening, just need a little more time."

"Now I'm really curious. I can't stand secrets."

"Sure you can. I bet you have plenty of your own. You going to share yours with me when I finally tell you what's going on?"

"Maybe – though some secrets are best left to lie. Do we really want to know everything about each other?"

"I don't know. Should I know more about you?"

"Just this. If you're not going to excite me with your plans, then you better excite me some other way, like on the quilted playground in the back room."

"Why Ms. Freier, I'm shocked. A nice girl like you enjoys that kind of stuff?"

"You bet, lover, anytime."

On a Friday night, several weeks later, Addison arrives at Tuck and Britt's place unannounced. *At a time like this,* he thinks, *phone and email don't do it.* After a hearty welcome, a mug of joe in hand, Addison opens up. "First of all, the toxicology report is back. Bubbles was drugged at the time she died. Second, the Investigator's report is back. He's told me all he can but it seems to be mostly speculative. According to Dr. Kammer's notes, Bubbles told him there was one more thing she had to do in order to free herself from the past. She wouldn't say exactly what it was, only that once done, she planned to kick drugs forever, and go back to me, be a good wife, even a mother someday. That's it."

"Jesus. What an awful thing for you to hear," says Tuck.

"Yeah, it is – but in spite of what she wanted, it wouldn't have worked. I cared about her but I'd had enough. She'd tried to kick the habit too many times before, each time supposedly 'forever.' I no longer believed her. She was seriously addicted."

"So how do they explain her ending up in the lake?" asks Britt.

"Investigator Stalk isn't sure. He can only speculate. She was a user. Buzz Takher was a dealer. She probably owed Buzz money. From what she told Dr. Kammer, it sounds like she was already planning to rob the Powers long before she was admitted to the clinic. She could have taken my old hat and coat with her when she signed in. To tell the truth, I have so many clothes I wouldn't have missed those things for quite a while. She knew I still had the camp key and security code from when I worked there. Stalk thinks Buzz wore the coat and hat to look like me, picked her up at the clinic and drove her up here so she could steal from the Power's camp and use that to repay him. Paying him off may have been that last something she told Dr. Kammer she had to do before going straight. It's all guess work but it does sort of make sense."

After a short silence, Tuck asks, "How do you think she ended up drowning?"

"I don't think Buzz drowned her because he would have grabbed the stolen goods first. I don't know. I mean, why would she have been on the ice when she could have walked out on the driveway? It's sad how some people die without leaving any clue behind, just quietly disappear, their stories left untold –"

"Or they leave a trail but we can't find it," adds Britt. Tuck mulls all this over but some things are best left unsaid. *It's beginning to make sense. When Bubbles didn't return to Buzz with the promised loot, he put the screws on me.*

"Do you think she knew what was in the box?" Tuck asks aloud. "And if so, how? Did she have a connection to someone in that household?"

"I don't know. I don't understand." says Addison, setting down his mug and dropping his head into his hands. "This whole thing is like some terrible dream. One minute it's tucked safely away, the next, it comes stalking along – a long, dark shadow trailing me." Tuck stands up, walks to the window, gazes out into the night, sees only darkness behind his reflection.

Turning around, he stares at Addison and says, "We expect to understand everything eventually – but perhaps there are things out there we're not meant to know. I guess we have to accept them for what they are and shift focus to something else."

After Addison bunks down on the lumpy sofa, Tuck and Britt retire to bed where they continue to talk, but in whispers. "Don't you think it odd that he claims to care about her but would never have taken her back once she had gone straight? It almost sounds like he's making up excuses."

"No, I don't think it odd. I'm starting to see my brother in a new light. He is extremely sensitive and very troubled."

"Like you?"

"Like I was. I'm beginning to find direction. I'm not sure he's found his yet but I think he's on his way."

"Funny thing to say about a brother who is a successful and wealthy architect."

"You're right, I sound arrogant. That's not what I mean. My brother's happiness matters a lot to me. I'm not sure he has ever enjoyed a whole lot of it despite his seeming success. I only hope he finds it now, whatever form it takes."

The next morning Addison is up and out of the cabin early. He leaves a note on the table: "Gone for a walk, back later." Rising early, Tuck picks up the note, reads it, then puts it down and tiptoes out of the cabin to go to his workshop where he puts in a couple of hours of writing before breakfast. The fiction is going well. So are other things. Smiling to himself, he thinks, *I hope my brother is finally finding his way as well.*

Summer

Shimmering warm air, engulfed in five minute deluges, then moments later, bursting forth in steamy sunlight reflected off clouds of stinging bugs and wet roads. Bright rays bounce up from a gentle stream; wavelets of light slide up the trees; Cardinal flowers hide their brilliance in shady nooks; a mink undulates over the rocky shore; there runs a creek, it cools our feet and helps the dogs escape the heat. Gold and red flowers spread their gay coverlets over green fields; bits of color break off to flutter into the blue: butterfly wings tossed by a gentle breeze; a garter snake, all yellow and black, wiggling through the grass. High overhead, royalty surveys a lake-dotted kingdom: eagle eye scanning for a meal, white head and tail leaving no doubt as to his title. Swallows, like flying arrows, skim low over the water scooping up dark gnats. Rusty deer shyly dip their heads for a drink. Lavender evenings filled with sounds of a veery's trills, the hum of mosquitoes, the quiet of stars.

Chapter 43

"You did what? Why? Why didn't you tell us, let us help you? I can't believe this," bursts out Tuck who has stopped in to check on his parents.

"We didn't need help. That's why we didn't tell you. We're just ready for smaller quarters; that's why we sold the house. Just because I'm ready to retire and shut the store, doesn't mean we're broke you know. We wanted something a little more manageable," answers Justus. *I fear he does protest too much,* reflects Tuck.

"Why not sell to the SuperPig?"

"Over my dead body. My clothes are too good for the likes of them. I'm selling the inventory to a downstate discount store."

"When's the house closing?" asks Tuck.

"A month from now."

"Have you found a new place yet?"

"No, but we're working on it."

"Actually we did find a lovely apartment in the senior housing building but your father refuses to take it because of the address," contributes Fawn.

"Uh-oh. What does that have to do with it?" asks Tuck.

"Now Fawn, we don't need to divulge everything; no need to bring that up."

"But she did. So now I want to know. What's the matter with the address?"

"This is the matter if you must know. The building is on its own road and it's named Memory Lane. I'm not that old. I refuse to be relegated to the geriatric set that lives for memories and nothing else." *Jesus,* thinks Tuck, *so much for aging gracefully.*

Trying to suppress a smile, Tuck makes a suggestion. "If you like the place, why not use a box at the post office for your mail. That way, nobody will ever know. I didn't even realize that was the name of that road. Most people just call it the Sears Building after the founder."

"Oh that's a wonderful idea." says Fawn with enthusiasm. "Let's do that. After all, it's a nicer place to live than anything else we've found."

"I'll give it some thought," comments Justus with a finality that stops any further discussion of the matter.

"I hear the Taglongs are buying a vacation house up here. They found a place yet?" asks Fawn.

"In the new development. Talk about names. Every street there is named after something that's been destroyed: Fox Run, Hepatica Road, Pine Lane, Orchard Street, Rock Ledge. That was blasted to pieces two years ago. It's like driving past tombstones, a virtual goddamned cemetery."

"Watch your language son. You know we don't tolerate that kind of talk around here. But, I see your point. It's sort of sad."

"When do the Taglongs plan to come up?"

"They've been here already. Eileen went out for a walk in the development. Complained nobody talked to her. Probably because she wears her stylish hat pulled so low over her eyes she can't see anyone above their knees. Bit of a problem when you're trying to meet folks. She did look sophisticated, maybe that's all she wants anyway."

Heading home after visiting his parents, Tuck thinks about their keeping secret how impoverished they've become. *What a shame; selling the family home just because my dad wouldn't admit to money problems. We would have found a way to help. Pride has a dark side. Some secrets should not be. I guess it's time I be more honest with Britt as well, tell her about the book. At last, I can publish under my real name. Now that Buzz is dead, I'm a free man.*

After supper that night, after Tibetta is settled in bed, after he relays to both Britt and Addison the astounding news that their parents are selling the family home, after all that, Tuck is ready to surprise Britt with his long held secret project: writing. Addison has gone for a night walk, leaving his brother and Britt a bit of privacy.

"Ready for a big piece of news? Remember when I told you I had found something which turned me on, besides you that is?"

"How could I forget? I've been curious ever since."

"Well, this is it. Byron and I are coauthoring a book: *Victory on the Head of a Pin.* It's due to be published soon."

"What? What are you saying? Well knock me over with a feather."

"No idea I was doing that?"

"Absolutely none; didn't know that kind of thing even interested you." And then the questions come pouring out. "How did you get into that? Since when have you been writing? How did you work with Byron without my knowing? Why didn't you tell me? Where did the idea come from?"

They talk for hours until Tuck says, "You know, you said you'd tell me your secret when I told you mine. It's time."

"I said maybe, if you remember."

"True, but secrets aren't good, at least most aren't. Don't keep me guessing."

"Oh Sweetie. My secret isn't so nice. We're so happy right now. I don't want to spoil everything."

"As long as you stay with Tibby and me, I can stand anything. Now though, you've got me worried. What's it about?"

She gets up, walks over to the stove, turns around to face him and says, "Okay, here goes, but you won't like it. First I need to go back to when my godson, Davie, was ill with cancer. I've already told you part of the story, how I sat by his bedside every week and watched him die, inch by inch, over two years. It was excruciating. Never again I told myself, will I let myself get that close to a child. His loss was intolerable. But now, in spite of my intentions, I'm in love with another: Tibby. She is like a daughter to me. The problem is – we'll never have children together. I had an operation, a tubal ligation, after my Davie died. I couldn't face risking such a loss again."

It knocks the wind out of Tuck. He says nothing. Britt watches his face. After a moment he gets up, walks over to where she stands, arms dangling by her sides, and clasps her in a mechanical hug. All is silent. She's right, he's devastated. *Why did she keep this from me? How could she do such a thing? We've come this far, gone through so much – now, the most special thing we could have done together – if only she knew – Tibby is not my – I will never have….* They remain standing. Tuck stares over her head into the beyond. It's at least five minutes before he can speak without betraying emotion. "We've come through a lot together. This is sad indeed but it's not a reason to give up on what we have. In fact, isn't it possible to reverse that operation?"

"Possibly but it's not a sure thing and we could never afford the cost. Thankfully we do have Tibby."

"You were torn up by your godson's death or you'd never have done that."

"I know but I should have told you before. Every time you talked about having our own child, I wanted to cry. I wish we could too. I've waited too long to confess – afraid to lose you –"

"It's better out. Hon, I would have married you anyway. You need to know that." Tuck closes his eyes, his shoulders sag. He sways ever so slightly, fatigue washing over him. He vaguely recalls Pitt's raspy voice proclaiming: "Which lies to reveal, which to conceal. To squeal or not to squeal, no one escapes the deal."

The next day at Tuck's parents' house, more truths are surfacing. Having finally decided to lease the apartment in the Sears Building, Justus and Fawn are busy packing their possessions. The sooner this sorrowful move is behind them, the better. Fawn considers. *While Justus is distracted by packing, I'll tell him what I'm thinking about doing. Maybe he won't pay it so much attention.* Justus is taking pictures down from the wall, and Fawn is boxing up trinkets when she eases into the subject in a chatty sort of way. "Did you know Britt is opening her store soon? It looks nice inside. She's planning to design clothes especially for North Country women. She's going to sew them right there."

"Right. She'll never make a go of it in this town."

"But she has some good ideas."

"Takes more than that – takes business savvy. I know of what I speak, having operated a successful store for many years. But, what the heck, let her have fun while it lasts." Suddenly Fawn sees a way to bring up the touchy subject she really wants to discuss. *I'll present it as something I want to do for fun, not because we so desperately need the money.*

"It does sound like fun. Britt asked if I would like to help her. Just for fun. I thought I might try. It'll get me out with other people and maybe I'll get to know Britt a little better. Probably won't be for long, anyway, as you said."

"You want to go out and work? You don't have a clue what that means. It's not the kind of thing my wife should be doing. How do you think that will make us look? Ridiculous!"

"I wouldn't do it because I have to but because it would be an amusing pastime. I'm getting a little tired of going to Esprit's all the time."

"Well, that's one good thing anyway. What does Britt want you to do there? I can't imagine how you could help, never having worked before."

"Sewing. She wants me to help make the dresses. I used to do a lot of that when the boys were little. Remember I made their pajamas, shirts and pants? I enjoyed doing it. Once they got bigger, though, they wanted store-bought. I've missed it."

Justus does some thinking. *Maybe people will see this as Fawn just helping out her daughter-in-law. Looking at it that way it might not be such a bad idea. And if Fawn is out of the house part of the day, I'll have more time to sneak out to the woods and study wildflowers.*

And so begins Fawn's new part-time job as a seamstress. She and her daughter-in-law work long hours together. Britt applies herself not only to the business but to learning to be a better listener with a more open mind. It pays off. She's growing fonder of Fawn as the two discover they can work together.

Britt's new store, Peak Colors, begins attracting customers. One day while Britt is standing in the front room by the cash register, the door open to welcome summer inside, Pitt and Rat trail by and glance in her direction. "It's over the moon with the dove and the loon," are the words that drift back to her as they pass. *Not sure what that means but it sounds magically right to me.* A smile lights her face. If it stays this busy, I may cut back on my city work and focus more energy here in Meltmor. Just then, Pitt and Rat return, heading back the other way, words, like shadows, trailing their steps: "Boom, boom, ready the broom, keep up your guard, never presume."

Chapter 44

"How are your parents liking it here?" asks Tuck of Britt.

"They're pretty happy. Especially can't stop talking about their invitation to a dinner party at the Ravens. They were thrilled to be introduced to several wealthy camp owners. They've described the Raven's Nest to me at least twenty times already with comments like: 'Bet you didn't know the shortest way to their camp is via the lake?' or 'The Ravens sent a special boat to pick up their guests at the club dock.' Then my mother informs me, as if I didn't already know, 'They have a valuable collection of rare paintings which they showed us.' And she can't get over the fact that the steaks and flowers for that evening were flown up from the city by private plane. Mother was particularly impressed with the centerpiece. This is exactly what she said to me, 'Imagine a table so big that they used a tandem bike for the centerpiece. The Ravens are tandem people you know.' She can't stop talking about them."

"Now be generous, Britt. If you've never before heard of these Great Camps, their size and luxury can come as a bit of a shock. It's no wonder she can't get off the subject."

"Guess you're right. Only their assumption that I know absolutely nothing about where we live really bothers me. They've never heard a word I've said to them about this place."

"Sure, that's irritating but let them enjoy their moment in the sun. The Ravens are an unusual family. They pay little attention to class distinctions, but not all of their friends are like that. The Raven's Nest may be one of the few Great Camps your parents will ever be invited to. Don't be too hard on them."

"You think so?"

"Yeah, I think so. It will be a real letdown. Got to feel a little bad for them."

"If that's the case, guess I should be a little kinder."

The next morning, Britt is at her shop when Sue Tower comes in. "Got my first mushroom-dyed scarves ready. Want to see them?"

"Of course, lay them out here. Fawn," she calls to the back room, "Come see what Sue brought."

"Don't get your hopes up; I've never done this kind of thing before. Not sure if it's what you're looking for." She spreads four silk scarves down the length of the counter.

Britt examines them closely. Finally she looks up, smiling, and says, "Sue, how exciting. You're a natural. This one especially," she exclaims, pointing to a golden toned scarf filled with the wandering lines of vines and leaves, "It has such flow, such vibrant tones, like walking through the woods at sunrise. The others are good but this one will go over big at A Thread Ahead."

"Really?"

"Really. Can you produce more like this one?"

I'll work on it. Takes a bit of practice to get the hang of it."

"But you're on the right track. If you can make five more like this, I'll take them to the city. Our Boutique will buy them outright. Think we can get $200 apiece. The Boutique gets 50%, you get 50%. Does that work for you?"

"You're kidding. Two hundred dollars?"

That's right. You've got something rare here – mushroom dyed, beautifully designed, rich in color. And, we have the customers. But remember, you get one hundred out of it, not two hundred."

"A hundred dollars! Wow. Wait till Stu hears this."

"The others aren't bad either, but don't have quite the same elegant flow. We can keep these here on consignment. I would have to charge a lot less for them. Meltmor customers don't have much money for scarves like these,"

"Works for me. Nice to sell some here as well. How much do you think you could get for them?"

"I don't want to hurt your feelings but while our boutique customers are wealthy and used to an upscale market, most of our rural customers are not. How about thirty dollars apiece, you get 60%?"

"That would be great. I am so excited you like my work."

"It's not so surprising. I think we have a lot in common, including our taste in design. I had a feeling you would do something good."

"It's funny. If you hadn't convinced me I could do this, I'm not sure I ever would've tried. But, tell me, how is business going? Getting many sales?"

"Yes, it's happening – slowly. Lots of people checking us out but not so many from around the lakes."

"That's not surprising. They do all their shopping in the city where they're sure of trendy fashion. Had much newspaper publicity?"

"A photo and line or two covering the opening."

"That's unfair. I hear Mayor Sly is hugely enthusiastic about the SuperBig – brushing off complaints about its trashed parking lot, illegal dumping, nonpayment of taxes, exploited employees and such. Instead of focusing on the problems, he's promoting favorable press. Rumor has it he's getting some kind of payoff."

"I believe it, hear he's dirtier than a junkyard dog but no one on the town board will speak up against him. Typical." snaps Britt.

"What do you mean? Typical of what?"

"Typical of folks who don't take their jobs seriously. Board members are supposed to question things. All too often, they cave to the herd and just follow along. It's easier that way."

"Guess that's why you'll never see our husbands selected for boards," says Sue. "They're wildly free thinkers – don't worry about approval except from the owners. Caretaking's a perfect fit for the two of them."

Fawn speaks up, hesitantly. "That's what they like about it? Funny, I never really could figure why anyone wanted that kind of work. But, when you put it that way, it sort of makes sense." She thinks of Big Moe, as she has so often has in the last several weeks. *Maybe that's what I see in him, that he's not worried about others' opinions, just does his own thing.*

When Fawn arrives home that evening she decides it's time to tell Justus about her cleaning job. *Like Moe says, a life lived as illusion, is no life at all.* They are sitting down to supper when she brings up the subject. "I've got something to tell you. All those times you thought I was going to Esprit's séances? I wasn't."

Justus stiffens, his face tightens, his brows shoot up. "And –?"

"I was working: cleaning."

"Cleaning! Why?"

"I wanted to help with our budget. The store was going badly and I needed more food money to make ends meet. I didn't tell you because I didn't want to hurt you. Nobody, well almost, nobody else knew."

"Interesting. So why are you telling me now?"

"Because – because I'm tired of living a lie. I'm too old for that." *At least some things I won't lie about anymore.*

"Well Fawn, this is a shocker." Fawn lowers her head, focuses on the hamburger she pretends to enjoy. He stares at her for a long time, as if he has just discovered she lives in the same house. Finally, he speaks up, "I'll be gosh darned. I'm sort of impressed, didn't know you had it in you. And to think, all that time I thought you were sniveling off to Esprit, the great deceiver who forces her girls to buy outfits from her own catalog store, the control freak who rules over her followers in the disguise of a loving leader. She's sure got them all hoodwinked. Glad you're finally seeing the light." Still Fawn says nothing. *I should defend Esprit. Sometimes her predictions are right but Justus is right. I'm not the follower I used to be.* "I'm impressed alright," he goes on to say, "And you're right about something else. We're too old to go on deceiving each other. Are you still cleaning?"

"Yes. I go once a week to Dr. Sterling Sears's Camp. Don't want to give that up either." *Nor give up Moe. God forbid.*

"Okay Fawn." She waits for the explosion, but none comes. "Fair enough. I appreciate your telling me," he responds.

"Here's another thing." Justus tenses again, not used to Fawn speaking up like this. "I'm worried about you. What are you going to do all day, now that the store is closed and we no longer have a house to work on?"

"Don't worry about that. In fact, as long as we're playing at true confessions, I have one too, but you better not laugh." Now it's Fawn's turn to worry. "I've taken an interest in the study of Adirondack wildflowers. While you've been working at Peak Colors, I've been out exploring the woods and fields."

"But that's great. What's wrong with that? Big Moe does it all the time." *Oops.*

"I'm hardly Big Moe," he says with resentment. *Know that well,* she thinks to herself. "But he's the one who got me interested when I went along on that nature walk with Tibby's class. Sort of a silly hobby but I became intrigued by the variety of plants that grow up here."

"I don't think it's silly at all! I'm glad you've taken an interest in those things. We should all know more about the place where we live. Maybe you'll take me along one day and teach me something about it."

For the first time in years, Fawn feels close to Justus, feels a surge of love for this vulnerable man. Does he feel it too? He does. Their new found honesty begins to repair the broken bridge.

"I don't know if this would interest you," offers Fawn, "but I heard that the Bartons are looking for someone to get their wildflower gardens back in order. They're selling, you know. They want the place in tip-top shape."

"Listen, Fawn, I don't need charity. We're doing fine financially since selling the house," he shoots back, falling into old attitudes.

"I know that." she answers, "I thought you might like to do it as a part of your hobby, just for the heck of it – not for the money."

"Well. That's different but what in the world will people think?"

"Who cares," says the new Fawn. "Isn't it time we stop worrying about that? Do what we like?"

Justus isn't sure. Regard of his neighbors has been a standard to live by for as long back as he can remember. But, a crack is starting to appear in his facade. *It might indeed be interesting but work as a common laborer? – can't do that. I'll talk to Tuck, see if he can find out more – know he'll be discreet.*

Tuck is astonished when his father tells him of his new interest. *What's happening to my parents? I thought I knew them so well but I've done to them exactly what they did to me: pigeonholed them, never expecting them to break out of their box.*

Tuck visits Stu and asks about the gardening job. The wildflowers have been neglected for some years, the Bartons having little interest in that kind of thing. The realtor, however, told them it would be in their interest to revive the gardens, the planting of native flowers being the new 'in' thing to do. They do need someone, part-time, to take the job. Until now, nobody has expressed an interest.

"What about hiring Justus as a consultant instead of a gardener? He would both advise and do the work?"

"Justus? The Justus that's your dad? He knows about flowers? I'll be damned."

"Yup. Apparently he's been studying them and learning quite a lot. I never knew either until recently."

"Sure, but why a consultant?"

"Because that position sounds better than gardener. It's the only way he'll accept the job."

"Okay – guess he's welcome to try. Nobody else has applied."

Tuck returns home, hoping the title will allow his father to accept work he would enjoy.

"Dad, how would you like to be a wildflower consultant for the Barton place, or whatever they call it now?"

"Consultant? That has possibilities. Maybe I should give that a shot."

That settled, Tuck returns home to lunch with Britt.

It happens that Mr. and Mrs. Power are visiting the camp together for a change, superficially reconciled after the announcement to build a new hospital wing in her name. Mrs. Power is out for a short walk on the wood's path near the main camp when she comes upon a terrifying sight. Turning around, she runs back to find Byron, much as she hates turning to him for anything at all. "Come quick, I need you right away." He follows her back down the path to the object of horror: a chainsaw resting on a stump, a can of fuel next to it.

215

"Look at that. What more evidence do you need? It's time for Tuck to go."

"Go? Go where? What's the matter?"

"Matter? That chainsaw. That murderous weapon. I've heard all about these things and how they're used to slaughter innocent people sleeping peacefully in their beds. And now Tuck has one."

"Good God woman. Have you never seen a logger at work? How do you think he cuts all our firewood every year? What did you think he was using to thin out the woods?"

"A regular saw like everyone else."

"Everyone else doesn't use regular saws, as you call them, today everyone else uses chainsaws."

"But they're so dangerous. Why one of these guys could come in the house some night and saw us all to death."

"Yes. Guess one of them could though I hardly think it would be the weapon of choice. Most people would be reluctant to lie quietly in their beds while a murderer sneaks up the stairs with a roaring chainsaw to cut off their heads."

"Byron, that's not funny. This isn't a laughing matter."

"You're right about that! A little commonsense would be in order here Pru. Get a hold of yourself. Chainsaws are as much a part of North Country life as cocktail shakers are a part of yours."

"Chainsaws – drowning – dark, shadowy woods – seems to be all life is about up here," sneers his wife.

"That's part of it, but there's a lot more than that," Byron responds. *Fortunately though, you know nothing about the rest.*

Chapter 45

Hospital bound, siren wailing, an ambulance flies along the road, pushing trucks and cars out of its way. In Meltmor, where everyone knows everyone else, any siren is a cause for alarm. Folks wonder who the freight-on-board may be and which colleague has been mowed down by fate's latest swipe. Those listening to police scanners, which many do, learn the news and pass it along. In no time at all it flows like water, flooding through the café and bar crowd, then down the street to post office patrons, gas station customers and grocery shoppers. "Ace Loneby fell off the roof at the Greene River Hunt Club."

"Ace? Can't believe he'd go and do a dumb thing like that. Slam maybe but not Ace." Ironically, however, it is indeed Ace who has fallen from the shed roof and slammed the ground so hard it shattered his hip. He is in for a long and painful recovery. Blanche must decide what to do. *I will stay on at the Club and keep earning while he is still at the hospital in rehab.* Visiting members generously offer to care for the baby while she prepares meals. Slam, a good, hardworking man when not drinking, does his best to make up for the absence of Ace. When, a few weeks later, Ace is able to leave the hospital and finish recuperating at their trailer in Meltmor, Blanche takes a leave of absence to stay home and care for him. At first he needs a walker, daily rides to rehab and help with meals. The Club's workers' compensation covers many expenses, but not all. Members take up a collection for the Lonebys and locals hold a spaghetti supper fundraiser with the usual suspects playing their foot-stomping bluegrass.

However, money disappears like water from a leaky bucket. It's the prognosis that worries them. Ace is so badly injured a return to caretaking, or to his winter job working in the ski shop, are out of the question. He will walk with a severe limp and the help of a cane for the rest of his life. Not easy for such a macho man to accept. What's to be done?

After a few more weeks, Ace achieves some degree of independence and Blanche returns to cooking at the Club, commuting back and forth each day. At first Ace stays in their trailer and cares for the baby. Eventually he is able to drive again. Laundry, cleaning, childcare and meal preparations make up his days. "Hell's bells, never thought the time would come that I'd be a goddamned housewife." he complains to his frequent visitors.

A new head caretaker is hired to replace Ace and take over their beloved cabin. A month later, friends bring trucks to the Hunt Club and help Blanche move out of the cabin that had been the summer home to the Lonebys for the last several years. The move goes smoothly, not so Blanche's emotional state.

Several months later, Tuck and Britt, unlike Ace and Blanche, see their lives take a turn for the better. They've saved enough for a small down payment. "Can't wait to move away from Camp Reedmor and have our own place again," declares Tuck. "Byron has been good to us but we need our privacy back."

Lengthy searches produce unaffordable real estate until, reluctantly, the realtor is convinced Tuck and Britt really don't have much money. Bobbi finally breaks down and takes them to a rundown cabin in foreclosure. The wreck of a place is surrounded by stately pines which Bobbi recommends cutting down to allow for more sunshine. *Not on your life*, thinks Tuck. The front yard is littered with rusted cars, old tires, empty gas cans and broken tools. This neglected property, located on the edge of town, is exactly the fixer-upper they can afford. Bobbi, a disappointed realtor rushes them through the closing. One person's luck is often another's lack thereof.

And so they buy the pile of tumbled down detritus, for it is little more than that. Britt has severe reservations. Her parents are appalled. But Tuck sees the potential, slows down on his writing and devotes nearly all his free hours to rebuilding the cabin. First he cleans up the property, hauling several loads of junk to the dump. The dump master shows him an old discarded wooden door with the iron knocker still attached. Appreciating its beauty, he had set it aside in the hopes that someone could use it. Tuck is the man. Perfect. Tuck brings it back to their new home. The previous tenant, lacking firewood, had chopped up the original front door, to burn in his woodstove. The newly acquired wooden door makes for a handsome entrance. It seems to deliver a message to passersby, "This is now a home, come knock on our door, be welcome."

"I read once that a front door should open to a grand view of the living room," Britt comments to Addison who is visiting Meltmor to see their new purchase. He doesn't exactly agree.

"That may work for an elegant city dwelling but up here, form follows function. As you know, extreme weather is the norm. You need to enter the mud room first: it's a place to shed coats and dirty shoes and a space to store all the jackets, vests, boots, gloves and hats that North Country living demands. Also, don't forget, the temperature often drops to -20^0 or -30^0 below freezing. You need transition space between your living area and the outdoors." Addison has a few other suggestions: large south facing windows for passive solar heat, a covered walkway from the woodshed to the house, a bedroom wing that can be closed off to save on heat and especially important, a screened porch to shelter against the myriad of summer bugs. Britt relents. By now a veteran of several Adirondack seasons, she adjusts her architectural dreams.

"I guess this won't be quite the stylish house I envisioned," she says.

When not "consulting" at the Bartons, Justus offers to help. It's a way of showing support for Tuck without openly admitting that some things this "wayward" son does are not all bad. More help comes Tuck's way when every week on Tuesday afternoons, he drives to the Greene River Hunt Club. There he picks up Slam, whom Tuck finds refreshingly lacking in pretense. Slam spends his one free day helping Tuck restore the house. Toward evening, this loyal assistant puts down his tools, walks into town, hangs out with the guys, drinks a bit, or more than a bit, then staggers along the abandoned railroad track out to Ace and Blanch Loneby's trailer. There he is welcome to spend the night. Ace drives him back to the club on Thursday mornings.

Rory Taglong, lacking manual skills, frequently comes to watch the work in progress. Tuck notices a canoe on top of his father-in-law's car. "Learning to paddle are you?" he asks.

"No, I don't want to get into that kind of thing but I do think carrying around a boat will bring more respect from the locals." *After looking down on us small town folks, he's sure changing his tune. That's crazy, putting his boat up there as a way to get respect from folks! Does he really think that will work?* laughs Tuck to himself.

Weeks go by. Slowly the cabin takes on new character. Small square window panes fill the gaping frames; weathered boards from a collapsed barn bring rustic charm to the interior. Britt's reservations start to crumble. She is delighted with the improvements. *What an amazing man, this partner of mine: caretaker, writer, house builder. What other surprises has he 'tucked' away? Sometimes I'm still not quite sure who it is I married.*

In addition to the house, the infrastructure also needs attention. The well water tests out as acceptable, the septic tank is an unknown. Before getting a certificate of occupancy, Tuck needs it dug up and inspected. One day, when visiting Ace, he mentions this. "That's it. Tuck, that's it. That's what I can do. I can't walk so good but I can still drive. I could get myself a small backhoe and pick up odd jobs for people – like digging up septic tanks. There's an old piece of equipment no longer used out at the Hunt Club – wonder if they'd let me have it to fix up?"

"If you can do that and get it ready in the next three months, I'll pay you to come out and find my septic tank."

For once, something happens exactly as he'd hoped. Club members, glad that Ace has a chance to get off disability, gift him the old, outdated backhoe. Ace's plan turns out even better than expected. No sooner does he acquire the equipment than he learns the local grave digger is retiring. Someone needs to take his place. "Hot damn. I'm not fussy. I'll dig graves, septic tanks, driveways; it's all the same to me. Things are looking up."

Pitt suddenly appears on the scene. Rat, no stranger to digging, sits on his shoulder; they speak in one voice, "Dig deep and things look up."

Six weeks later, the backhoe, bolted together, is in running order, sort of. It is loaded on to one of Tim's flatbeds and driven to Tuck and Britt's new place. "Shouldn't take long to locate the old septic tank; maybe it's even still good enough to meet regulations." Ace digs. The result is spectacular. Instead of the septic tank he unearths a 1955 Chevy hooked up to the sewer line. "Can you beat that? You got to admit someone was quite creative. Seems to have worked alright, for a while anyway. Shall we rebury it? Who will ever know?" says Ace trying to save Tuck money.

"I'm afraid I'll know. I'll call Hood to come take it away. It stinks so badly I hope they'll accept it at the junk yard. Whew."

Hood comes but finds little humor in the situation. Holding his nose, he complains bitterly of the odor. "Mebbe a rottin' dead bear smells worsen, but me doubts it." However, in an act of neighborliness, he removes the hulk without charge. "I do this for you this time, but once only. If you dig up anythin' else dead 'round here, don't be callin' me. Ma Jane'll have somethin' to say when she sniffs me acomin' down the street tonight."

Ace is not the only one to suffer a trauma that summer. One day when the phone rings, Britt answers to hear, "This is the emergency room at Meltmor Hospital." A quick review of where all her family members are flashes through her mind. But, before panic sets in, she hears, "Do you know a Pat Smith and her daughter Katy?"

"Yes, I do. What's happened?"

"There's been an accident, Pat Smith is hurt. She says she hates to ask but you're the only one she knows who could help. She wonders if you can pick Katy up at daycare and bring her to your house for the night. We'll call back later when we know the extent of Pat's injuries."

"Of course I'll do that. Wish her the best and tell her not to worry. Katy will be fine here for as long as she needs to stay. Our daughter will be delighted." She hangs up. *Our daughter? Did I just say that? I did.*

Katy's mother, working as a window washer, had taken a fall, plunging to the ground from the top of a ladder. She is less well known than Ace so her accident elicits less attention. "After all, she's but a welfare queen, duping the system by working to supplement her state check," is the general 'herd' opinion of those living in blissful denial of the role luck plays in their own good fortunes. Pitt and Rat also find the criticism glib, "No matter renown, luck up, luck down. Short ride, fast slide," they warn.

Britt calls her in-laws. "I'm coming in early today to pick Tibby up from your place and get her friend Katy from daycare." "Katy? Isn't that the daughter of that woman who got flooded out? How come Katy's going over to your house? Hoped she and Tibetta weren't getting too friendly."

Britt, once more irritated with Fawn's reaction, explains the situation, then drives to town, picks up the girls and brings them home. "I bet you'd both like a snack. Why don't you look in the fridge and see what you can find." A minute later, Katy lets out an

"Ick. Why are the eggs so dirty?"

"I don't know," says Tibetta, "They just come like that from the farm."

"Yuck. That's disgusting. My mommy's eggs don't come from a dirty old farm; they come from a store. Hey, where's your TV?"

"We don't have one."

"No TV. What we gonna do all day?"

"We could climb trees, explore the woods, draw pictures, stuff like that." Tibetta is amazed to discover that her friend has never been in a boat, never been on a hike, never skied and doesn't know how to swim. Folks live so close and yet so distant from their neighbors. A small town holds amazingly diverse cultures.

Britt foresees a lot of questions and explanations cropping up in the next few days. *It will be good for Tibby. Maybe she'll realize how lucky she is in spite of the fire, how privileged she is compared to some other kids – something I was oblivious to when I was a child – in fact didn't really take in until recently.*

Katy ends up staying for three weeks while her mother recovers from a broken leg, broken arm and internal injuries. Katy and Tibetta each love having a "sister" for the first time. They spend hours with their arms around each other, their heads together whispering little girl secrets and bursting out in frequent fits of giggles. Tibetta likes showing

Katy how to build a fort in the woods, catch frogs, make leaf boats to float down the nearby creek. She wonders why her friend has never done these things before.

"Depends what family you're born into," explains Tuck. "Would you know how to stay by yourself after school every day, how to keep busy until one of us came home, cook yourself a meal? I'll bet Katy does." Different folks know different things.

When the hospital finally releases Pat, her brother and his wife come from the city to pick up Katy and her mother and take them back to the Bronx. The little girls' giggles turn to tears when the moment of parting comes.

"You can phone each other and stay in touch. The city should be a fun new adventure for you, Katy," says Britt, trying to cheer them up. Katy is inconsolable.

After Katy leaves, the girls stay in touch by phone – for a while. Tibetta is distraught when Katy tells her about life in the city: how she has to share a room with her mother who lies awake nights in pain, trying not to disturb her daughter. "I can hear her crying," Katy tells Tibetta during one of their calls, "She thinks I don't but I do. Anyway I can't sleep none – our room's really, really hot. My uncle is always yelling at me and my mom tells me to make myself scarce, get outside and play but there's only this one playground here with a fence around it and no trees to climb and no grass and it's really, really hot out there and boring too. Anyway, I hate it 'cause the kids pull my pigtails and tease me and it's unpretty gray cement and I fell down and hurt my knees real bad and everyone called me a crybaby."

She's not the only one who cries. Tibetta hangs up in tears as well, asking, "Why does she have to live there, why can't she come back here? Why are people so mean?" Why indeed?

Chapter 46

Tuck is planning to take his family to an island for a camping trip. "Thanks for letting me have your old canoe and rigging. Addison and I used to love sailing this thing when we were kids. Be great fun to teach Tibby how to do it," he says to his father.

"I don't have room for the rigging and leeboards at our new place so I'd have thrown them out if you hadn't wanted them. Not many people interested in sailing canoes anymore," responds Justus.

"Glad you didn't," says Tuck as he continues filling the boat with gear, "Think you can paddle this canoe out to the island? I'd never fit all our camping stuff plus Britt and Tibby into my own boat. Maybe you'll stay for supper with us, let me paddle you back afterwards?"

"That sounds fine. I used to camp when I was young. It's been a long time since I've done anything like it."

An hour later they set out for a distant island on Cedar Bluff Lake. Justus paddles the Old Town canoe filled with camping gear and rigging. In the other canoe, Tuck paddles stern, Britt bow and Tibetta, nestled down in the middle, dips her own kid-sized paddle in the water now and then, confusing the paddling rhythm but delighting in "helping" propel the boat.

By five o'clock they have landed, unloaded, set up the tent and are cooking bean stew over the campfire. While the meal is heating, Justus wanders down to the shore. Sitting on a rock, relaxing, he slowly becomes attuned to his surroundings: shimmering orange reflections of the sunset, flattened mountain silhouettes, and a beautiful bird song, one that thrills him with its melody. He gets up and hurries back to the others.

"Come down to the shore. You've got to hear the bird singing there. It's quite astonishing." *My dad excited about a bird song? Wonders never cease.* Tuck, Britt and Tibetta trail him back to the water's edge. Across the lake wafts the lovely trilling of a hermit thrush, nightingale of the northern woods.

"I bet you never heard anything like that before." declares Justus. Tuck, reluctant to dampen his excitement, is nevertheless amazed that his father could have lived his whole life in the Adirondacks and never before paid attention to a hermit thrush's song.

"I've heard it before but, agree, nothing could be prettier."

Serenaded by the thrush as well as the haunting call of loons, the family eats its meal in silence while mist swirls over the darkening lake and a splinter of moon rises in the eastern sky. Britt tries to enjoy the scene but is constantly swatting at mosquitoes, squirming in agony from their bites. "Ready to give in and put an unfashionable bug net over your head?" asks her grinning husband.

"Okay. I give up. But, how come the rest of you aren't attacked?"

"I don't know. We seem to be immune. Maybe there's something bitter tasting in the Rising family blood. Here, slip this over your head. You don't look bad at all. In fact, maybe you can find a way to decorate these nets so they become more fashionable."

"Right. But once wrapped in netting, there's no way to sip my wine."

"Oh yes there is. Drink it right through the mesh, Adirondack style."

After supper, Tuck and Tibetta paddle grandpa back to the landing, returning over the lake through the thickening mist. It's hard to see much at all. "It's scary out here Daddy. I can't see anything. There might be monsters around."

"Monsters? We don't have monsters in our lakes, only friendly fish." Just then a loud slap near the canoe knocks Tibetta's pint-sized paddle out of her hands. She cringes but doesn't shriek, having just been informed there are no monsters in the lake. Tuck's chuckles reassure his daughter there's nothing to fear. "Now that was a beaver slapping his tail, warning his friends about us. He must have bumped into your paddle. Maybe the beastie was looking for a little wood to gnaw. Let's go back and see if there's anything left for us." It doesn't take them long to retrieve the paddle, undamaged, nor does it take long for Tibetta to join her dad in the giggles.

"A beaver?" she squeals, "Why's he doing that? We wouldn't ever hurt him, would we?"

"No, but he doesn't know that. Animals have to be on guard all the time. That was a warning signal to his friends and family." Just then a barred owl starts hooting from the shore. "Hear that? That's your friend calling. Isn't it fun to know he's out here with us?"

"I remember him. We heard him before when you took me out walking at night. Call back to him Daddy." And so Tuck does, the owl and Tuck hooting back and forth across the water, their voices mingling through the misty moonlight.

Next morning, the family is awakened by bright sunshine beaming into their tent. "There's a light breeze blowing today, good time to show you how to sail a canoe." Tuck secures leeboards to the canoe's gunwales, steps the mast into the hole through the bow seat, settles his family on the bottom of the boat, Tibetta in her lifejacket, and they set out. "Whoa, this is tippy." exclaims Britt nervously.

"I think it's lots of fun," says Tibetta. Her dad sits on the stern seat, steering the boat with his paddle. They sail around for a while, Tuck reminding his crew to lower their heads each time the sail crosses the canoe. Once Britt relaxes enough to ease her white-knuckle grip on the gunwales, he starts explaining the rudiments of sailing.

"If you want to go someplace upwind, you have to tack to get there. That means sailing back and forth across the wind, pointing slightly up into it each time. Zigzag enough times and eventually you'll reach your goal. It's not as direct, takes a little more time, but it's a more interesting challenge – like a lot of other things." The rest of the morning is spent teaching the family how to sail. Tuck lets Britt try first. It's tricky. To keep the canoe upright, she must lean far out over the rail opposite the sail but at the same time, be ready to bounce back to the middle if the shifting lake breeze suddenly lets up.

"Why in the world did you think I'd enjoy this? It's terrifying," Britt's laughs after the first tense lesson is over and Tuck has landed her safely back on land. Tibetta, however, at the tender age of six, shows a good deal of skill and finds it exhilarating. "This is fun Daddy, why doesn't everyone sail canoes?" she asks.

"Don't know. Maybe it's too much work. Most folks prefer the ease of running a motorboat."

The following day Tuck is up first with hot coffee at the ready when Britt, bleary eyed, crawls from the tent. Huddled inside her bulky sweater, she settles down on a log near the fire, wraps her hands around a hot steaming mug and murmurs, so as not to wake Tibetta, "Coffee never tasted so good."

"That's what I like about camping," Tuck quietly responds, "makes you appreciate the little things in life." Later with everyone up, fed and ready, Tuck's picnic stuffed in his backpack, the three of them embark on another venture. Following the shore line, they paddle up the calm, sunlit lake, passing several camps and boathouses along the way. It's like a tour through history with some camps dating back as early as the 1880s. They range from bark-wrapped Great Camps with multiple buildings to several more moderate in size and decor. All include boathouses and most display stunning rustic craftsmanship. To Tuck's delight, a few vacationing individuals are sitting outside reading books. More fascinating to Britt is a trim looking woman out on a dock with an instructor leading her through yoga stretches, faces turned up toward the rising sun. "I never realized this kind of thing goes on out here, not a bad lifestyle. I could go for that," comments Britt. They see other camp owners just sitting on their docks, enjoying the quiet and the view.

"Country people aren't the only ones who seek nature's peace. As Thoreau once said, 'In wilderness is the preservation of the world,'" says Tuck. They land the canoe at the far end of the lake and follow a path leading to a small mountain. Tuck, in the lead, has taken but a few steps when he suddenly stops and points out a dew-laden spider web stretched across the trail. "Look at that, I guess Mr. Spider didn't get much sleep last night. That is a big construction job for such a little guy. Let's duck down and stoop under so we don't destroy all his hard work." Thirty minutes later Tuck calls a halt so Tibetta's short legs can have a rest. "How many birds and animals have you seen so far?" he inquires of his family.

"None." says Tibetta. "Where are they all?"

"Oh they're out there alright. Let's sit here quietly and see what moves back in around us." Before long they hear leaves rustle and a robin is spotted searching for worms. This is followed by the chatter of a red squirrel. To their delight, along the path, stepping quietly, comes a doe followed by a fawn. *Doesn't get much better than this.* Tuck smiles with contentment. Once rested they continue their hike, slowly climbing to the top of Cedar Bluff Mountain where they stretch out on the rocks to view, with a sense of accomplishment, how far the lake looks from up there.

"What I really brought you up here to see," says Tuck as he points toward the high cliffs across the lake narrows, "are the peregrine falcons nesting over there. Watch a few minutes and you'll see them fly past going some 60 miles per hour.

"I've never heard of these birds," observes Britt. "They are incredible. What are they called again?" Tuck is pleased by her enthusiasm.

"Peregrine falcons. The name is said to mean wanderers. In the late sixties, these birds were extinct in the east. Now they are back thanks to the Endangered Species Act. Seeing them flying about like this makes me ever so slightly hopeful for the future of wild life."

Britt unpacks peanut butter and sliced orange sandwiches, passing them around while the family continues watching the falcons streak by. Tibetta is eating lunch when, looking down, she sees a slender beetle with long antennas. She moves her feet out of the way and calls Tuck to come see. "What's that Daddy?" she asks with excitement. Tuck reaches down and picks up the beetle which has a pebble, at least half its size, clasped in its legs.

"Wow! I'd say this is a paranoid pine borer – afraid someone will steel his property. Must be he's been hanging around people too long." He is happy that his child is learning to notice things small as well as large. After lunch, they hike back down the trail and paddle back to the island.

That night, weary from a long day, they gather around the campfire and listen to the night sounds. Tibetta fights sleep as she leans against her dad. Loons call, a few frogs croak and their friend the owl sends out his greeting. Suddenly in the distance they hear the howls of a pack of coyotes. "Yikes. How scary. I'm sure glad we're camping on an island." comments Britt.

"They wouldn't bother us even if we were on shore. Actually, I love hearing them."

The next morning, they pack up and leave. Tibetta has made stacks of drawings which are carefully stored inside a dry-bag along with their clothes. They are home by late afternoon. After putting everything away, Britt says to Tuck, "That Nordic Track machine that was given to me, I think I'd like to keep it at the store. Would you take it there tomorrow?"

"Sure. But, what brought that on? I thought you were big on exercise."

"I am. After our camping trip though, I've become acutely aware of the beauty of this area. I think I'd prefer to get my exercise outside where I can enjoy it. If the machine is at the store, other people, like your mother who is suddenly interested in getting in better shape, can use it."

That evening they get a call from Stu. "The Winston Historical Society wants to buy the Barton place but only if I agree to stay on. Works for us. The Cedar Bluff Lake Association has to give its approval before the sale can go through but it's looking good. The Society would lease or sell the cabins to members only. Even though it will increase the number of people using the place, it will still continue as an exclusive enclave – exactly what the lake folks like."

"Congratulations, sounds like your job has been secured."

"Yup. We're relieved."

A further surprise comes after Tuck hangs up and the phone immediately rings again. This time it's his brother who bursts out, "Guess who's buying the Barton place?"

"I already heard. How'd you know?"

"Because I've been trying to make this happen for some time. I'm a longstanding board member of the Winston Historical Society. I've felt for years that it should be more active about preserving Great Camps.

227

This is a first step. The Barton estate, soon to be renamed Barton Reserve, comes fully furnished, including eight antique guide boats. We'll be keeping it pretty much in its original condition. It's a real coup for us. Of course, to be honest, there's a bit of self interest at stake as well. I've been wanting to find a weekend getaway on Cedar Bluff Lake but I didn't want a large estate. This way, I can buy into the Barton Reserve and use one of the cabins without having to worry about maintenance." Tuck hangs up. *Interesting. Think this confirms what I had suspected about Addison. Time will tell. I almost hope I'm right. The guy's life has not been easy.*

Part III

Four Years Later

Chapter 47

"Tibby, baby," Tuck says as he sweeps his gangly-limbed weeping daughter into his lap, "tell me what happened." Between the sobs of a 10-year-old, the garbled story comes out.

Mrs. Power had invited Tibetta over to play with her children, only, "she doesn't let Winnie and Norm do anything – can't go in the woods or build forts – it's so boring – we have to sit on the porch and play games and we can only swim when she's watching – she doesn't even let us have water fights. I brought Red in his cage and we played with him for a while but then Winnie started complaining that she was jealous cause I got to go out in the canoe by myself so I told her I'd take them out only Norm said they weren't allowed and Winnie said she didn't care she was going anyway and Norm said he wouldn't and I left Red in the cage on the dock and Norm yelled names at us and said he was telling his mummy and Winnie and I paddled around for a while and we were wearing our lifejackets and we heard her mother screaming at her to come back 'cause it wasn't safe and when we got back she told Winnie to go change her blouse 'cause it was dirty and she told me I was a bad girl and to go home. I picked up my squirrel cage and looked inside and Red was dead – lying on his back with his head all twisted weird and Mrs. Power said it served me right – and Red is dead and he was my best friend and I don't have him anymore and I want him back." Tibetta breaks down again, burying her tear soaked face in Tuck's shirt.

Tuck's anger threatens to boil over. He knows Norm is an obedient but unhappy child whose jealousy no doubt, got the better of him. But it's Mrs. Power who, dangerously controlling, is the real culprit, clipping her children's wings, preventing them from making discoveries of their own. *She's a miserable woman,* thinks Tuck, *an angry Goddess who knows just how to zing the arrows. Why would anyone put up with a wife like that? At least when Byron brings the kids to Reedmor, he lets them explore to their heart's content. And what am I to do? I can't always protect Tibby from cruelty – come to think of it, guess I've also been cruel.* Remorse sets in as he remembers batting at squirrels in the Reedmor's pantry. *How much I'm learning from my child.* Tuck hugs Tibetta even tighter.

"It would be better not to visit Camp Reedmor anymore when Mrs. Power is there. When Byron comes alone with the kids, you can play with them all you want," he advises. It is the best he can do. Tibetta, wracked with sadness, begins to realize that her dad can't fix everything; he can't stop the hurt; he can't make things better. Tuck, holds her tight as his mind drifts. Byron is a good man but he can't protect his children anymore than I can protect Tibby. Byron's a generous guy, sharing credit with me for our book's success. I think he likes me but that doesn't mean my position here is safe. Royalties are meager, I need this job. If I talk back to Mrs. Power, for sure I'll be out on my ear. Around here, I'm a caretaker, not an author. I guess it's like they say, 'fame begins 50 miles from home.'

Not a week later Tibetta is invited to spend the night at the Ravens. "They're having a party to celebrate their 20th wedding anniversary. They want their children to have a few friends over as well. Do you think she should go?" asks Britt. "I can't bear to see her hurt again."

"The Ravens are good people. She'll be fine. In fact, she needs to go and find that out," says Tuck. Arrangements are made for Josh to pick Tibetta up and take her to the Raven's Nest. Josh stops first at the liquor store.

"Got my order ready for the Ravens?" he asks.

"Surely do. Four cases here, I'll help carry them out to the car. I added a bottle of Jack Daniels for you. Keep these orders coming my way and I'll keep adding something for you on the side." Josh doesn't argue, he could go for a little upper at the end of the day, sure Tripp wouldn't mind lowering the bottle level either. He then drives to the Risings and picks up Tibetta. "I've got to meet guests at the airport. You up for coming with me?" he asks her.

"Sure. I like planes."

They arrive at the airfield in the Raven's SUV. Josh's license is checked, a gate opens, and he drives directly onto the runway, bypassing security checks. A corporate jet wheels up to the small square box of a terminal; stairs are rolled out and two well attired couples descend the steps. Josh introduces himself as well as Tibetta. "She's going with us to visit the kids. What about your pilot? Is he staying?"

"No. He'll probably get coffee and head back to Philly." The pilot is busy unloading their luggage. Josh goes over and takes it from him, grabbing a Diane von Furstenberg bag in one hand and a Vera Wang in the other. He piles everyone into the vehicle and drives them to the launch site where the Raven's antique mahogany Chris-Craft is tied up and waiting. After stowing liquor cases and luggage in the cabin, he gives a steadying hand and helps the women aboard. The men display their manliness by making the transition on their own. Skidding on their slick leather shoes, they nearly topple overboard. Josh starts the motor and speeds up the lake. A white wake trails them, breaking the quiet reflection of purple evening clouds.

"Any problem with pollution in these waters?" asks one of the men as they motor along. Before Josh has a chance to answer, the man's wife intercedes.

"Now darling, let's not spoil the visit by discussing anything unpleasant." With which lame demand he obediently complies. Approaching the far shore Josh points out the Raven's dock.

"How simply divine." the women marvel. "Look at the filigree woodwork and decorative balconies on the house. I've heard about these homes. Just delightful. What a view. Love the way it's situated right on the shore. Marvy!"

"That's not their house, it's their boathouse," pipes up Tibetta. The women quickly backpedal.

"We know Honey, we weren't born yesterday."

The men, sitting towards the stern, exchange glances. One of them saus, in an aside, "Country pipsqueak better learn not to correct the queens, they don't easily forget."

And then comes the oft heard comment that even annoys the good natured Josh, "How lovely it is. I'm sure you don't half appreciate what a magnificent place you live in." *That's why I live here, dummy*, he mentally retorts while smiling graciously. Soon thereafter, Josh pulls out his phone and calls Bill Raven.

"In case you haven't seen us, we're almost to the dock." Bill, dressed in white pants and navy jacket with brass buttons, walks down the hill to welcome them. Before landing, Josh passes out the Raven's Nest rule books which explain exactly what is and what is not allowed while visiting.

Later that evening, guests from around the lake, dressed in gowns and tuxedos, arrive for cocktails and dinner. Josh is responsible for safely docking their handsome antique boats. Rory and Eileen Taglong, are invited. They rented a power boat and driver to deliver them to the party. Lila and Mark Raven, Norm and Winnie Power along with Tibetta and two other guest children, sneak appetizers from the tables and giggle at everyone. Odd snippets of chatter float at random through the air.

"Simply charming, my dear, just divoone – You know how every bride must have a silver pitcher, well that is what I wanted to give Julia but she already had one, inherited from her grandmother."

"You have no idea how inconvenienced I was – the chauffer delayed because his daughter got sick and had to be picked up at school. You'd think that wife of his could have done it for him but no – claims she couldn't leave her job. I've seen the pitiful little girl – looks sickly all the time. Wonder what they feed her?"

"This party is simply fab!"

"Darling, did you see Esther's new gown? Just flown in from Paris, a little tight on her, but I'm sure the seamstress can fix that later."

"We just got in from our fourth safari; it was dreamy, all those gorgeous big animals spread around the park – I'm not crazy about so many natives close to me but it was a true wilderness adventure – I especially loved having breakfast served outdoors every morning."

"The staff, you know, I guess we simply have to put up with what we can get. It's not like the old days when these people knew their place. By the way, how is your caretaker? Is he suitable?"

"My father always said: 'Never give up the servants.'"

"We're thinking of building a new wing. Addison Rising wants us to use sustainably certified wood. I was reluctant at first but hear now that it's all the rage."

The chatter carries over the lake and out to the loons who give up talking and escape under water. Mrs. Power is there receiving praise for the hospital wing, made possible thanks to Byron's generosity.

"Oh, I was so thrilled to do that. You know how I adore children; they are so darling, so delighted I can help the poor Meltmor residents, after all, they don't have much else to be proud of." Byron is noticeably absent. "Just a little under the weather this evening. He sent his apologies. He's dreadfully distraught about missing the party."

"This is boring, let's go exploring," exclaims Mark.

"Hey, you're a poet," laughs his sister as the children, having stashed their pockets full of appetizers, go whooping off into the woods. Tibetta loves visiting the Ravens. When she used to play at the Power's house and other "lake" children or city kids came to visit, Mrs. Power would send her home. Here she is included. But, Tibetta is a bit embarrassed that her father is a caretaker. She pretends otherwise.

"Where do you live?" asks one of the visiting children.

"We have a camp on another lake, Camp Faraway," she tells them, having picked up a knack for making private jokes. "It's far from here, you wouldn't know it." Becoming aware of the perils of class discrimination, she does her best to avoid being its target. Other families are not like the Ravens.

Meanwhile, Tuck and Britt are enjoying a quiet evening at home. After supper they watch a movie together before settling into talking ideas, dreams and observations. "I hurt for Tibby. God is that Mrs. Power a number. She knows bloody well that Norm killed Tibby's squirrel. He's going to be a mess if she doesn't watch it. Her poor kids;

not allowed to have any fun at all. When Addison and I were young – a little older than Tibby, fourteen or so – we used to go camping on the islands. We'd take the canoe and sneak around spying on some of the Great Camps. Addison was fascinated by the buildings, I was fascinated by the kind of life those people led: lying around on their docks, butlers in uniform bringing them lunch; the mail boat delivering letters; guests flying in by sea plane; special instructors to give the kids swimming and sailing lessons. We were awfully envious. Hope we've raised Tibby with enough sense that she doesn't feel the same way." Only of course, just like her dad, she does.

Chapter 48

At 10 that evening, Tuck and Britt are still up talking when the phone rings. "Uh-oh. That's not good. Might be an emergency." Tuck picks up.

"This is Mother. Your dad had a heart attack. You better come to the hospital right away. I called your brother but got no answer. Try to reach him if you can but get over here as quickly as possible."

"Oh no. When did that happen?"

"About two hours ago. I waited to call to find out how he's doing."

"How is he doing?"

"He's hooked up to all kinds of stuff but resting quietly. Seems comfortable at least." Remembering his brother planned to come up to the Barton place for the weekend, Tuck drives over to Addison's cabin and knocks. When the door opens, Tuck blurts out the news. "Dad's had a heart attack. Mother tried to call but couldn't reach you."

"Damn. How bad?" Tuck fills him in on the little he knows.

"I had the ringer turned down – forgot to turn it up again. Thanks for coming over."

"Come on. I'll give you a ride."

"Right – um, I think I'll take my own car, take me a few minutes, you go ahead."

"That's crazy. I'll wait, might as well ride together."

Addison falls silent, looks at his brother for a second, then looks down at his feet and shuffles a bit. Hearing a noise from the back hall, Tuck looks up to see Byron emerging from the bedroom. In a restrained voice, he addresses Addison.

"We might as well tell him, Addie."

"You don't have to. I've suspected for a long time. Truth to tell, it makes sense, sort of glad to know." says Tuck. This is followed by a long silence. Finally Addison explains that he gave Byron a ride over to his camp and needs to take him back before going to the hospital.

"I'll be right over after that," he assures his brother.

"Good. See you shortly then."

At the hospital, Fawn surprises Addison and Tuck with her self control. They stay late that night until Justus is settled into the ICU. The doctor is reassuring. "Good thing you brought him here when you did," he says to Fawn. "Think, with a little luck, he'll recover nicely. For now, he needs to rest. This is the best place to do it. The nurses can watch his monitor. They'll let me know if anything changes. Time you all go home and get some sleep."

The next day, Josh brings Tibetta back. Tuck is up at the hospital. Britt tells her about Grandpa, that he's doing better and that she can go see him in a couple of days. Tibetta, with the naiveté of youth, believes what she hears. She is not overly upset. Then Britt resorts to what all mothers do, makes comfort food for the two of them: tomato soup and grilled cheese sandwiches. They sit down to eat and Tibetta, reassured, happily babbles on about her visit to the Ravens. Later, Tuck calls.

"Things have taken a turn for the worse. I'm staying here for now. Don't say anything to Tibby. Could you and Tibby do me a favor though, and go out to the Powers later this afternoon – take down the bird feeders for the night? I don't think I'll be back in time and the last thing we need right now is bears showing up at Reedmor." *How can he be thinking of things like that at a time like this?* wonders Britt, *– or maybe that's exactly what we do need to do to keep our cool when the going gets rough.*

Chapter 49

A few days later, the latest news makes its way around town as well as into Britt's kitchen where she is having a second cup of coffee with her sister, Shelley, who is visiting again.

"It just shows there's no point worrying about the future. Here we were all upset about Justus when in fact he has been doing fine and instead it's Slam who dies."

"Who was Slam?" asks Shelley.

"The nicest guy you ever want to meet but he had a big problem: liquor. He did seasonal work for Ace at the Greene River Hunt Club. He'd lost his license for multiple DUIs. The remote location of the club made it difficult to find a ride to the bars in Meltmor. He was a good worker when sober, so good the new head caretaker at the club kept him on after Ace left. Slam even helped remodel our house. Tuck liked him a lot – told me Slam only complained of one thing: women. He could never connect with them. One date but never a second."

"So how did he die?"

"I'm told he was in town for a dental appointment. He always stayed at the Loneby's trailer if he needed a place to spend the night. Unfortunately, after the trip to the dentist, he made a second one – to the Town Trough. He was half in the bag by the time he left to walk the old railroad track leading to the trailer. Guess he didn't realize that a flood had taken out the bridge. He fell twenty feet and slammed his head on the rocks below."

"God, that's horrible," says Shelley, lifting her skinny arm and shaking her silver bracelets into place.

"Yeah. It was that damn liquor. Takes me back to my days with Jim. Remember him?"

"I do. Seemed like a good catch. I never did understand why you two broke up."

"Because – well – I never talked about it. I was ashamed, but, in hindsight, I realize it wasn't me, it was him. He was a boozer and every time he started drinking, he also started getting on my case. No matter how I tried to please him, there was always something else. Eventually he began hitting me. Somehow I found the strength to break up with him. I never told anyone this before but it's why I get so uptight about drinking. Unfortunately, there's a lot of it around here. On a Friday night you see guys toting so many six-packs you'd think their arms would be stretched below their knees."

"Does Tuck drink a lot?"

"He used to. He still drinks and it worries me all the time but he doesn't drink like before."

Only half listening, Shelley casts a critical glance around the dark paneled room, taking in the lack of window curtains, the debarked tree trunks supporting the open loft bedroom, the stained pine slab furniture and the wide polished barn board floors.

"Sis, I like your new home okay but it's not very mod. Ever think of putting in wall-to-wall white carpeting? It would lighten up the place; give it an aura of sophistication. You could make cute white matching curtains for the windows."

"White? You've got to be kidding. White? In this place? It would get dirty in no time."

"But I thought everyone had to take their shoes off before going inside an Adirondack home?"

"Most do. But remember we also burn wood. That gets a lot of ash flying around and in the summertime, windows are open letting dust blow in. Country windows don't have curtains. Windows here are for letting the outside in, not keeping it out." Shelley throws up her hands, rolls her eyes and changes the subject.

"So what's with that weird painting? Looks like a dismembered tiger?"

"That's one of Inky Washburn's. She had to drop out of the local gallery and take a job waitressing. She's been totally rejected by the art world folks, gotten really depressed, completely quit painting."

"Then why do you have it?"

"Because we like it in spite of what others think. She's wasting her talents working as a waitress but she sees no other choice."

"If I were you," continues Shelley, "I'd do something about Tibetta's room. It's not very girly-like with that deer skull on the wall with its orange hunting cap, and peace stickers plastered all over those gray paper wasp nests hanging from the ceiling."

"It's her idea of fun. Look, it may not be typical of a girl's room but it's hers and it's the one place where she can do what she wants."

"Well, if she were my kid, I'd clean that room up in a heartbeat. So – how come you like living in Meltmor?"

"I just do. In fact our parents enjoy coming up to their place here too. Dad says he never realized how much friendlier a small town is than the big city. He told me it's a nice change from sterile malls, chain stores, parking lots and the constant rumble of subways and traffic. He even drives over to the Senior Center and volunteers. He was amazed to find a lot of seniors ride bikes. He's thinking of getting one himself – thinking anyway. Who woulda thunk it? Our dad now believes there should be a decree forbidding towns to grow too big. 'If you want real community,' he declares, 'make it a no growth town. Keep it under 10,000 residents.' Mother's in seventh Heaven with all the gallery openings and music events. Sometimes she even takes Tibby along. Nice for Tibby to have two grandmas around."

"I bet they party a lot too, at the Great Camps – "

No, I'm afraid not. That didn't last. Tuck predicted it. You know Mother, never passes up a chance to meet the rich and famous. She's quite a social climber. The Ravens, the first people they met up here, exceptionally warm and friendly, not hung up on class but they're not typical of the lake crowd. The Ravens include our parents at parties but nobody else does."

"Social climbers? Our parents? Never occurred to me. Oh well. Seriously though, what is it that attracts you to this life?"

"It's hard to describe but, like an iceberg, the greater part lies out of sight. You need to dive deep to find it."

"Well, myself, I'm not into diving," laughs Shelley, "but you seem to have taken to it. Like your intuition about Sue Tower. Our Thread Ahead customers are eating up her mold-dyed scarves. I think I'm even going to raise the price to $250 apiece."

"Not mold, Shell, mushroom-dyed."

"Whatever," responds Shelley, as she pats her carefully glued-down coiffure.

"Come on, let's get over to Peak Colors. I'm dying to show you the improvements: better display space, a larger fitting room and an enlarged sewing area. I just have to put on something different before we go. You know how it is, customers pay attention to what we wear," she says disappearing into the bedroom.

"What in the world? Now – that's really out there," exclaims Shelley when Britt reappears a few minutes later still dressed in black shorts and white tee shirt but with overalls made of see-through netting covering her from the neck down. Perched all over the netting are fabric blue and white birds.

"A tribute to swallows," Britt explains. "They are highly efficient consumers of the mosquitoes and black flies which cause such misery. This is a bug net with attitude. Hoping it will go over big." Shelly's mouth opens in astonishment.

"Well Sis, I'll be damned," she finally ekes out, "you've clearly been living in the country too long. Okay, let's go."

240

Britt takes her sister in the truck, a new adventure for Shelley who looks down and sees an ice scraper and roll of toilet paper on the floor.

"Good grief! What are those things doing here?"

"You can never be sure of a weather change in the North Woods, even if it's summer – and the roll of toilet paper – good for emergencies. It's standard fair in Adirondack vehicles," her sister replies.

Arriving at the shop and after looking around, Shelley remarks, "At first, I wasn't too sure about expanding our business. But it seems to be working well in this crazy town."

Meanwhile, at the Hunters' Hub, Tuck, Ace, Josh and Stu are also in discussion, this time about the death of Slam. "Heard that Slam was going to meet up for a second time with a woman from Cliff Rock. He seemed happy, even introduced me to her, nice looking chick hanging on his arm. First time he'd spent more than one evening with the same woman. Then he had to go and get sloshed. Guess that's why he missed the bridge walking back to your trailer," says Josh.

"What's really crazy is that he spent his spare time making model bridges. Even made the bridge that was no longer there when he walked home and fell," says Ace.

"His way of making connections," adds Josh. "Should have paid more attention to real bridges."

"Jesus. What irony," comments Tuck.

"Poor bastard," says Stu, he tried so hard to connect with women. Not his fault they're all so damned difficult."

"Ahh, stop your moaning, Stu. If you're looking to put the blame somewhere, it's certainly not with the women."

"So who's organizing the funeral, and where?"

"Slam has no family so Jane Slanter took over and arranged it along with Tim Berson. It's at two o'clock tomorrow at Tim's place. Slam used to say that whoever in their band died first, the others should play at the funeral. That means Blanche sings and Tim plays guitar but they'd like someone to play Slam's drums as a tribute to him."

"What the hell. In honor of Slam, I'll give it a try. Don't know much about it but I can keep time. No family huh? No woman either – sad. Who's going to say a few words?" says Josh.

"Norton Smithers, president of the Hunt Club, said he'd do it. Nice of the guy as none of us are much good at that kind of thing," comments Tuck.

"Is anyone else coming from the club?"

"I doubt it. Folks didn't hold much sympathy for Slam; a good guy but few knew him as anything but a drunk – and yet – he was so much more. Blanche checked out his room and was dumbfounded to find he had a beautiful collection of tiny model bridges. Made of wood and metal, they were detailed and precise replicas of area bridges: twenty of them. She plans to display them at his funeral. Another overlooked artist. Who knew?"

"Maybe we should see if a museum would like to have them: a memorial to Slam." Pitt and Rat sit eating breakfast in a far corner. Ma Rose rules at the Hunters' Hub and she now requires the two sit in the back of the room to spare customers any whiff of this unorthodox duo.

Finishing off a sizeable meal, Pitt gets up to leave, Rat riding his shoulder, cleaning his egg encrusted whiskers. First though, Pitt detours by the guys' table and adds his own two bits to the conversation: "Bridges and drunks need inspections, beware any failed connections."

And in another part of town, in a small apartment, Justus, with Fawn's attentive care, is making a smooth recovery from his heart attack. The two of them sit talking over their morning coffee.

"Too bad about Slam. Tuck liked him a lot, though why I never could figure," says Justus.

"Maybe just because he was a nice guy."

"Nice isn't enough in this world. What did the guy ever achieve?"

"Why does everyone have to achieve something? Isn't managing to be nice a kind of achievement in itself?" Fawn replies, reflecting the influence of Moe's thinking. "Slam never had a bad thing to say about anyone. He was full of compassion for others."

"It's all well and good to be compassionate Fawn, but you have to be more aggressive in this world if you want to take care of yourself." *Our conversation is going nowhere,* thinks Fawn. *I love this man for his very vulnerability – feel sorry for him. Unfortunately he lacks the warmth to spark my life.*

"Look, for instance, at all that Addison has achieved. Now there's a son we can be proud of. Designing the Prudence Power Pediatric Pavilion, using sustainable building materials in his great camp design. That's all the rage these days. Hope he remarries soon and chooses a better wife."

"But Tuck has also been successful. The book he and Byron wrote has done quite well."

"That's not the same. After all, who reads anymore? Today it's all about movies. A couple of years after publishing, hardly anyone even remembers his book or that he was a ski champ. I mean, we have a son

242

who actually likes caretaking and that's what folks know about him. Oh well, at least, between that and Britt's work they are surviving." Justus holds up his cup, a signal for Fawn to refill it. *Such gestures are all he has left to give him a sense of control,* she realizes. *At least I can do these things for him.* "I guess it's fate." Justus continues, "After years struggling so hard to build the family name, we have to watch Tuck slide it backwards again."

"I wonder why Britt and Tuck don't have their own children. Tibetta is a dear, starting to look more and more like her Uncle Addison, but I wish she weren't the only one. I hinted to Britt a couple of times that they should see a doctor but she brushes off the suggestion. When I mention it to Tuck, he gets mad so I don't dare say anything anymore." Changing to a lighter note, Fawn continues. "At least Britt is doing well with her business. I actually enjoy working at the store sewing dresses. Lots of people come to her shop so it's very social."

"Then why don't you give up the cleaning job at Dr. Sears and spend more time sewing? That's certainly a more respectable occupation than cleaning."

"I would but I'd be letting Dr. Sears down. I don't want to do that." *And I'm not about to give up Moe.*

At the funeral Norton Smithers, a frail, slightly hunched, white haired man, dressed in a dark suit, adjusts his wire rimmed glasses and reads a few kind words in Slam's memory. Though he hardly knew him, he felt compelled to do his duty and help out by conducting the service. Blanche sings one of Slam's favorites songs, "Help Me Make it through the Night." Wrenched by emotion however, she is barely able to make it through the first verse, breaking and stumbling over the words. In a chorus of support, the others pick up the tune and the music swells in a motley collection of cracking voices. Then, a few toasts are proposed. Folks are respectfully somber until Tim and Blanche strike up livelier music. Josh bangs haphazardly on the drums. The rhythm propels Pitt onto the open floor where he kicks up his heels and does a jig, Rat grinning from ear to hairy ear.

"What's that all about?" the mourners ask.

"Ah," says Pitt smiling into his beard, "For each there's a plan, best dance while you can." This time, it's the men who take up the boot-stomping rhythm as they thump around the floor in an effort to hide their 'unmanly' tears; the women stay seated, openly expressing their grief, willing to acknowledge it as a part of life.

"This one's for you Slam," they sing out. And in the corner, a stranger sits alone quietly weeping.

Part IV

Seven Years Later

Chapter 50

At eight o'clock on a Wednesday morning, Blanche Loneby enters the Hunters' Hub and drops her stocky body down onto a chair. Ma Rose clomps over to her table and says, "You're looking mighty weary, girl." Blanche puts her arm around Ma's waist and leans against her.

"It's the constant commuting to the Club. It's getting me down. Must be over 20 miles each way. Much as I love the job, I look forward to winter when I can work the lunch counter at the ski lodge. Takes me only 15 minutes from our trailer to get there."

"Guess we all have our problems," says Ma as she smiles down at Blanche. "Me, I just turned 78. What a wreck. I'm like a dilapidated house in need of repair. Instead of windows, plumbing and insulation, it's eye drops, diuretics and sweaters. I put on a smile the way you put on a coat of paint; looks good on the outside, doesn't fix the inside."

"Why Ma Rose, I never heard you talk like that before. What's bothering you?"

"I'm worried about this place. I'm tired of keeping it going but don't want to see it close. Feeling stuck, you might say." Just then the door opens and Sam, right off the night shift and looking tired, walks in to take a seat at the counter.

"See that? He needs a lift, needs a smile, and needs a cup of coffee. If I close, I'd be letting customers like Sam down. How can I not be here for that?"

"Did you ever think of selling?"

"Yes I have but there's not enough profit in it for any serious investor and anyway, I'm picky about who I'd want to run it. Got an offer from the Toast Host chain but God forbid, I'd never sell to them; see it turned into a clone of all their insipid lookalike shops." Ma Rose walks behind the counter, smiles at Sam, pours his coffee and asks, "Hard night Sam?" Blanche remains where she is, unmoving, staring at the floor, her thoughts elsewhere. Ma Rose looks at her friend across the room, smiles to herself and thinks, *I'm not so daft yet.*

You know, I'm tempted to do something totally crazy, thinks Blanche, *and I think that sly old Mama knows it. I'm not up for all the commuting anymore and it seems like half my pay goes into gas. Like Britt once said, if you want a thing a lot, sometimes you have to give up something else, be irrational. Think I'm ready.*

That evening, a weighty talk takes place in the Loneby's trailer. Early next morning, before customers arrive, another weighty talk takes place at the Hunters' Hub.

"You clever old fox," bursts out Blanche.

"Why not? You're the only one I know who can follow in my tracks," replies Ma Rose.

"I might make some changes though."

"Change anything you want except I hope it stays a place where everyone feels welcome."

"I know a way to make that happen," responds Blanche. "I'll keep a special seat ready for you whenever you want to drop by. Customers will love it if they think you might be here."

"That would be real nice. I'm like an old tree that no longer sprouts twigs, don't mind holding out my branches, they just don't hold many leaves anymore."

"But you're sharp enough. Look how you've managed to slide this place off your shoulders onto mine." The well matched pair, both broad in the beam as well as attitude, wander back to the kitchen where Ma begins explaining the operation. A month later Blanche has taken over the Hunters' Hub, agreeing to pay for it in monthly installments over the next 5 years. Her greatest challenge is the teenagers who invade the place. "Ought to lock them all up till they turn twenty," she is heard to mumble.

"You got to laugh along but keep a firm hand," advises Ma. "Eventually they'll acquire some sense and those who don't move away will be the future decision makers in our town."

"Now there's a scary thought," says Blanche as the door opens and four kids explode into the Hub, 17-year-old Tibetta amongst them. "Hey, why aren't you kids in school today?"

"Teacher conference, day off," Tibetta answers as her friends snicker amongst themselves. They settle at a table where they dig into plates of junk food. Tibetta leaning back and opening her mouth, attempts to catch a doughnut hole pitched at her across the table by a scrawny, unkempt boy who looks no more than 10-years-old to Ma Rose. He is, in fact, 18. Tibetta leans too far and her chair crashes over backwards. Jumping up, she sweeps off her cap and takes a deep bow, at the same time scooping the dusty pastry off the floor and popping it into her mouth. The kids love it and roar with laughter.

"Ugh," comments Blanche in disgust.

"Did you see that boy's hands?" asks Ma Rose. "I wouldn't eat anything he touched for love nor money. The floor's probably cleaner. Someone should teach him a little hygiene." After a brain-clogging breakfast of Coke and brownies, the jaunty gathering trounces out in a burst of joyous energy. "Got to admit though, I like that Tibetta, she's full of high jinks – makes me laugh."

At five that evening, Tuck and Britt sit down for a talk with their increasingly unruly but lovable daughter. "So, teacher conference, huh?" Tibetta looks down at her supper. "Take off that cap so we can see you. You know, if you want to go to college, you'll have to do better than that," says Tuck. "Mack and Roy are failing school. You could have tried persuading them to stay in class rather than joining them out hiking."

"Jeez Dad, you know the saying, 'If you don't like what you're doing, try something else.' I don't like math so I tried something else today." Britt hides a smile. *How is Tuck going to handle this one?*

"I hear you Tibby, but don't put too much stock in clever sayings. They have a nice ring but they're often more damaging than helpful. Think for yourself; don't let others do it for you."

But you didn't like ski racing and quit. I'm just doing the same thing."

"Okay, you're right, I did, but you're a little young to make that kind of decision. If you give up something with a good future, you better make damn sure you know the consequences. You don't know those – not yet you don't. Luckily I had your mom to help me through the rough times. Don't want you having to struggle like that."

"Yeah, yeah. Still, I don't think all sayings are bad. A lot of them are really good."

"Like name one," says her father as they begin to tangle, much as he had done so often with Justus.

"Well, like – like – um, like the early bird catches the worm."

Quick as a flash, Tuck responds, "The early bird catches the worm but too soon to bed misses the stars."

"Right. But you can't eat stars," banters Tibetta.

"But it can inspire you to greater wisdom."

"Who needs wisdom?" counters Tibetta.

"You do."

"How about this one, 'If you want something done, ask a busy person?'"

"That's just a way to make people feel guilty about taking time for themselves – society enslaving its members to endless toil."

"Oh Dad, what a grump you are."

"Call me what you will, I'm telling you here and now. School's where you belong, not out playing hooky. You need to go to college."

"Anyway, I hate having my life defined by the school bell: ding, class over, ding, walk to the next class, ding, lunch time, ding, recess, ding, class again, ding, assembly, ding, time to go home. I'm programmed like a robot." *Good girl, she's thinking,* reflects Tuck. Britt adds her own two cents.

"Things could be worse. Think about your friend Katy and the life she leads; her mother abused by an alcoholic brother, living in a crime ridden neighborhood, too much violence to go outside at night, trying to survive in a notoriously dangerous high school. You don't know how lucky you are."

With the superior attitude of youth, Tibetta doesn't respond but, supper over, simply pushes back her chair. "Can I go now?"

"Depends where."

"Over to Ginny's so we can study together."

"That's okay. You can take the truck but be back before dark. You have school tomorrow and some makeup work to do." Tibetta, baseball cap jammed back on her head, slams out the door.

"Teenagers!" Tuck and Britt exclaims simultaneously.

An hour later, Tibetta and her boyfriend Jock are cruising along by the lake and sharing a beer. "Better slow down girl, this road is curvy, sort of like you," he says.

"Hmm, who's the fast one around here," she answers seconds before the truck skids on the sand and hurtles off the curve.

"Watch out." she yells as they hit the end of a bridge railing with a terrible scream of metal and breaking glass. The truck comes to rest half on solid ground, half hanging over the river below.

Chapter 51

The phone rings at Tuck and Britt's home. "Hi Mom. Now don't get mad but I had a little accident. I'm okay but I'm at the police station. Can you come get me?" Tuck and Britt can't get her very easily as Tibetta has the truck. They call Stu for a ride and in less than a half-hour they are at the station talking to Sam.

"Little lady's gotten herself in a heap of trouble drinking beer and speeding around with her boyfriend in your truck. They hit the bridge railing out on the Cedar Bluff Lake Road. Jock Slanter broke his arm and is in the emergency room as we speak. His parents are there with him. Your daughter got her cheek slashed but refuses to go to the emergency room."

Sam takes them to see Tibetta who is sitting slumped in a white plastic chair, a bloody gauze dressing taped to her face. "Okay Tibby. What were you doing drinking and what were you doing out at the lake? You told us you were going to be studying."

"I was but we got done early. Jock and I were going out to look at the sunset." *Touché,* notes Tuck, *she knows how to play me.* Britt lifts one corner of the bandage and peeks underneath. "We better get that stitched up or you'll have a scar."

"I don't care. I don't want it fixed."

"That doesn't make sense. You're a beautiful girl. Don't let your face be marred."

"Don't care if it is. I won't do it."

"I think we should let her decide, Britt. It's not the worst thing if she has a small mark on her face." *I think I understand where Tibby is coming from – a scar with meaning.*

They learn that the truck's left front headlight and fender got bashed in, that it had been towed to the Hood 'n' Wheel but can be, with repairs made, ready to drive again. Tibetta is released into the custody of her parents. Stu drives Britt and Tibetta home and then drops Tuck off at the emergency room to find out about Jock's condition.

Tuck finds Jock's parents, Hood and Jane, standing outside the front door taking a cigarette break. They are surprisingly calm. Tuck approaches, saying, "I'm sorry about all this. Apparently my daughter was driving. How badly hurt is Jock?"

"Looks like his pitchin' arm is broke bad."

"His pitching arm?"

"Yeah. And he's just got a baseball scholarship to help pay for college."

"That's terrible. I don't know what to say."

Tuck tries to talk with them but it's a bit awkward so he finally asks if it's okay to go see their son. Stopping at a cubicle in the emergency room, Tuck pulls aside the curtain and looks in. Jock, under the influence of painkillers is asleep, his arm in a cast propped on his chest. *Not much point my hanging around, I might as well leave.* Stu drops him off at home where he finds that Tibby has gone to bed. Tuck and Britt's talk about the situation finally ends with his saying, "This is what Tibby's going to do. I had told Jock a while ago that I'd give him a summer job helping at Reedmor. He won't be able to do that now. Tibby was going to apprentice with your sister in the Thread Ahead but that's not going to happen either. I want her to take Jock's place this summer and turn over all her earnings to him for his college fund."

"Isn't that a little severe? Tibby admits she was drinking and going a little fast. She said she's sorry"

"Tibby lied to us. She had no intention of being home by dark. She was drinking. Do I think I'm too severe on her? Not a bit. Hadn't I just finished talking to her about consequences? Time she learns what that means. The little fool. Why did she have to go and do something stupid like this?"

"I know you're disappointed but she's rebellious. Like someone else I know, she's trying to find her own way. We can't expect to control all her actions."

A month later, in June, Tibetta and seven other young people stand assembled before Tuck. None have ever worked as caretakers. "For starters, the shirt has to go," says Tuck pointing to Henry who had the words, 'Save a plant, Eat a vegetarian' scrawled across his front. "You can find a spare in my shop for now. Your role here this summer is to be as unobtrusive as possible, don't start conversations with the owners or their guests and always respond pleasantly when spoken to. If something pisses you off, come to me about it, not anyone else. Furthermore, you need to adhere to the caretaker code: what happens here, stays here. If I get word of you talking in town about anything that goes on at Reedmor, you'll be fired immediately."

"How about saying back to me what I told you." They do their best. "Good enough," says Tuck. "This can be a fun summer for you and help pay for college as long as you don't screw it up by doing something dumb. The snow melted late this year so a lot of chores had to wait. We don't have much time left to get them all done. July 4th weekend is zero hour: the Powers, their household staff and guests will be arriving. You two," he says, pointing at a couple of hefty looking guys, "I want you to get a ladder, start at the main building, clean the gutters and pull all fallen branches off the roofs. Do the same for the guest cabins and sheds."

"Tibetta. You're to clean up the paths, pick up the branches and litter that have blown down. Stick to the paths within a twenty minute walk from the buildings. We can worry about the rest later. When that's done, get the wheelbarrow, rake up pine needles and spread them all along those walks." Tibetta finds it humiliating to work for the family whose kids used to be her playmates.

"This sucks," she says under her breath, "After this summer, I'm never doing this again. I wonder how my dad can stand it."

Looking at two more guys, he says, "You told me you have some carpentry experience. I want you to come with me. We have a lot of repairs to make from winter damage to the outside of the guest cabins." One of the boys is Roy, the failing student who Tuck thinks has potential as a carpenter if given a little guidance. *For now, I'll keep him close to me.* "You all," he says addressing three boys waiting nervously for instructions "start staining the decks off the main building."

Off to work they go. The days tumble by, seeming to speed up with the approach of the 4th. Gardens are tilled: plants put in; fences repaired, firewood stacked; docks put in; outdoor furniture set up on decks, docks and patios; canoes, kayaks and guide boats suspended in the boathouse are lowered into the water; powerboats are brought over from winter storage at the Lakeside Marina; rooms are cleaned; gallons of water stocked; food supplies hauled in; deer repellant sprayed on the flowers; lawns mowed; the bowling alley spruced up; and on and on. One of the last chores involves climbing ladders in the great room of the main building to take the glassy-eyed big game heads down off the walls.

"Mrs. Power is bringing up her guru and several of his followers, the Maha-something or other. He's a vegetarian so she wants all these slaughtered animals removed from the walls. We'll put them back up later."

The day before the urban battalion moves in, Tuck gathers his summer staff for reminders and updates. "Remember, you don't use the same paths the Powers and visitors use; you stay out of the way as much as possible and don't start conversations with anyone, even if you've had a friendly talk before. There are clear boundaries here, be sure you understand them. You'll see things you won't believe. That's because in the eyes of Mrs. Power and visitors you're invisible – mere underlings, and your opinions don't count. What you see doesn't matter to them. Some things may make you want to laugh – don't. When you leave here at the end of the day, no peeling out down the road, no whooping it up. You can do that when you get home. So far, so good. You've done well until now. The goal from here on in is to make sure everything runs smoothly at Reedmor without anyone being aware of all we do to make it happen. Anticipate problems, take care of them quietly, stay out of the way and above all, watch your attitude."

That weekend, Reedmor is engulfed by a tsunami of urbanites, most of them followers of the Maha-something or other, and a gaggle of city staff: maids, butlers and cooks. The spa cabin is bustling with activity, massage therapists, saunas and hot tubs getting a workout. Tibetta is assigned to help the chef serve gourmet tidbits to this blessed crowd. Snacks and lunches are delivered wherever and whenever guests suddenly crave them, sometimes on a porch, sometimes on the docks, often in their cabins. Evenings, everyone gathers in the main dining room to share a feast and ooh and aah over the scanty delicacies daintily perched on gold rimmed porcelain plates.

The staff is kept running. One family complains to Tuck that the cabin is missing an air conditioner. One of the staff is sent to explain that air conditioning is not needed if windows on both sides of the building are opened. He opens them, letting a fresh breeze blow through. In five minutes, to this city family's amazement, the stuffy cabin is cooled down.

Another pair of visitors calls on their cell from the dock. They want to take a canoe out on the lake but its "missing the motor." A staff member radios Tuck. "We actually do have a small electric motor we can mount or I'll paddle it myself. Tell them I'll be right down and they can choose," he responds.

One woman says being in the Adirondacks reminds her of going away to camp when she was fourteen and making terrariums. She would love to have a terrarium to take home. Tuck sends Tibetta into town to the feed store which has fish tank supplies. "Pick up a small aquarium, bring it back and go dig up some mosses, wintergreen, partridgeberry and other things to fill it. Let me see it when you're done, then you can take it over to her cabin."

And so the summer days pass with a variety of visitors, events and dilemmas. One of Tuck's workers is approached by an older, immaculately dressed gentleman heading up a group of three men and two women. "Which trail would you recommend we take?" he asks. The worker casts a quick look at the women's foot ware: leather moccasins and dainty sandals, their versions of hiking boots. He directs them to the flattest shortest path. Seeing that each is carrying a short heavy stick he says, "We have hiking poles if you would like."

"No, that's alright. These sticks are for protection; understand you have bears up here. Just want to be prepared." The worker starts to smile and explain but suddenly, remembering instructions, catches himself and says nothing.

An emergency midnight call comes through to Tuck where he is spending the night in the caretaker cabin as he often does when it gets very busy. "Someone's in trouble out on the lake. Something awful is happening." Certain what the problem is, he heaves himself out of bed and before even going out the door, his suspicions are confirmed when he hears the loons hollering over the water. *Thought so. Well at least this one is easy,* he laughs as he makes his way over to Cedar Cabin and explains the scary sounds to guests who, shaking with fright, have locked their bedrooms to keep the intruders out.

On another day the chef requests Tibetta take a snack over to Fern Cabin. She arrives, knocks on the door and hears "come in." At first, on entering, she thinks no one is there. But then, her eyes adjusting to the darkened interior, she realizes to her horror, that in the corner, a naked, flabby, gray haired woman is standing yoga style on her head. Flustered but well trained not to show it, Tibetta swallows hard before simply asking, "Where should I put this, Ma'am?"

"Nice going," Tuck tells her upon hearing the story, "you're learning a skill that will serve you well in the future. You've got one more year of high school; let's see if you can use your experience to get back on track."

Tibetta lost her license for six months. Hood had wanted to sue the Risings but his wife, ever compassionate, persuaded him not to. "Tibetta is giving her full summer earnings to Jock and her uncle Addison is adding to it so that Jock will be able to go to college as planned. The doctor says that by next year, he'll be as good as new and playing again."

Summer ends, fall slides in with earthy tones and crisp edges. Tibetta, as if taking a clue from her surroundings, becomes mellow and more grounded. Autumn hints of the coming of harder days. Storms lie ahead: tough winter weather and new challenges for everyone.

Chapter 52

Rat has curled up on Pitt's sleeping bag. Illness leaves him droopy, his ears falling flat on his pointy head. Pitt sits by the fire, worried. Not again – no more losses – not this time. He gets up to take another look at Rat, pulls a large dirty handkerchief out of his pocket, lays it lovingly over his hairy pal and murmurs, "Don't leave me pal, not now."

Lost in reverie, Pitt drifts back: *Oh my Mattie, my angel, ever faithful to the camp owners – ordering her out in that storm – damned party crowd – got to have their midnight feast – if only I'd not been tied up with the generator – never let her go outside. Act of God be damned – act of inhumanity – trees crash in storms – fall on the unprotected – curses on the privileged – never be a caretaker again – never – Mattie and her unborn – the past is past but never done – can't lose Rat.*

The past is bothering another person as well: Tibetta. "Dad, I love mom but I'm wondering about my real mother. I want to find her. You've never told me anything but don't you think I deserve to know who she is, what she's like?"

"Let me think about that. Sometimes it's best to let things lie." *Lie, the big lie, of course it must all come out someday, of course, but, not yet, please, not yet.*

The next morning as soon as the family leaves home, Tibetta to school and Britt to her shop, Tuck picks up the phone and dials Addison. "We've got problems. Let me start by saying that there's something I never told you earlier because you had enough troubles on your plate already but – you've got to hear it now. For a long time, I dealt with a blackmailer who knew Tibby's history and threatened to reveal it. It gets worse. He claimed that Tibby was actually his daughter, not yours, and that he would lay claim to her, even have his DNA checked to prove his paternity if I didn't pay him hush money. The guy had an accident, died, so that threat is gone, but now we have another. Tibby wants to find her biological mother."

"You're kidding. You should have told me before. His daughter? Who was the bastard? How much did he get from you? Tell me more. No, on second thought don't, not now. It's all too much. Damn. Damn. Damn. What do we do about Tibby? You've got to talk her out of this."

"I'll try, but you know Tibby, she's not easily deterred."

"Yeah, I know. But if the truth comes out, God knows what it will do to us. Look, you've cared for her all these years, you probably know best how to handle this."

"But I don't."

After a fruitless discussion, Tuck hangs up. That evening he takes Tibetta for a ride and tries to persuade her of the potential problems that could arise from her search. On returning home, Tibeta goes to bed early to get ready for an early Saturday start with friends. They are going on a camping trip.

"Did it work?" asks Britt after Tibetta is asleep.

"No, not at all."

"Then why not let her go ahead with her quest? I won't be hurt. It's a natural enough desire on her part. She needs to find her own way."

"I know that, but – I'm afraid you'll be hurt."

"I assure you, I will not. What I will do is try to be there for her as she travels her path of discovery. I love that child; no matter how she reacts I'll help her cope."

"How about me? Will you still feel the same?"

"You know I will. I've stood with you this long, and you with me. Surely nothing can come between us now."

"I hope you mean what you say because there is something we need to talk about. Come curl up with me on the sofa. I need to hold you close while I talk."

And with that, long held secrets start to gush forth: secrets that include adopting Tibetta from Addison and Bubbles, inventing the love-child story, writing under a pseudonym, blackmail and deception. Britt lies curled in his arms, stunned and speechless, the ground knocked out from under her. Denial comes first. *This can't be. It's some kind of mistake. He couldn't have lied to me all these years. Surely this is just a dream, a nightmare. I'll wake up in a minute.*

Five minutes later she wakes up, not to a prior life built on false assumptions, but to a new one: out of focus and askew. *Tuck deceived me. The fool. Addison lied too. What about that? What do I do? Where do we go from here? How will this affect Tibby? And what about his parents? Why, why?*

"Why Tuck, why?"

"Why'd we do it? Drugs, and shock – fear – pity – Addison's wife sliding into addiction, her god-awful decision to give up their baby – pity for the child – wish to spare her finding out what a messed up mother she had, a mother so out of control she was willing to give away her child and steal to feed her addiction."

"But you must have realized the truth would surface eventually? You could at least have told me."

"That was another fear: fear that you'd be turned off by the whole sordid story and leave us."

"Oh for God's sake. As if sitting on this kind of secret could ever make for a healthy relationship. How the hell did you guys get in so deep?" There is no answer, nor does Britt expect one. They sit unmoving, each trying to balance the moment, baffled how to go on. Finally Britt speaks.

"Tibby will be devastated. How do you plan to tell her?"

"I've been thinking about that – constantly."

"Well, you should tell your parents first, or better yet Addison should explain to them. After all, you did it to help him. He owes you."

"What about you? How does all this hit you?" Tuck asks.

"Like a hammer shattering glass. I need time. Would I have married you if I knew your deception with regard to Tibby? I can't say, maybe not. I was different then. But now? You've accepted my deception – never telling you I couldn't have children – how can I object to yours? I'm in for the long haul. I'll do my best to pick up the pieces," says Britt.

"I'm not the same person anymore either. In retrospect, it was a mistake to keep you in the dark. When do we get old enough to know what to tell, what not?"

"Maybe never."

"Could be you're right," agrees Tuck.

"Where do we start?"

"I guess I'll call Addison back and ask him to break the news to our parents. I think I should go over there with him. It won't be pretty. Once they know, we'll tell Tibby. I think it should be only you and me telling her. Would you do that with me?"

"It's going to be rough but, as I said, I'll help."

The next day, Addison arrives at Tuck's place. Britt is at her shop. Tuck reveals the full extent of the blackmail and the death of Buzz, though not his own part in it.

"What do you think? Could Tibby really be Buzz's child?" asks Addison, incredulous at the idea.

"I'm not sure but Britt thinks she looks more and more like you so there's hope there. The only real proof will be a DNA test."

"Okay. There's too much going on here all at once. Let's first talk to Mother and Dad – tell them about Tibetta, but nothing about Buzz. This will be joyous," Addison spits out, the sarcasm rolling off his tongue like burnt oil.

258

When the brothers arrive at their parents' home, Justus and Fawn welcome them with a certain reserve, unsure what they are going to hear. However, no matter what they had imagined, it doesn't begin to stack up to what they actually learn. The whole twisted story, minus the blackmail, is revealed. His fuse lit, it doesn't take long for Justus to go off.

"Dishonesty like this – it's a disgraceful blot on the family name. With all we taught you about decent behavior, what made you think such outrageous lying was defensible? Look what you've done to the family. Misleading everyone about Tibby! How are we ever to live it down? I am deeply ashamed. This is the final blow. I am shocked and disappointed with you both." With their father gone ballistic and their mother saying little, there is no point in staying longer. The brothers get up, kiss their mother goodbye and tell her they will be in touch later.

With the boys gone, Fawn says nothing. Instead, going to the kitchen, she makes a pot of coffee and brings a cup to Justus. He takes a sip, takes another, requests a shot of rum and then finally turns to her.

"Well Fawn, I don't hear you making any comment. I suppose you think this is all just fine."

"No I don't. It makes me sad. Why didn't they feel they could tell us earlier?" Before Justus can answer, she continues, "Perhaps because we are too judgmental."

"What's that have to do with anything? You have to hold your head up in a community. You don't do it through being dishonest."

"Maybe not you Justus, but we're not all as strong as you. I think the boys didn't want to hurt us. That's why they did what they did."

"They've never particularly cared about that as far back as I can remember."

"Maybe they did. After all, Tuck adopted Tibetta to keep her in the family, and he tried to protect his brother and us by not letting anyone know that Bubbles wanted to give up her very own child. If they hadn't worked out this scheme, we never would have had a wonderful grandchild."

"But why didn't they just come out and tell everyone what they were doing?"

"Bubbles," responded Fawn, "would never have consented to anyone knowing she was so far into drugs that she couldn't take care of her baby. She had signed Tibby over to Addison, thinking he would make arrangements for an agency to take her. She was unaware that Tuck planned to adopt her from Addison – and claim she was a child from a European affair."

"Good God. Maybe you're right – for a change. All this time we've been on Tuck's case about that affair. He never said a thing to defend himself," reflects Justus with some contrition.

"We have underrated Tuck. He did what he thought best. Isn't that all any of us can do? Haven't we also kept things from each other, only to discover later we didn't need to?" Fawn reminds him as she tries to soothe Justus's hurt feelings. However, she can't help but be aware of all she is still holding back. Slowly the afternoon passes, the sun sinks lower, they talk, the room fills with shadows – shadows that reach far beyond the walls.

Tibetta returns Sunday evening from her camping trip. She bounces into the house, dirty, disheveled and happy. Her good mood soon to be deflated. "Why all the gloom?" she exclaims.

Tuck and Britt sit Tibetta down at the kitchen table, taking their places on either side of her in an effort to offer protection – but little protection is possible. Tuck begins to explain the true story of her origins. She is furious, exploding in wrath.

"You lied to me. You're mean. I hate you. How could you have done this? Uncle Addie is a coward. He's my father? I don't want him for a father. I hate you all!" She runs off to her room sobbing loudly. As if a tornado has just torn through their house, Tuck and Britt are left dazed in the wreckage. They hear her cries of agony, wracked with pain. An hour later, after their daughter has quieted down, Britt goes to her room and sits down on the bed where the distraught Tibetta is lying, face buried in the pillow, too exhausted to cry anymore. Britt quietly strokes her back.

"It's hard isn't it?" she murmurs.

"It's worse than that. Everyone lied to me. How could you do that?"

"Actually, Sweet Pea, I didn't know until Friday."

"Then don't you hate them all?"

"No, I'm upset but I don't hate anyone for it."

"You should. They lied to us, Mom. They lied and I'm leaving home and never coming back."

"What good would that do?"

"Teach them a lesson. They're so mean."

"You know, don't you think we've all made mistakes, done sneaky things?"

"Maybe. But not like this."

"Might have felt like this to other people."

"Like who? You mean like Jock?"

"Yes. But you're not the only one who's done it. I've also kept secrets. We've all done it."

"Yeah, but I paid for the time I lied. I had to work a whole summer without pay. Adults don't get punished for their mistakes."

"Tibby, if you trust me at all, then trust me on this. Adults do pay. There's a lot of suffering going on in this family right now – a lot of pain and a good part of it is because everyone is so worried about you."

"Why? I don't believe –"and another sob breaks forth.

"Because everyone, Uncle Addison –"

"You mean my stupid-ass father."

"Call him what you like, Uncle Addison, your lifetime dad, your grandparents and me, we're all torn up with worry this will be too much for you to handle."

"Too much? You think I'm a little kid? Can't handle stuff? I can handle a lot."

"I know that, and you've proved it before. But now there's something else to think about for both of us. Forgiveness."

"Forgiveness sucks. Why should we forgive anyone?"

"Because at one time or another we've all made bad decisions and others have forgiven us – and because if we don't, we'll wear ourselves out dragging around our anger. What's the point?"

"But I thought Dad loved me. I thought Uncle Addie did."

"They did and they do. That hasn't changed. You have no idea what they've been through to ensure that you were kept safe in this family where your grandparents, uncle and dad could raise you. That's not something you do for a child you don't love."

This is followed by a long silence until Tibetta mumbles in her pillow, "Oh Mom, I'm so sad."

"I'm sure you are but, you'll see – with time you'll feel better. Get some sleep now." Britt returns to the living room. Deep circles under Tuck's and her eyes show the toll of the last couple of days. Nothing but sleep will erase such troubles and so, with no further words, they also retire for the night, exhausted and wondering what the next morning will bring.

Chapter 53

The next morning brings peace. Tibetta appears for breakfast. Tuck is staying home for the day, as is Britt. "Do you want to go to school today? It's your choice. If you want to stay home you can."

"No, I want to go," she says, barely eating breakfast and gathering her books together. "There's the bus, gotta leave." Tibetta kisses her dad and Britt, and runs out the door, sealing their day with joy.

"Do you think she'll be okay?" asks Tuck.

"I think she'll be okay but right now she needs to talk to friends, not us." replies Britt. "And we should talk to the school counselor and let her know what's going on. Tibby is going to need more support than we can give by ourselves."

"Hon, we're so lucky to have you aboard steadying the ship. You're the ballast keeping us on an even keel." Tuck gives her a hug.

"That heavy? And here I thought I was keeping my weight down. Let's go for a walk." Along the way, they meet Pitt coming from the other direction. Rat is lying slumped over his shoulder.

"What's the matter with Rat?" asks Britt.

"He's been sick but I think he's slowly recovering."

"Hope he's up and at 'em soon." With that, Rat raises his head, and emits a series of faint squeaks.

"What was that he said?" asks Britt.

"Flies in the pudding, lies in the pot, some hide below, some rise to the top." answers Pitt.

Part V

Two Years Later

Chapter 54

On an unusually warm fall morning, Tuck and Addison, jackets hanging on the backs of their chairs, sit drinking coffee at the Hunters' Hub. Jane Slanter comes over to their table. Smiling shyly, she hands them menus and asks if they'd like some breakfast.

"Jane, you working here?"

"Sure am. Just started last week. Business is picking up so Blanche hired me to help. I'm loving it. Know what you want to eat?"

"Well, that's great and great the business is going well. I know what I want," says Addison. "You've got a lot of new things I never thought I'd find here, like a yogurt-granola-fruit parfait. I'll try that."

"It's all Blanche's doing. She wants to attract more tourists so she's adding fancier foods."

"Hope she won't stop serving the old standbys," comments Tuck.

"Oh, she'll keep those. What do you want?"

"My usual: two scrambled, sausage and fries."

"I'll get that right out to you." Fifteen minutes later, she returns with their breakfasts.

"You might be interested to hear what else Blanche is doing. We both wanted to keep on volunteering like we used to, so she came up with a way to do it. We'll be having musical evenings here once a week to raise money for victims of the latest town flood. We feel so sorry for them. You'd think twice was enough but it seems like these floods just keep on coming. Anyway, we'll get local bands to come play. Blanche is anxious to get back to singing so this way she can perform as well. I'll donate my waitress earnings from the night and the cook is working for free as well. Come on down and listen. Live music, good food and a worthy cause. Can't beat it."

After she walks away, Tuck starts talking about the state of the environment. "What's it going to take to make folks take climate change seriously? You'd think after their homes had washed away two or three times, the message would sink in. The rate at which we keep burning coal and oil reminds me of the way the previous owners of our house used the front door to fire up the woodstove!"

"Speaking of the environment," comments Addison, "I see Tim Berson's sustainable lumber business is finally taking off. Remember when we told him that once certified wood became the 'in' thing, people would be beating down his door? Well, now that it's fashionable, he's selling very well. He's doing what he wanted, giving a lot of guys jobs, even offering them health insurance. I just saw one of his boats heading up the lake fully loaded. I think it was on its way to the new building site on the north shore."

"You've certainly helped the green construction trend. Now that you're so recognized, folks can't wait to claim you as their own personal architect. They love boasting about doing business with the 'famous Addison Rising.'" adds Tuck.

"Oh get off it brother. It's all a bit embarrassing."

"I can imagine. Isn't it strange how some people are greatly praised for doing the right thing, even though they only do it because it's trendy, while other less fancy folks get shafted for their efforts?"

"Like?" says Addison.

"Like, let's see, like Josh sitting over there. One of the Raven's guests wanted Josh to take him fishing but refused to let his gear be tied down in the canoe – said it wasn't necessary. Josh reminded him how easily canoes tip over but the guy said, 'Not to worry, I'm not some landlubber, sonny.' An hour later, the intrepid fisherman suddenly lunged to one side while netting a fish. Splash. Over they go. The guy was ripping, berated Josh up and down for not preventing the dunking. Josh quietly righted the canoe and pushed it to the dock. The guest swam to shore, rushed up to his cabin, put on dry clothes, then took a few minutes to spread a story about his clumsy guide tipping them over. Josh swam back and made several dives to the mucky bottom to retrieve the guy's gear. In the course of doing this, he slashed his foot on a knife the fisherman had left unsheathed. Finally finished, Josh climbed out on the dock where Mr. Big Shot was checking everything over. 'Looks like it's all here. I suppose you're going to want to get your foot stitched up. How long will it take you to drive to the hospital?' he asked. Josh told him it was about a 45-minute trip. The guest responded by throwing a 20-dollar bill at him and saying, 'That's for the ER bill. You should be able to get back here by one, enough time for us to go out again. Remember, I still haven't caught any fish today.' Never a thank you, never a thought to the problem of an injured foot, never a word of apology."

"Did Josh tell Bill Raven?"

"Nope, you know how it goes, caretaker's role is to keep everyone happy, not complain. Bill would have been more than sympathetic if he had known. He's good goods. Josh is funny about it though. When telling me this, he said, 'You can't blame that guest too much. After all, he's a banker and bankers think the rest of us are put on earth to cover for their mistakes.'"

266

"Wow. Poor Josh. Sometimes you get the wrong end of the deal no matter how hard you try."

"And then there was Slam. The Mountain Museum was excited to acquire his bridge collection. He finally got the recognition he deserves but only after he died," continues Tuck, "In some ways you've gotten a bad deal yourself."

"You too," Addison replies. "You've not had it so great."

"No, that's not true. I've had some good breaks: Tibby, Britt, my job, my writing."

"I guess I could say the same for myself. I've been lucky meeting Byron," responds Addison. "He's the kindest, gentlest man you could ever know and yet his home life has been a misery. He told me what happened with his marriage. Mrs. Power cut him off after she had the children she wanted. He's been without love or sex for years while she was out sleeping around with any big honcho she could nab. They negotiated a deal: separate lives in the same house; married in appearance only so he could help raise the kids. Their son Norm stuck to Mrs. Power like glue, believed every nasty thing she said about Byron – never ventured out on his own. He's a mess now – in an institution. Winnie was more rebellious, closer to her dad. She seems to be the stable one. Mrs. Power's going back on the deal, wants a divorce so she can marry her 'big oil' man from Texas. She put a detective on Byron, found out about us and now she's hitting him up for all he's worth."

Suddenly a truck pulls up in front of the Hub, its horn blasting continuously. Walt leaps out, the horn still going, and bursts through the door. "Okay jackass, fix the goddamn thing right now." he yells at Josh who is sitting at the counter, grinning into his coffee cup.

A police car screeches to a halt outside, red lights flashing. Sam jumps out and strides inside. "Walt. Stop that horn, pull the fuse or do something – now or I'll ticket you for disturbing the peace."

"Me? It's that jerk there. He's the one who did it, crossed the wires in my truck or something. Give him the ticket, or does being your brother give him special protection?"

"Don't give me any of your lip or I'll write you up for contempt. Get out there and do something to stop that racket."

Walt stalks out, and starts fiddling around with the truck, unsure exactly what Josh had done to make the horn keep blasting. While he is under the hood puzzling over the problem, peacekeeper Ma Rose, sitting next to Josh suggests that to avoid trouble, he would do well to clear out while the clearing is good. Josh, heeding her advice, throws down a couple of dollars calling out "keep the change." and speedily exits the Hub. Customers enjoy a hearty laugh while Tuck explains the long standing feud to Addison.

"It's gone back and forth for years; the last thing that happened was Walt greased Josh's windshield wipers. When it started to rain, he turned them on, couldn't see a thing and nearly ran off the road."

"Hey, not to change the subject, but how do you think our parents are doing?" asks Addison.

"Okay I guess. They're surprisingly cheerful but disappointment lurks in their future. Mother is still on our case about having more grandchildren and she's constantly wondering when you're going to remarry."

"Leave them their dreams. Some truths are best left buried. And Tibby?"

"You probably know more about her than I do. She's good about calling from the city but now that she's away at college we don't see so much of her – miss her a lot. Hoped she'd go to a more rural school, always thought she liked country life – never thought she'd choose a city school."

"Well, I must admit, I do get to see her fairly often. It was awkward at first but she's working through her mixed feelings. A good girl for sure. I think she has inherited Bubbles's artistic talent. I try to remind her that her mother was a good woman who just made some bad mistakes along the way," says Addison.

Tuck breaks in, "You know Tibby asked us about her name. I told her the story, how Bubbles called her that before turning her over to the adoption agency, hoping because of the association with Tibet and things sacred, it would bless her with a kind of spiritual protection. Told her I liked the idea and kept the name. By the way," he continues, "We might as well drop the DNA test idea. Tibby has grown to look so much like you there's no mistaking she's family." Tuck looks at his watch. "Uh-oh, got to get going. I'm supposed to read parts of my new book to the 5th grade this morning."

"How's the book doing anyway?"

"To my amazement, quite well. On a kid's level, the idea of two marionette children breaking away from their parents to see the world on their own seems to have appeal. I hope they'll get my message: think for themselves, take care of the planet."

"If it's doing so well, why don't you quit caretaking and just write?"

"Thought about that but the truth is I don't make enough with royalties. Besides, working as a caretaker keeps me grounded in the real world, keeps me humble – "

"Grounded for sure," breaks in Addison. "You don't get much chance to get away – ever."

"True. A lot of people say that to me. Why is everyone so intent on getting away? Away from what? Why are so many folks always on the move? It hasn't been easy getting where I am but I have pretty much achieved what I want. Why should I want to get away from it?"

"Brother, you have an answer for everything."

"I wish! By the way, my old teammate, Storm, turned up the other day wanting to know how I was doing. Said a lot of my former ski buds were worried about me when I quit. Imagine that? And I thought they only cared about my winning medals for them. Bit of an eye opener. Storm and I had a great time together. He's working as a sports announcer. Okay, now I'm really late. See you," Tuck says as he rushes out the door.

Addison sits brooding. *We sure do follow tangled paths. Takes a lot of energy. I'm beginning to understand my father, why he's content to live quietly and do less. Must be sort of a relief finally. Now that Tibby is nineteen, she should be thinking about her future. Wonder in what direction she'll go? How hard her path will be?*

Chapter 55

"Hi Mom, it's me. You said I never call you so here I am." Britt signals Tuck to pick up the extension.

"Hey Tibby girl, how's life in the big city, how are your classes going?"

"Awesome! Love it here. Classes are great, especially art. And, guess what? Next semester I'm signing up for drafting. Uncle Addie was showing me what he does and it's sort of interesting so I thought I'd try this course."

"Do you often see Uncle Addie?" Despite learning that Addison was not her uncle but her father, Tibetta prefers to continue calling him uncle. After all, Tuck was the one who adopted and raised her, Tuck was her dad.

"Yeah, he's taken me to the symphony several times. I never listened to that kind of music before but now I'm really getting to like it, though I do have to keep from laughing at the way the conductor leaps around – sort of like a bull stung by a bee. Sometimes I visit his place but mostly he comes over here and we have coffee together. Hey, guess who I met? Winnie Power. She's going to the same school. It was sort of crazy running into each other after all this time. She seems nice, not at all like her mother. We're getting together next week." *Fathers, lovers, daughters, friends – the carousel goes round and round,* thinks Tuck.

The following week Tibet, so nicknamed by her college friends, sits at a table in the Tyler Tea Room awaiting the arrival of Winnie. Refusing the more sophisticated urban look, she wears jeans and a white tee shirt under a short, gauzy, flowered blouse. A tiny turned up nose seems at odds with her high cheek bones and angular face. Her blonde hair, cut short, gives her a boyish appearance. Winnie prances in like a frisky pony ready to kick up her heels. She's wearing a flouncy white miniskirt over black tights topped off with a burgundy tank top. Her straight blonde hair, dancing about her neck, gives her longish face an aristocratic flair. She smiles and joins Tibetta at her table where they get off to a good start by discovering they both like jasmine tea. After being served, they begin the challenging task of getting to know each other again.

"It's sad about my brother. He's got serious problems and is in an institution. It's all Mummy's fault. She really messed him up, messed us all up."

"What did she do?" asks Tibetta.

"She tried to control us every minute of the day, constantly telling us we were upper class, better than other people, shouldn't associate with 'guttersnipes,' tearing down our dad, stuff like that. Norm got so he didn't dare make a move without first checking with mummy. He finally got so afraid of everyone he wouldn't go to school anymore. Dad was easier with us but Mummy was too strong for him, she always got her way. We just tried to keep out of her path. Now they're getting divorced, probably should have a long time ago."

"That's so sad. I'm sorry."

"It's okay. I've learned to live with it. Mummy was the one who stopped my playing with you – said you were from a different class of people. I resented her for that. Guess I still do – for that and a lot of other things. I try to love her, but I had to get away. Does that make sense?"

"Makes sense to me," answers Tibetta, not quite sure if she really does understand.

"When I was a kid," I realized that Dad liked your family a lot. That made me wonder."

"It's funny. I always thought of you as rebellious," says Tibetta. "Of course, I was jealous of you too. I thought you didn't like me when I was never invited over any more. I hated it the summer I had to work for your family, I felt like some kind of slave. I remember you weren't around very much that year and I wondered why but never dared to ask."

"I was mostly traveling in Europe with my uncle. I did see you working at Reedmor a couple of times but was sort of afraid to talk to you with the way Mummy was and all." Winnie pauses a moment, staring at Tibetta, then goes on to say, "Can I ask you a personal question?"

"Sure."

"When you came to work for us that summer, you had an ugly slash on your cheek. Now I can hardly see it but I did always wonder what happened."

"I don't mind explaining." Tibetta recounts the details of the accident that evening. "Mom wanted me to get it stitched up so it wouldn't show later but I didn't want that. It was sort of my own personal battle scar."

"Makes sense to me. I got a squirrel tattooed on my ass. Mummy was raging. I did it as a protest against my brother's and her cruelty.

Here, look." Winnie stands up, and to the astonishment of the other tea room customers, lifts her skirt, lowers her panties and flashes the tattoo at Tibetta.

"No way." exclaims Tibetta, "My squirrel, the one Norm killed?"

"That's the one." The girls laugh, put their arms around one another and exchange big hugs. The rest of the afternoon, conversation jumps from one subject to another, the girls sharing recollections as well as some of the practical jokes they both enjoy playing on others.

Finally Tibetta asks, "So, what are you going to major in? Do you know yet?"

"I'm not sure but I think I want to go into some kind of humanitarian work. Make up for my mother's lousy attitude. What about you?"

"I'm going to do something related to the arts but don't know what. I can't be a studio artist. There's no money in that." The girls talk and laugh together until late into the afternoon.

"Hey, remember when they found Addison's wife in the water that spring. Wasn't it weird? Did they ever figure out what happened?"

"My God. I thought everyone knew." exclaims Tibetta.

"Maybe they do, but I don't." Tibetta proceeds to tell her how Bubbles left the rehab unit and what they think happened. Then, on impulse and because she and Winnie are hitting it off so well together, she goes on to talk about her own past and learning that Bubbles was her biological mother, Addison her father.

"That's so incredible. I can't imagine what it would be like to hear stuff like that about your past. You must have been a mess."

"I sure was but I've been working through it. Things are getting better. I have a good family. That helps."

"Guess it would. Wish I could say the same for mine."

"But I think your parents love you too, in a different way. You know, while I was telling you all this, something strange occurred to me. Maybe I'm crazy but when I was little, I crawled out on the ice at your family's camp. It was black ice so I could see right through it. There were turtles and grasses and fish but there was something else – it's coming back to me now. It's sort of strange."

"What was it?"

"Well, when I was out there, I thought I saw a mermaid with long wavy hair. I'd forgotten all about it until talking to you just now. I'm wondering if it was my mother I saw? Wouldn't that be a weird thing, to have seen my mother under the ice?"

"No shit, that's way freaky."

"When I think about it now, I'm pretty sure it was a real woman and they did find Bubbles's body that spring."

"Yikes. That gives me the shivers."

"Maybe not. Maybe it makes a kind of sense. I almost like to think it was her."

Shortly after this, the girls break up and go their separate ways, but only for that afternoon. A bond is established. They continue to see each other often. One day, Winnie calls Tibetta to ask if she'll help her with a plan.

"My mother sent all these cocktail dresses to me to wear at college. I know she means well but she doesn't get it, they hardly fit my lifestyle. What do you say I pack them up and we go out some night and give them away to the hookers standing on the streets? I feel sorry for them, might give them some fun this way."

"Winnie, you are stark raving mad. When do we do it?"

They decide on a date but also decide it might be safer to take a guy along with them. Late one chilly evening, the three students take a subway to the city's red light section, cocktail dresses folded in a colorful embroidered cloth bag. It's easy to spot the prostitutes; they sport only the briefest of clothes and lots of goose bumps. The dresses are received with hardly a thank you and a good bit of rudeness. "I thought we were doing them a favor but they don't seem to appreciate it much. Wonder why?"

Tibetta is suddenly startled to see her old friend Katy standing on the corner. She rushes over to her, gives her a hug but then doesn't know what to say.

Katy rescues her, "Guess you didn't know I earn my keep this way, didja?"

"No, guess I didn't. Are you doing okay?"

"What d'ya think?" Katy answers, yanking down a black, leather strip of skirt that barely covers her butt. She is emaciated rather than slender, with thick makeup applied in an attempt to cover her bad complexion. "What you doin' down here anyways?"

"We came to give away some dresses. They belonged to Winnie. We'd love to give you one."

"I don't need no handouts. Least I'm makin' my own living. Your parents are probly payin' your way in some high class snooty college. Right?"

Tibetta is devastated; her face flushes as she half mumbles a reply.

"See? I knew it. I don't need you lookin' down none on me. I do it on my own, no help from nobody."

Tibetta stares at her own fancy shoes, puts one foot behind the other as if to conceal them, tears up a bit and turns away. *It's true, Katy's right. I've had breaks that she never did.*

Turning back, she says, "Katy, I'm trying to understand. I think you have a lot of courage, more than I might ever have." Then she turns to Winnie and John who stand by lamely holding the partially filled suitcase of fancy dresses, "Let's go, I need to get out of here."

"You know her?" asks John, the guy who came with them.

"I do," says Tibetta. "She's an old friend." Suddenly everything feels wrong. "We're out of place here, don't belong. Did you hear what she said to me?"

"Sure, but you can't let things like that bother you," says Winnie.

"Yeah," echoes John, "What do you care anyhow, she's only a hooker."

"No she isn't. I mean yes she is but that's not all she is. What she says is true. We've had all the breaks."

"Hardly," says John, "but, even if we have, be glad. Don't beat yourself up about it. Hey," he suddenly exclaims, "look at that one over there. Now there's a piece if I ever saw one."

"Shut up John. You're a pain in the ass."

"What are you squawking about all of a sudden? I came down here like you asked. Now you suddenly want me to leave with all these sexy babes slinking around?"

"Yes, we do. You know, Winnie? I think this wasn't such a good idea. I think you and I can do better. Come on John Boy, we're leaving."

But John is smiling broadly, a woman in black shorts, net stockings and halter top hanging all over him. He takes his time disentangling himself.

"Okay, okay, I'm coming. You girls have no sense of fun."

"That's fun? Seeing women earn a living like that?"

"Sure, they love it and that last one really went for me, saw it in her eyes right away."

At the station, John reaches for his wallet to buy a token, reaches here, there, pats his front pants pocket, his back, his jacket his shirt. "Oh no, my wallet. It's gone!"

"Mr. Sexy huh? Now we know why she went for you. Sucker! Here we'll pay." They ride back uptown, a more thoughtful trio than the one riding in the opposite direction a few hours earlier.

Chapter 56

Large bold words parade across the front page of the morning paper: "SuperBig goes out of Business."

"Well, well," says Ma Rose who is enjoying a leisurely breakfast at the Hub, "Are we surprised? Don't rightly think so. Same old story. Big business going to save the town, oh yeah, the big boys going to march right in and tell us how to do it, only they don't care nothing about our town, only about their profits."

The door swings opens; Justus, Fawn and Tuck enter. "Welcome Risings. Don't often have the pleasure of seeing you all together," booms Blanche. "Don't you look bright and cheerful," she says to Fawn, "like your hairdo. That short straight cut suits you well."

"Why thank you. Britt made this dress and Tibby persuaded me to cut off the perm."

"Beautiful. Have a seat; I'll be right over with menus."

After they order breakfast, Fawn says, "I've been thinking lately, life never happens quite the way you think it will. I mean, look at that. The SuperBig out of business. Your store forced to close down – "

"I was not forced to close," protests Justus, "I was ready to retire."

"And now poor Fred and all the other workers losing their jobs. What are they going to do?" continues Fawn as if her husband had not just spoken.

"Deal with it," declares Justus, "They'll have to face reality like we all do, that's life. Better not start complaining either. No one listens anyway."

"Whoa Dad, that sounds gloomy, not like you at all."

"I don't know about that. I've always believed in keeping your shoulders squared and your head up regardless what happens. But, do people listen to me? Do they listen to each other? Not much. You, for instance, you've never listened to me." Then in a softer voice he adds, "Maybe you were right."

"I heard a lot more than you realize and I do agree about people not listening."

"Glad we agree on something," says his father.

"In fact, that's the reason I write. I'm hoping that someone somewhere will read me. Putting it down on paper relieves me of any great need to talk. Of course, there are other reasons not to talk much, like Big Moe for instance, the silent one. He's more attuned to the natural world than to people, takes what he can from each day, doesn't worry much about tomorrow." *Did I just see my mother blush? Now that's interesting.*

"Put that way," his father replies, "I can sort of understand why you choose to do what you do. I guess you're not all crazy. A certain understanding creeps in with age, and what I'm beginning to see is that each of us has his own private world, as if we're in separate bubbles. Oh, I didn't mean to put in like that – rather it's like we're all in separate glass spheres looking over at one another but unable to enter the other person's reality."

"That's a cool description, Dad. It's sort of the way I see it too. I've always thought that –well, that we each must travel our own personal paths. We won't know when we reach the end so we best open our eyes and enjoy the trip."

"Not bad, Tuck. I guess we have more in common than I thought. I've been hard on you but it's paid off. You've turned out once more to be a son we're proud of."

"Of course we're proud of him, always have been," Fawn adds, stretching the truth a mite. "Remember when I told you what Esprit said?" There is a noticeable groan from Justus and Tuck.

"Don't worry. I don't need her any more but not everything she says is laughable. Remember, she's the one who said that you, son, would become well known again and yet unknown at the same time. She was right. When you were no longer a skier, you became a successful writer, only anonymously. No one knew it was you. Now, using your real name, you're a recognized author."

"Esprit? The one who makes her followers meditate in shirts from her family's store emblazoned with 'Esprit's Girls'? How spiritual is that?" asks Justus.

"Now, now, we're not all perfect. A little tolerance goes a long way. In fact, I feel sort of sorry for her. With her graying hair, pale skin and skeletal frame, she looks almost translucent, as if she's disappearing in her own spirituality. Still, I think she offers something useful to her followers: a fantasy to hang on to when life gets too tough for her followers. People need that kind of hope to sustain them. And did you hear she got an award for being the most spiritual counselor?" At this, both Justus and Tuck burst out laughing, loud and hard. Even Fawn's mouth turns up in a bit of a smile.

"I was glad to see you break away from her. You're thinking for yourself now, standing on your own two feet. You don't even seem to need me for that anymore," says her husband.

"Oh dearest, that's not true. I don't know what I'd do without you."

"Don't go getting upset now. I meant that in a good way," explains Justus.

"Look what a beautiful day it's turning out to be. Justus, would you take us out to the Barton place so we can see the gardens you work, er, consult on?" asks Fawn.

"I think we can do that." Turning to his son, he asks "Have you got time?" He doesn't really but Tuck, sensing the occasion is important, feels compelled to go along. He takes the truck, his parents take their car. They meet at Barton Reserve where Justus takes them on a tour to see the beautiful wildflower landscape he is creating. After a half-hour's walk, his father feels winded and they stop to rest. Sitting on a bench, they breathe in the flower scented air, bask in the sunshine.

"I feel so free out here, unbound by duty, like I'm sailing on the wind," observes Justus.

"And where does the wind take you?" his son asks.

"I don't know." Justus leans on Fawn's shoulder. *Now that's something he hasn't done in years* she thinks to herself. His weight becomes heavier until it's hard for her to support him. Turning her head to look, she suddenly realizes his eyes are closed.

"Quick, something's wrong with your dad." Tuck jumps up, grabs him by the shoulders, pulls him upright and feels for a pulse. There much of one. Pulling out his phone, he dials 911.

Justus is vaguely aware of the words "ambulance" and "emergency" but sounds fade as his arms rise and his feet blow back behind him. He is lifted on the wind, flying over the garden of wildflowers: golden black-eyed susans, purple vetch, white daisies, and his wife, like a red rose in her colorful dress all bending and swaying in the wind. She is waving farewell. In great peace, he waves back and, like a flower petal riding on the breeze, floats away. Four days later, the family lays to rest this high principled and well-meaning father, husband and village elder.

Chapter 57

One winter's evening, Tuck and Britt are sitting down to supper when the phone rings. "Hi Dad. We get a long weekend for Presidents' Day. I'd like to come home. If I take the train to Cliff Rock, could you come pick me up? I've got stuff to tell you."

"Stuff? Do we need to be worried?"

"You'll see. I'd like to wait until I get there to talk about it though. Can you pick me up on Friday at noon?"

"You bet; it'll be great to see you. Not even a hint?"

"Well, not about that but I did see something exciting the other day – peregrine falcons nesting on the ledge of a skyscraper. They've adapting to city life and doing just fine here. Isn't that cool? Hey, by the way, how's Gram doing?"

"Which Gram, city or country?"

"Country. I had supper the other night with my city grandma and grandpa. They're fine and really nice to me. Sometimes though, I get a bit bored hearing them go on and on about which big show they just saw and which they're going to next. It's Gram Rising I worry about, especially with Grandpa gone. She's never had it too easy."

"I think she's doing okay, working more hours at the Sears Camp but it seems to agree with her pretty well."

"Good. I'm glad. So, I'll see you on Friday then."

Tuck hangs up, saying to Britt, "I hope she's not pregnant, planning to get married or doing something crazy like that."

"My God. What a scary thought."

Friday comes, Britt and Tuck drive to the train station, joyfully gather up their daughter and bring her home. "Mom. Your hair has grown so long and wavy. You look different."

"Guess I passed the bobbed look on to you. You've cut your hair sort of the way mine used to be. What happened to the curls?"

"Got rid of them. I like it better this way. What do you think?"

"I think it suits you just right." After Tibetta phones her friends and after a late lunch, Britt bursts out, "Okay. You've made us wait long enough. Tell us what's going on."

"Remember I told you I met Winnie Power? Well, we've become friends. We're both trying to figure about majors and jobs and stuff like that. We've come up with a plan."

Tuck and Britt both breathe an audible sigh of relief. "What's that for?" asks Tibetta.

"We were afraid you were getting married."

"Married! Yeah, you guessed it! That too. I met this dude at a bar and we're getting hitched." Tuck and Britt exchange looks, their worst fears realized. Then Tibetta starts laughing. "Just fooling. That's rare. No, not hardly. I've got better things to do. Actually, Winnie wants to do some kind of social work so she can help other people and I want to be part of the environmental movement." *Ah,* thinks her dad, *we didn't do too badly raising her.* "I was pretty sad for Katy – remember her? – when she told me about the cement playgrounds in the city. We met Katy again a while back and it reminded me of that. So, what we're thinking is to start a group to raise money for more green playgrounds in the city's neighborhoods where volunteers could teach city kids about nature and gardening."

"Wonderful," exclaims Britt. "Good thinking," adds Tuck. *Our little girl has grown up.*

"The school is going to help us get started. I'm excited about it."

"No wonder. It's an excellent idea."

"But that's not all."

"Is this the marriage part?" jokes Tuck.

"No Dad. I'm not ready to get tied down. What I've been trying to figure is what to do for a job when I graduate. I've been thinking a lot about the green playgrounds and it gave me an idea. I like the drafting courses I've been taking. I've decided to go into urban planning."

"Urban planning? That sounds good except it would mean you'd have to live in the city, surely you don't want that?"

"Actually, I do." Tucks spirits sink. *Our daughter, choosing the city when she could live in this beautiful place?*

"Why? Why the city?"

"Because the city's exciting. I love the roar and rush, all the stuff going on, the galleries and concerts and going to the theater. It's awesome. You always taught me to look for the best in my surroundings. There's plenty of good stuff going on here."

"I thought you were interested in environmental work?"

"I am. I've been thinking. The reason people move to the suburbs is because cities are full of asphalt, cement, pollution and dirty air. If I become an urban planner I could work on fixing some of that – help clean up the core and stop the spread of urban blight. I'd build lots of spacious green corridors, small ponds, and parks full of trees, flowers and play equipment. If kids had safe and beautiful places to play, it could help them to a better start in life."

"But what of your artistic talent? Aren't you throwing all that away?" asks Britt.

"I don't think so. It would actually give me a perfect way to sketch out my ideas so others could see the possibilities. I would put band shells in some of the parks, where free theatre and music could be offered. Spread the arts around so more people could enjoy them." Tibetta is maturing fast, making choices of her own, choices beyond the sphere of her parents. Over the course of the weekend, exchanges take place, emotions bubble to the surface along with arguments, each person voicing opinions on how Tibetta best plan her life. It's a big letdown for Tuck. *Where did the last 10 years go? Doesn't she care anymore? Has wilderness no value for her?*

Britt consoles Tuck. "We may not see her wings but she's soaring out of the nest, taking off on her own. The city seems to inspire her. She'll do fine. Think of the falcons. Like she said, you've always believed in making the best of things. She's learned that lesson well. Remember when she first discovered about Santa? Instead of being disappointed, she found it thrilling that we had let her in on the adult secret. She couldn't wait to help play Santa for other children. A girl like that will do well wherever she lands." Rat and Pitt, never at a loss for words, conclude, "Young and old in the country thrive; those in the middle find the city alive."

Late one evening, a day after Tibetta returns to college, Tuck says to Britt. "My head is muddled. I need a night walk." An hour later, he is far out on Cedar Bluff's windswept ice. Out there, in the quiet, he reunites with time and place, past and present. *Maybe the things we shared are not lost on her after all. Maybe it's time to trust and let her fly.* He wears his well-worn Carhartt jacket, wool pants and heavy boots. Eyes focused ahead, his gaze shifts from moon to ice to shoreline and back, always searching. A thick cap sits low over his ears. Perhaps that's why he doesn't hear the footsteps coming from behind. Britt suddenly appears in ski pants and a blue winter parka, the hood pulled up to block out the wind.

"Hey, how did you know where I was?"

"I followed your footsteps."

"I'm glad someone has. Is something the matter? Why are you here?" he asks in alarm.

"Not really. Guess I'm out here because I'm coming about, just like our daughter." A big smile lights up her face as she kicks up first one foot, then the other, to show him the well insulated Sorrel boots he gave her those many Christmases ago.

"Wow. I've never seen you put those on before."

"I never have." Tuck puts his arm around her.

"You'll get cold."

"Not like this. It's only a chill wind when you don't dress for it."

Tuck feels the warmth coming from his wife. They cling to one another as a full moon rises, coyotes howl, an owl hoots and the ice booms. "Guess what I have?" he finally says, breaking the spell.

"I haven't the faintest idea, a sandwich, a thermos, a handkerchief?"

"No, something I've carried in my pocket a long time, waiting for the perfect moment." With that, he pulls out the small cassette player she gave him, also many years ago.

"You still have that thing?"

"I have." He flips it on. A string band slides into a lilting waltz. "Ms. Freier, may I have this dance?"

"I'd be honored," she says, "to dance with the finest caretaker a family could ever have."

He takes her in his arms and looking down, sees her upturned face smiling back. They swoop and swirl across the icy ballroom floor, their feet crunching softly on the frosty snow. "It's all okay, isn't it?" she whispers.

"It is." he answers as the moon lights up the sky, the ice and the waltzing couple but not the shore, where silent woods stand still and full of shadows.

"Rat-a-tat-tat, rat-a-tat-tat
We may know this but
We don't know that
Lickity-split, lickity-splat
Heed the words of Pitt and Rat.
Nothing much is –
Where we think it's at."

About the Author

Author Caperton Tissot has a background in pottery design and production, healthcare and environmental advocacy. After retirement, she was finally able to do what she had long dreamed about: write. Her abiding interest in small communities and natural history is reflected in her seven published books. These include history, fiction, poetry, memoir, and recently short play writing.

She has written for both printed and online journals and newspapers as well as for the local historical society.

She and her husband live in Saranac Lake where Tissot enjoys balancing an outdoor lifestyle with an indoor writing vocation.

More information at: www.SnowyOwlPress.com.